ALSO BY ROSE SANDY

The Calla Cress Thrillers Series

Book 1: The Decrypter Secret of the Lost Manuscript

Book 2: The Decrypter and the Mind Hacker

Book 3: The Decrypter: Digital Eyes Only

Book 4: The Decrypter: The Storm's Eye

Book 5: The Decrypter and the Pythagoras Clause

The Shadow Files Thrillers

The Code Beneath Her Skin

Blood Diamond in My Mother's House

THE DECRYPTER AND THE BEALE CIPHERS

JOIN THE ARMY OF FANS WHO LOVE THE CALLA CRESS SERIES BY ROSE SANDY...

What readers love about the Decrypter books

"**Takes you on a ride** and refuses to let you off until you reach the very end." *Marie*

"A brilliant read! I recommend this to anyone who enjoys mystery, suspense, thrillers, or action novels. The **detail is astounding**! The historic references, location descriptions, references to technology, cryptography....this author really knows her stuff." *Fran*

"An **action-packed adventure**, technothriller **across several continents** like a Jason Bourne or James Bond movie, but with an actual storyline!" *John*

"**Brilliantly written**. I loved the very descriptive side, which was a good way of visualizing and getting to terms with each new place, as the action takes place in several different countries." *Sean*

"The **description is so rich**, so immensely detailed that it just draws you in completely to its world." *Denise*

"There is **great tension and chemistry** between the two main characters, Calla and Nash, that has you begging for more." *Pam*

THE DECRYPTER AND THE BEALE CIPHERS

A CALLA CRESS THRILLER

ROSE SANDY

SILVER GRAVITY

*For all those who are curious about our world,
its mysteries, history and the technology that runs it.*

NOTE TO READERS

If you are new to the Decrypter Series...

Each book in the Decrypter series can be read as a standalone novel, but the series is best enjoyed in order. The novels are fast-paced, action-adventures steeped in history, espionage, and cyber defense in a world evermore digitally dependent. The books explore a world where technology and science are at the forefront of humanity.

If you are new to the series and want to get your head around the characters and action quickly, here is a little catch up:

The story so far...

Calla is an agent with the **ISTF**. An acronym that stands for the **International Security Task Force**, a 500-person strong intelligence body, created and massively funded by the UK, US, France, Germany, and Russia. It came into existence before 2000 to help fight expected problems with Y2K—not in how it might influence business and commerce, but how criminal organizations might exploit it. The agency works covertly overseas and domestically, gathering intelligence around sciences, technologies, and high-tech artifacts that threaten global security.

Abandoned as an infant, **Calla's** life's quest is to search for her parents. When she finds them, she learns **Stan** and **Nicole,** her MI6 parents, left her to save her from those who would seek to exploit her unique abilities thanks to a heritage of genetic engineering. An attractive woman, aware of her looks but still quite unsure of them, **Calla** is a product of being an orphan for as long as she can remember. Though she was raised in a good home by good people, the fear of abandonment persists.

Both at **ISTF** and at a day job as a **British Museum** curator, **Calla** holds prestigious positions she's earned through her many talents, including an unusual mixture of old and new, anthropology and hi-tech. Even more important for her success, though, is her unique skill at breaking codes, earning her the nickname of the Decrypter.

Now head of **ISTF**, with the code name *Red Fox,* **Calla** has been cleaning up one tech and scientific criminality after another, especially havoc created by former **ISTF** head **Mason Laskfell**. **Calla** believes technology will develop at a rate so much faster than humans can cope.

Helping her on her escapades, both professional and personal, are two individuals. Formerly in the military, **Nash** is an NSA security advisor attached to the **ISTF** and is also quite attached to **Calla. Jack** is a remarkably successful tech entrepreneur who has a fondness for Calla and a love of the excitement surrounding her in discovering rare artifacts, advanced technologies, and sciences that appear around the globe. Superior to anything humanity has seen, these discoveries are mostly unknown to man and are protected from exploitation by a group of tech keepers called the *'operatives'*.

Recently **Calla** and **Nash** married secretly and lost their unborn baby to a dangerous enemy. They have sworn to confiscate any **operative** technology or science that remains at large.

And so, our story begins…

CAST OF CHARACTERS

Oskara Almano: Assassin for hire. Leads a group of mercenaries

Margot Arlington: Former Governor of Indiana and later became the US Ambassador to London. She ran for president and lost to her fellow Democratic candidate Aaron Seeburg

Fiora Benassi: Jack Kleve's sister

Calla Cress: British Museum curator and head of a secret, multi-government spy organization, the International Security Taskforce (ISTF). Code name - *Red Fox*

Stan Cress: Calla Cress's Father. Former MI6 agent

Mama & Papa Cress: Calla Cress's adoptive parents who raised her

Lent Cyrus: Psychiatrist from Miami, with family scattered across the globe

Capt. Kaden Delgado: Ex-naval officer commander hired by Nash to command the Scorpion Tide yacht

Allegra Driscoll: International Security Force (ISTF) board member, Foreign Affairs guru

Peregrine Esperson: Socialite from New Mexico related to Thomas Jefferson Beale

Marree Johnson: Marine biologist from Hawaii. Daughter of the head of the FBI in Honolulu

Jack Kleve: Serial Technology Entrepreneur. Chief of Science and Technology at the International Security Taskforce Technology Adviser. Code Name - *White Wolf*

Soma Kleve: Agent with the African Intelligence Agency (AIA)

Kaarlo Kleve: Agent with the African Intelligence Agency (AIA)

Mason Laskfell: Former head of ISTF and chief of ISTF's research, signals intelligence and linguistics divisions.

Halona Osa-Menglian: Former technology student at McGill University.

Sheik Amir Salib : Oil tycoon and was trained for military combat by Nash Shields

Massoud Salib: Sheik Salib's son. Artificial intelligence and technology developer

Scarlett: Personal assistant to heads of ISTF and Calla Cress

Aaron Seeburg: The US President and a Democrat politician

Nash Shields: Former Marine currently employed by the National Security Agency, the NSA. Attached to ISTF. Code name - *Silver Jaguar*

Tiege: Calla's favorite security operative. Works both for ISTF and the operatives

Ashton Vaxon: Former ISTF chief of science and new technologies

Lucy Weisheng: Child prodigy interested in new technologies and codes

Sue-Lyn Weisheng: Lucy Weisheng's mother

Zeng Weisheng: Lucy Weisheng's father

FACT

According to a pamphlet published in 1885 in Bedford County, Virginia, Thomas J. Beale described how he buried treasure in a secret location. After entrusting a box containing three encrypted messages to a local innkeeper named Robert Morriss, Beale departed, never to be seen again.

The innkeeper opened the box twenty-three years later and gave the three encrypted letters to a friend before he passed away. That friend spent the next twenty years trying to decode the messages, but he only solved one, which details the buried treasure's contents and its general location.

There have been countless attempts to decode the two remaining cipher texts and find the treasure since the pamphlet was published. All have failed.

CHAPTER
ONE

HALONA'S FISTS were no contest for the firearms they had brought against her. Her brow drenched in sweat, she scowled.

On the gunman's forehead was a headcam. In tactical gear, armed with a weapon that could take down a small army, he moved and accepted orders from an earpiece.

Halona slammed her back against the wall as an icy shiver crawled down her spine. Her father had always said if anyone wanted to find Beale's treasure, they would have to solve the puzzle. For 200 years, no one had.

He had repeatedly informed her never to share what they knew. Now, his voice coming from downstairs was deafening and unmistakable. "Run!"

A bullet whispered past her ear in a high-pitched whine. Her feet bolted to the edge of the door she hadn't remembered closing. Trembling fingers fumbled with eagerness, then slipped on the door handle as she tried to break through it and shut it behind her.

"Halona Osa-Menglian, the oracle herself! I'll make this very easy for you," a large man belted as he reached the top of the stairs. Halona ran a palm down her homemade skirt depicting her forefathers' beliefs, the Wampanoag Native American operatives of Massachusetts.

These guys knew who she was.

She wasn't an oracle. Just a damn good technology person like any other girl. Her family shared the operatives' secrets. Too much sometimes.

The man slapped a clip into his gun.

Her feet itched to run, but when she heard her father bark at the intruders, his tone distorted with anger and dread, she held still. "Who are you? What do you want?" Halona asked, trying to disguise the crackling in her voice.

"You know what we want. I'll give you two minutes to speak. If you know what's good for you, start this very moment by not resisting. Hand over what we need. The telescope. The decryption. In that order."

Halona scowled. "The Beale Ciphers hide the truth from people like you. What makes you think I would tell you anything?"

He approached, and the gun jammed closer into her neck. Its cold steel made her shudder.

"Will make this quick. Give us what we demand," he grumbled.

Halona shook her head and stared at a second man, whose sneering eyes made her insides raw. Caramel skin, amber eyes, his nostrils flared at her as he grunted forward. His long hair would fit no visor mask, so he hadn't bothered. He had to be the leader here.

As he advanced, in all of two seconds, his breath was so close, and she almost felt she would suffocate from his glare. Nearly two heads above her, she drew back. Fighting dread and everything within her will, she charged toward the balcony door.

There were more of them downstairs—three men and a woman with pistols.

"Amano, she's the one," the man assured in his earpiece. "We've found her."

Just what did he mean by, 'she's the one'? Who were these men? If she ran, she could find her way out and down the house the hard way.

It was time, she decided.

Her chance came when her father's rifle blasted a warning shot toward the two attackers. Enough time to distract them for several seconds, as they turned their aim toward her father.

Halona landed a lucky blow on the first guy who gained in on her.

He pivoted, stunned by her strike.

One by one, the men filtered in.

They meant business.

Her eye caught that of her father's, now struggling at the foot of the stairs, as the assassin charged in her direction.

Instinctively, her limbs gathered strength.

CHAPTER
TWO

NOT TOO FAR AWAY...

THE SUN'S hue dimmed from bright yellow to a deeper gold as it sank below the horizon of the New Mexico desert. Clouds lit from below picked up the colors of the sky.

Calla Cress and Jack Kleve had been in the cave for an hour and yet had not found the wall paintings Jack's contact, Halona, had told them about.

"What time is it?" Calla said.

Jack held up a smart phone whose screen glowed green and blue lights shone into his magnificent dreadlocks. "Just after six. The sun's still up, though. We should get out of here before dark. We don't want to be held in here overnight," he said.

"I'm going to look around a little more," Calla replied. "Why don't we split up and try to find the paintings?"

"Sure," he said.

She was out of her depth here, and she didn't know where to begin. No history account recorded these wall designs. Intelligence circles provided her with information, but nothing about the cave was on record. A ten-minute discussion with an antique dealer in a shop in London had told

Halona and Jack that an ancient telescope held important secrets. It was relevant to the relationship between the US and the world, and it all had to do with these caves. Were they chasing a myth? Unsourced, sketchy at the least. It's all they had to go on today, and for Jack's sake, she would carry on. He believed something was in here. God knew they'd found enough unregistered artifacts in their government careers.

Jack drew out a nano-scanner that could penetrate moist rock for age and mineral content as Calla climbed over rough rocks, following a path through the cave. In the inner sections, Calla felt a jerk on the rope tied to her waist as she turned a corner and ducked under dangling ropy lichen. The rope would lead her back if she strayed too far.

Leaving the dim light of the entrance, she stepped deep into the cave's obscurity. Enormous, she didn't want to be stuck in here and struggled forward through darkness. She walked over loose sand, occasionally grabbing at rock and earth formations. As she turned around a bend in the cave, she felt her way through a head-high tunnel. Calla had progressed into the inner cave, about fifty feet by her guess, when she spotted more light from an opening above.

Stepping forward, she bent under a low-lying plant that had grown out of the wall of the cave. Brightness came from above. Almost through to the other side of the space, she caught sight of a cleft in the wall. Treading carefully, she tried to peer into it, then halted when she realized it continued into nothingness. Calla stopped to examine her surroundings.

A low voice grew from behind her. It was Jack.

"This is one maze, huh?" he said.

"Indeed."

A rock plunged suddenly from the ceiling in front of them, descending quicker than she could blink. It smashed into the floor, inches from her feet, with a resounding crash.

The sound caused her to flinch, and it took a second for her to realize what it was, and she withdrew.

"You okay?" Jack said.

She glanced at him and nodded.

When he held out his hand, she grabbed it, sidestepping jagged rocks poking from the ground. They progressed to a new cave room. As they entered, blackness now surrounded them on every side.

"Where do you think they are?" Calla asked.

"Halona only said the painting fills the wall," Jack replied.

"The wall must be here somewhere. Let's keep looking," he said and touched her shoulder.

She looked at him. "Yes?"

"Be careful."

Calla nodded and smiled. "I will."

She could determine what lay ahead. Light coming from the area far above and forwards was just enough for her to see. She advanced into nothingness and felt like she was on a smuggling operation inside a treasure mine. The passage then opened to a new level. She clicked the switch on the flashlight a few times to turn it brighter.

Footprints were visible on the floor of the space. Not so fresh either. Piled up in ridges, sand mirrored that of around the edge of a beach.

Wet impressions extended a few feet and then turned and continued back out the way she had come. A large, deep pit in the dirt in front of her made her stop. Then she looked behind her. She paused. Her eyes were arched so steeply they hurt for a second. The cave wall paintings were archaic and colorful, several feet high, all hand-painted in ancient ink. The paint was rich and cracked in places. Still vibrant and detailed, at first glance, they appeared fresh, as if staring out of another time. Carved or etched into the wall, a kaleidoscope of the sky, there was a series of long,

long panoramas in a setting so remote and so savage. She would never have believed it possible hadn't she witnessed it.

"Jack! I found them," she said.

Jack rushed in behind her.

Calla's eyes wouldn't leave the scene before them. Her mouth tightened as she stared at painted reds, greens, blues, and hues of black that wound through as well.

"I've seen nothing like it," Jack said, approaching slowly.

"It's a code," Calla said, smiling. "Encrypted."

"In the mural?" he said, grinning.

"Yeah. They're messages. Ancient words and numbers intertwined with images," Calla said.

"Well, if anybody knows, it would be you."

"So you were listening?" she said.

"I always listen to you. You're full of interesting stuff."

She gave him her full attention. "Is this what the telescope you mentioned helps decipher?"

"Yes," he replied.

"Plus, you said the telescope could be a crypto machine. I still haven't seen it, you know," she said.

He cocked his head. "You will soon. There was much that man in London told Halona and me. Think that's where you come in, the Decrypter."

"Not sure if I've ever liked that term, but I will take the compliment from you."

Jack anchored his attention on Calla. "Halona sent me what she could and instructed me to locate this place. It's sacred to her ancestors. Do you know she is a descendant of the first Native American known to have spoken English and helped the Pilgrims who traveled to this continent?"

"No, I didn't know that. Just genius. Look at all of this. Imagine what the world would do if they saw this. Leonardo da Vinci has a competitor with this wall mural. The paintings merge with an ancient language," she said. "I just don't know the alphabet."

Jack's eyes lit up. "I'll take some pics, and we can use Halona's telescope tonight. She brought it to London once, you know?"

Calla's body twitched, and she faced Jack with wide-open eyes. "Did she?"

She studied the script, then peered up at Jack, who took photos on his secure phone. Her focus returned to the wall. The discovery was important but unknown to man. What they had seen here would raise questions, perhaps attract the wrong characters. Halona's ancestors must've painted the code to hide the designs that from afar depicted a scene of the moon and stars, the heavens.

Glancing over at Jack, she barely caught him cringe at the sight before them. "Like many ancient cultures, one of the predominant reasons for creating art was the intention to please the gods, who would bless them because of it," Calla said.

"I suppose that makes sense, but why this kind of writing?" Jack asked.

"Native American craft reflects religion and is based on a deep connection to nature, however not in these paintings. There's something special going on here. They're intertwined with numbers. Arabic numerals that you and I use all the time in mathematics."

Calla could read it. She didn't know why. There was a sequence of figures. One, two, three. Ten. One, two, three. Ten. One, two, three. "Two, seven, six, eight, three, four," Calla whispered.

Jack focused on her, possibly puzzled by her quiet mumblings, then snapped a few more photos. He continued studying the compositions.

"Jack?"

"Yeah?"

"I see something here. Come," she said, pointing to the wall. "Those marks on that wall between the rings. I can read them."

Calla glanced up, her eye catching a gap in the ceiling. A geyser of dirt and rock burst from beneath Calla's feet, snapping the entire ridge of the wall. As she'd feared, the caves were ancient and not stable.

She ducked until her hands found crumbling soil beneath her. When she looked up, a split had torn through the entire mural.

Dirt and pebbles trembled as the ground rattled, so hard it felt like it was cracking.

She fell back as the tremor ripped up the ground beneath her. "Jack! Watch out!"

He spun in time.

Taking a breath in and out like a wheezing man in the cold, Calla shrunk back as more dust from above dropped to her face. She sneezed and watched the debris gather, and a low rumble growled behind them. Heaving dust nearly suffocated them. Her nostrils burned for breath as she dug her nails into her palms. They had to get out.

Jack seized her arm as a heap of debris and rocks piled behind them. Without hesitation, they ran. Calla's throat burned from the dust. Her eyes watered constantly, and she wiped her runny nose on her sleeve. The tremors in the floor rattled her teeth, calling her back to attention. "It's too fast!" Jack called. "It's collapsing! We need to move!"

"Faster!" Jack screamed as a boulder dropped from the ceiling and rolled in their path.

She cringed as their boots scuffed across rock and dirt, her hand still in Jack's. Calla quickly released the rope around her waist.

A sharp odor of water and earth surrounded them. They hurdled over giant stones and dodged falling rocks.

Early evening light from outside the cave shone a path before them. They were now steps from the cave's entrance. It loomed before them. A colossal archway of stone, crevices, fallen rocks, and rubble waited ahead before they reached it. They stopped for a moment, clinging to each other's sides as the ground rattled underneath them.

When fresh air hit them, and they surfaced through the archway of the cave several moments later, a mighty rumble of rock and debris crashed behind them, completely blocking the entrance.

Calla drew in a sigh of relief, her loose hair blowing in the light wind. They took several moments, gulping in the fresh evening air. She froze, eyes wide, trying to comprehend. "We can't tell anyone about this. What we saw there could change civilization. Modern thinking. Just what was Beale trying to do? This place was sacred to so many people—ancient landowners. Thomas Jefferson Beale started something he should not have. He must've come here, and this is where it all began."

Jack rubbed his eyes with the base of his palms. "I don't know what I'm going to tell Halona."

CHAPTER
THREE

WITH HALONA'S hand behind her, she wrenched hard and pushed. She slumped back, and with one abrupt move, rose to find her way through the door.

Her feet hurtled past her telescope on the roof patio. Taking all of three seconds to snatch it, she slotted the telescope into a collapsible size, then threw herself over the rail and down the duct of the house's side that led to the backyard.

It was two floors down, but she realized her life depended on it. It seemed like an eternity before she landed in one enormous bump, nearly fracturing a rib. Halona fell with a bone-rattling smack, her arms windmilling through the air until she struck the dirt. Pain wound through her joints. She couldn't move and didn't know with what sense she'd done it. Halona was sure it was the end.

Barefooted, she hit the ground running. The sound of feet slapping the earth, the crack of briars, the hiss of dry grass, the snap of twigs surrounded her. She had to keep moving.

Her feet hit the ground hard as a bullet zipped past her, and she took no time to think. Panic rose to her chest, but she wouldn't stop. Feet did the talking when they charged away from the only home she had ever known and into the desert blackness.

As fast as her legs would allow her to move, she reached the path and sprinted. Halona would put the telescope where no one would find it. The caves. Her ancestors would protect it. If Jack had had any luck, he probably had found what she had told him about.

CHAPTER
FOUR

"THE BEALE CIPHERS are one's even GCHQ can't crack," Calla said, eyeing Jack. "Does Halona still have the telescope?"

"Yes, we're supposed to meet her tonight. She knows we're visiting the caves. Her family is Native American, as I mentioned. She's a descendant of Squanto, from the Patuxet tribe, an interpreter that guided the Pilgrim settlers at Plymouth during their first winter in the New World," Jack said.

Calla thought about what they'd just learned. No matter what happened. From there on, they would reveal nothing about this place—this ancient key to a complex cipher. If it was in the wall paintings, Calla could read some of it, but she needed something else for the rest of it. Perhaps something like a crypto machine. The secret protected many, and it would have to remain that way.

"Halona sounds fascinating, Jack," Calla said. "I really want to meet her and see the telescope. You took lots of snaps right."

He nodded, raising his phone and moving to where they'd

left their backpacks. "Plenty here to fill a tabloid paper. I'll encrypt it now and send it to my server. The telescope is supposed to help read these ancient ciphers. Something in its mechanics. Halona only loaned it to me to study it when she came to London, but I suspect she'll tell us a little more about how her family gained it and what it really means. She can trace back her family's connection to Thomas Jefferson Beale's time."

Calla smoothed down the hem of her shirt and pulled her dark hair out from where it cascaded down her shoulders. She slung it into a ponytail. "I've always considered the Beale Ciphers a hoax. After all, many have struggled to understand what they say. Some people suspect they reveal where a great treasure is hidden."

"Truth is," Jack said, "the ciphers expose something many would appreciate. Especially you. At least that's what I think." He straightened his shoulders. "You've come to this point many times. You've asked yourself many questions over the years. Cal, this might help you figure out something that plagues you—you've always had to watch over your shoulder. Perhaps if we continue with this, we might find out just what was behind the Beale Ciphers and a little more. Like Halona, your ancestry is just as mysterious."

"Is that what Halona told you?" Calla asked, raising an eyebrow. "I know she told you more about this place. It's okay. Jack, I know you dated her," she said, smiling at him. "You're a fascinating guy, both you and Nash. You both do something to women."

"Yet I missed out on you. My best friend is beating me to it."

"Nash and I are..." she began. "You'll always have me, Jack. And Nash. Tell me more about Halona," Calla said.

"We met in Canada at university, just before I finished my Masters at McGill," he replied.

She could tell Jack did not want to talk about it. The squirm at the corner of his lips gave him away. He'd broken it off when he met Calla, and she wondered if he regretted it when Nash had come into her life. After that, Jack had dated no women, but Calla knew one day he'd find the one and she'd be there, right behind him, supporting him.

The sky filled with a bright orange flash and the blast of a gunshot echoed across the desert that could be heard for miles. Her ears rung and Calla zipped her head.

Jack's eyes bulged "What was that?"

"Someone who shouldn't be here," Calla said.

A second gunshot exploded, and they took shelter behind rocks outside the cave. Footsteps pounding in their direction made them glance at each other in silence. Soft padded, it meant the person was barefooted.

"Someone's in trouble," Calla said. "Stay here with the equipment. Let me go check."

"Be careful," Jack said. "If you're not back in seconds, I'm coming right behind you."

Calla proceeded down the hill outside the cave. And then she saw her. A young woman, hair flying, out of breath and on foot. The woman surged in her direction.

Whoever was after her had some serious weapons.

CHAPTER
FIVE

HALONA'S EYES darted to the right, where she saw one of the most exquisite women she'd ever seen. Olive skin, emerald-amber eyes, dark hair, and an athletic physique made the woman appear powerful. Yet gentleness shone in her glistening eyes as she looked at her. It was hard to tell if the woman she was looking at, with dark, cascading hair, was Caucasian, Asian, perhaps Latin American, French Gypsy, or Indian descent. She housed a beautiful mix of cultures in her tall stance.

This had to be Calla Cress, the incredible code breaker and expert in ancient languages and history. Halona couldn't meet her when she was in London, but Jack had told her how the prolific British Museum curator had been in such demand the government had recruited her to work on puzzling ciphers.

Halona flew toward her as, behind her, gunshots sounded.

With footsteps hurrying behind her, she turned for a millisecond and bumped into a solid stump. It wasn't a rock. Her eyes widened.

The bullet hit hard.

No one could've prepared her for the pain, the piercing, the choking of her blood. Then she felt a gush of warmth on her side, a strange mixture of fire, ice, and agony that clouded her vision into blackness.

CALLA STUDIED THE WOMAN.

This had to be Halona from the pictures Jack had shown her.

She charged in Halona's direction, who now peered at her and gave out an exhale of relief. Calla had never met her in person.

When Halona was about two feet from her, she crumpled to the ground. Halona's skin was dark around the eyes, and she maintained a plain stare.

Trundling eyes in hollow sockets, Halona had striking Native American features. Out of breath, her chest expanded and collapsed.

"You're okay, now," Calla said, with a quick glimpse around them for assailants.

No answer.

It was then that Calla saw red. A bullet had grazed the side of Halona's stomach, and she was losing a lot of blood. Halona had her hands in fists and stiffened in agony.

Calla dabbed the injury, trying to make the blood stop. Halona couldn't move and hauled her behind a rock.

The footsteps became more pronounced.

Calla took off her jacket and held it against the flesh wound, then lifted her chin when she noticed the first man surface behind a boulder and head in their direction. "Stay here," she said, gently placing Halona to the ground.

Calla rose and examined the gunman.

He lunged for her, and she struck a boot in his middle.

He dropped to the gravel, groaning.

Calla hauled him to his feet and studied him as he came to. This time, she had no tolerance. She thrust a fist in his jaw, and he spat blood.

Eager to protect her new friend, Calla kicked the pistol out of his hand, claimed it, and then positioned it toward him.

He jumped upward, and like the coward she knew he was, he turned to his heels and hurried back the way he'd come.

Calla waited. Would more follow him? She didn't know, but Halona was in grave danger.

She rushed back to where Halona lay. Her breathing had quieted down, yet the horror in Halona's eyes had not gone away.

"You can't let those guys get to them. Pl... pl... please promise me you won't allow them to have it. You must protect our secret. The land's secrets," Halona said.

"Get to what? The paintings?" Calla asked.

Halona shook her head slowly as Calla drew closer. She didn't look good. Despite the frailty of her body, her eyes sparkled with light. Her voice was a whisper, a hiss of rusted machinery. Eyes bloodshot and her breathing slowing, Halona wanted to say something.

Calla put her ear to Halona's lips. What she learned made her freeze. It couldn't be. No, it couldn't. A fluttering attacked her stomach. She then heard footsteps stomping behind her.

Jack's brown eyes filled with such pain it tore at Calla's

heart as he spoke. "What happened? Halona? Oh my goodness! What did they do to you?"

Jack's voice was now hoarse with pained emotion. The horror in his eyes was hard to bear. He dumped the equipment and rushed to their side. Then his eyes fell on Halona, and he kneeled at her side and cradled her head. "Who were they?"

There was no response from Halona.

"I don't know," Calla said, her voice almost a whisper. "Halona doesn't look good. We need to help her, take her back to the truck, and drive her to a hospital. She's in incredible pain and losing a lot of blood."

Anguish was visible in Jack's eyes, and his brow wrinkled. He lifted her in his arms, and Calla kept the jacket pressed on her wound.

Halona's breathing slowed down.

"We need to hurry," Calla said and picked up their belongings with one glance around them. "She must've had something they wanted. Something to do with the cave paintings and Beale's ciphers. It has to be. I think you were right about the telescope, but we can't worry about that now. She needs help. Let's go."

"This is a lot bigger than I thought," Jack said, carrying Halona.

Calla's mind seesawed back and forth. "We have to keep it a secret. The code belongs to the land, to her ancestors, to history. We can't tell anyone. It's too dangerous now."

Convinced Halona wouldn't survive the trip to the hospital, Calla bit her lower lip and checked on her pulse. "Jack! She's stopped breathing."

He placed Halona on the ground, and Calla began CPR. After a few pumps to the chest, Calla opened her mouth to speak, but her vocal cords refused to cooperate. Sweat beads gathered on her forehead, and pain stung in her gut, agony she never wanted to experience again.

This time, it hurt even more.

SEVEN

THAT WINTER, BÖNIGEN,
SWITZERLAND, 5:00 A.M.

VIEWED from the highway on the drive, Bönigen was a world away from most places Calla knew. Picturesque houses dating back to the sixteenth century reflected the majestic mountains in the deep blue waters. North of the Alps, Bönigen lay on the southwest side of Lake Brienz, on the steep mountainside. Minutes from the resort town of Interlaken, rural life blended in harmony with nature. In the distance, she glimpsed the extensive mountain train network where Europe's highest railway station, Jungfraujoch, brought most visitors to the municipality.

Nash Shields stood next to her, his frame tall. Sandy-brown hair neatly tucked away behind a beanie hat, reminded Calla of the desert. Well built under his mountain anorak, Nash liked to stay comfortable. At six-foot-three and a half, a head above her, she liked how his lean build and posture spoke of years of military discipline, though that didn't rob him of the sparkle in his engaging, deep-gray eyes. A security agent at the International Security Taskforce, or ISTF, and a former marine, he had spent significantly more time in combat and a special forces secret unit funded by the NSA.

That's why she needed him today. He could teach her how to breathe calmly with discipline and skill in ice water.

Years of exposing himself to both hot and cold temperatures as a field agent had taught him that the act of breathing in ice water was a skill that could save lives.

Nash had practiced the art, and after months of practice in bitter temperatures, his breathing had strengthened and had become much deeper. She wanted to know how. If only she had possessed the courage to jump into the ice water all those years ago, Lucy would be alive today.

Though he didn't talk about it much, Calla knew Nash had joined an exclusive covert division of the NSA before he'd moved to London, the KJ-20 Ops. He trained with them but later refused to join the missions of the elite group. Possibly because he'd known they were training assassins, as well as recruiting for the president's secret service.

A special operations arm for combat military and cyber-technology defense, the KJ-20 Ops gave the government options for cyber security when military or diplomatic actions weren't viable or politically workable. They were deadly and very good at what they did. Nash had been their best.

Buried deep in the NSA and reporting to no one on paper, the KJ-20 Ops didn't know who set the assignments or the missions. The US president didn't know they existed or that they operated on government payrolls. Most of their funding came from covert units of the military budget. The money was too little to miss, yet enough of it to train the first three in extreme conditions—Nash Shields, a woman, and one other agent. Three top-tier agents in US intelligence.

They'd been climbing for several hours, and the air was thin. Cool air touched Calla's exposed face as the brittle crunching of their footsteps made their way toward the lake. Passing meadows and picturesque wooden houses, they were panting, bundled up in down jackets and sturdy walking boots, while taking one of the network paths of marked hiking trails.

The snow was powdery as they approached the furthest end of the lake. Seclusion was what they needed. Gray clouds hung so low they were almost on top of them now as a chilly wind sent snowflakes sideways.

It had been a challenging climb, but Calla didn't know what Nash was planning. She caught sight of the lake and took in a deep breath. If it hadn't been for the water, let alone the ice, perhaps Calla would've been a bit more confident.

This morning, this side of the lake was now abandoned. Sometimes, it was used to train Olympians.

They wore four layers, but this was necessary. Their last layer was a wet suit. One by one, each of the first three layers fell off until they were in wet suits.

A clean, raw chill greeted Calla as she stood, her feet planted on the banks. She would be in the water for a long enough period, and her breath came out in a fog as she observed the lake.

Calla inhaled again, filling her lungs with cold air. She was about to get wet. This was going to hurt. Her feet were inches from the frozen lake, and a slight ozone flavor of frost melting on her tongue intensified.

Nash squared his toned shoulders, and Calla wondered if he knew how attractive he was. Come to think of it, when wasn't he?

"When one breathes," he said, beginning the first lesson, "it creates heat, and the warmth slowly melts the surrounding ice. So the trick is to breathe. If not, the cold will eventually freeze your lungs. Learn this technique."

"Okay."

"Before a mission like this, we'd all hold our breaths. Stay under for as long as we could. It's not exactly something I'd recommend doing at home," he chuckled.

Calla wasn't sure how to react, so she kept silent.

Nash dipped into the frigid water, reached for Calla's arm and pulled her in. "After your body has reached a point where it can't take anymore, it will oxygenate your blood again, awakening and calming you, like meditation."

When Calla hit the ice-cold water, shivers pierced through her. It seemed as if the lake was darker than the sky, and she could not tell where the surface was. As the seconds went by and her new reality became more apparent, she wished it were a dream.

Nash held her gaze. "Hey, I'm right here."

She took a deep breath and told herself it would be okay.

"Come on now. This is supposed to be relaxing your mind, not intensifying it," Nash said.

She choked.

"It will calm you and clear your mind but certainly not kill you. It's a skill you master that will help you not fear ice water, and it can be done," Nash said.

Calla didn't feel calm. It felt as if her lungs were going to give out from the memory of losing Lucy. She closed her eyes and rested for a moment and took another deep breath, then opened her eyes.

"Let's try to swim," Nash suggested.

Shallow near the edge, they walked with ease until the water was shoulder deep.

"You did it, Calla, but you need to calm down on your breathing. When you inhale that quickly, you can't control your actions."

"You realize this isn't altogether easy, Nash? It's like winter in my ribcage," she said, gasping.

"Then let's train you some more with just calm breathing."

"Okay," Calla responded.

"We'll keep going," Nash said. "I'm going to be here the entire time."

She nodded.

Nash made her feel like she could do it.

"All right, Calla. We'll start training again. Just breathe."

"I'm in ice water. I can't."

He looked around and led them to the edge of a slab of solid ice. "Hold on, and I'll provide you with air."

"I can't—

"Just relax."

She edged against the floating ice and started breathing as slowly and calmly as she could.

"You can do this, Calla," he urged her.

He was a few feet away and began inhaling. "You all right? Ignore the chill. Master it. Let your mind master the dread of the cold and the fear of death," he said.

"I need oxygen."

"Keep breathing. You're doing great. You're getting your body used to it. It's not that tough," he encouraged.

Was it the altitude? Why couldn't she relax? She did as instructed and took a deep breath. It wasn't easy, but she eyed him as he held his breath for long, with ease. Then he released.

"I'll do that again, and when I can't hold it anymore, I'll let you know. Then you do the same," he told her.

Mentally, she gathered her courage. "Okay. Let's go."

Surrounding ice cracked slightly as they further toward the middle of the lake. Her hands still shook, but she ignored them. She was strong and could take on whatever she needed rather than fear it.

"Okay, we're in deep enough. Let's try something new. Float on your back and breathe. Just like you did before," Nash said.

Calla nodded and closed her eyes. She sensed the sun on her face before submerging herself and leaning back. Soon she was floating, and the water felt like icicles on her skin. Within seconds, ice needles pricked and poked through her. They burned and hurt, and her teeth chattered. "Nash," she croaked, her voice hoarse.

"Yeah?" he responded.

Her body ached from pain, and she struggled to breathe, her senses paralyzed. "I can't do this."

"I'm here, Cal," Nash said, floating by her side. "Control your breathing. It's the first rule to conquer your fear. What is it you dread so much?"

She could barely see him through the glare of sunlight now appearing behind the mountain.

"You can't quit. Keep going," Nash said.

"I'm sorry. I'm sorry to waste your time."

He eyed her carefully. "That's enough for today. You've done enough breathing. Next time, we'll take it one step further and have you under. That's when meditation and control kick in."

They returned to the lake's bank, and he helped her out.

Calla was still panting when he handed her a towel and blanket from his backpack. As she reached for her knees, her head sank. It was too painful to hold herself up anymore.

He offered her a drink of water, and she took it as he sat beside her and wrapped his arms around her. "I'm sorry, Calla."

"It's not your fault. It's mine," she said.

"You're still in shock. But from what? Calla, tell me what happened. You've got to believe in yourself."

Taking a deep breath, she acknowledged his soothing voice. "I lost someone a long time ago and couldn't save her because I was afraid of the ice lake. I thought if I came back here and started on a different part of the lake with you, I could face that fear."

He raised an eyebrow. "You will, Cal, but when did this happen exactly?"

"Maybe I need to show you."

CHAPTER
EIGHT

CALLA STOOD AT THE WINDOW. This was the only winter home Calla had ever known. Many things from the time Lucy left were unclear, and much was still hazy in her mind. Lucy hid and was never found.

A dullness settled in her rib cage. The feeling of heaviness wouldn't flee as clouds of tepid air curled out of the chalets' chimneys and roof vents on the other side of the lake.

Bönigen was a village that gave Calla tranquility. Today, as most times she came, the sunlight glittered off a thin layer of sparkling ice on the outdoor surfaces of the beautiful chalet. A horizontal blanket of snow, delineating the left and right sides of the lake, reflected the sun. Like most homes here, the cabin had a small, private dock in the middle of a nearly two-kilometer lake with an ice bank on the other side separating it from its main body.

The view from the dock to the big house of the chalet was impressive, overlooking two arms of the lake, south, and north. Its large windows let most of the light inside during the day. Dawn shrouded the interior in obscurity.

Snow had stopped that morning when they had returned

to the chalet. Growing up, Calla's guardians had bought the holiday home when she was barely a teenager. When Calla started her British Museum curator job in London, she vacationed with them every winter and knew she owed them much.

Nash grazed her skin with a fingertip on her bare shoulder after they had showered and warmed up. Warm towels caressing their drying bodies, Nash wrapped his arms around her from behind and held her close as they both stared out the window.

It was the first time he'd used his body to show what he felt about her. Calla knew they were going to the point of no return. She liked it and gathered confidence from Nash, but she didn't know how to process her feelings toward him. Not yet.

She shifted around and settled into his broad chest. He kissed the top of her hair, and she drew back gently to look at him squarely.

"Is that where it happened? Is that where you lost Lucy?" he asked, looking at the lake.

"Yes. Lucy and I were childhood buddies. I was sixteen. She was ten. Every winter, my foster parents, Mama and Papa Cress, and I came here. There weren't many children in those days around here. It was natural that we connected. She was an exceptional child, but then one day she played by the lake, and we never saw her again."

Calla drew in a deep breath and moved toward the bathroom, a tear welling in her eye. "I promised Lucy's mother, Sue-Lyn, I'd say hello on this visit. I have to do this next bit alone."

"Okay," he replied, observing her. "I'm right here, beautiful if you need me."

"I know, Nash. And thank you."

She dressed quickly, finding her warm sweater, winter

boots, and a dry anorak. "I won't be long. Make yourself at home. Mama and Papa Cress always keep the chalet stocked. I'll see you shortly."

Calla left the chalet on the small path and progressed toward the residence next door. Magnificent chalets, surrounded by a weather-worn dock that swayed in the current that drew her attention.

She had to do this and took a set of stairs down toward the lake. It didn't look so threatening, not when Nash was here with her. Her hands went limp when she approached the frozen water. Then she examined the area where she used to play hide and seek for hours with Lucy, a game that never grew old with young girls.

Lucy had been good at it and played a little too close to the water. When they couldn't find her, Calla remembered jumping in. to look for her. She didn't know how long she was in the ice water and recalled nothing. Later, they told her she had been in the water for several minutes, then passed out.

That day Calla learned her body stiffened when in contact with freezing water. It was as if her body's neurological functions just stopped working. Was it an inherent genetic thing she didn't understand? She didn't know if she ever would.

Guilt stung at her core. Even now.

The hairs on her arms rose. She shouldn't have come here. It had only brought unwanted memories. Her nostrils detected the fresh-baked cookies their neighbor Sue-Lyn, Lucy's mother, had just made. She rubbed her hands for warmth in the brisk air. It was all coming back now—the details of how they had lost Lucy. Eager for a break from England, Calla visited every winter break. The plan had been to watch Lucy for the afternoon. A special girl, Lucy was one many would call a loner. To Calla, she wasn't. She was a friend. Once, Lucy had told her she'd learned of a lady in the lake. The lady was afraid of her powers. Of course, it was childish talk, but Lucy to Calla was someone wise beyond her years.

Calla turned when she heard Sue-Lyn approaching the water's edge. "It was always wonderful to see you two girls play together. Lucy took a special liking to you, Calla. You were the big sister that she never had."

Calla managed a weak smile, and Sue-Lyn returned the gesture. "You should stop blaming yourself, Calla. Lucy left us, and it was not your fault."

"Thank you, Sue-Lyn. It has been hard for you. You lost both Lucy and your husband. I'm always here for you." Calla took her hand. "I wonder if I could ask you a favor. Lucy once gave me a note that she had something for me in that room. I've never dared find out what it was, but I made this trip so that I can face the past. Could I have a peek around if that's okay with you?"

Sue-Lyn's eyes glistened. Pain stained them. "Of course, Calla." She dropped a box of fresh biscuits in Calla's hand. "Help yourself to more too before you leave. Get some for that gorgeous man I saw you with earlier, and please lock up. I need to go to town. Please also say hello to Mama and Papa Cress for me."

"Yes, I will."

Sue-Lyn ascended the trail back to the house, then turned for a moment. "And Calla, remember you're always welcome here. It wasn't your fault. Lucy is gone. Even though it was the hardest thing I've ever had to do, somehow I've found closure."

Calla felt as if daggers had hit her. She had never had the closure she needed, especially because Lucy's little body was never found. Why could she not let the guilt go away? She'd been trying to protect Lucy like a sister, and she had done a miserable job.

Sue-Lyn and Lucy's father, Zeng, had never changed the

place since the day she'd left. Zeng had been quite successful in business, from what Calla recalled. Several years ago, she'd learned that he'd gone missing and had never returned. The pain must've been unbearable for Sue-Lyn, who never faltered and always had something positive to say.

Eyes stinging with hot tears, Calla peered out toward the water and headed to the house. Everything was still in the room, from the drawings Lucy had created when she was younger to the pencils she'd needed for school and the posters Lucy used to have on the wall.

Lucy had been a mature child ahead of her years. Her parents came from China, and she was a first-generation Chinese American who had often come to Switzerland for holidays. Perhaps it was their way of keeping her spirit in this place. A place suspended in time.

Calla advanced swiftly, and she headed to the door at the end of the room. She had always seen the door but not once ever asked Lucy or the family about it.

Her hands fumbled as she turned the key in the door, which slid to one side. Dust and darkness greeted her, and for a second, her mind refused to register precisely what she saw.

CHAPTER
NINE

CALLA REACHED for the light and flipped it on. Nothing could have prepared her for the sight.

A deep, narrow room, well lit, collected some of the most advanced computers she'd seen in her life. The far wall had a desk. On it was a touchscreen computer. As Calla approached, she couldn't help but marvel at the DNA sequencer. From the looks of it, it had been twenty years since someone had used it.

"This is incredible," she whispered to herself.

Calla ran her hand over several large glass tubes. On the counter stood another computer. This one, however, didn't work. "What happened here?"

She inspected the touchscreen that showed a date, just a series of digits, so far in the future. When she touched the screen, the motion replaced the date with a different date. Inside the folder were blueprints. The first and second pages were sketches of a cliff building. When flipped open, the prints exhibited a super-structure construction on many levels in a crag, snowfields, a lab, and a few outbuildings.

Calla opened every single file until she found something

that made sense. Most notable were prototypes for all kinds of cameras that would rival anything at the ISTF agency.

She took her time investigating, wondering just what else on Earth was here. Her number one instinct was to find Sue-Lyn and ask.

Calla closed the door, locked it behind her, and kept the key in her pocket. She advanced downstairs, then stopped when she peered out the window. Outside the house parked a dark car. She'd seen it there when they'd driven here with Nash.

Waiting behind her rented Audi, its plates and windows were concealed.

Her phone rang. "Yes?"

"Miss Cress, we need you and Nash at the ISTF London offices. Something urgent has come up," the team's executive assistant Scarlett announced.

"Okay, we'll be back in London as soon as we can."

Calla approached the window, and as if by instinct, whoever was behind the wheel looked straight at her.

The car began its engines and crept to the end of the road. In all five seconds, it disappeared around the corner.

TEN

EIGHTEEN MONTHS LATER, PORT
OF SILVA MARIS, CÔTE D'AZUR,
3:27 P.M.

DAY 1

NASH MOVED SWIFTLY through the control room of the 553-foot-long flagship yacht. He liked to check things twice, everything from the mini-submarine that could submerge down to 50 meters underwater on good days. He could not be too careful, especially with all the guests onboard.

Next, he inspected the intruder missile detection system and stepped out to the double helipads. He would let the crew check the twenty-five guest cabins, the main receiving room that for tonight had been turned into a dance hall. The decks of the two swimming pools and hot tubs were clear of threats.

From the deck, Nash took the stairs that led to an inbuilt pool with a retractable roof. He smiled to himself. The yacht was original. He would never have imagined living on a futuristic boat reminiscent of a stealth warship or submarine. Scorpion Tide had been a wedding gift from Calla's actual parents, Stan and Nicole Cress.

Satisfied the inspection was done, he assured himself that like many things on this yacht, the master bedroom and the yacht's bridge had armor plating and bulletproof windows, all in bright and white shades.

Calla's parents had thought of everything when they'd constructed a ship that even had a garage to fit several vehicles. Lined side by side were three cars, a silver Maserati that Calla drove, a four-wheel drive for rough terrain next to a Jaguar F-Type, and a Jaguar XE.

Among other skills, Artificial Intelligence was a fundamental interest of Nash's, and processes around the ship could alert their smart phones.

Before finishing his inspection, he checked the counter-drone systems that detected and mitigated rogue drones should any enter their airspace. There was no sense in having a security system that wasn't up to date.

Nash smiled to himself. The yacht's operations included defensive and offensive options. He was taking no chances. Not anymore. The yacht, run by him, Calla and Jack, was a home, and was possibly the safest place for them.

He nodded to Delgado, who was as thorough as he was.

Captain Kaden Delgado, a former vice admiral of the US Navy, commanded the Scorpion Tide. Nash had had simple instructions for Delgado. "Hire a crew of ten and get up to speed with the technology, as it changes fast."

The former vice admiral of the US Navy was nothing like Nash had expected. Perhaps he'd predicted an older, gray-haired man in uniform. Delgado was nothing like that. He was an aristocratic gentleman with almond-shaped, coffee-colored eyes and a focused face. He had pale skin, thin lips, and a white mustache. A creasing brow arched over his square face, and a dancing Adam's apple moved when the fifty-five-year-old swallowed.

Nash took one look at the outside facilities and knew this yacht could take care of any threat. Having spent several days now at sea, he was satisfied. He was ready. Ready to marry Calla. Again.

They'd parked the yacht at the dock in the South of France with its entire crew moving through the ship, making sure everything was working perfectly. Right now, he was going to agree to anything Calla needed if it meant his family would be safe.

He smiled, bringing a picture of her to his mind. She was beautiful. Long ebony hair, green eyes, and slim, with athletic curves, he couldn't stop admiring. Nash didn't even see himself as resourceful as Jack, yet he did what he could to look after her, letting nothing get in the way. It seemed to work for the exceptionally talented woman she was. Calla was an independent spirit, which he liked about her. She didn't need a man to protect her.

Fast strides carried him through the ship. Everything was in perfect order, and he'd give the crew their next set of orders.

When he reached the lab office on the second level, he sank into the leather chair, relaxed, and crossed his right leg over his left, then rested his elbows on the armrest on each side of him.

He connected to the secure network and waited. Something was not right. Using the satellite feed, he fast-forwarded the images. Margot Arlington, head of the Congressional Oversight Committee for the National Security Agency, the NSA, used the same IP address that had wiped out the database collecting the agency's employees' data only two days earlier.

He ran a code to clone the IP address. It was fraudulent. He would have to hack into the dummy server, the only way to find out who was helping her. The fake IP was expensive and could've been a computer or a digital cash system. In trying to think of a reason for a citizen and government employee with so much capital to make a mess of government accounts, he came up with none.

Nash switched on the video feed on Margot Arlington's computer.

Margot was in her office and stared into the camera, confident she wasn't being watched. Like most days when he'd been asked to spy on her several months ago for laundering money, her short black locks were impeccably styled. She was of mixed-race origins, he'd read in her file. Though born in the US, a former presidential candidate, and US ambassador to London, her roots were equally Polish and Zimbabwean. To this day, Nash didn't know which side she favored most.

It took Margot a moment to log into a computer, and she did so with a unique key code. The screen froze, and Margot frowned. She waited for activity to resume on the screen and then spoke to a man who went by an avatar who said something in a digitized voice.

Margot nodded.

Just who was he? One thing Nash knew, the avatar had surfaced in intelligence circles when a notorious criminal by the name of Mason Laskfell, and former head of the ISTF, had been shot. By Margot.

As Margot's tiny microphone flashed, Nash watched it. He had installed a micro listening device that transmitted wirelessly to his system from her desk.

Nash froze the feed and forwarded it again. A line Margot assumed was secure was his way in and had been for a week. He had to know what she was up to. She'd been trouble from day one. Now he had a plan.

Nash sat and expected for her to sign out when she was done. He would then run a look into her screen window. Something was missing.

He delayed some more, then zoomed in from his mirroring laptop. Someone had left Margot a little surprise. He shook his head. It was an invoice with a note.

Since you contributed so much money to the service, obviously, you could afford the additional cost for the same level of security. We will add the following to your account:
Tracking device — for when you leave the house.
GPS/Cell phone tracking — for when you're running.
Warrant activation-simulation — for when you use the phone.
Receiver — so you can listen in on your office phone.
This invoice is a one-time service charge and can be reinstated anytime you want.

He paused and reread it. Margot had created many enemies over the years. This had to be one of them, but someone valuable to her. It sounded like a joke but probably wasn't.

Nash had no choice. The NSA had to know where the money was coming from.

ELEVEN

MARRAKECH, NORTH AFRICA,
11:23 P.M.

MARRAKECH, with its ancient architecture, temples, and souks, offered much, but Oskara Amano wouldn't be distracted. That could all wait.

She had never understood Lent Cyrus's fascination with Marrakech, but it didn't matter. As long as she paid her debt off, Oskara would go anywhere with him. Only privileged hires ever saw him. She was one of two.

An evening breeze whistled through the palm groves, making her hungry and eager to taste Moroccan and Mediterranean dishes she'd seen the staff prepare earlier. She had to give it to Lent. He usually spared nothing, not even a cent, and his *palais* perfectly blended a traditional Moroccan style seamlessly with the ultra-contemporary taste. Here was a magical North African retreat boasting lush, landscaped gardens and creatively designed terraces.

She took a deep breath. Her eyes wandered to the floor-length windows that accessed a roof terrace. Over the years, the hands of an ancient craft worker had fashioned white slabs of terra cotta building blocks, into an intricate mosaic of geometric patterns, like a carpet. Now, in the dim light of dusk, the floor looked like a deserted hotel lobby. Birds' chirping and cawing were the only sound that broke the calm quiet that surrounded the villa.

She ran her hand over her hunting knife and waited on the terrace of Lent's palace in the foothills of the Atlas Mountains. A contemporary residence, its classical architecture, Moorish arches and intricate tile-work, made her itch to inspect it further.

The house's unique ambiance intrigued her and was previously the family home of Suhada Mahdi, Lent's father, Oskara, had heard it whispered Lent owned the biggest shipping company in the market whose headquarters were in Bordeaux, France.

The corporation placed an eagle statue, which was the design symbol of the Mahdi's Maritime Empire of Suhada, at the front gate entrance, and these days it was referred to everywhere Lent went.

Lent had designed this place to tempt, ensuring all rooms had private terraces with panoramic views of the gardens, the pool, and the nearby Atlas peaks.

Why had he brought her here and not his usual residence in Miami? If she had to guess, he was on the run. She'd seen the files herself. Files she'd paid good money for someone to hack. Oskara constantly checked on anyone who hired her.

"Your men should have killed them when you had the chance. Now, that girl has passed on more things and could ruin everything we've worked for!" Lent shouted, storming toward her.

Trained as a psychiatrist with a private practice in Miami, few would know of his connection here. A tall afro-haired man, powerful in build and stature, Lent watched his prodigy, her, and turned on the Eye—a rotating high-tech desktop camera. Oskara couldn't understand why. After all, they were in the same room.

Silent and motionless, he stood like a figure carved from mahogany. Proud of his heritage, half Moroccan, half African American. Oskara had been told his father was born in the tiny village of Iblis in the Draa Valley, and his mother, Atlanta. Lent had always been proud of his family. Still, when he had been first sent away to attend boarding school, he would later confess that he was glad at the time that he was not representing either the African American or the Moroccan sides of his parentage. The rumor was he'd later abandoned both parents and changed his name. Lent Cyrus had a better ring to it.

The wind blew at his afro, obscuring his features, cooling him off after a long day under the scorching sun of Marrakech, the summer capital of Morocco. As he sipped the last of the Moet, Oskara wondered if he was not ignorant of some cultures the ancient peoples of Morocco had held in contempt, as he had grown up in the lap of luxury.

He studied her, the person he had trained.

Was this it? Would she see more of his anger? She wondered if he would be better off in a psychiatrist's chair, taking his advice rather than giving it. How his two worlds connected would always be a mystery. Oskara held her head high. She was talented and had come in handy and had helped to locate the guardian family. "I'm sorry, Lent."

Lent observed her.

Had it been a good idea to take on his contract? He was a man of many tastes, and she wondered if her black hair and enormous eyes the color of burnished iron threatened him as she stared back at him. Perhaps it was because she was well built, and her cream-colored skin, thin eyebrows, and firm chin rarely gave away her SAS training.

Often, she intimidated men with her words. Her commitment to intense and extended training demands had seen her as one of the few women recruited by the special forces.

She knew one thing. Lent had often monitored how she fought and attacked. He wanted to be proud, but it seems he couldn't even feel anything but sorrow for how much he had spent on her further training.

"I didn't train you to lose. Not to lose the fight to a woman who can imagine, and feel like we do," Lent said. "Your men should've been able to finish off Halona Osa-Menglian and her family."

It was a tone that Oskara wasn't comfortable with. She raised her chin. "She had help. I'm not sure who."

Lent walked back to his chair and sat down as he breathed in a deep sigh. "We need to decipher the Beale Ciphers. Thomas Jefferson Beale has a connection to my family."

She watched him and sometimes wondered why she had come to him. She wouldn't venture, but he was right about one thing. They had lost something great in New Mexico. They had come so close.

Lent stood and moved around the low table. "Perhaps there's another way." He glanced up. "I won't fail the same way they had. The same way Mason Laskfell did. Oskara," Lent said. "What you don't know is I've watched Cress all her life, and she doesn't disappoint. She's not predictable. The very moment Halona, a gifted guardian of secrets, ran into the line of your path, my vision was blocked."

"Your vision?" Oskara asked.

"Yes. It was delayed. My cameras have most of Calla Cress's life on them. I've watched that girl for many years. She's one I'd like to have in my chair. But for now the Eye's camera on her life will do."

"What do you mean you've watched?" Oskara asked.

"Think of me as a god. What I'm telling you is that I have ways. Cress's life is on my hard disk."

"How does that work? How can you have Calla Cress's life on your hard disk? No spy cam can… And if so, how?

How does it work? Plus, how can it possibly have her entire life?"

"Same way I've watched you and many others." He raised an eyebrow. "Calla Cress was one of those children for whom I waited. For years, the operatives lived in this dual reality. We can barely show the things we can do to a very primitive world. We can help this world and can change it. People I care about own the Beale Ciphers' secrets and their decryption. People think the ciphers lead to a monetary treasure, maybe, but they lead to so much more."

Lent rose and shuffled toward where the Eye on the desk stood.

Oskara peered into it, her insides taut. "You're saying Calla Cress knows the secret?"

"Yes. She can destroy what we've worked for, and sometimes, she can detect the cameras and avoid them. It's almost as if her mind becomes aware. Mason Laskfell used to say she can access a certain part of her mind that helps her and alerts her to danger. When this happens, she blocks people and the cameras," Lent added.

"We couldn't hear what Halona whispered in her ear?"

"Correct."

Oskara felt as exposed as a rabbit crossing a plowed field with a hawk circling overhead."Just how were you able to have a camera on her life? How could you…?"

"Oskara, they're so many things you don't know about the operatives. They understand secrets, your secrets. Operatives have access to all the world's scientific knowledge. Years ago, in one of my old labs, we could manufacture liquid electrons in a simple drinking water glass. My cameras are up there on satellite points, ready to capture anything that anyone will show me. They bounce from one electric source to another that has an open door. They can jump from one metal to another and capture anybody's life, and yours included. I have so much to show you. Come with me."

The Eye swiveled its round frame on the desk tabletop. Moments later, it stretched its neck.

"Go to that terminal," Lent said, pointing to a row of screens by the far wall of the room.

Oskara approached the counter. Cameras and monitors, each displaying different scenes and angles, rose. She took in a profound breath before she spoke to the voice recognition unit. "Show me what happened in New Mexico."

The system's response was instant.

TWELVE

SOUTH OF FRANCE

THE COASTLINE'S paleness reflected the moonlight above. With her wedding dress on and for the few moments Calla found alone, she stood at the Scorpion Tide's railing and took it in.

The small private port da Silva at Eze was a tiny marina. Normally, they restricted it to residents' boats, but the Scorpion Tide was a boat most flocked to see and could command favors thanks to Delgado's connections.

Tucked away in the corner of Cap Roux, Monaco was only five miles away. Eze sur Mer was where they'd spent the afternoon, and once the party had settled on the yacht and the guests had been dismissed, Nash had promised them a small after party. They would follow a steep drive up Nietzsche's Path to the perched village of Eze, comfortable and majestic on the cliff above. Calla was certain she would see the best views of the Côte d'Azur.

Holidaymakers and parties ebbed and flowed in all directions along the glistening coast. Music from celebrations, the laughter, the dancing, the merriment lifted her spirits. Pale light from the moon above the water and the serenity set an incredible coastal mood. Tonight was the last night of their wedding festivities. Calla loved it here, and the partying was not done.

The South of France had its perks, and for one week, Calla wanted to make the most of it. As strange as it sounded to her mind, she was marrying Nash for the second time. Only ten months after the first. Any bystander would think it was ludicrous, but not them. Tonight was special.

From where she stood on the yacht, Calla could see the top of a hill overlooking the ocean, where a church steeple poked above the village center. Its lights illuminating, it was minutes from the Exotic Garden, a major attraction at Eze and one she had never seen. Calla was eager to visit the restaurants, artisan shops, and world-famous hidden churches, plus a secret hiking path that led down to Eze beach.

Calla settled a hand on top of the yacht's railing, her white dress fluttering in the ocean air. Hair free of its usual ponytail and dropping down her back, it fanned down to her shoulders.

She took a deep breath. The Scorpion Tide docked out in the Mediterranean Sea on an exclusive boat pier cost a fortune, but it was the perfect privacy they needed.

Stan, her biological father, had thrown the wedding party for them on their yacht. And now, Tiege, her favorite operative and master of her security at ISTF, had made a quick plan with Nash and Jack for tonight. In Eze, they would go to a secluded villa for sale called Le Clair de Lune, one of the finest in Eze.

Nash, athletic and handsome, approached her from behind. She felt his breath on her bare shoulder. He was so close now, so personal, and she could sense his body heat.

"You're beautiful," he whispered, his warm breath on the back of her neck causing a shudder down her spine. "You ready, Mrs. Shields?"

"So, a second step at this?" She asked.

"I would do it repeatedly. Our first wedding was, well…

we eloped and kept it secret for many months, from everyone. I don't want to run anymore or hide who we are."

She smiled. Nash, now top security adviser at the NSA and ISTF, stood and whipped her around. His body lived in a gym, in the field, and with her, and it showed through the elegant tux he wore. He seemed born to wear it.

With his sandy hair and expressive gray eyes, he made a woman's heart race. The fine-boned structure of his pleasant face and broad-shouldered frame were as attractive as the rest of him. Tonight, as always, she admired his torso and the way his slim-fit tuxedo jacket stretched tight across him to hug him, combining luxury fabrics and razor-sharp cuts.

Yes, he was attractive, but it was his intelligence and courage that shone through his eyes. Nash was loyal to two things, justice and to the people he cared about. Nash had a charm most women could not resist, but he was devoted to her, and it made her feel safe. She looked into those crystal gray eyes, and Nash moved closer.

He grinned, showing a row of perfectly white teeth. "I've been looking forward to this for a long time. Come," he whispered. "It's time to go."

She nodded in agreement.

Together, they walked up the stairs.

Nash smiled, and the hard masculine lines of his face intrigued her. "And so, Mrs. Shields... I like the ring of that. Calla Cress, whose married name we never use. Head of ISTF and *the Red Fox*, you ready to make that jump?"

"No, they'll still know me as Miss Cress there, The Decrypter. I can't get used to that nickname, but it means we stay safe in ISTF. It's on a need-to-know basis for most people, I'm afraid."

He smirked. "Some things never change."

Tiege pulled up on the dock in a Bentley. Jack and his girlfriend, Marree, were already in the car.

Several moments later, as they drove away from the pier and up the coast into the small inlet, the view took her breath away. The Bentley sped along the winding seaside highway and then curved inward toward the hills as they approached the modern villa.

The car pulled up in front of the entrance, and Calla, Jack, Marree, Nash, and Tiege stepped out and joined the butler, who greeted them at the door. Trust the men to hire an entire staff tonight to show the villa a potential buy for them in its authentic form. But she had already made her mind up. If Nash wanted this home as a getaway from the Scorpion Tide, then why not. Villa Clair de Lune's ocean views made her itch to explore.

They entered the vast lounge where music played, and a catering staff waited. Two bars were at either end of the pool and the men stopped near the doors where a table with appetizer trays and drinks was at the ready, but Calla could not eat anymore.

Calla and Nash moved to a magnificent balcony overlooking the Mediterranean Sea. "I actually never thought I'd ever get married, not after what happened with my parents," Calla said.

"It's too late now, Mrs. Shields. Any regrets?"

She stared at him. "No. Not at all."

"I would marry you over and over, no matter how many times you push me away," he said.

"I'm sorry, I did that, Nash. It's just when we lost the baby, doubts about this life overcame me. ISTF, the missions, but I know now we can only have what we want if we eliminate what we don't."

He kissed her hand and drew her close. Nash had given her a second chance at normal. He took a step closer to her, tilted her chin up, and his lips met hers. He kissed her slowly.

"We will, and we will do it together. And one day, you and I will—

"There you two are," Jack said, bursting onto the balcony. "We were wondering."

Nash grinned.

"You two are inseparable," Jack said, "which is why I need to speak to you."

Marree and Tiege drifted behind Jack.

"Calla, Nash," Jack began, "I've got a gift for you."

Jack handed Nash and Calla two small gift boxes. "This is a little wedding present for you. This is what I call the future. Telepathy powered by the rhythms of your pulse and brain signals. You can talk to each other with your mind, and it gets exciting… in the bedroom. Tiege and I have been working on this for a while."

"Open it," Jack said.

Nash let Calla dig her hand into the package, and she drew out an electronic device. "A watch?" she said.

"Not just any watch. An old concept with new tech, new thinking, e-telepathy, to be exact. The non-creepy version," Jack said. "I also have one and had tested it for over a year."

Jack had wrapped the outside of the watches in leather; and lined the insides with a clear film. Carefully, he took both watches and removed the film, then turned one watch over and tinkered with the back. Finally, he placed the watches into their hands. "You each get one. Want to use them?"

"Intriguing. You saying I can use my mind to communicate? How does it work?" Calla asked.

Jack pressed a button on each watch. "Think of it as a remote control that can map waves from your brain and trigger an emotional response that is then transmitted through waves all the way to the chips in this watch and vice versa, depending on who you're speaking to. See that?" he said, pointing to the watch's frame. "It's got communication to my satellite. You can talk to each other through a line of communication created following the rhythm of your pulse. As the watch connects to your nervous system and links to your nerve activity, it triggers a connection. Think of it as Bluetooth on steroids. If enough of us have the same watches, it functions very much like a chat forum, through emotions. That's why I picked the Scorpion Tide because of the impressive line of sight to that satellite and security. But it shouldn't matter wherever you are in the world. What do you think?"

Calla didn't answer. Her eyes were searching his, her lips trying to form words of awe and gratitude. "It's impressive, Jack. But then again, I can't remember anything that wasn't impressive that you created."

Jack's eyes lit with excitement. "Try it."

Calla admired Jack. His intellect, his loyalty, and friendship. He was the best friend anyone could ask for, and she knew she had hurt him when she chose Nash over him. He had remained loyal to the core.

"Of course," Calla responded with a smile. "It's a little weird, but what isn't in our world? We'll have to get used to it."

"It's great, Jack. Thank you," Nash added.

"I've set it up, but let me show you how to use it." Jack leaned in. "Watch it for a few seconds, and it will load the program. Think about what you want to say, and it will transmit via my private satellite."

Calla watched Jack as he engaged with this satellite software on his phone. "Thank you, Jack."

She felt all eyes on her -Tiege's, Marree's, and Nash's. Calla took a deep breath and engaged with a thought, a word she wanted to send Nash. When she saw his smirk, she knew. The watch worked.

Nash leaned in and whispered in her ear. "I hear you loud and clear, beautiful."

She giggled. "It's working, Jack," she said, twisting her wrist to admire the mechanics within the gadget further. If she wanted to, she could just speak to Nash silently. "Does it work when we are in different countries?"

"As long as my satellite is up and running and these two settings are engaged, you can be in Siberia and Nash in the Pacific, and you can still communicate."

So far, they had only communicated a few words, simply to test it out. It was strange talking through her mind over a watch signal on GPS.

"It's the latest thing in telepathy research," Jack added.

Nash turned to Jack. "Can I speak to you for a sec?"

NASH TOOK Jack to one end of the balcony, away from the group. He fiddled with the watch in his palm. "Means a lot to me. I wouldn't have been able to do this, you know, marry Calla if I knew you were not okay with it. You and I have a very long history, and it says a lot that you'd do something like this."

Jack ran a hand through his dreadlocks. "Nash, we've been through this. She chose you a long time ago. It's just right, and it's what I want for you. You're a brother to me. Yes, I won't lie. There was a moment when I wished it would've… that she would've, but that was a long time ago, and that's not what friends do. We stay together through everything. I couldn't be happier for you."

Nash raised an eyebrow. "You certain?"

He acknowledged the concern. "I'll find my girl one day," Jack said.

"Sure you haven't found her yet?" Nash replied, eyeing Marree where she stood with Calla.

Calla joined them as Nash turned to her.

Jack straightened his tux. "Go on, beam her in. Or you might prefer to wait till later."

Nash bent and leaned into Calla, his lips nearly touching her cheek.

She closed her eyes, then opened them, laughing.

With a knowing smile, Jack backed away in stitches. "Now I'm wondering if this present was a good idea."

FOURTEEN
MARRAKECH

THE SCREEN DIDN'T LIE. Oskara watched in horror as Halona sprinted to the cave, her men in pursuit. Halona shivered from the cold, and the wind blew her hair wildly. Her bare feet seemed to have no resistance against the rocks and dust, as she scuttled to a wide cliff where she met Calla Cress and fell to the rocks at her feet.

The machine continued its work. Screen after screen, it showed what had happened next, and then it paused as if someone had turned it off. The monitor flickered with static before it went blank.

Oskara swung to the other screens. They, too, were blank. The system had ceased working right when her gun had fired, and Cress moved toward Halona's injured body. Then nothing. Complete blackness.

"Is that all you have? What happened next? Do you have more on the cameras?" Oskara asked.

"No," Lent said. "Not anymore. There's nothing, and she has the one thing I've been searching for all my life," Lent responded.

Oskara wiped sweat from her brow. She knew what she had to do. Make sure the secret would stay a secret.

FIFTEEN

ISTF HEADQUARTERS, LONDON,
11:08 P.M.

ISTF ANSWERED to no directive or jurisdiction, a fierce unit upholding international law. From now on, Scarlett was the law, and no one would suspect the little secretary who took phone calls, booked private jets and hotel accommodation for all former and current heads of ISTF, starting with Mason Laskfell, then Allegra Driscoll, and now Calla Cress.

Scarlett had paid her dues.

ISTF worked alongside the Secret Intelligence Service, but that was all about to change. She admired how the organization responded swiftly to eliminate cyber crimes, and even if it had five hundred permanent staff and stepped up where Interpol, the CIA, and MI6 left off, nobody had ever asked her to step up.

Scarlett had been an assistant for far too many bosses. Not any more.

It wouldn't be easy to get in, but she had every access she needed to bypass the building's smart technology security.

Most people here called themselves code breakers. Others called themselves security agents. A handful had no job descriptions but went by a code name, a color followed by an animal, and Red Fox was the highest agent code, belonging to Calla Cress, now head of ISTF.

Scarlett pulled out her phone and inspected the high stone walls. It would take everything she had to run past the reinforced steel gates, and she knew where every unregistered escape tunnel was.

Her feet moved faster, her dark suit against the shadows, keeping her invisible. She hurried through the main floors.

Certain no one had followed, she walked up to the security guard outside the main entrance of the security room. "Red Fox has sent me to check on the firewall protocols for her office," she said.

The security guard shrugged. He checked her credentials by scanning her palms. They were accustomed to Scarlett's visits here, and she wouldn't expect anything else but access.

"You can go through," he said.

"I need the night's password. You know, finish the job. You know what they do to those who aren't thorough."

The man set eyes on her for a few seconds before he reached for a piece of paper, jotted down the password, and gave it to her. "Be sure to shut down when you are done in there."

Scarlett smiled. "No problem."

He instructed other patrols to ignore Scarlett until she was out of the server rooms.

Scarlett had already hacked the Internet-connected devices, each running one or more bots around the entire building. Control over it was now hers.

"I'll be two ticks," Scarlett said to the man.

She progressed into the server room. A long line of server farm computers greeted her. The best in the field. She banged, hacked, and shut them down. The most expensive equipment in the world wasn't all that great if you were Scarlett. These servers' activities were usually secret. Now *she* was the secret.

Scarlett proceeded to the satellite connections in the adjacent room. The easiest target. She disabled their terminals, but she could not destroy them. She might need them. Finally, she turned to the easy pickings, the regular connection hardware.

Guards covered every inch of the building. Scarlett disconnected every secure line and used the guards' password to hack into the security guard's communications. "This is for all those late nights," she whispered before she sent the security team the fake coordinates for tomorrow's schedule.

"CAPTAIN!" one of the security guards yelled from the terminal's interface.

She heard it in her earpiece.

Scarlett froze.

"Sir, I think something is wrong with our GPS," one of the security guards said.

Scarlett hacked faster.

"Okay. Seems we're good now," she heard him say.

There was one more thing. Agent Red Fox's office needed one thing, Scarlett needed to be inside and plant a bug on the office's command center. She worked like her life depended on it.

Finally, she was done.

Scarlett nodded to the security team on her way out. They nodded back.

In all of three minutes, she was on the street outside the building. The entire network, the entire building, was now offline.

She smiled. She'd left no trace of her attack. There was only one thing wrong. She could've made more money out of this, but then again, this wasn't about money.

DAY 2

WHEN THEY GOT to the master suite, Calla took in her surroundings with a smile. Extravagant window drapes cascaded over expansive windows and misted the room with low lighting. The dark wood contrasted with the linens on the bed. Set in Provence colors, the furniture was various shades of blue and yellow. The curtains were a swirling pattern of aqua and violet blending, and the floor was a swirl of the two.

Calla ran her hand across the bedspread and patted it for Nash to join her. They settled on it together. A plate of cheese, fruit, bread, and wine were on a small table, and Nash let Calla start on the meal. "I know you're hungry," he said, smiling.

Calla's eyes lifted at him. "not really. It's late."

"I know what you mean," he whispered, picking at the bread with her.

"I think I should be the romantic here right now," she said, biting into a piece of aged brie. "Feels like we haven't had a moment together. Something's been on your mind, Nash. What is it?"

He stopped chewing. "I prefer not to do this tonight, but there's something I saw. An account I've been monitoring for months and had had no activity for more than a year has suddenly received several transactions in the last couple of weeks. I didn't want to tell you because, frankly, a part of me wants to forget we have a new Mason Laskfell, but the other part feels that something he was up to before he died still lives. I don't want to be surprised."

"Mason? But he's dead. We got him," she said.

Nash wiped his mouth with a napkin and looked straight into her eyes. "I don't know. I wasn't going to tell you about the transactions. Think they're going into his old account. We've just been through so much, and certainly not tonight. It's not what I want for us to think about. I'm going to investigate it and keep you out of it."

"It's written all over your face. Nash, I care about what you care about. We'll figure it out. We always do. I get you don't want to talk about it tonight, but you're going to have to tell me what's going on soon and tell me what we're up against."

Nash's fingers tickled her thigh, watching her, admiring her for a moment, then he smirked. "I have a lot more on my mind right now, like trying this new watch Jack gave us."

She laughed. "Then let's try it, shall we?"

Her hair fell in her face, and he swept it back, cradling her face in his hand.

Pulling her closer to him, her lips pressed gently against his.

He dragged down the straps of the dress, and his hands traveled over her back, sliding down her spine until his arms encircled her, holding her close to him. Nash ran his palms through her hair, and his hands slid down her neck, over her shoulders, under the straps, and he caressed the curve of her back.

Calla passed her hands over his back, feeling a sequence of

smoothness and strength. Pulling her lips from his, she passed her tongue down his neck to his collarbone, where she felt his pulse race.

Nash swallowed hard and searched her eyes, his gaze burning at her. "I love you. You and me against the world, no matter what," he said.

She wrapped loose arms around his collar and felt the heat of his body, his skin as his hands ran up and down her back. She stroked his hair as his arms folded around her. The watch illuminated and fired up the software.

No words were necessary.

SEVENTEEN

THE SCORPION TIDE YACHT,
FRENCH RIVIERA, 3:22 A.M.

THIS TIME, Jack knew something was wrong. He progressed down the stairs, then slotted the card through his room door and entered his cabin. Something had been bothering him about the way the code sequence readings appeared almost eighteen months ago. The day with Halona, who had died in their arms, had not gone well.

Many days after that, they had found Halona's village, and they learned little. All they were told was that the family disappeared and had never been heard from again.

For the last several nights, Jack had been observing the code sequences he had coined after he'd discovered the wall paintings with Calla in the cave. What his machine could do was scary, unheard of. The photographs they had taken in the caves continued to frustrate him. All those codes, those numbers, a key to decryption.

How Calla figured the sequences out was beyond him. Now she would have to use that telescope to finish the task, but it was too dangerous. That's why he had hidden it. They had made a bargain. One takes one part of the puzzle and hides it from the other. They each had taken a piece of

Halona's secret. He was to hold on to the telescope. Calla took the key to decrypting the cipher.

The images from the cave bothered him. Also, where had Halona's telescope come from? The method the telescope used was unbreakable to his knowledge and that of many of the scientists he worked with. Just how had Beale done it? Why the caves? Who painted the drawings with such a sophisticated code? They had spent the last few months trying, and maybe it was time to let the issue go. They had gotten nowhere, and Jack wasn't sure why he'd thought of the cave code tonight.

He heard a noise behind, then pivoted.

Alarm welled in him.

His body froze mid-stride, and his mouth fell open. It wasn't possible.

Jack gripped his throat and pressed a hand against his breastbone, then took several seconds to digest the appearance of the intruder.

This man was dead. He had to be.

It was several moments before he spoke. "You're supposed to be dead," Jack said.

"I may have been gone a long time, but I'm not dead," the man in front of him replied.

This couldn't be happening. Jack had seen the man die. He'd gone to his funeral as much as he hadn't wanted to. His grandmother had forced him to. He'd been bitter toward the man for dying. But now, this man had returned. The accident had happened. It had. Yet, as he stared at the man, he sounded different. Nothing about his being here made sense. He looked old. Besides long hair, his face had wrinkles and ridges. The man he believed would never return was nigh unrecognizable.

"It's not possible," Jack said as he tried to recall everything about him.

"What's not possible?" the man asked.

"You died. I saw you die. I was there. Not even you can come back from that." Jack said. "I didn't want to, but grandmother forced me to attend your funeral. I was livid!"

"I know," he responded before Jack could continue. The intruder then reached up, scratching the stubble on this chin.

Jack swore. Somewhere in his memory, he could see the blood on the man's shirt from where he'd been shot.

"Supposed to be, but not really. I'm alive, Jack," the man stated.

Jack made for his gun in the drawer but was suddenly cut off.

Behind him, it caught him hard. The knife went deep into his shoulder.

He screeched; the pain monstrous.

"Stop moving, and it won't hurt," the man said, patching his shoulder by ripping a cloth from the bedsheets and pressing it to ease the bleeding. "Now, look what you made me do. I need you to come with me," the man said.

"Why?"

"There'll be enough time for all your questions, but we better go. My employer is not patient."

The pain from the knife wound eased. He had expected much from this person, but to have a betrayal like this and a knife to his shoulder, something he hadn't seen coming, was torturous.

Just where had the other men come from? How had they even gotten onto a yacht as secure as the Scorpion Tide?

Jack lifted his chin, trying to ignore the pain and the blood on his shirt. "Who do you work for? The Shadows?"

"The Shadows are a myth," he replied.

"Who and how much did they pay you to do this? Your motivation is always money."

"One million sterling. You fetch a hefty price, Jack. I always knew you would," were the immediate words that left the intruder's mouth.

Pain resurfaced in Jack's shoulder and he breathed deep. "What's your agenda in this?"

"I'm here to collect evidence."

"What kind of evidence?"

"My employer will answer that."

Jack pulled up his sleeve to reveal blood that had trickled down his shoulder as two more men helped him up, blocking any desire for movement from the look of their pistols.

His mind went over the past few days to retrace his steps. The Scorpion Tide was impenetrable. Just how had they done it? How had they slipped past Captain Delgado's security? And Tiege's? Nash's? Somebody must've helped.

He set his arm down on the counter where his own blood had spilled. Jack couldn't remember how it had happened, how he had parted ways with this man, but he remembered his death.

Now he doubted his memory.

Jack now felt faint. His drawer was inches from his bed, but he would need to circumvent the men.

"Let's go. My boss won't be that gentle," the first man said.

Jack eyed the drawer with the gun. "Go? Where are we going?"

"Move now. Questions later," was the man's response.

Just who was this employer? Jack had to think fast. Then he heard a noise above him.

With the Scorpion Tide guests still on board for Calla and Nash's party, going strong into the night, his ambushers had planned the moment perfectly, somehow knowing to slip in with the guests.

No one would hear him if he didn't get to the panic button by his bed.

He took his chances and lunged for the door.

A woman in tactical gear blocked his path and laid a blow on his bad shoulder. He zipped round as a second clout on his head nearly knocked him out.

She seemed like a vision as he slowly came to. With every training in him, he leaped for the first guy, then slammed a boot into the groin of the second goon.

The attackers moved quickly. With his hand over his hurting shoulder and the last of his strength, he put as much power into his swing as he could and sent a guy flying.

He prayed he'd make it to the panic button, but couldn't get to it fast enough. In his wild state, the pain almost made him forget why he was running.

Jack thumped to the hard floor that nearly concussed him. Somewhere in the commotion, he knew they had destroyed his laptop, his watch. The telepathic software was ruined. Dead.

The four ambushers' only option was to wind duct tape on his feet.

His brain overloaded from the knock, his vision blurred, a sharp pain ran up and down his arms. He gritted his teeth and prepared for death as his world went fuzzy. How could this, his father, a man he thought was deceased, do this to him?

The last thing he saw were two gloved hands gripping more firearms.

EIGHTEEN

CLAIR DE LUNE VILLA, EZE,
6:27 A.M.

THE CELL PHONE RANG. Nash stretched for it as Calla stirred from her sleep. "Salib?" Nash said.

He'd called again, as he had promised. Nash rose and moved away to the balcony as a golden sunrise appeared over the horizon. He wasn't sure how Calla would take this.

She stirred and rose slowly from the bed and looked out over the water where their yacht docked.

Nash nodded with a smile and pressed his ear to the receiver. Salib's call meant one thing. His theory was correct.

"Nash, it's time. Can you make it? I know you're tied up. It's been an important week for you."

Sheik Amir Salib. For years, Nash had been his go-to for security matters. Salib, a tycoon who practically ran Kuwait, was an old friend. The sheik attracted all kinds of wrong people with his wealth and influence in the Middle East. Every inch an aristocrat. The man had a heart of gold, and Nash knew it. Salib's time in the army had given him a special appreciation for men like Nash.

"Sure?" Nash said.

"Yes, my friend. I hate to bother you after I've just seen you get married. You sure this won't be a problem?"

Nash felt his heart sink. He'd spent little time apart from Calla in the last weeks, but she would understand. He could finally find the people who had targeted his unborn child only months ago. "What do you have for me?"

"A leak in the NSA linked to a deflector in ISTF shared details about Calla. We don't know who. What I've intercepted involves *The Danvers Project*. An MI6 project kept off ISTF records related to the Beale Ciphers," Salib said.

"I can take care of that. Send me everything you have."

"Nash, I'm also under some pressure. You'll need to act fast."

"Why?"

Salib's tone changed. "Money is moving again. Billions of it."

Nash drew in a breath. "I knew they'd compromised the bank account. I have a team working on it and need some information before I put more men on this. What help do you have?"

"An old acquaintance from my days in the Eastern Block of the Kuwaiti Army," Salib said. "He's no longer active with military cover duties, but I'll go there first and see what I can find."

"Okay."

Salib's breathing intensified. "Nash, it has to be done tomorrow. How soon can you get here?"

Nash checked his watch. "I can be there by this evening. I'll take the first flight or charter a jet."

"Don't. My corporate plane is on standby in Nice. Nash, tell me honestly. Can you do this alone and keep ISTF out of it? Something isn't right with the picture. I would never ask if it wasn't important. You've been more than a brother and saved my life twice. But can I ask you for a favor?"

"Anything," Nash replied.

"Before Mason Laskfell died, he deployed men across the Middle East and into Africa. I'd like one of my men to go in with you and check out this situation, this site, a lab, from where my son has gone missing. That's how this whole matter started. I want to know what he was working on. We found several files on a spy program, but they destroyed much of the evidence in operations. I don't know how you do it, but I know you're good at what you do. I need my son back."

"I'll look into it. We'll figure something out, Salib. I don't want you to stress anymore about this. Let me think first before I go."

Salib hung up, and Nash moved to where Calla stood.

"You have to go, don't you?" she said, moving to the balcony in her nightdress.

He held her close. "One of Salib's men says there could be a western intelligence breach working over the Middle East and North Africa. I have to leave. It involves his son too who has gone missing, but… I can't leave you alone like this."

"Nash," she said. "You can. I care for Salib and he trusts you."

How could he tell her Salib had protected them from something even more dangerous all those months ago? "I'll complete this as fast as I can. I promise, Okay?"

She nodded and pressed her lips to his. "Okay."

Nash seemed to struggle with what he would say next. "I won't be able to contact you. Not until I complete the mission."

"I know. Not surprised. You were never meant to be in one place," Calla said.

"Really?"

"Salib is a good man," she said. "He needs you."

"In this industry, there are no sure things."

"This industry?" She laughed. "You mean spying and going after the bad guys. I would hardly call it an industry."

"That's the closest thing we have to an industry. Not sure exactly how else you would classify using high-tech, combat tactics, and satellites to protect those that will pay. Our lives are not so normal. I don't want to leave you," he pleaded. "Not so soon after last night, or any night for that matter."

"It's not like we haven't been married before," she said with a giggle. "I like Salib. What does he need you to do? What's the job? I know you don't do it for the money, Nash, and your missions are not cheap for any billionaire. When they call on you, they will pay for the best and must be in deep trouble."

"He needs a team and security. I think it is personal again. The usual. Something I can't talk about. He has billions of dollars at stake, always has. He's like the Robin Hood of the oil and technology industry. Cal, I don't know how long the mission will be, but we can keep in touch with Jack's new software and these watches. This time I'll break the rules."

She nodded, looking at the watch. "When do you fly?"

"Later today."

She pressed her lips to his. "Sh… I wouldn't be good to you if I didn't let you go. You need to do this. Besides, I have Jack, Marree, Delgado. We'll just sail the Mediterranean till you come back. I know you can't tell me exactly where you're going. It's for both our safety."

Nash smiled. "I'll be in touch as soon as I can."

She pressed him to the bed. "Do you need to leave right now or does Mrs. Shields get one last request?"

OSKARA RAISED her chin and observed the Eye, the camera device on the counter. "There'll be no turning back."

"You have my permission," Lent said. "Use whatever is in our power to make sure Cress never interferes with my plans ever again. It's time we teach ISTF a lesson."

Oskara thought about Lent's orders, and her head cocked.

"Time to find out what Cress knows," Lent said, moving toward Oskara.

For years, they had hired her to carry out people's undesirable work. Work they didn't care to do themselves. But Lent was a different boss and Oskara had stuck around more than she usually would.

Oskara never cared who hired her. Lent had employed her like all her other missions through a secret contact, and he'd also paid for her artificial intelligence training ten years ago. That one slip now meant she had to pay off a debt to him.

The camera rotated.

"This will be a tough mission, but if you do it, I'll be willing to pay whatever you want."

"Find out who she's associated with," Lent said. "You're

dealing with British government intelligence now, so use what resources you need."

"Anything?"

"Yes. I want an information-gathering mission. Find out if she has any friends, lovers, or intelligence circles she runs in. If she does, find out who they are, and we'll go from there."

"Lent," Oskara said. "You can count on me."

"That's what I like to hear. She'll turn soon enough," he said. "You either buy into the Beale Ciphers, or you end up dead. She knows about the girl in New Mexico. It's been over a year, but now we are ready. Calla Cress and the man Jack Kleve are who we need. ISTF pronounced Halona dead upon arrival at the hospital. They put the family in a witness protection program of some sort. I've been hunting them for the greater part of last year. My patience is running out."

"She won't surrender. We'll have to squeeze the information out of her. That'll include changing the world as she knows it," Oskara said. "And my men in London are on it. Scarlett was an easy plant."

A smile spread across his face. "I know. Watch that one, though. Scarlett may be more useful than we know."

"Leave it to me," she added. "I want us at the head of the game. I'm eager to get back into the swing of things."

The camera swiveled as if it had a mind of its own.

Oskara observed it. Why did Lent always insist on recording every session with her?

CHAPTER
TWENTY

LONDON, 1:27 P.M.

DAY 3

CALLA CRUISED the Maserati through the Westend like a ghost, not caring to stop at Great Marlborough Street to run an errand. Had she been too quick to let Nash go?

She didn't want to feel like this. Empty and Calla couldn't remember Jack saying goodbye. Perhaps he and Marree had been busy after the wedding.

Calla missed London, even if she'd spent most of her child-hood hating it. That feeling seemed to have faded, replaced with a dull numbness.

She cruised the Maserati to the ISTF offices on the Mall. Opulent houses converted into a high-class office block were a familiar sight. Her phone was off most of the trip back to London, something a Red Fox Agent hardly did, but she needed to think, and needed a distraction.

When her Maserati stopped in front of the building, a knot in her stomach unraveled. Startled, she glared at the building's secure entrance.

Leaving the car in the loading zone, Calla strode into the

building. When she rounded the corner past the lobby, she saw people running.

Then she heard the commotion. First, a gunshot followed by a leaking gas can.

Calla zipped her head round.

She was dodging debris and brass until she saw an agent lying face down on the ground. He didn't respond when she called out to him.

She put her hands under his shoulders and dragged him from a collapsing wall.

He slowly came to, and she set a shaky hand on his cheek, then wiped dust and debris from his face.

"What happened?" she asked.

"An attack," he said, his voice heavy and scratchy.

She was torn between her duty to determine where the attack came from and her desire to save those evacuating. The building was emptying quickly. In fact, hardly anyone was in the building now.

"I need to call the emergency services," Calla said.

"No! Red Fox, I'm okay. Calla," he mumbled. "You need to get out of here."

"Who's behind this?" Calla asked.

Thundering boots on the floor behind her alerted her senses.

"Looks like it's you," said an agent, approaching her. "Miss Cress, you are under arrest. You may remain silent."

When she saw the numbers they came in, Calla rose slowly as the agent handcuffed her and read her her rights. "What is this all about? Why are you doing this?" Calla asked.

"Your questions will be answered, but from what I can tell, you've been planning this for a while," the agent replied. "Bringing down ISTF."

"I don't know what you're talking about," Calla replied.

"*Au contraire.* You knew exactly what you were doing. In

fact, I talked to Scarlett, your assistant. She says you planned our attack."

"That's not possible," Calla said, twisting from the cuffs restraining her, and tried with great effort to snap them open.

The agent pulled out a gun and cocked it. "My orders were to bring you in as soon as you arrived. It looks like you have no choice, Cress. Give up and hand yourself in. It will go smoothly for you."

"Not like this," said Calla, twisting as she saw Scarlett scowl and head toward her with a pistol.

His words had left her speechless, and her stomach churned. Was Scarlett part of this? The arrest was unusual. Her ISTF agents were usually loyal and sincere people. This guy she'd never met. Her fight was not here, not now, not until she knew what was going on. And since when did Scarlett carry a gun? Suspicion stirred in her gut, and her belly clenched.

"Run!" the agent she'd saved screamed.

She gulped a quick breath, and with a pop sound, she was free from the cuffs. Calla seized Scarlett's handgun, released a shot in the air, and sprinted out of the building toward her Maserati.

She fired up the engine, leaving a string of sirens behind her.

Ahead, she could see her destination.

CALLA TRIED Jack's phone from her in-car system, her heart thumping. She was in a heck of a lot of trouble.

No answer.

Nash was off the grid, somewhere between North Africa and the Middle East by now.

Marree's phone was off, too.

What had happened to ISTF? A bomb? An ambush?

Someone had destroyed the agency and pinned the blame on her. She sped the Maserati through Central London.

Buildings, rooftops and streets on the Mall were in a perpetual mist. The fog reduced the world to a flat vista of gray and never-ending mist hung over the city like an unbroken veil. The sound of the wind on her half-open windows was like an invisible hand rapping the glass, like the slap of skin meeting skin.

She closed it.

Calla had to get to Jack's lab, a concealed and bolted up warehouse off the M4 motorway. No one knew about that place. There, she could think.

When she got to the warehouse, a man waited as he lit a cigarette. Jack's longtime acquaintance, a spacecraft designer for NASA. A shadow fell over his dark gray eyes, as he sported a modish look fashioned by neat, dark-blond locks.

What was he doing here, a long way from Florida?

Primarily known as Tad in their conversations, he had been a close friend of Jack's growing up in the Seychelles. Something had happened along the way. The men stayed in contact, but not this close. Certainly not enough to know where the lab was.

She parked the car and headed toward him.

"Can I help you?" Calla said.

He raised a brow ridge. "I'm Tad," he said.

"I know."

He stood in front of her, discarded the cigarette, and pushed large hands deep in his pockets. "You could let me in, Calla. You know, Jack would be upset if you don't."

Taking a deep breath, she said, "After you."

His eyebrow rose again, this time with an amused and mischievous smile. "Jack sent me."

"Thaddeus Evick," Calla said, raising an eyebrow as she used a hand to unlock the lab's palm recognition system. "What's a NASA engineer and technology analyst doing here? You're a long way from Florida. Jack has mentioned you perhaps two to three times to me, and not once did he tell me you knew where this lab was. Which begs the question, what are you doing here? Why now?"

His eyes narrowed. "I don't have time to explain, Calla. You must listen to me."

Calla took in a deep breath. She would give him the benefit of the doubt. Maybe Jack had sent him. But then, where was Jack? She was certain he and Marree were still in France on the Scorpion Tide.

"I'm here to help," he replied.

She swept aside her tangled emotions. "I need a quiet place to think, Tad. I can't do this right now. Just need a place where no one will disturb me," Calla said.

"I know. I can help," Tad said. "Jack didn't show up for a call we were scheduled to have last night. It was a crucial call. He knew I was coming to London. I've been trying to reach him for over twenty-four hours, and it's not like him. I'm embarrassed to say I was jealous of Jack's work for years, and the last time I saw him, I put a tracking device on him. Even though I meant to spy on his work, kind of like how we did when we were kids, I saw strange activity on his GPS tracking device, and it led me to this place."

Calla wasn't sure if she should believe him. The lab was a secret between her, Jack, and Nash, but it seemed believable enough that Tad would've tried to spy on anything Jack had been working on. She was out of ideas for the moment.

Calla saw something change in Tad's face, as if his features were straining. Something was wrong, like a magnet pulling at Tad. He held on to the lab's iron door to keep himself on his feet.

"What's wrong?" Calla asked.

"I'm in trouble," Tad said. "I need to find Jack, too. I was down at ISTF earlier and saw what happened. When I saw the ambush, I had to get out, just like you. Seems like you and I think alike because we both thought to come here."

She raised an eyebrow. "So you followed me?"

Tad was gasping for breath, as if he was being squeezed.

"We need to contact Jack," Calla said. "It's not like him not to respond to any of my messages. I have to do something. I need to get out of here. If you found this lab, then others won't be far behind. Besides, you wasted your time trying to track the lab. Several weeks ago, we changed our plans about this place."

Tad's voice was insistent. "I can take you to where we can

get help. ISTF has a mole, and now they are after you. If you come with me, I know someone who can explain this. I believe it has to do with Mason Laskfell and when he led ISTF."

"How did you know about that?"

"You forget Jack and I were once close" he said.

"Not that close from my recollection."

It was the second time Mason's name had come up in twenty-four hours. First with Nash yesterday and now. As much as she didn't want to let the situation get out of control, she had few options. No one was reachable. Perhaps this was not the best place to be. Someone had compromised ISTF, and she was certain Scarlett wasn't working alone.

"Let's get out of here," Calla said. "It isn't safe to be here."

They jumped into the Maserati.

Tad was quiet in the passenger seat and she didn't know what to make of his presence here, but instinct told her to be careful. "So where to?" she asked.

"Bristol."

"Why are we heading to Bristol?" Calla asked as the Maserati zipped on the motorway.

Tad looked at Calla. "The person who can explain this is over there."

"Who?"

"Jack's father."

"I thought Jack's father died."

"So did all of us. I'm sure it'll all make sense when we see him. He's been in touch with me," Tad said.

"What happened? I mean, between you and Jack?" Calla asked.

"I went to NASA," Tad replied. "But I got bumped down a few years in grade because of the new Space program. So after a few years, I did something crazy. Jack refused to help me."

"Jack would have his reasons," she said. "I know it."

Tad studied her, and then he spied through the rearview mirror. "What is it?" she asked.

"Thought I saw something," he said.

"Damn it. What do they want now?" Calla said, checking her rearview mirror for a few seconds.

"Look out!" Tad screamed.

Calla turned in time to see a dark shape ahead, a black van heading for her front.

The Maserati sped onto Clifton Bridge, a long stretch of pavement, two lanes of car traffic in each direction, running between stone concretes spanning the River Avon.

She slammed the brake as hard as she could, but the car seemed to speed up. She swayed toward the side of the bridge as a Range Rover, with dark windows in front of her. Calla felt a jolt as the engine made harsh sounds; the side dented. Within a few moments, she had the car working.

"Can you lose them?" Tad asked.

"Watch me."

Calla stared out and shifted gears. The car had hit a structure in the middle of the bridge spanning the Avon. Clifton Suspension Bridge had never looked so scary. Her vehicle, barely functional, was in the middle.

On either side, agents waited for her.

She started the engine and had to get across the bridge and get far from these people.

The torn tires squealed as the vehicle sped forward toward two black Range Rovers with tinted glass.

In the rearview mirror, she saw the dark vehicles closing in.

The Maserati sliced past the first vehicle and struck the second in the rear, squeezing past both cars toward the end of the bridge. The tires wouldn't hold out for much longer. She knew it. In all of three seconds, the car halted hundred meters from the end of the bridge.

"Can you swim?" Calla said, giving him a quick glance.

Tad's breath came in short bursts. "It's suicide."

She winced. "Take it you've never lived much. You either stay here and try to be part of this inexplicable situation, or you can come with me."

"Calla, stop! This is madness. Let's talk. They sent me to talk to you," Tad said.

Calla slammed the brakes.

The car screeched to a halt.

She felt her throat tighten. "They? You know about this?"

"Not everything."

The muscle in her left eye quivered. Was Tad part of this? How had these people penetrated her life and screwed it up in less than twenty-four hours?

Calla found her gun. It wasn't her style, but she pinned it to his arm. She had to know. "Tell me everything, Tad. Now."

Tad lowered his gaze. "They have everything on Jack and you. Tell me what you found in the caves in New Mexico. Where is the telescope? Then maybe I can talk to them."

ISTF field agents had stepped out of the three Range Rovers and were making their way toward her damaged Maserati. They had trapped her from either end of the bridge.

Calla watched Tad, her heart warning her. "What on Earth are you talking about? What has New Mexico got to do with anything? Tad, are you working with them? And just who are they?"

Tad said nothing. She'd been set up twice in one day. The agent in London had been correct to tell her to run. And now it looked like she could trust no one.

She had one thought. Fast currents below her were more inviting than sitting next to betrayal.

Calla set her hand on the door handle and placed a gun in its holster, securing it. There was only one way to do this. She had to brace herself. With one heave, she kicked the car door open and sprang out.

"Calla!" she heard Tad yell.

He would have to face the agents alone. They would not take her like this. She lunged onto the railings of the structure, as agents behind her aimed. She slid her foot to one side for a better grip and lifted off, closed her eyes.

All she could do was imagine her landing.

CHAPTER
TWENTY-TWO

CALLA COULDN'T APPRECIATE Clifton Suspension Bridge's engineering when bullets hit the surrounding waters, fired as warning shots. Its pillars going deep wouldn't be enough to shield her and spanned the River Avon, linking Clifton in Bristol to Leigh Woods in North Somerset.

One of Bristol's most recognizable structures, it marked a turning point in the history of engineering and symbolized a city of original thinkers and an independent spirit.

Calla thrashed through the currents toward the edge of the Avon's banks with gun, still in its holster, weighing her down.

She didn't do guns, but what choice did she have?

She hurried and didn't stop when she reached the grassy banks of the river, then charged forward as fast as her feet would allow. The sound of a car motor and hurried footsteps pounding behind made her sprint.

They had waited for her.

She choked back fear and kept running until she reached an empty lot at the end of the open field. A chain-link fence that enclosed it had a tall gate. She tested the sagging gate and found it was unlocked. It screeched as she pushed it open and hummed through it into the small field inside.

Calla skidded on the muddy earth as her feet hit the ground. Pain piercing through her, she ignored it and struggled to crawl to a stand, and continued to the timbers at the other end of the field. She plummeted forward and her ankle already felt like it was on fire. She picked herself upright and hurried as fast as she could. Calla jumped a second fence, then ran toward the trees.

Brushes in Leigh Woods were scratchy and prickly, but Calla pushed leaves out of the way as she sprinted toward the other end of the forest.

Branches scratched her knees as she ran past them, but she kept going. Agents were on her heels and the thought of being cornered was terrifying. She had no coherent plan. Calla could only offer brief resistance with her injured ankle. Her e-wrist-watch had stopped at 4:45 p.m. Which meant telepathy was out of the question. Perhaps the watch had been damaged in the fall.

While on the bridge, her GPS had shown an ISTF safe house. The agents she'd left behind her would have vehicles and might know of it, but she needed supplies.

The woods ended at a tree line and connected to a secluded meadow.

She saw the distance behind her. They would catch up if she didn't move. There were no escape routes or hiding places yet, so she would have to continue to the safe house and hope, as with all ISTF safe-houses, this one hadn't been compromised.

A two-story house. Late Victorian, the home was set within quiet grounds with a window stuck half-open, either left on purpose or in a hurry. Good. She scuttled and drew the window open the rest of the way, then slipped in.

She glanced back, hurried from the window, then moved

forward through the house. Where was it? Each ISTF house had a safe with supplies.

With her heart in her throat, she checked the entire house. She needed something else. There were more guns here, perhaps keys to the car in the garage, but she was after something smaller. A stiletto blade. Or a knife. Something she could throw as a distraction. She imagined where it could be stashed inside a box underneath the kitchen sink. Guns paralyzed her, because when she fired, she never missed. She never knew how she'd gained that skill. The idea of a safe house was to be ready and use anything as a weapon if needed.

These old houses made noises. She crouched and advanced, careful not to make a sound. What if there was somebody in the house? Shaking her head, Calla couldn't think like that. When she reached the kitchen, she paused. Listened.

In training, she had learned that most newbies come from the front door. Calla had heard them shouting on the bridge, about calling in other agents in the area.

She crept to the utility cupboard under the sink and opened it.

Found it. Perfect. Calla put the small blade down in her pocket. Her heart was already pumping.

Voices murmured.

She turned and glanced over the countertop.

Two agents were in the small kitchen. One was leaning on a cupboard. The other was pacing. They were ISTF. Her men, and a face she would never forget—a woman from New Mexico all those months ago.

Calla had found the assassin's name on MI6 files. The woman only took the deadliest missions and had been in New Mexico. She was here for blood. Of Japanese descent, she shot to kill just as she'd killed Halona.

Calla breathed as slowly as she could.

Two more men entered with a man whose hands they constrained and had a hood over his head. It took several seconds to digest the information. The man on the right pulled the hood off the man's head and pushed him forward.

Jack!

His eyes met hers. He was injured, and his face was empty of all expression.

Calla choked back a heavy lump in her throat as the woman, she was certain, was Oskara Amano, held a gun to Jack's back.

"Out now, Cress!"

Calla backed into a table with chairs. Instinct made her seize one. One distraction would do it. Maybe she could get to Jack before Oskara moved. Would she do it? Would the perfect-shot assassin pull the trigger? It was a risk she couldn't take, and knew all too well Jack could take her on, but he remained numb.

Something had happened to him.

Calla felt anger return and pushed the chair into space. It flew out, spun, and crashed into Oskara.

As the chair hit Calla's assailant, she plummeted to the ground.

The other men didn't move. They were not after blood. They were after information.

Calla took a moment to seize Jack from the two men with a kick in the gut to one man and blow to the jaw of the other.

An agent fired a warning shot, and smoke filled the room.

She ducked, bringing Jack to the ground with her.

Their shots came quickly, but she grabbed a chair to her chest to shield their fire.

A bullet grazed her arm, and she thanked heaven silently.

Agony shot through her for several seconds. It was a minor flesh wound, and she rolled on the ground as another bullet hit the chair. She would not lose Jack to them and shoved him around the table, through the smoke, until they got to the side door.

Calla used every well of strength in her to charge through it with Jack then snapped the door locked behind them.

Jack had been set up. Her mind raced through details, trying to understand who would do this to him. Everything. All she knew about Halona, what Jack had told her about the ciphers, swirled through her mind. She had to know what they wanted from her. They couldn't know what she knew. It was information she kept to herself, for herself. It was between her and Jack.

She seized his arms and searched for injuries as bullets hammered the other side of the door.

His mouth was bleeding. Were those bruises on his jaw? It hurt to look at him, yet her own wounds were throbbing again. He could barely speak and she reached down to his side, then saw an injury on his shoulder.

Men fired at the door. It wouldn't hold much longer.

Calla pulled Jack down.

It would be only a matter of seconds before the other agents reached the safe house.

Jack seemed to register the situation for a moment, then shook his head slowly. "My shoulder. They must've given me some serious drugs. It kills. I can't see or stand straight. My father…" Jack began.

"Try not to speak, Jack. We need to get out of here. We can get to the car. Can you move? The car is in the garage."

She checked the shoulder wound. Bandaged. The drugs they had to have given him had not only sedated him; they had dazed him.

He needed to get to a hospital, and his face grew pale with pain.

More gunshots fired at the door.

"Jack, get up. We need to go."

Heavy as lead, his body wouldn't budge.

She fished a water bottle from a cooler in the far corner of the second room and looked at his wound. The knife had broken the skin and pierced his shoulder. He was in extreme discomfort, but alive.

He had lost a little blood, which was a good sign. If it hadn't been for the drugs, he would have moved easier. Then a blast.

Agents hammered at the door with ever greater fervency.

She had to take him with her. But how? She had to think fast.

"I'll get us out of here, Jack."

Jack gave her a good stare. "Calla, go. If they were going to kill me, they would have by now. They want something from us. Us being together is more dangerous than apart. If we split, they'll never get what they want. Information from us."

"No." Tears stung her eyes. "Jack, no. I can't leave you."

Jack's voice was firm. "You have to."

"I've lost too much in my life. I really can't lose you, Jack."

He winced. "You won't. I promise you, Cal."

Tears welled in her eyes. They wanted the key. The code sequence she'd read in the caves. They wanted it from both of them. If they split, the assailants wouldn't get what they wanted. Jack was right.

Why did her brain find patterns, rhythms, and sense in chaos? Calla didn't know. She just could. This had to be what they wanted.

Calla had never understood how her brain could calculate data faster than any other human she knew. Even as cryptanalysts were in growing demand more than ever before, Calla had a natural gift. That's why ISTF had recruited her. Now they had turned on her for the very reason she was hired. If they would threaten Jack, their head of science and technology, then whatever they wanted, they wanted it badly.

A gush of blood rushed through her veins. "I can't leave you. For one, Nash would never forgive me, and I'll never forgive myself."

"Nash loves you more than life," he said. You've got the watch, let me see it. Looks good. I can always find a way to reach you. Also, the chip attached to your nervous system will help."

When the outer layer of her eye received transmissions and stimulation, it sent it to a nerve that projected images directly into her eye. The nerve acted like an intelligent central processing unit. Jack had her spend five hours at the ISTF headquarters several months ago and she'd memorized every criminal database in existence. That's why she knew who Oskara was. She had read her file in two seconds by connecting to that nerve.

"You sure, Jack?" Calla asked.

The door was nearly down, shredded by bullets.

Jack raised his chin slowly. "That nerve in your brain is my best work. Use it to connect to information you need. You'll find me. Whatever happens," he also touched her wrist and showed her the watch. "We also have this. Keep it safe and you can stay in contact with Nash and I. I programmed it for the three of us. Just us. Cal, find out what they want. Who they are. Keep it from them, but we have to split. That means Nash too. They'll go after him too."

The tears were uncontrollable now. "But we always work together. We figure everything out together."

"Not this time, sweetheart. Go!"

"Nash is on mission."

"Good. It means he is off the radar. You can't contact him. These guys will harm anyone connected to you or me."

While she didn't want to believe him, she knew he was right.

The door crashed in and almost flew off its hinges as

Oskara reappeared. Now, she aimed the gun point-blank at them. Her eyes were empty. Her mission, shoot for information.

In a swift movement, Calla reached for her gun.

Oskara fired first.

Calla dodged, and the bullet missed her. She turned and shoved Jack out of harm's way.

She met Oskara in a fistfight, this time wrestling for the firearm.

Calla crushed a fist in her chest.

Oskara pushed with all her strength, trying desperately to overpower Calla. She proved to be more than Calla had expected and thrust her against a wall, the gun secure in Oskara's hand.

It was time for the stiletto knife to wield the weapon away from Oskara's hand.

Then an agent appeared at the door, gun at the ready.

Calla launched a hard kick in his chest, sending him cartwheeling. Her focus turned back to Oskara, who'd moved to where Jack was. Oskara's revolver was pointed blankly at Jack's pained body.

Think fast, Calla!

Calla moved in the line of fire, turned to dodge the bullet, but not in time to prevent where it landed.

Fire exploded in the tiny room.

She turned too late.

CHAPTER
TWENTY-THREE

THE BULLET RIPPED through Jack's jacket. It was a clean bullet hole, straight through the fabric. The pain was an inferno as he cried out in agony.

Calla's eyes went wide.

Oskara had struck him like a freight train. It wasn't supposed to go like this. Jack was supposed to live.

She thrust forward to his side, her mind trying to process everything that had happened. She'd never been in danger like this. Never known this deep emotion. *Not again. Not Jack! No!*

Faint, every muscle in her went numb, weak as time slowed.

More agents filed into the room and seized her as she tried to get back to Jack's lifeless form.

ISTF? She didn't know. She didn't care. Rubbing her forehead and shaking her head, a heaviness expanded in her core. Her eyes burned with a well of tears, unable to leave Jack on the floor as the men pinned her down and cuffed her.

These agents were supposed to protect her. Jack was gone. She heard one man call out to Oskara. What he said was a blur.

Oskara dropped the gun to the floor as more agents arrived and surrounded the house.

"She's in here. The mission is complete. We have the fugitive. Red Fox in custody, White Wolf down!" she heard the woman say. "First, she blows up ISTF, and now she's killed the technology chief, Jack Kleve, White Wolf."

Calla couldn't believe what she had just heard, as the agent's force was more than necessary. She didn't want to resist. Not anymore. Not with Jack gone. She looked at Oskara in disbelief.

They wanted her, the head of ISTF. This Red Fox, like all other Red Foxes before, had compromised ISTF, and she'd not been there to witness it.

Calla didn't want to be a hero, not today. Not after what had happened to Jack. She took a deep breath, closed her eyes, and felt herself slowly rising. Her heart was torn in shreds, wrenched at losing Jack. She felt numb, hot emotion threatening to overwhelm her. She had to know.

Calla turned to get one last look at Oskara. "Why?"

No response, all scorn.

Calla accessed her brain chip, sent the visual information, and ran them through a database via a microscopic nerve that Jack had implanted in her brain. She closed her eyes and could see it as it scanned Oskara's details.

Calla digested the information through her signal that connected the chip in her brain to the operatives' headquarters. She saw the information it sent back to her. Oskara had wanted Calla for months, and owed money to many terrorist organizations, including one run by Lent Cyrus, a tycoon of dual North African and American descent, a relic collector, treasure hunter notorious for having searched for the Beale Ciphers.

The report she saw in frame said he liked rare antiquities,

things with a history, myths and hand tampered with gene-editing science. She was this guy's prey.

Oskara owed him. He'd found Oskara via another name on file: Thaddeus Evick.

Hatred warred with guilt, ate at her. It was a desperate attempt by terrorists to get what they thought they deserved, but she had never known the magnitude of what knowing Beale's secret would amount to.

Several hours later, the car pulled up to a building outside London, ISTF's detainment center. How had ISTF turned into a hostile organization on her watch?

They transported her to an interrogation room, small, with high ceilings that reached high to black metal light fixtures. The walls were made of white tiles, three metal doors, one in the middle of each wall. A barred window with a metal grill at the top made her shiver.

Full of tiny little desks and cubicles with dozens of files and papers neatly stacked to one side, she had used this very cubicle often as Red Fox. For criminals.

DAY 4

THE TRUTH COULD GET her killed. Calla had never been a good liar. The only way she could think to make them listen to her was to tell the truth. The interrogation room, with three CCTV cameras, hi-tech interrogation centers and forensic tools, had been used many times before and usually with her on the other side of the desk.

CCTV cameras narrowed on her, recording and transmitting everything to senior ISTF officers. IP based surveillance systems with audio recording made the job easier, and Calla knew it well.

She almost laughed at the irony of having fitted gadgets and equipment to record. She'd commissioned for their best interrogators in the business, she and Nash had hired and trained every single one.

Hands on the table in cuffs, Calla couldn't go through this. She'd been set up, and Calla watched as lights came on bright and blinding. There was a committee of them, and they would surely blame her for the explosives that ripped through the ISTF building.

She'd heard that the attackers had hurt no one. Miraculous, because they had evacuated the building a few minutes before the blast, except for the boardroom. That's where Allegra and Tiege usually worked.

Every single eye was on her.

She could only hope that her father, seated as her council and former MI6 operative, had a plan.

A tall, curly-haired gazelle-like woman pressed the button on the wall and a screen came alive on the other side of the room. It started recording. Calla's eyes met her father. Stan, her father, had been her 'one call'.

Was Jack right? Should she not contact Nash?

She held back a choke. Was Jack really gone? The memory of the gunshot crawled back to her mind, and she felt sick. No. The only way she could protect Nash was not to contact him.

Stan hadn't hesitated when she'd called. He knew these things well as a former MI6 agent of high caliber. His emerald eyes, mirroring her own, pierced into her. He was calmer than she was. How could he help? No law governed ISTF.

Stan was glaring back at her with a knowing look. Lights were on her, and they were ready to begin.

"Could you please state your name, age, and occupation for the record?" the light-haired man said, who had been introduced as their ISTF spokesperson.

The only thing that helped calm Calla's frantically beating heart and unstable breathing was the sight of the watch on her wrist. It was her connection to Nash. She needed him. What would he say? If ISTF had compromised, all they knew.

"Calla Cress, twenty-eight years old. Occupation. ISTF Red Fox. British Museum curator."

"A proper day job. Do you want me to state what you at ISTF have asked me to do over the years?"

He ignored her quirkiness and continued reading like a robot. "What do you have to say about these claims?" he read them out. "Conspiracy to bring down ISTF…"

Calla shook her head, and she refused to listen to the rest. What good was being an operative, a genetically enhanced race that hid in plain sight? What could her talents do for her now?

"I have nothing to say," she managed.

"It's obvious, Miss Cress. You're withholding information you could have given us minutes ago, and it would have saved us hours of time. Yet, you haven't given us anything to work on," he said.

Calla lifted an eyebrow. "What exactly do you need?"

"Why blow up ISTF's building? Why kill Jack Kleve, agent White Wolf?"

"I did neither of those things," she said. "If you even know what we do at ISTF, you would check the surveillance camera and find out that explosion occurred before I was even in the building. Jack Kleve…"

She could barely say his name without her throat tightening. She had to stay strong and fought back burning tears.

"This is preposterous," Stan said, the only ally she had in the room.

"Your turn will come to speak," the one in the middle said.

Calla opened her mouth. "No need. It's obvious I've nothing to say. What can I say that I haven't said already? You give me no proof."

She paused, not knowing who she could trust, then scanned each face in the room.

"Here is the security recording of a meeting between you and your personal assistant, Scarlett," said the lead interrogator. "We have had to cover up the mess in the media, but right now you are Britain's most wanted undercover agent."

He held up a blue box to her. "We know ISTF has been

breached, been infiltrated on your watch as a Red Fox. You as ISTF head ordered these infiltrations," he continued.

She swallowed the lump that had formed in her throat. "I ordered a full review of ISTF systems. Nothing more," Calla said.

The man nodded and pressed a button on the desk phone. "Send in the security team. There's evidence that ISTF has been breached. We'll find out what's going on and we'll not let any actual damage to our systems get out of hand," he continued. "Thankfully, no one has been hurt. Except sadly, Jack Kleve, at your hands. The gun used was your ISTF gun."

This can't be happening!

They dictated a list of smart technology breaches to field agents, most of which were utter nonsense and could only be disqualified by the one person who could get her off the hook here. Jack.

Someone had set her up, and she had to find out who. She had to get out of here. It would mean being a fugitive, but for now that's all she needed to do because someone was about to lock her away, without an identity, for a long time.

"There's more evidence from your office," he said.

Calla didn't have the heart for this. She'd been mourning Jack for hours. She couldn't explain the agony she felt at losing him and was desperate to reach her husband. ISTF punishments for criminals were challenging. They put you in the system and lock you away.

They would manufacture criminal activity from thin air to protect the covert agency. She was still fighting the system, and now she'd become its most recent victim.

Prison authorities were told not to ask about ISTF. MI6 usually handled the paperwork to keep the agency off the radar.

"If ISTF was breached, it wasn't by me," Calla said, staring at Scarlett, who had entered and was at the back of the room.

The interrogator's eyes never left Calla once. "This isn't the only recording. There's a myriad of other recordings that show your involvement. We have evidence of you ordering these breaches and using video surveillance to get information that you later used to order the attacks. You've caused a lot of damage. Don't think you're going to get off as easy as you might have hoped," he continued.

She held back a choke. "I do what I do to protect the ISTF and our country, our world, from this sort of criminal activity. Even the prime minister can tell you that. This is a setup."

Scarlett's glare was more than Calla could take.

"Then there's the issue of murder. Jack Kleve was one of this institution's greatest assets. You killed him because he knew of your plans and he tried to stop you. You'll most likely be locked up under full security protocols and you'll never see daylight again," the man said.

This wasn't happening. Murder by a woman who'd only fired a gun twice in her life?

Could it be that easy to manufacture lies at ISTF, the agency that had hired her for her expertise?

Calla took a deep breath and shot up from her chair. "What if I don't want to go to prison? Not until I find the real guilty people in this picture?"

The room watched her.

"Blood is on your hands for the murder of Jack Kleve, chief technology officer of ISTF."

"I did no such thing. You hired agents. Just what is ISTF up to? I don't know what you stand to gain here," Calla said, staring at Scarlett.

This time, her father gave her the nod, and she knew it was time to move.

It would take two moves.

One for the front lights control panel, and one for the back one.

Her brain could see it. It could will it, and therefore she would do it. Sometimes she couldn't control what her brain could do when she was in danger. Programmed to protect herself and others, her nerves kicked in.

She braced herself to cut the lights. Calla had to be fast and had only used this maneuver twice.

It worked each time. Her pulse raced, and she caught the eye of the security man by the door. Calla connected to his thoughts via a wavelength she barely understood. An operative mind control ability Calla never wanted to use, and few knew she could. It acted like hypnotism, just from a stare.

His hand went to the command panel and hit a switch. Instinctively, she picked up the whirr of the electronic locks going through their cycle.

In darkness she made her move. Two snaps and the cuffs were off. No one would think to watch the door.

She heard gasps around her, her eyes focused as if using night vision, as she passed through her interrogators.

Soon, she crossed the lobby and hopped on the elevator. Calla looked both ways before it closed and rode it to the ground floor. When she stepped out, Calla hurried for the nearest exit and smelled the familiar scent of her father.

She turned down the hall toward him, sprinting.

He drew her into a hug. "Go do your thing, Calla. You were born an operative for a reason." He kissed her forehead and placed a firm hand on her back. "Go."

Within minutes, she was outside the building.

CHAPTER
TWENTY-FIVE

SANTA CESAREA TERME,
SOUTHERN ITALY, 5:27 P.M.

THE PLAN WOULD NOT BE simple. Extract Salib's son Massoud from the hands of an enemy they did not know.

Sheik Salib had insisted. Nash picked up a broken signal from the son's phone. His last communication had been in Abu Dhabi.

Nash tried Jack's watch again, just like he had done the last ten times.

It failed to connect to the satellite.

He then tried his cell and the Scorpion Tide, but all he got was a flat signal. He hadn't been able to reach Calla since he left her and had ached to go back the minute he'd left.

She never had her phone off. Strangely, he couldn't reach Jack either.

Nash slapped the watch back on his wrist as he advanced through the left-wing corridors of the safe seaside house he'd arranged in a town where most people went about their business discreetly.

Santa Cesarea on the Adriatic coast was positioned well for most of his missions. He took one look at the low, green-forested hills against white cliffs at the water's edge glittering in the water below. Resting on the hillside, tiny houses seemed to have grown from the rock. Wooded areas and meadows ended right in the emerald water.

As Nash moved, he took one look at the vaulted ceilings and cladding in the stone walls, powerful enough to stop a bullet. He then progressed onto the large arched veranda, excellent for monitoring for intruders, chosen specifically for that purpose.

Sheik Salib came into the room. "You okay, Nash?" Salib asked.

Nash drew in a sharp breath. "I can't reach my wife. I have this feeling something's wrong. Sure, I know we agreed not to be in touch when I'm on a special assignment, but…"

Salib watched Nash. "I can see how hard it is to leave a woman like her. She is the most beautiful woman I have ever seen, and you are a fortunate man. I'm grateful you have left her to help me out with my minor dilemma."

For now, he ignored the nag, and turned his attention to what Salib was saying. "I'll call the others," Nash said.

Nash was in the briefing room when his team arrived.

"We're going to throw in everything we have at this one," Salib said.

"What did you find out about the host in Abu Dhabi?" Nash said.

Salib's confidence was evident as he spoke. "He goes by the name of Ahmed Salim. That's just an alias. He's dangerous, and his identity changes often. Seems to be an expert in top-end, spy warfare, and artifacts. Probably able to uncover secrets we've been keeping."

"How do you know this?" Nash asked.

"I've a friend in the CIA who's been helpful to me," Salib responded.

"How does your contact know him?" Nash said.

"She worked with him."

Nash lifted an eyebrow. "She?"

"She's now a politician and consulted a lot with the CIA. I felt their relationship went beyond business," Salib said.

Nash thought for a moment. "You mean he had a romantic affair with a US politician?"

"Yes. They were lovers," Salib said.

Nash ran a hand through his hair. "This guy's terrible news," Nash said.

"Yes. He served time for treason. But they pardoned him when the state needed his skills, then he jumped ship."

"I know you think he has Massoud. How did he get into Kuwait?" Nash asked.

"He came to Kuwait City and made inroads, then took a job with a radical group. He defected and then left the country with his team. This was about seven months ago. He's made quite a name for himself. People look to him to make them money, and he's made a ton of capital selling information, and government secrets. That's the way I would do it."

This time Nash paced the floor. "How many individuals are on his team?"

"We don't know exactly, but I would say, thirty people. The team has already taken the buildings around the fort in Abu Dhabi. My men feel it is secure enough to land near there," Salib said. "We're landing stealth choppers soon. Two groups are on their way."

Nash followed Salib through to the balcony.

"We'll meet them there," Salib said.

"I need all the intel you have. I'm going to have to change some people around," Nash said. "Okay. We'll push forward. We can't wait. We'll complete the mission in seven minutes, tops, but we need to move now."

"Like the old days," Salib said, smirking. "You and I have had a lot of fun. You're the one man I trust with my life. By the way, you still have not visited the vault. What's in there is yours. Your family is like my family Nash."

"I'm not ready to go to the vault. Not yet."

"All right. You heard the plan," Salib said, turning to the team that had joined them on the terrace. "Four small teams will handle all the exits."

"Everyone else will go in and take the main base through the front," Nash said. "We'll deal with the stairs. We've placed snipers on the roof. They'll take out any enemies who attempt to leave the main building with Salib. I'll be leading that team. Let's go get this guy."

CHAPTER
TWENTY-SIX

LONDON, 6:26 A.M.

DAY 5

CALLA HAILED a cab the traditional way. No traces. "Please drive," she instructed the cab driver.

Stan had slipped her a wad of cash and brought her backpack. The true MI6 agent that he was, he knew exactly what she needed.

Calla kept her face to the left, staring out the window as the cab headed north.

"I'll get off here," she said and paid the man when they were a suitable distance from Central London.

"But there's nothing here," the driver said, moving onto the hard shoulder of the motorway.

"I know."

He shrugged, took the money, and drove off.

A morning chill entered her bones as she waited for the road to clear before she wound her way to the open field.

Rain slapping her face, she found the tree, its bark wide and unmarked. This was it.

She thought hard before she made her moves. Was this really happening? Was she really now a fugitive?

She took in a deep breath and stared at the tree for several seconds. The goal had been to create a bunker, impenetrable and entirely invisible in the heart of London, but oddly inaccessible through Central London.

It would be a hike from now on. The operatives had scrutinized anyone who dared know about it down to the last pair of underwear. They had done every background check from credit and driving records of anybody they'd hired or exposed their lives to, be it a nanny, a driver, a pilot, or a chef.

High-tech gear serviced by a fiber-optic cable buried eighteen inches under the facility would detect movement by sending an alarm, and the cameras were like eyes ready to spy on any activity as well.

She found the opening in the ground and typed in the code. The door opened, and she descended.

The operatives had blended heat detection and television cameras around the bunker, all hidden using artificial intelligence.

Calla hastened.

The analytics feeding into the cameras and security systems had learned the difference between a falling leaf, an errant deer, or a plain intruder.

She slowed down, dodging the humanlike sensors, knowing where each one was. The sensors gave precise coordinates to drones that could be deployed at any minute, and she knew not to linger.

Calla opened a second gate, taking her to the basement and made her way into the darkness, careful not to wake the drone armed with a thermal payload, and could track down anything in the small compound. If triggered wrongly, the security team would be out in a flash.

It was not her favorite place in the world. Dank and with a

distinct smell to it, but this was her only way into the building, through the basement and down the long tunnel.

The tunnel led her through a dark hallway that became more impressive and less like an afterthought.

ISTF, the police, and a few intelligence agencies had to be on the lookout for her. Most times they just responded to an ISTF alert without questioning, so she had to be careful.

She was now an international security threat and there was only one place to hide, one she never thought she'd ever had to use.

Too tired to stay on the run any longer, she hurried to the far side, then placed her hand against the wall with a steel control panel. It opened.

The brick wall slid to one side as if on rails, revealing a small hidden passageway.

As she made her way in, Calla saw lights in the distance.

She advanced. When she neared the light, her breathing intensified. She'd only ever been here once. The London Cove bunker. The only place she would find anyone she could trust.

What had started as a brick tunnel steadily turned into an aluminum-lit hallway with fluorescent lights. Motion sensors in the walls stirred as she progressed toward the end and stopped. Hands flat on the wall, the palm recognition software made it move.

She now stood in front of a second steel door and pressed her hand on the panel beside it.

A red light surrounded her. Then she heard a voice from a speaker. "Password?"

"Agent FDCO1223."

The steel door slid inch by inch and then shut behind her.

"Thank God, you're here. Stan has been calling every few minutes," a bright face said when she moved into the space.

One of the Cove managers, who two-timed as an MI6

agent, just an analyst, not a field agent, approached. "They're all waiting inside," she said.

"Sorry, I had to evade quite a few people. Any word from Nash? Allegra? Tiege?"

"You better come in."

Next to the entrance was a plaque. It read:

Agent FDCO1223 and Agent FD1222
founded the Cove

No matter how many times Calla came to the secret operative base, one of many littered across the globe, it never ceased to amaze her that another world existed within the world. A world of people who knew the secrets of science and the Earth.

The bunker was neatly organized and computer-controlled from every angle. Divided into medicine, nanotechnology, cyber security, and more sections, large displays controlled every operation.

They had turned most cameras to the entrances and exits, including one into the ISTF building, now blank. The building which had survived the blast only knocked out a small section next to the lobby.

Behind every terminal in here, an operative specialist worked tirelessly in case of threats to operations. Engineers had built the computer systems as if nothing on Earth inhibited them. Software engineers carved code, and researchers put it all together.

Calla recalled Jack loved it here. She felt a heavy load settle in her gut and, for the first time since losing Jack, she collapsed to the floor. Calla didn't know how long she cried. Tears of doubt dropped to the concrete.

The room and those in it melted into silence.

Jack was no operative, but he'd been one of them.

Calla looked up, feeling like a stranger—it was clear from the minute she entered.

Metal doors slid back and forth with a big sound. Calla rose and moved through a doorway into a round room with screens on every surface known as the 'Mission Room.'

Three men and a woman followed her in.

"Calla, I'm so sorry," he began. "Jack only ever wanted to protect those he loves and the operatives' knowledge. Do you need more time?"

She shook her head slowly.

"We're so glad you made it out of there and have everything ready. We've refurbished your operative suit. It's right here in the Cove, the most secure and serviced bunker in the world. We have an air filtration system, which was overhauled last year, the newest in the world, on a gold standard," the operative said with pride.

"Thank you. I don't know if I need the suit," said.

"Take it. It keeps you safe and is bullet and fireproof. We've also got a car prepared. Tiege has been in touch and is on his way."

"Oh, right then."

"Okay, you better come through. They're in the main hall."

An immediate feeling of warmth came over her body, making her relax for the first time in hours. No matter what happened, she was safe.

For now.

TWENTY-SEVEN

HOW TIEGE and Allegra had made it to the Cove, Calla wouldn't ask, not today, not now. She was glad to see Allegra, a former ISTF interim head herself.

Allegra had access to all kinds of influence and power.

Each wing in the Cove housed several doors, with scientists, agents, and other employees whizzing around. Like a high-tech factory, most rooms had rows of tables, machines, and a giant map that displayed everything going on.

The place sometimes felt like a spaceship, with the other noises breaking in and out of each room every so often.

Screens lined each wall of the mission room, showing each recent update from MI6, ISTF and the Metropolitan Police.

Tucked into their newsfeeds, the situation was worsening. Whereas they'd released information on her to the agencies, they'd let a little out in the public to not compromise ISTF's own functioning. However, everything about her identity was threatened.

She shuddered and turned down the hallway, then strode into the mission room. Greeted by an operative, a screen was on with a map of the Earth displaying several cities worldwide.

It had been almost hours since she lost Jack. ISTF, and indeed her own life, was in extreme danger.

"What's the latest?" Calla asked.

"Truth is. Someone has come after you and brought ISTF down, too. They want to leave you no options. Someone with a terrible vendetta has tried to destroy it and pin it on you. We don't know who or why," the first analyst said.

Calla leaned in. "Start with Oskara Amano. Who her clients are. Where she trained. Where she's been for the last several years."

"We've learned they sent Oskara to kill anyone connected to the Beale Ciphers and gather intelligence therein," Tiege said.

"Jack and I went after those. We found nothing, no treasure. A woman died when she handed me knowledge of an artifact, a telescope of some sort that Jack had known about. We do not know where this telescope is. You see, she handed it to Jack, not to me."

"Did it look like this?" Tiege asked as he pulled up an image on the screen.

"Yes," Calla said. "That's it," she said, nearing the screen.

It was the spitting image of the telescope Halona had given them.

Calla rotated and faced Tiege. "Yes. What exactly is it?"

"I have a suspicion, Jack knew, and that's why they came for him. You need to find out, Calla," Tiege responded. "That telescope went missing over 200 years ago from one of our coves in the United States. This is the first time we've heard of it resurfacing since our records began, and you know our records go back at least 2000 years," Tiege said.

She anchored her attention on the screen. "I'll bet. What's puzzling me is the Beale Ciphers date to the 1800s. This telescope is older. What's the connection? I wonder if it's to do with an ancient code. In New Mexico, Halona Osa-Menglian told Jack something neither of us understood, but they killed her for it."

"That must be what they want," he said.

"Tiege, they've killed my best friend. I don't know what more to do except to find out who did this. Do you know how to contact ISTF securely?"

"Only a few people who're still loyal will talk," Tiege said.

Calla's posture went limp, as if all her bones had dissolved away. "Everyone is scared. The Beale Ciphers have been a mystery even to the operatives. Some think we wrote them. If we didn't write them, who wrote them? Beale? Is he real?"

"There's a code in the Beale Ciphers leading to a treasure, maybe gold, silver, jewels, wasn't it?" Tiege said.

Calla shrugged. "According to popular fiction. This whole thing cannot be about a treasure that's worth, not even £50 million, in today's money. There's got to be more to this to draw fighting power like they used against us. Jack and I found caves with wall patterns written in sophisticated code while we were in New Mexico. It was a strange code, and I'm still trying to figure it out. Jack and I hadn't even talked about it since. Is that what this whole telescope is about?"

"Maybe the code in the cave inspired Beale," Tiege said.

Allegra drummed her fingers on the table. "Halona had something she was hiding."

Calla took an involuntary step backward. "She died before we got to the hospital. Took me days to come to terms with that. And now, Jack. They shot him in front..." A profound emotion made Calla choke on her words. "I've asked myself many nights why these people hunted the poor girl. The only connection I can find goes back to us at ISTF. Halona was guardian to her ancestors' art, which inspired the code, then the cipher. They only passed it down in her family."

"So when she died, she passed it on to you and Jack," Allegra said.

"But neither Jack nor I understood it fully," Calla answered.

"That's why you need the telescope." Allegra insisted. "It acts like an Enigma machine when you use it to read the code. Did she tell you anything more?"

Air stalled in Calla's lungs. "That's just it. Whatever she told Jack and me, I swore not to repeat. I intend to find out without breaking a promise to Jack. I never break my promises."

"Fair enough," Allegra said. "We trust your instincts."

"Looks like the telescope has two lenses, one facing up and one facing down. Does it mean anything?" Calla said.

Tiege's response came as soft as his brown-eyed gaze. "It is an ancient telescope, more ancient than the first known telescopes."

"Can you tell me about its build, Tiege? What else do we know about it? The operatives' records must have more," Calla asked. "What else do your records say?"

Allegra thought for a second before she spoke. "It used to be part of a larger one. It's got Native American writing on the side. There's some information in Spanish written on the handle. It says here that the ship that carried the telescope to the Americas was called *'La Diosa.'* Another plaque says *'Illa y Del'* on the side of the wood. Its owner used to use a telescope to encrypt codes written in the stars."

"The Spanish used the telescope in America, the French in India," added Tiege, "and the Dutch in Europe, and only three of its kind were made, two were destroyed and never to be found. That's when the operatives noted it. Rumors from locals said it held a strange, powerful mystery. Nobody knows where the telescope ever came from originally. That wasn't all. It also enables the creation and the reading of the code, unbreakable, known as the 'Unhindering Code.' Only the telescope owners and those who built it knew this. The trail ends there."

"Until Halona brought the telescope to Jack in London," Calla added. "They went to the antique dealer in London who knew about codes. He couldn't help. That's when Jack brought me in."

Allegra had a little furrow between her eyebrows as she thought. "So Halona couldn't read the code either?"

Second thoughts poked and jabbed at Calla like a sharp stick. "Halona once told Jack she saw me in a dream and that only I could read the code. As if they wrote it for me to unearth. I didn't believe her, of course, until I recalled what I saw in the caves. Drawings, hundreds of them in beautiful colors marked by symbols and numbers. It was beautiful. I could read them, but not all of them. The telescope is the only thing that could read that code perfectly. That's why Jack and I kept it far from me. We knew that code must not be read. This was all about a year and a half ago.."

Allegra rubbed her chin. "So that's how you came into the picture. Jack needed you to help."

Calla nodded, then turned squarely to face her. "Who checked out the telescope according to the Cove's records?"

Tiege shot Allegra a glance before responding. "Mason Laskfell, the then head of the operatives. He'd just taken over the role of Red Fox, the chief at the ISTF as well."

"This is far beyond what we think. Why did that science terrorist take the telescope in the first place?" Calla and took a moment to breathe.

It was as if she was in two places at the same time. She saw Jack's body on the floor as it had happened; it had been so vivid. Scary. She saw herself crying and couldn't stop. She then saw Jack take the telescope. Keeping it far from her mind. It was what they had agreed. She could read the key, but it was the telescope that exposed Beale's codes.

"If you let some time pass, it will get easier. You'll find the answers," Tiege said. "I'm so sorry about Jack. He was my friend too and someone I learned an awful lot from."

Allegra put an arm around Calla. "We'll do everything we can. What about Nash? Does he know?"

Calla shook her head. "It's best that Nash doesn't know. He'll try to come for me. That will put his life in danger."

A puzzled look crossed Allegra's eyes. "But you need him. Don't you?"

"I need him to stay alive," was all Calla could manage.

Allegra cocked an eyebrow in surprise. "In the meantime, we need that telescope. There must be a connection between what you and Jack know and the ambush at ISTF and Mason Laskfell."

Even in death, Mason Laskfell wouldn't leave her alone. Calla drew in a quick breath. "I don't have time."

"We'll provide information and help. We can only do this if you trust us," Tiege said.

"I don't have the telescope, but I might have an idea where to look," Calla said.

"Okay," Tiege replied. "Where do we start?"

"I'll go alone," she said. "I can't lose anyone else."

Allegra paced with her to the door. "Calla, let us know what you need. We'll get you safely to the Scorpion Tide. Delgado has the boat on standby in Dover port. There was a complication in France but he believes the security threat to the yacht is over."

"Yes, my father told me," Calla added as a weight seemed to press on her chest, robbing her of breath as she moved toward Allegra."Allegra, thank you. You know, when you told me about ISTF, I never once imagined it would end like this."

"I know."

Tears stung her eyes. "Jack's not supposed to die. I know little about his family or who needs to know. I trusted Jack more than most, and I still do. However strange that sounds. I know he had his secrets. And I respected him for it because I had my own too. Now our secrets are what can save us."

Allegra took her hand. "Are you sure you don't want me to find Nash? I have my ways."

Calla shook her head as if it would bring her clarity. "I've lost my best friend. I can't lose the man I love too."

"Okay," Allegra said, her hand gripping Calla's for comfort.

"I have to find out what they wanted with Jack and why they took him away from me. Allegra, you, of all people, told me never to run away from a fight. Never to hide. To defend those who can't defend themselves and to be faithful to who I am. The only way I know how to be true to who I am is to find out who did this to us and who did this to my best friend. I have to find that telescope before someone else does."

"Mason Laskfell planned so many things even before we got rid of him. This is just one of them," Allegra said.

Calla nodded in agreement. "He knew if anybody took over as head of ISTF, it was a death warrant. He would rather destroy ISTF than have anyone else lead it, and he'll use anybody. I have to find who that anybody is."

TWENTY-EIGHT

A POLICE BLOCKADE was in effect on all highways, searching cars randomly. Tiege had promised to keep the cops at bay by hacking into their systems. Airports were also an enormous risk.

Calla checked her appearance in the mirror of the Audi rental the operatives had organized for her, her hair tied back in a baseball cap. Using the power of her hyper-computer car, she gripped the steering wheel with her hands and sped onto the A20 motorway.

"What time is Delgado docking?" Calla asked Tiege in her earpiece.

"Should've arrived by now. I'd give him five," Tiege replied.

Congestion on the motorway slowed traffic. As Calla waited for the lane to clear, she pulled over onto the hard shoulder. Her GPS navigator popped up on the screen with a review of her location and a blue line leading to where she was to meet Delgado. A red X highlighted Dover.

As her GPS traced the blue line, it turned into a thin red string, then a thick red line. This wasn't looking good. The motorway split for the A26 toward Dover. That was the best route.

Calla continued.

She was close enough to hear the constant sound of sirens on the roads up ahead. The lights changed to red again. Within minutes, she made the turn for Dover. It didn't take her long to reach the marina parking at the port when she arrived. Calla pulled the Audi off the road and into the marina, then jumped out of the car and headed to a dock entrance.

A chime sounded from the Audi in-car systems, still linked to her phone, alerting her to a message. "You have company. Hurry!" Tiege warned.

First, she reached into her pocket to find her new secure phone and called Delgado's cell.

The phone gave a static ping. She walked forward and tried the phone again, leaving the shipyard with a glance over her shoulder.

She thought about the rental. Although she could abandon the car at another location, Tiege was resourceful so far. He had probably taken care of the rental pickup, so there was no problem.

The Scorpion Tide was visible to Calla. Her yacht was setting sail, the motor just revved. A port worker opened a large barrier to allow the large yacht to enter the marina.

"The yacht is ready. I'm leaving the car," she said in her earpiece to Tiege.

"Okay," he replied. "Be careful, Calla. Any word from Nash?"

"I don't want to put his life at risk. Not after what happened to Jack," she said.

"Allegra and I'll stay peeled for any information," he said. "Let us know what we can do."

A black van was pulling in. Then a bullet thudded into the bonnet of the rental, and gunfire peppered at her position.

She froze.

The van was still speeding up. It was too late to do anything. The van drew her attention as it stopped.

Anxiety constricted her chest as Calla ducked. "Damn it!"

She charged toward the water, saw a speed lifeboat, unstrapped it, and pushed it. Calla jumped on and shot off, leaving a puzzled lifesaver gawking at his stolen boat.

"I'll take care of it and return it!" she yelled.

She made it to her boat as Scorpion Tide was turning. She kept focused, speeding the boat toward the yacht's tailgate and slowed at the ramp where a crew member met her. With ease, she climbed the ladder's metal rungs.

In stealth mode, Delgado started the yacht's engines as she hurried to his control deck, as the yacht gained speed.

"Where to, Calla?"

"South, have you ever sailed her to Africa?"

"There's always a first time."

"Are you fueled up?"

"Always, ma'am," Delgado said with a smirk.

It was going to be a long journey. They had no choice.

CHAPTER
TWENTY-NINE

10:26 A.M.

HE COULD HEAR the metallic clanking of crates shuffling in the van each time it navigated a corner. The van came to a sudden halt.

All Jack could feel was steel against his hands and rubbing against them. He pulled at them, but the tightness and painful nature of the cuffs made it impossible, no matter how much force he used against his hands. The rough, continual movement of the van stirred his senses, and the pain in his shoulder didn't feel as bad as it had before. God knew what drugs they had used on him.

Wind from outside against the side of the van and the constant tug at his cuffed hands, his tongue, and the mud—or was it his blood—made his stomach queasy.

Waves of agony pierced his shoulder as if it had been broken. His hands would get numb from the lack of blood, so he tried to move them. His back ached from the bumps that he felt against the tin walls of the van.

Each time he felt the end of the cords against his hands, he yanked and fought them.

"Back from the dead, Mr. Kleve," a tall man with a big afro said.

Jack looked up, his senses slowly coming to. It was the first time he had seen Lent Cyrus. If memory served him right, ISTF had put Lent away twice, both times in relation to Laskfell.

"What?" Jack said between breaths.

"You were there when the technology was first developed," Lent said.

Jack tugged at the cords and cursed under his breath. He pretended he didn't hear the man and focused on his head. It hurt and was all limited. God, it hurt.

"I was shot. There's no bullet wound. What happened?" Jack asked, keeping all hints that he was in dire pain at bay.

"I wasn't born yesterday. Amateur stuff. Thought death could work well on you." Lent said, humoring him. "You were there when gene editing first became a thing among technological and science circles."

"No… no," Jack argued, eyes now unfocused.

"Yes, you were."

"No…" Jack hissed.

"Yes, you were."

The man had moved to Miami and become a tycoon. That's all Jack remembered from ISTF records. It had served Jack well to understand every enemy that had worked with Mason Laskfell. Lent was what he called a viper, maybe even a copycat, but more dangerous. He had no conscience.

Jack didn't respond.

"I see you're going to be quiet," Lent said.

"Okay, so this is how this one will work. My understanding is that you've created a startlingly simple method for cutting and pasting DNA. I need you to finish what you started at ISTF. Your genius means I can finish something I started years ago. Promises are important where I come from."

"But friendship isn't," Jack said. "You've betrayed a lot of friends and left a lot of bodies along the way, Mason Laskfell included."

Lent's eyes wouldn't leave Jack. He smirked. "Well, that's their fault. I need you to complete this. I know that there are short sections of DNA that need adjusting. If my memory serves me correctly, you found some of this DNA in bacteria, and they help fight viruses. I also understand they can change the genome of many organisms. Isn't it right that they use a protein called Cas9?"

"What's this about?" Jack asked.

"Revolutionizing our understanding of biology and curing deadly genetic diseases," Lent added.

"Something tells me that's not the only reason why you need me to finish developing the technology, is it? There is something more." Jack said.

Shadows extinguished the light that surrounded Lent. Darkness closed in around him.

"You catch on quick. Yes, there's more," Lent said. "Your intelligence and research in this area are ideal for what I want to do. We'll use it to cut out the offending DNA sequence. The one that supposedly makes us vulnerable. She needs it."

Jack's tongue felt too thick to form words. "Who?"

"Peregrine."

"Who's Peregrine?"

"The woman I loved and lost, and the rightful owner of Beale's treasure."

Jack narrowed his eyes. What was the psychopath on about? "I see."

"Yes. People with my brains, your brains, we deserve to be in control," Lent said.

Jack clenched his jaw so tight he thought his teeth would crack. "What happened to Peregrine?"

Tension tightened Lent's neck tendons. "None of your

business. I'm a pragmatist, Jack. Everything I fought for, everything I tried to make better, it's all going to be gone if I don't finish developing this. Everything will go back to the way it was, but I'll be in charge. And I'm not afraid, unlike you."

Jack couldn't believe what he was hearing. "Are you trying to reverse Darwin's theory? Identities gone, baldness gone, life span on the rise, the ability for the average man to care for himself, gone!"

Lent grabbed Jack from behind. "Yes, yes. I know what it's all about. But I only care about the last principle. I don't care about all the rest. Something big is coming, and you and I can be at the heart of it."

Jack tugged harder. He had to get out. "If you have me, then you got into ISTF. She helped you, didn't she? I mean the woman Scarlett? Why have you let ISTF believe her? This can't just be about DNA research."

Lent took a seat in the back of the van as it revved its engines. He leaned in closer to Jack, and Jack smelled the strong cologne. "True. I have lived a life that's very much like yours, Jack. I have seen the world. Just like you, I have been to war zones and come home. It changed something in me, and I have a hard time connecting with people. I have this sense that I'm going to create something revolutionary. People in the world deserve it. Just like you, I've had to make hard choices, and I'm not afraid to make them. That's why we should be partners."

"Not on your life," Jack said.

"I'm sure I can change your mind. What do you know about the Beale Ciphers?" Lent asked.

"Not much. An amazing find by a certain Mr. Beale."

"He was a great man. Peregrine's great-great-great-great-grandfather," Lent said, putting him into a headlock. "And I may not be the man she married, but I'll always be the man she loved. As you can see, you and I have exactly the same dilemma in life."

The man was deranged. In love with a woman who had possibly left him for another man, and now it seems she was dead.

Lent's voice was calm, steady. "I know how to make this easier on you."

"Enlighten me before you choke me to death. You've already tried to shoot me and wedge a knife in my shoulder. I'm intrigued by what you're going to do next and who else you will use to get to me," Jack managed in rasps.

Lent turned to look at him with a strange eye. "You'll not like it."

"Really?" Jack said.

Lent shoved a boot hard in Jack's stomach. Jack dropped to the ground, breathing unsteadily as the van jolted suddenly to the side. It took a moment for Jack to figure out what had just happened. A second goon jumped into the back. "We are under attack," the man said. "They've found us."

Jack made a sudden motion, and then the lights extinguished as the rear of the van went dark.

"They got in by hacking our systems. Must've put a virus in our networks," Jack heard Lent say.

Jack heard a thud and then a struggle.

The driver shouted.

"Take them out, the rear doors! No, the front doors!" Lent shouted.

A thump, a crash, and a minor explosion.

This wasn't good.

CHAPTER
THIRTY

THE SCORPION TIDE

EYES BURNING, Calla slammed a fist into the table of the main lounge. A hot tear dropped to the glass, and it caught her reflection. Hair disheveled, hands shivering, her gaze fell on the watch Jack had given her. Calla had never felt so alone. She hadn't grieved Jack. She would have her answers if she could get to where he kept his secrets, where he first learned of the telescope and the ciphers. What they shared had cost Jack his life. She wasn't giving up now and owed it to him.

This was the third time she'd lost someone so dear to her. She had grown up without her parents, and close friends were the only family she knew. Jack and Nash had always come first.

God, was Jack really gone? Nash was all she wanted. What would he do if he knew what was going on? Only he could comfort her. He didn't know what had happened to Jack. How would he take the news?

Death had visited her. Again.

It had once taken her boss and adviser at the British Museum, then… her unborn child.

"Damn it!" Another hand rammed into the glass.

This time it smashed as a crew member popped her head through the door. "Calla? You okay?"

She nodded. "I need to see Jack's cabin. Please unlock it for me. I'll be there in a few minutes."

"Yes, Calla. I'll also make you something to eat as well. You look like you need it."

Food was the last thing on her mind as she sank into a chair to catch her breath.

She kept her wits about her and proceeded upstairs to the third level, where the master suites were. Jack's cabin was at the opposite end of the hall from the master cabin that she shared with Nash.

She overrode the lock with her palm scan at the entrance and noticed a scratch by it. They had followed Jack here. That's how they got in. Scarlett was the only person at ISTF who had been told of the seven-day wedding plans, and had signed an NDA to keep details at bay.

What had possessed Scarlet to betray them? Someone who had worked for Allegra for years and had proved nothing but trustworthy. That's why they had brought her into the fold and kept Scarlett as Calla's PA.

The door opened, and she inspected the suite. A small safe stood in the far corner. Calla opened the smart lock requiring an iris scan, removed Jack's wallet, and discovered a brown paper inside. She scanned the room and noticed blood on the carpet. Not much.

Next, she moved to Jack's bed and then checked out the ensuite bathroom. On the floor where she found a discarded shirt, she sank down and drew it to her nostrils. The scent of her friend still lingered.

Hot tears burned in her and fell on the blue jersey. How had anyone gotten to the Scorpion Tide? It must've happened after Jack had gotten back to the yacht from the villa that night.

Scorpion Tide was very secure. The only way they could've broken in was if someone had let them in.

Who? How? It wouldn't have been obvious for Jack to sniff out the breach, since the rest of the crew had gone through a rigorous vetting process. Now he was gone.

Had it been Scarlett? Slowly, Calla rose and went back to the main cabin suite.

By morning, they would be in Mahé.

There, answers would unfold. It was where Jack was born, a place he talked little about, but equally a place important to him.

Calla recovered several papers from a drawer where he kept his gun. She noted research and prototype tracking numbers across the top of the documents in the drawer.

Jack had also marked the notes he'd made with a series of formulas. She knew his research was usually never out in the open. This had to have been scribbled in a hurry.

What had Jack been working on? Usually, he had three or four projects going.

She heard a noise by the door and set her hand on her gun. Calla hated guns, but maybe after Nash had convinced her, they gave her a sense of security?

Quiet but distinct, the shuffle at the door stirred her. "Delgado?"

"Calla. I'm so sorry about Jack. Are you all right?" he said, stepping into the room. "The first officer's taken over. I wanted to see if you are okay."

The thin thread holding her nerves together frayed. "For now. Yeah. Jack's been…"

Delgado raised a chin and glared at her, empathy filling his eyes. "I know. Allegra filled me in."

A hot tide of disappointment stung the back of her throat. "They're after me… they won't stop until they have me. It's important we don't contact Nash now. I'm desperate to, but I fear it may bring him to their attention. Everyone around Jack and I is in danger and I'm so sorry to put you in this position."

Frown lines marked his brow. "When I took this job you became my family, Calla. You've not put me in any situation. I came in to your lives with my eyes open because I believe in what you all fight for. Jack was my friend too, so we're in this together. We're all behind you. Because we believe in you."

She nodded. "Thank you, Delgado. That means a lot to me."

"I'm sorry, Calla. Jack is… was one of the people I admired most. You, Nash, and he are a tight unit. I'm so sorry."

Calla had to concentrate hard to form a coherent sentence. "I'm hoping Mahé will give me answers. Jack was born there, and lived there until he was a teenager."

She showed Delgado the GPS information. "Someone wants something from us. Something only Jack and I knew. I don't know what we'll see when we get to Mahé, but I'm hoping that something Jack knew can help me."

Delgado nodded. "I'll keep Scorpion Tide under the radar. And Nash? Where is he?"

"I don't know. We can't tell him yet what's going on. For his safety."

Calla heard a noise from the floors above.

"Oh. I forgot to tell you," Delgado said. "Marree has been on the boat since Jack disappeared. She didn't know what to do after she discovered how they had left Jack's cabin. The night it happened, Jack, Tiege and her returned from the villa in good spirits after your wedding. Security systems show that each went their separate ways at some point that night on the yacht. The intruders cut the cameras in all three of their cabins."

"We need to keep her safe," Calla said. "We should drop her off in Calais. It's too dangerous for her on the Scorpion Tide and especially where I'm going."

CHAPTER
THIRTY-ONE

THE LAST TIME someone opened the electronically controlled door to bring him his food, Jack had gotten a good glance at the surroundings and the security shift. There were three security guards assigned to him. One had even been in the van. All were armed.

He didn't remember how he got from the van, in what looked like a country far from home, from the few glances he got out the window.

The place was like a high-tech lab hidden in some sort of natural structure. No natural light came into the facility. However, there was not an ounce of darkness anywhere.

Well lit from every corner and with the highest technology set up, this was a facility, perhaps a research center of some sort. The building had a tech setup that made him dream of possibilities. The walls were white and technology-enriched, with glass sheets behind them.

The air was comfortable, too comfortable. White walls lined the corridors, and lights on the ceiling gave off a bright white glow. It was almost too bright. The few people he'd seen moved in a hurry, busy about the corridors or around computers in glass booths.

Jack shook off a nagging feeling. What on Earth was wrong with him? They had kidnapped him, and Calla was probably worried sick.

His wound had healed slightly. He couldn't recall many events, but he remembered one thing. The gunshot. He was certain the bullet had hit him. How could he be alive? Unless they used blanks. And yes, he remembered how it wasn't the bullets that had made him fall but the blow from the guy who had been standing behind him. It had been a choreographed setup. They wanted to make Calla think he was dead.

He pulled off the watch and examined it. The software now had a glitch, but if he had a paperclip or a thin piece of metal, he could fix the GPS connection to his satellite that would trigger a telepathic response from either Calla or Nash if the watch was still connected to their pulses.

Where was he going to get something like that?

The room was minimalistic and practically void of any extras beyond a bed, a desk, and a connected toilet with necessities.

Stacked in a cabinet by the bed were a fresh pair of clothes and shoes.

All white, just like the ones everybody wore in this facility. Jack suddenly heard voices coming up the stairs outside his room and then past the door.

Was he the only prisoner in this place?

The voices moved on, and then more came back down the hallway. They were coming to his room as they did every two hours to drop something off or check on him.

The camera in the room's corner was always on him, so he had to be careful. The next time somebody came in, he would make his move. All he needed were a few electronic pieces he could insert into the watch to make it work and connect it to Calla and Nash.

The place was oozing with new technology and if he could find a control room or similar, he was sure he could find what he needed.

After two more hours, Jack heard the door to his room creek open. He got into position.

The door swung open, and three men in silver suits emerged.

"Ah, I see we've made you comfortable," Lent said. "We need you to cooperate. You certainly don't want to be here, do you?"

"You've a great setup in this place? Just what do you do here?" Jack asked.

"I wouldn't complain; just answer our questions, and you might be on your way," Lent said.

"What do you want?"

Lent was a tall man with an impressive afro, broad shoulders and Middle Eastern features against dark skin.

He made his way into the room and took a seat in the chair beside Jack's bed. "Ever heard of gene-editing technology?"

"Maybe."

"You're one of the main gene-editing pioneers. You have something special. Well, how about I take you and show you? I'm sure you'll be more receptive when you see what we do here."

It was Jack's turn to talk. He was more interested in what they did rather than his speaking to them. "Gene editing? Of course, I know about it. Is that what you're interested in?"

Lent sighed. "It'll change the world. The world needs better medicines and to alter disease genes. There'll be an endless purpose for the human population with gene-editing technology."

Jack eyed him. "But who's asking?"

"Forgive my rudeness. I haven't introduced myself. You can call me Lent Cyrus. I run what we do here, but I also understand you have something else I want. The telescope and what that girl in New Mexico told you about it. That little trick back there by my trusted team is going to come in useful. With Calla Cress assuming you dead and the fact that I'll stop at nothing to hurt those around her, she will lead me to the telescope."

"Why do you need the telescope? I thought this conversation was about gene editing," Jack said.

"And so you did," Lent said, now rising and strolling to the desk, where he picked up a device that pulled down a screen on one side of the wall. It was impressive. A feature that even he hadn't spotted, a division that merged into a viewing screen and a casting monitor. "Calla Cress has less than three weeks to give me what I want. That's all the time I can give her."

With that, Lent left the room, his men behind him.

It was now or never.

"Hey," Jack called to the last guy. "In the jacket I was wearing when I was unceremoniously brought here, if you look in the inside pocket, find a folded up piece of pink paper held together with a paperclip. It has a series of numbers that open my laptop you took from the Scorpion Tide," Jack said.

"Why are you so cooperative now?" the man said to Jack.

The man moved from the room and returned several moments later, then searched Jack's pockets.

He put the paper clip on a table next to Jack, who took the paper in his hands and turned to the door. In one swift moment, he dropped it on the floor, slid it with his foot, and shifted it under the table.

"I'll keep this," the man said, taking the paper, oblivious to the clip. "Don't think you're going to get off easy if we don't get what we need. If this paper doesn't pan out, we'll know quickly."

They must've thought he was that naïve. The man left the room and slid it locked by punching in numbers on the lock outside the door.

Damn it!

He hadn't gotten a good look at the door coordinates the man had fingered.

Jack reached for the paperclip. He stood there. Then he heard the door open again.

DAY 6

MARREE SEARCHED the top drawer where the kidnappers had left scratch marks. Calla entered the room. Her face was a mask of concern.

"This is where they hid the bug they used to kidnap Jack. It must've happened when you and Nash were at the villa. How did they get onto the Scorpion Tide?" Marree said.

Calla answered with a shake of her head. "I don't know, but I have an inkling it must've been someone at ISTF. I'm so sorry, Marree."

Surprise rendered Marree speechless. "I don't understand. Who would do this? I've been on the yacht for two days, unsure what to do, where to go. Finally, I contacted Allegra to see if I could find out anything."

Calla's chest tightened. "And?"

"Nothing." Marree looked at Calla squarely. "When we returned to the yacht, I came into his room that night. It must've been moments after it had happened. And then…"

Calla grimaced, fighting her own tears, then took in a deep

breath. "I'm so sorry, Marree. Whatever happened, we will find out. You need to stay strong, and we need to make sure you stay safe. Anyone connected to Jack now is a potential target. "

"Where are we going?"

"Marree, we're dropping you off in Calais. It's too dangerous. I'm a fugitive, and I shouldn't drag you into this."

There was determination in Marree's eyes. "I can help, Calla."

"I know you can, Marree. And the best way you can help me is to stay safe until I know what's going on."

Delgado moved into the room. "We'll reach Calais in twenty minutes. Marree, the crew will take you to shore in a safe boat."

Marree searched Calla's eyes. "Please let me help."

"You can. I've organized a car to meet you in Calais and take you to a highly secure hotel in Paris. I'll contact you when I know more."

Marree nodded.

Several minutes later, Delgado pressed a button near the ramp on the lower level of the yacht, and a lever rose. Behind it were two speedboats. He prepared one and summoned the crew member to get it out to the water. A crew member took it from there.

"I should warn you, Marree, you might get wet," the crewman said as he helped Marree get into the seat.

She looked back at Calla.

"You'll be much safer off the Scorpion Tide," Calla said. "I'll be in touch as soon as I can and will also make sure Allegra alerts you of anything."

When the crewman had taken Marree, Delgado closed the yacht's garage and looked at her. "You ready to disappear off the grid?"

She nodded.

"No better time than the present."

THIRTY-THREE

A BLINDFOLD CAME off Jack's eyes, and the light nearly blinded him. His shoulder ought to have hurt more, but whoever had dragged him here made sure his shoulder wound pain subsided.

God knew what Calla was thinking. When they shot him, he had seen her face. They wanted to make her believe he was dead. Why?

He examined the watch on his left wrist, the only personal belonging his kidnappers had left with him.

Somewhere along the way, satellite communication had broken. Without resetting the communication on the telepathic software, he couldn't contact them.

Computers were all set up, recording every move Jack made.

A man in tactical gear, with a dark mask over his face, entered the room. Though Jack could barely focus on what was going on, he tried. One look at the interrogation setup, and he had to stay calm if he was to pass their tests.

The man slapped an electric band around his right wrist and pressed him down in the chair.

"ISTF doesn't have a tradition of listening," the man said.

"Try me," Jack said with a grin.

"But we have other ways…"He stopped mid-sentence and played a video on a screen opposite Jack's chair.

A girl with dark hair and eyes in a blue dress was running in the video.

Soma? How? Just how much did these people know about him?

It had to be her.

He had been told that someone had adopted Soma, and his grandmother never denied it.

Soma was younger than him, but after he left for university in Canada, he had never heard from her after his father joined a shady intelligence agency in Africa.

She had disappeared from his life.

"You have a lot at stake here. Chances are you thought she was dead, along with other people you have not been in touch with. Your sister is alive," Lent said, entering the room.

"I thought this was about gene editing."

Lent sighed. "You'll soon find out what it's all about. Most things are never too far from home."

His entire past was unraveling in front of him, led by an organization he had no connection to.

After he moved to Canada for University, Jack had called his father a few times asking about Soma. His father said he was doing undercover work, developed a drinking habit, and had tried to find out what happened to Soma.

The second to last time he had seen his father was when the man got caught up with pirates in the Indian Ocean, who did their worst when they held his father for God knew what and threw him overboard. Jack had not been there and came too late.

The pirates asked for a ransom for his father's life. Then

they sent him the video of what they had done to him. That was the last time. Now, his father had facilitated his kidnapping on the Scorpion Tide two days ago.

Lent's chin held high and eyes focused as he approached Jack. He reached for what looked like a lethal needle, an interrogation piece used by the worst of them.

"Tell me what you know about the Beale Ciphers," Lent began. "Your sister can live. Not the sister in New York, but the one you thought you lost years ago."

Jack's eyes grew wide. He knew nothing about the code. Calla could work it out, but he could stall them if they had his sister. "I swear I know nothing," he repeated. It was a lie, but he didn't want to find out if he was right by being wrong.

"I don't need your little 'I know nothing'. I need your knowledge and genius, and please don't make me take them out of you. I want the telescope's location and the names of those who could have decrypted the data sets found in those caves in New Mexico. When that's done, we'll talk about a gene-selecting process I want you to complete."

Jack raised an eyebrow. "How do I know if she's alive?"

"Soma Kleve is alive. But not for long, and it all depends on you."

Jack felt his body shaking, and he thought for a moment. It sounded like these guys needed a bioweapon, which had been something he feared about his research. Could he imitate a gene-editing process for them that couldn't stand the test of time?

Lent approached. This time, he took a gun to Jack's head. "Didn't think that I wouldn't know about your plans, did you?" he asked. "If you want Soma safe, you'll do as I require."

"If I do this for you, I want to see that she's alive."

"I've watched her every day of her life since she was a

baby. I have a habit of scouting out prodigies and talent. A thing I picked up from an old friend, Mason Laskfell."

"You're sick."

Lent laughed. "I am attracted to geniuses and polymaths like you. You slipped out of my hands, but Soma didn't."

THIRTY-FOUR

2:33 P.M.

CALLA COULDN'T WAIT ANY LONGER. She proceeded to Jack's cabin. They had taken him by force, but Jack had sent a signal from this room. How and what did it say? Calla had to know.

"Code red. Infiltration. System compromised," she read on the phone that had dropped under his bed.

Jack sent that message from this room. And Delgado had located the phone.

First, Calla took a minute to look around.

Jack's cabin was perfect for his needs. He had to have notes, research, code in some form to have sent the message.

She discovered the safe to be empty, cleaned, hacked, and moved. Jack must have been doing something in secret. The trapdoor under his bed was a small space, and it had papers with notes on the ciphers and the telescope.

Jack was a talented hacker. It gave Calla hope.

"This is all I could find," she said, returning to the captain's control deck several moments later. "How did they breach our security? Jack found out, but he didn't have enough time to warn us. That much is clear,"

"He didn't have enough time, nor did he have any option," Delgado replied.

Calla's frustration was getting the best of her. Her eyes darted from side to side, every movement of the surrounding air a threat. She couldn't bring herself to accept it. "ISTF framed us for a crime we didn't commit. And now they've done worse to Jack to prove that they are capable of anything. What was Jack trying to tell us?"

The captain maneuvered Scorpion Tide in silence as Calla let out her frustration. "I believe it's time you find out, Calla. Jack would've wanted you to. He would've wanted you to clear both his and your name. They've turned you into a fugitive. You can't give up now."

She knew Jack would've fought to find the truth. He had been brilliant, a new breed of rogue that made him dangerous for the powers that be. They would want to make an example out of him.

"Someone betrayed him," she said. "I'm not exactly sure why."

THIRTY-FIVE

MAHÉ, THE SEYCHELLES, 6:27 PM

DAY 7

THE SEYCHELLES HID many of Jack's secrets. Calla remembered the Seychelles, an archipelago of 115 islands in the Indian Ocean. A small island with Victoria as capital and major port, the French had settled here on the island in the seventeenth-century, and then the British established a presence in 1814 and formed an outpost on Mahé. The first permanent settlers were the French. Since then, though the French-speaking African nation had been the largest group, Calla could see the British continued maintaining a firm existence.

Tiny white buds bloomed on palm trees as their branches covered the small hillside of the island like a blanket. A breeze carried the scent of the flowers as birds sang.

She took a stroll through the road from the house she believed was Jack's to the beach. It had been guesswork between her memory and Delgado's navigation skills, but from the pieces and the conversations they always had, this had to be the place.

Calla assessed what she knew. Jack was born on the main

island and traveled the world, but there was nowhere like home. They both had known it. She could see why as she stared at the wonder in front of her.

Jack, a daredevil and helicopter pilot, who once told her how, as a kid, he would disappear in the ocean of the famous rocks of Seychelles, between the inner reefs of the Comoros Islands and Aldabra.

Calla headed onto the beach and stared out at the ocean. She felt his presence, and as the cloud formations drew in, was she ready for what she would find? It wouldn't bring Jack back, but it would give her answers.

Jack had to have brought the telescope here. The pact had been simple. Calla would hide what she knew about the decryptions in the cave. He would keep the telescope. As long as the two were on opposite ends of the globe, they were safe. Not anymore.

She stared out at the ocean, where a slap-up of white curls in the ocean breeze looked like a merman. "I just... don't know how to start."

Calla turned to the house where Jack had grown up, a beach hut and a modest garden surrounded by a stone wall. She noticed wood carvings on the walls. They were spirals of flowers and small animals.

Would his grandmother come?

The memory of Jack's Grandma brought Calla back to what Jack had said. "She was a wonderful woman, exquisite, but she was always nagging me. She said that my father was a monster."

When Calla stepped into the house, it was quiet, clean, serene.

His secret lab had to be in the back and perhaps through the floor.

Adamant about surveillance issues, Jack had secured the perimeter.

She set a palm on the door, thankful that Jack had taken every step to make sure he used biometric locks and facial recognition to open doors.

She inspected the lock that required just a touch of a finger and smiled when the door clicked open under her touch. Jack was always a step ahead. He must've known something was wrong and made sure his high-tech gear confirmed her identity.

If she had to guess, Jack had programmed a code to reset the alarm.

Scanning the microscopic memory chip under the skin behind her left ear, she found it. Exactly where she would've put it. A quick reset of her alarm would alert her if someone followed her.

Her subsequent investigation would be the generators. This was what powered the small remote house with the security details that Jack needed. Everything from satellite phones for backup to prevent any unforeseen disasters.

Jack had come up with most of his best ideas while working as a boat boy, and one genius invention paid for an education many only dreamed of. Many corporations still wanted him because of his talent.

Just where was the telescope?

Calla moved further through the house, lifting the floorboard in the master bedroom, and checked on the low hanging shelves, and filed through enormous computers next to a line of low servers. She opened the back door and scanned some more.

Palm trees swayed slightly in the wind that blew from the sea, and the air was crisp and invigorating.

A few minutes later, she heard a truck pull up in the yard in front of the house, crunching sand as it parked. Calla moved to the door when a voice came from the truck, and she turned to see Grandma's silhouette.

Jack's grandma was beautiful, as Jack had described her. She was tall with flowing, matted afro hair. Grandma walked toward her, carrying a basket of flowers in her hands. Her skirt fluttered in the breeze as she reached out to take Calla's hand.

She hugged Calla and gave her a basket of blossoms; some that Calla didn't even know the names of.

A few looked like teardrops or gardenias. There were pink orchids and yellow ones. Grandma patted her arm in her grandmotherly way, and Calla knew she wanted an explanation.

A few minutes later, the two women stood alone on the small beach, staring out at sea with the same thought in their heads. Jack.

"Lovely flowers for a delightful girl," Grandma said. "Thank you for contacting me about Jack. My grandson only ever said good things about you. I'm so sorry to have lost him. Did you ever get together? I had a feeling you'd be a wonderful woman for him. He was very fond of you from what I gathered."

Calla felt as if a dagger had pinned her to a wall. "Jack and I were good friends, but we never got together that way, Grandma. In fact, I married his best friend."

"That might explain the slight sadness I saw in his eyes. You were such a good friend to him. He told me you had a key to this place."

"I was hoping I would never have to use it," Calla said. "Like all of us, Jack had his secrets, she said, looking back at the house. There are few he told me about. This was one of them, and he told me if anything ever happened to him to come here."

Calla swiveled toward Grandma, waiting for her to speak.

She didn't say a word.

"Jack told me you said his father was a monster," Calla explained. "I don't understand. How?"

"Jack was my favorite grandson. I have four, but none of them are like Jack. His father, my son, was also a very complicated man. I haven't seen him in years. Some tell me he's dead. I don't know."

"I'm sorry," Calla said.

"I loved Jack more than anything in the world."

"I understand," Calla said. "I never knew my grandparents. In fact, I didn't even grow up with my parents."

Jack's grandma moved to the water, and Calla could see that her legs were shaking. "He's never told me any personal thing about his life."

"He had his secrets, but I'm glad he shared some of them with me," Grandma said.

She stared out at sea. "Calla, I had to share him with the world. It needs people like Jack, who think differently and want to give back to science. I shared wonderful private moments with him, and it was my duty to protect him. I don't know what you would find on this island. He left little here. Jack was not happy here even with a place that's as gorgeous as this."

The older woman started walking toward the house.

"Is there anything that Jack would have left here on the island beside the house? Memories, old friends, anything, Grandma?" Calla asked, following her.

Grandma stopped and turned around. "You must leave now, my dear. There are bad people about."

"Okay, Grandma," Calla said in a quiet voice. When she looked closer, Grandma's eyes filled with terror.

They came without warning. Two gunmen and they got a hold of Grandma's arms. Grandma glared at Calla with eyes full of fear. She struggled against the grip of the man holding her. "Shut up! You know what happens if you make trouble."

Grandma couldn't make trouble if she couldn't breathe.

She clawed at his hand, then kicked at his shins, all the while trying to scream, but she couldn't make a sound.

Calla didn't feel her lungs draw breath when the man let go of Grandma for a second, and she sure as hell didn't hear Grandma's gasps and sobs when he pointed the gun.

Calla broke free from the fog of her panicked daze. She seized hold of one man's shirt and slammed him against the car.

Grandma didn't even realize that the man was still holding onto her.

He yelped in anguish when his back slammed against the metal. Calla kicked him in the groin, sending him flying into the driver's side door of Grandma's truck.

The second assailant took off.

Calla wasn't in the mood to chase. She took a moment to compose herself and checked on Grandma, who slowly rose to her feet. She was okay, but badly shaken.

The man's eyes had been scary, but the rest of him was harmless. It was his eyes that were dangerous. They were dark, but there was something else, something hidden.

If he was here, others were not far.

"We need to get you out of here," Calla said to Grandma.

She took her inside the house and fetched her a glass of water. "Stay here and let me check the outside."

It took Grandma some time to calm down. She stared Calla in the face, her eyes still showing panic. "How did a girl like you take that guy on? He was twice your size."

"I'll explain later. Are you okay? I need to make sure you are safe. I have to get you out of here before more of them come. That guy looked like a local hire and wasn't skilled enough. Someone more dangerous sent him. I'll be right back," she said.

Calla heard a sound and glanced up to see another man in black tactical gear standing near the truck with a handgun.

His head turned toward her, arms held at his sides, body straight, elbows locked, legs taut. Goodness, all of him taut.

Calla's nose twitched as the man's sweat wafted through the air.

It came without warning, without explanation, without motivation, without narrative necessity, but not at all unannounced.

She backed away as he lifted the gun.

In one charge, he had her hands behind her back and set the gun barrel to her temple. "You should've thought first before leading us to an old woman," he growled. "You better give us what we want before—"

Without a second to lose, she cut off his words in a twist that freed her arms and slammed fists into his neck.

He staggered to the ground and reached for her leg in a swift haul.

Calla felt her back slam to the ground. Every muscle in her compressed.

She shot to her feet and sliced a leg under his stubby feet.

He collapsed in a pile, and she fetched the discarded gun before setting a boot on his neck.

She pressed for a few seconds, cutting off his air supply. He went limp under her hold.

Calla squeezed harder. "No more hurting people," she said. "Now, I think you best forget about hurting Grandma. Are we clear?"

Anguish in his face, he nodded, and she let go.

He jumped to his feet, and the gun in her hand did the talking. "Move, and if you even look back, this gun will go off."

He scampered for the road of the beach house.

Calla wiped the moisture off her sweating face and hurried back to the house. She had to take Grandma and leave.

"We need to go now, Grandma. You were right about those bad people. I'll close up in a second after I check a few things."

A search of the house revealed nothing unusual.

Within moments, she put Grandma in her truck and asked if she was okay to get back home alone.

Grandma nodded. "Be careful. Those men look like the kind who used to make company with my son, Jack's father."

Calla nodded, and Grandma started the engine. "I'll check on you later."

When Calla returned to the house, she halted by the door, quickly scanning the basket of flowers Grandma had brought her. The door shut behind her and locked itself with a soft click. From the back patio, a tall figure in a dark shirt blocked the view of the beach.

The face was hidden behind a brim and a mask of thick, dark sunglasses. The clap of the figure's shoes was a steady beat, a metronome to their steps.

Even before she saw the face, she knew who it was. The door was her only exit, but an unwanted person stood there leering.

CHAPTER
THIRTY-SIX

CALLA'S MUSCLES quivered as a lump crawled to her throat.

"Hello, Calla," Oskara said.

"Something I can do for you?" Calla asked, her mind trying to calculate what Oskara would do next, standing in the doorway.

Oskara moved into the room, grinning, slow and deliberate, like they were playing a game. "I'm not here for you, Calla. I'm here to get the telescope."

"I see," Calla said flatly.

She had come with her men again. The tall one that had run off in New Mexico and the two local hires she'd just fought off.

Oskara's eyes flicked about the room. "Where is it?"

"Who wants it? Him?" Calla said, with a quick glance at the outside door to the beach hut.

They both knew who 'he' was.

Oskara swore to herself, then pulled a gun out from behind her belt. She pointed it at Calla. "Just answer my questions.

Where can I find your damn telescope?" Oskara asked. "I've seen it before. I know that woman gave it to you at the caves."

The doorknob twisted, and the door flew open. A second woman burst in.

Athletic, she pointed the pistol like a trained field agent. The woman's short black afro glistened even in the house's shade, and her brown skin contrasted with Oskara's pale white skin.

The woman lunged at Oskara, ripping the gun from her hands with a violent jerk.

Oskara yelped and jumped back in shock, dropping her phone.

The gun slid across the wooden flooring until it fell against the front door.

Oskara stumbled and fell to the ground, landing on her rear, and scooted for her dropped gun.

Calla leaped over Oskara and snatched up the pistol.

Oskara then drew a second gun from her holster. "Where's the telescope?"

Calla didn't answer. She only looked back and forth from the gun to Oskara's face. As soon as she saw Oskara's eyes, she knew she had to act fast.

A LOUD SOUND reverberated through the air as the gun went off. It was a warning shot. The sound was so loud it echoed off the walls.

Gunpowder. Oil. A metallic scent.

Calla hesitated as Oskara neared her. "Tell me where it is," she said. "I want that telescope!" she yelled.

Calla needed to distract her and took a quick look at the door when the second woman aimed a gun at Oskara.

The woman did not blink as Calla wondered who would fire first.

Who was she?

It didn't look like she was here for Calla. When the woman gave her a nod, she knew they were on the same side.

Oskara snarled. In one swift move, the woman pulled Calla to her and kicked the door shut behind her. "Come!"

They darted outside at full speed. Once at the back of the house, they bolted for the pier. The other woman was slightly ahead when they got to it.

Both women halted.

A man at the end of the pier stood sneering, with a long chain tied to two beasts.

Two panthers stood between them and the jet ski. The first black beast snarled and moved toward them, poised to spring at the woman with her. Calla had no choice but to trust her. She had saved her life.

It took all of two seconds to see the beasts charge.

"Any bright ideas?" Calla said, turning to her new companion, whose dark eyes peered into one beast.

Her afro, cornrowed to the nape of her head, glistened in the sun, and for the first time, Calla noticed her dark khaki combat pants below an army t-shirt and a bulletproof vest. "Who are you?"

"No time to chat, but you may call me Soma."

The beasts showed no fear. They advanced.

The first beast propelled itself at Soma. She and Calla took only seconds to decide to leap from their path, almost toppling in the water. Behind them, Oskara advanced to the edge of the pier. "The telescope!"

Calla was tiring of this game. She shot Soma a knowing look, who nodded back at her. Her physique was athletic, and Soma was a no-nonsense type. She knew what Calla was about to do.

Calla sprang into the air, charging toward the man. She executed a perfect kick, aiming her right foot for his temple.

He fell back and dropped the chain.

Calla landed back on the pier and pounced next to the amazed panther just before she reached for the chains and loosened them.

Angry beasts turned on their masters as Calla jumped a second time and landed with both feet on the pier. The wood cracked, sending planks flying into the air. Soma wobbled until she found a firm footing on the cracking dock.

Oskara, having found her way to them, blinked, lost her

balance, yet set a determined foot forward on the breaking wood.

"Now!" yelled Calla.

Soma and Calla dove off the side of the damaged pier and swam for the jet ski. Planks of wood littered the water from the broken dock. They dove off just as Oskara fired behind at them. They swam out to sea, leaving Oskara to trail behind them. The water was clear, light from the sun shining over the waves, but the shadows were dark. Calla could feel the current's icy grip around her, her skin tingling. She swam hard, her arms burning. Thrashing forward, the women reached the jet ski, and Calla came for the handles as Soma steadied the vehicle.

Calla swung her foot over and pulled her weight onto her jet ski, dragged the woman up behind her, and churned the engine.

"Welcome to panther island, as Jack used to call it," the woman yelled above the skis engines. "His neighbor should never have bred those animals here."

"Soma, why are you here?" Calla asked.

A bullet rang out.

"Don't think now's a good time," Soma replied.

As she drove the jet ski toward the yacht, Calla increased her speed.

They neared the Scorpion Tide's rear ramp, with enough distance now between them and their assailants. Calla slowed the machine. "You knew Jack?"

"Yes, he's my little brother."

"Jack has one sister, and I've met her," Calla said, her eyebrows knitting. "That isn't you."

"I'm Soma Kleve, and that wasn't Jack's sister that you met. Fiora was supposed to replace me when they came for me. The woman you think is Jack's sister is not."

Calla's jaw dropped. "What? Fiora isn't his sister?"

"No."

Calla shook her head, trying to take it all in. There was an indisputable resemblance between Soma and Jack. And for a moment it seemed as if Calla had Jack back. "How? How did you know to come here?"

"I followed Grandma, and when I saw who was following her, I knew something was up. Now, what was that telescope that deranged woman was yelling for?"

Calla lifted her eyes to Soma. As if she had just seen her for the first time. How many secrets surrounded Jack? She'd always let him tell her his deepest fears, hopes, and more, all in his own time. But why hadn't he mentioned Fiora wasn't his actual sister?

"I was there earlier today," Soma began. "I've run into Oskara Amano on a couple of occasions. She's a highly trained assassin for hire."

"I know," Calla said, wondering if Soma knew what had happened to Jack.

Where could she begin?

Delgado helped them onto the ramp and parked the jet ski, and threw each a towel before leaving them alone in the vehicle room.

Soma put her gun away and let a crew member help her onto the yacht's docking platform.

"Somehow, I'm not so sure Jack would leave things lying about so easily," Soma continued. "He was always meticulous and trusted very few. What's the telescope, anyway?"

Calla took a moment before answering. "You're right. Jack trusted very few, and his grandma was one of them. That's why she gave me the telescope, and Jack must get his spy tactics from somewhere, for she knew enough not to hand it to me in broad daylight, but in a basket of flowers," Calla said, drawing the telescope from the pocket of her small backpack.

"It's no bigger than my palm when collapsed and… it's something that got Jack killed. I'd only seen it once in a picture. Jack was working on something. I don't know what yet. I thought I'd find it here."

CHAPTER
THIRTY-EIGHT

CALLA SQUINTED as she studied Soma. Of all things she had expected to find in Jack's house, it wasn't a long-lost sister.

Once the yacht was safely out in the water, they settled into the main room. The videophone rang in the yacht's lounge, and Calla answered it. "Father?"

Stan's face appeared, a mask of worry and relief filling his face. "Calla, are you all right?"

"I'm fine, father."

"Be careful, darling. The wires are alert, looking for you. They won't mention ISTF, so the authorities have used the police as a cover, saying you're a cop on the loose."

"Well, that covers them but not me."

"Calla, as long as you're on the Scorpion Tide, no one will find you."

"I can't be on the boat forever. I need to find out why I was set up and what they wanted from Jack."

Stan's voice was firm. "Call Nash. Please."

"I can't," she replied. "If he gets involved, he too will be a target."

"You're as stubborn as your father. Listen, just say the word, and I'm there with you," Stan continued.

"I will, father, but not now, and please don't track down Nash. I won't lose a husband and a best friend all in one week."

"Okay. We've found out a little more. They drugged Jack and used his phone to get on and off the Scorpion Tide. I traced the leak as far as I could, but then it went cold. Jack's phone is missing, so be careful. I've worked with Delgado to rework the security on the yacht. You should be okay for now."

Calla took in a deep breath. "I found Jack's phone."

He hung up, and she turned back to Soma.

A distrust chilled Soma's eyes. "Tad, is that what you call him these days?"

"Excuse me?" Calla said.

Soma's shoulders went stiff. "Tad has always been in Jack's shadow, and now he has caught up with him."

"What do you mean?" Calla asked.

Soma put her gun on the table and stared at her. "Tad, as you call him, grew up with Jack, and yes, they were friends, but I'll not exactly say they were friendly. Tad has always been jealous of what Jack could do. And they were competitors. I wouldn't listen to anything he says to you."

"How do you know about Tad?"

The edge of Soma's mouth curled into a sardonic grin. "I've been following his activity for months."

"What about you? Why would Jack not tell me about you?" Calla asked.

"It's classified. Jack was on a need-to-know basis."

Calla ignored Soma's fierce expression. "Classified? Who do you work for?"

"The African Intelligence Agency, a secret intelligence division no one knows exists. It came into being as the colonies were breaking away from their European masters. They have been working undercover on the continent for years, training spies like me, funded by pockets of the West. But then broke off in the seventies."

"I see. So where did you grow up and—

"I was raised in South Africa and adopted into a spy family to be trained. This was before Jack was born. I later found out he found out about me. Must be connections in the British government that he gained over the years."

"But he never mentioned you."

"To protect you, I think. AIA has had many enemies over the years. Jack left Seychelles when he was older. We didn't meet until he was sixteen and I was twenty. It was brief. He was attending an American high school in Tanzania for a while before going to college in Canada. I was working undercover in the area. In case you don't know, some of these islands are a hotbed of criminal activity. The AIA separated Jack and me as infants. Our grandmother raised him."

"What about Fiora?" Calla said. "Where does she fit into this whole thing?"

"Fiora is not Jack's sister; neither is she mine. The AIA brought her into the family to replace me."

"Replace you? Why would anyone want to replace you?"

"The African Intelligence Agency wanted to recruit young prodigies. It worked with another overseas child recruitment program, and they had their eye on our family for a long time. They'd been watching my father. They knew or thought that somehow along the way, he had gifted kids. So they wanted us both in this program. Our grandmother intervened. It was too late for me, but she kept Jack out of it. For years she looked for me, and eventually found me and connected me to Jack, but we could tell nobody that we knew each other or had found each other, and we had to make Fiora believe she knew nothing and it has to stay that way."

Calla sank low on the sofa. "That would make sense why she has always spied on Jack and even sold his resources to criminals."

"Doesn't surprise me. Jack sent a message to me three days ago and told me to come to meet him here today. He didn't give me any details, but he told me about you and Nash, and he was leaving after your wedding. You can imagine my surprise when I arrived expecting to meet Jack, and I met his enemies instead. We need to act fast if we're going to find out what this telescope everyone wants actually does. You and Jack shared a lot, and it's the reason you're the target of this powerful organization. Is there anything that you can share? I can see what you're up against. I have a feeling that our enemy doesn't want to be found either. They want to find us."

Calla pursed her lips. "Tell me about Tad. How does he fit into all of this?"

"Tad was the reason they got to Jack. The two have collaborated most of the time on projects until Tad refused to return a favor. When Jack contacted me three days ago, he told me someone very dangerous was onto him and needed my help. He told me not to trust Tad and to be on high alert until we met. They were tapping into every communication, not just Jack's but others close to him."

Calla felt her throat go dry. "Soma, I'm sorry, but Jack's dead. He was mine and my husband's best friend."

Soma looked at her. "He's not dead. He can't be. If they killed him, why would he send me an SOS? I know that if he were dead, he wouldn't have sent me this message."

"When was this? When did you get the message?"

"Five days ago."

"Jack was still with us. Not anymore."

Soma pulled out a piece of pink paper from her pocket. "Jack and I use this communication device, and it prints out on pink paper anything that we might need to transmit. He sent this to me a few days ago, and I replied."

Calla relived the moment. "They shot him in front of me. I held him before they took him away. He's gone, and I'm being pinned for his death by what you've just seen there in his house. They want him and me out of the way, but they can't do it yet because they want what we have."

"What is that? The telescope?"

"Let's not get into that. We need to find out who that person is. They wanted something from Jack."

"That's why Jack is still alive," Soma said.

"Did you not hear me? Jack is gone. I know this is hard." This time, a tear welled in her eyes. Tears she had held back for Jack poured out. She missed him more than she could contain. Calla pushed back a sob and peered through tear-stained eyes. "I don't know if the telescope will help us," Calla said. "The telescope is only a key to solving the Beale Ciphers. But it makes little sense. The ciphers can't be all that this is about. And that woman, Oskara. She's an assassin—

"Whatever you and Jack shared, someone wants badly, and it starts with that telescope. The Beale Ciphers, you say… what are those?"

A blissful sigh of satisfaction escaped Calla's lips. "Where do I start? Three ciphers left by Thomas Beale that supposedly lead to a treasure. Two of the three ciphers have been deciphered. There is one more, and it remains a puzzle. But even if we get to the end of it all, the treasure is not considerably valuable as one would think in today's money."

Soma took in a deep breath. "Jack must've known more about the ciphers. And so do you. You are the world's best code breaker. Many have heard of the Decrypter, so someone powerful who wants what's in that brain of yours and what was in Jack's has sent that assassin. Which tells me they're after something you know or something only you know how to know. Calla, I need you to put everything else out of your mind. I want to find out who did this to Jack and why, and I'm counting on you."

Calla studied Soma. The sight of her made her feel like there was hope again, like maybe this nightmare was not real. She wondered why Jack had never told her about Soma, why he had kept her a secret.

Calla moved to a large cabinet and set a flat palm on the scanner. The safe slid open. Out of it, she drew out an object. "This is the telescope. Jack and I swore never to bring the telescope and the decryption of the ciphers together." She paused and looked upward for a second, talking to herself. "But maybe it's time we do."

THIRTY-NINE

JACK MUST'VE BEEN out cold, his head full of unanswered questions. He woke up in a dark room, thirsty, and his back was aching something fierce. He figured he'd been asleep for a few hours. At least he could plan his communication with Calla.

He thought he had hours before they came back. Jack turned when the man stepped into his cell. "You can't keep me here forever, you know."

"The time will come when Lent Cyrus runs out of patience."

Jack knew exactly what the man meant.

He dropped to the floor. "Can I get a medic? My shoulder is killing me."

The man rushed to him and placed a hand on his shoulder. "Knock it off."

Jack studied him and swallowed hard. "I can't help you if you don't get me the right medical attention."

The man looked at him curiously, and after a few seconds, he nodded and left, locking the door behind him.

Jack rose slowly and sat on the edge of the bed. He had

what he needed. The man's wallet. All he needed was a credit card. He'd find the opportune moment and get to work.

Since being dragged here, he had sensed that the only way that they would've been able to kidnap him and get onto the Scorpion Tide was because of cameras everywhere. Somehow, during the wedding celebrations that week, someone must've brought a spy cam onto the yacht. He had seen it and deactivated it, and that's what had triggered him to go downstairs to check his work in his cabin.

His fingers circled the paperclip still in his pocket. It had all the things that he needed to create a communication pocket and connect through a hidden network in this place.

Just where was he? Where had they brought him? This had to do with the Beale Ciphers and what he and Calla had found. It also had to do with Halona's telescope. Calla had to find out precisely what that telescope did. Calla's life was seriously in danger. He just needed a few hours to work out how to make the chip from the credit card and the paperclip to create a communication line.

"You're lucky, Jack. A doctor will be down here soon." the man said, returning.

Jack wouldn't listen to anything he said. He was going to stay focused and not let anything else mess with his head. They wouldn't get to him.

"We won't harm you."

"I'm not as dumb as you think," Jack said. "I know what you're going to do."

"You've no idea."

Jack didn't know what they would make him do, but it didn't look good. He had to make this guy quit messing with him. He needed a distraction to make this man leave so he could work out his communication plan.

"Why don't you tell me exactly what this thing is that I'm

supposed to make? I can't make anything I don't know about," Jack said.

The man grunted. "You can't change the fact you will do what we tell you to do, whether or not you like it."

The man had more information than Jack expected. It was probably worse than he realized. But it was what he needed to work through if he was going to do anything. He had to pry some stuff out of this man. "What have you done to Calla Cress?"

The man stared him in the eye. He said nothing. Then he walked back to the door. The man laughed as he walked back into the room. "We've only separated you from your illusions. And now you'll look for the truth."

The man opened the door and nodded to the two men waiting outside. "Have fun."

The two men took him out and down the corridor. He needed to stay focused and develop a plan to make some sort of communication tool that he could use.

"Just a little further," one of the men said.

The two men walked in tandem—one in front of him and one behind. There was no way to get past them, but he had to try.

They turned a corner and brought him to a door.

Jack's mind raced.

The first man pulled out a key card, swiped it, and went inside a large room. The other man shoved Jack in.

Jack didn't have time to think of anything. One second he was being led into the room, and the next second, the man had his hands on his throat. "Where's the telescope?"

Jack couldn't breathe.

He pushed Jack down on the floor and pulled out a coil of rope from the wall. "Where is it?"

Jack knew the telescope could create havoc, and it was the

reason they had hidden it. "I don't know. So that's what you want?"

The man walked him over to a small table. A remote computer was on top of it. "Start plugging in the coordinates of where we should begin looking."

"On the computer?"

Jack looked around the room. There were eyes everywhere. These men were answering to a much higher being. If he only knew where he was, he would fight his way out of here. It was a possibility, but it could be stupid if he did not know what was outside these walls.

Though the place was wrapped in windowless white concrete and all the latest in medical equipment, robotics, and robotics-for-medicine as any lab at NASA, it felt more like a prison.

He had heard trucks that morning outside the walls crunching and moving. Could have been pebbles, or could've been rocks, or equally could have been snow. There was no way he could know where he was.

Not a single window was in this place, a combination of steel and mirrors. He had to be somewhere freezing, as the radiators were never off in this place.

"The telescope makes calculations. Somehow, Beale knew about that telescope and failed to mention it. But that girl-friend of yours must've figured it out, the one you all call the Decrypter, the ISTF *Red Fox*," the man said.

Jack's hand reached out and fingered the keyboard. There was nothing connected to the computer. He swiped again. Not even a drive connector. "It doesn't work."

A quizzical look appeared on the man's face. "What? No!"

Jack smirked.

"It was working before you got here," the man said as he circled the table and worked his way around toward the door.

A confidence washed over Jack. "You need to restart your servers. Your computers can't work without them."

Jack smiled as they dragged him back to his cell. It was the time he needed to plan his next move. He had deactivated the servers. Now he had to channel their energy and re-establish communication with his satellite and then contact Calla.

CHAPTER
FORTY

CALLA LAID OUT THE TELESCOPE. She had never fully examined it. "This is what they sent Tad to get. He made it sound like he was after something else, but he was working for them too."

"Tad was always one to watch," Soma added. "But so was our father. They sort of took the same path."

The telescope was beautiful when pulled out from a set of seven circles. Made before most of today's technology existed, Calla inspected each ring and remarked on its unique features.

First was the former world currency sphere; silver, gold, and copper collected around the outside. Next were the zodiac signs on the other side, then the compass points and other symbols. Last was the stylized landscape on one side and then the ciphers on the other.

The telescope's lens was also a recent addition. The symbols were ancient, and Calla could only determine a few recent dead languages. It was the most beautiful thing she'd ever seen.

This was a crypto machine made to encrypt and decrypt

ciphers made in various ancient periods. Calla could identify some legends of the ciphers—the ones she knew, anyway.

She spent a few minutes trying to decipher the messages within the circles. After an extensive study of the rings, she noticed the leather set on an iron stand in the center of the telescope. The stand showed its history on the bottom.

Calla slid the lens onto the telescope's eyepiece, moved to the outside deck, and aimed at the southern horizon. She spied through the lens as small specks of dust circled over the land below. What she saw was not a cloud or even a stray bird. It seemed to be a way for the sun to meet the sky. The perfect part of the sky to watch a solar eclipse. The telescope was splendid.

Calla set the telescope at first forty feet from the eyepiece, then moved it to fifty feet, then to sixty, and finally to seventy-five feet. The image was becoming smaller, but she could not read the writing.

Taking the whole telescope in her arms, she adjusted the lens again, this time to the furthest it would go.

"I have never seen such a device. Where does it come from?" Soma said.

Calla shrugged. "That's what we need to find out."

Calla stopped her examination of the telescope and collapsed it back into its compact form. There was one question still on her mind. "When did Tad change? It sounded to me, like at one time he and Jack were close."

Soma answered with a tinge of regret. "Only when they were boat boys. But when Jack showed real promise, Tad wanted to prove himself too, and he's been trying to ever since. His jealousy must've gotten the better of him and then if he couldn't beat Jack at his own game, then he would destroy him."

They stood in the lounge silently, lost in their own thoughts for a while. Eventually, a crew member walked by, and she put away glasses behind the bar.

"I can't believe he'd do that," Calla said to Soma as the crew member walked away. "And Jack couldn't do anything about it?"

"Maybe we should go see Tad and talk to him," Soma mused. "If we can find him."

"Where would we find him?" Calla said.

"I don't know," Soma said. "But he likes to be where power lives."

FORTY-ONE

SANTA CEASREA TERME, SALIB'S
SAFE HOUSE

WHEN NASH ENTERED his room at the safe house in Santa Cesarea Terme, he took inventory of his surroundings. On any mission he took, rule number one was to check everything.

Nash shrugged off his jacket and hung it over the back of a chair. He checked his watch. He had been there under two minutes.

Dark with only a single light, a small computer lay on a table next to a lamp on a bedside table.

Nash moved closer to the computer, studying its display.

The computer played a message, and it was not from Salib. Nash couldn't guess at its origin, as if someone was trying to tell him something.

He moved to the computer and studied the technology. It was a significantly better system than the one he used at the NSA. Not good. Salib had said nothing about a computer or video terminal being here, and why would it call him? What was the external power source?

Nash scanned for power sources and his eyes stopped on a small box sitting on a table beside the computer. He examined the box, too small to run the computer. The electronics box was square, about the size of a postage stamp. The surface was black and rounded, like a smooth piece of polished stone, with a glass screen and a series of buttons.

Then he stopped, realizing that the power box produced a slight gleam of red light. A switch for an audio recording system was on top.

The computer kept repeating the same message.

"Mr. Shields, I've set up a surveillance system for you. Please don't be alarmed. It'll be activated after twenty-four hours. To view the system, simply press this PAUSE button."

Only Salib knew he was here. He wasn't sure what was being sent or why, but the confidence gave his heart a slight feeling of assurance.

Was someone watching them?

Salib was a thorough man and certainly would not have put this here. Nash rang his cell. "Salib? Could you come in here for a second?"

Salib answered the phone with his usual response. "Yes?"

"There's something here for you to see on the table beside my computer. You told me nothing about surveillance. Why is it there? What do they do?" Nash asked.

Several moments later, he heard footsteps, and the door opened.

When Salib entered the room, he saw what Nash was pointing to. He looked at Nash with a guilty expression. "Sorry, I forgot to tell you about it. I got a few reports that someone else works here in the area. I just thought I might get a surveillance system here to protect your life."

Nash raised an eyebrow. "Is anyone watching us?"

Salib shook his head. "No, this thing runs on an internal battery and will activate five hours from now. It's just a test. I thought you'd want the best."

Nash scratched his chin. "A damn good one, too. You don't stop surprising me and your investment in such tech."

"With this thing watching behind us, we will be clear of the area and back in the airport before they know what hit them. Think of it as spies sent ahead to give us any intel before we enter. I've loaded the place with several of these," Salib said.

He slapped Salib on the back. "You're full of surprises. Anything else I should know?"

Salib fiddled with a device he took from a drawer. "I got you a cell phone for the extraction, just in case. It's disposable and can be turned on and off at will. I want you to stay in touch. You just can't call me direct."

Nash chuckled, turning on the cell. "Got it."

With a single touch, the screen lit up. It activated with a small call to the carrier.

Salib also pointed out a camera built into the computer and a tiny electronic device. "They built the camera into the screen. You see what you're doing. It's a nice setup, huh? The electronic device is a motion detector. It's attached to your combat suit, but you shouldn't be able to see it." Salib walked over to the device and turned it off. "I need to always make sure I meet your standards."

Nash smirked. "Think we are ready."

FORTY-TWO

SCORPION TIDE, SOMEWHERE IN
THE INDIAN OCEAN

CALLA LEANED back in the seat. "I wasn't prepared for this. A betrayal."

Soma's eyes held a hint of disappointment. "Yes, it was our father who started this mess and possibly who told Lent about Jack," Soma glanced away from her to look at the panel of screens in front of her. "I wanted to find out everything about my father," she said in a quiet voice. "But I also wanted to do it in my own way."

Calla raised an eyebrow. "That I understand."

"Why do you think?" Soma replied. "Our father never really liked me."

Calla could feel it in her gut. The same feeling of rejection that she had come to terms with when her parents left her. Soma had a similar resistance. There was nothing like a parent leaving and a child not knowing why. Calla could see that Soma was struggling.

"What about your mother?" Calla said, remembering what Jack had once told her.

He had spent his first ten years with his mother and not his father, and Calla knew that his mother had been a good person.

Calla heard Soma sigh. "I don't know about my mother, really," Soma said. "My father left her."

"Well, it doesn't suddenly make everything okay if you're grown up and doing okay," Calla said. "Many would say I turned out halfway decent, even though I don't think I had had the best start in life when my parents left me. And it doesn't get any easier when you grow up, so I understand. When did you find out that your father was a spy, Soma? Mine is too," Calla said.

Soma squirmed under Calla's steady stare. "It's been common knowledge for a long time."

"At what point did you know?" Calla asked.

"Years ago," she said.

Calla could see that she didn't want to bring up a painful memory.

Soma bit a nail. "It was clear for a long time that the African Intelligence Agency hadn't been able to locate him. They actively went after him. But he was nowhere to be found. So I figure the only person who would know how to find him and could do that would be my uncle. But when he too went missing, everyone seemed to think that someone had found him and killed him."

"Except for you," Calla said. "You knew what was going on."

"I figured it out," Soma said. "That's when I wanted to contact Jack. I noticed something from the tone of things. Then I realized that the AIA's search for my father was a fake. He could've sold out long before the search. They'd been lying all along." She looked at Calla. "You knew Jack better than everyone else. I can see why you and Jack hit it off from the very beginning. I'm sorry for yours and my loss."

FORTY-THREE

PARIS

DAY 8

MARREE HAD REACHED Paris by midnight. The city's lights dulled in the early morning hours, bleaching towers and limestone facades, their geometry as regular as a child's crayon drawing. A city of lights, mist now shrouded bridges, and the River Seine, a forlorn reflection of the blue sky.

Marree had asked the taxi to drop her two blocks away, and she now walked up the Champs-Élysées Boulevard, her boots knocking against the cobblestone.

Traffic flowed around her, but none saw her. The air smelled of exhaust and the grease of cars. Her ears picked up the sounds of distant music from a closing café, the thrum of car engines, and the sound of her own breathing.

Why had she never told Jack the truth? All the lying about her past. Lying? No, perhaps she'd just failed to mention the facts. Now it was too late. Jack was dead.

Calla had sent her here to find the truth, and maybe she wasn't the only one with a hidden past. Why had Jack never told her about Halona? Sure, he worked for a secret agency, but there was something else.

The sun dawned as Marree stood staring at the river and thought of Calla. She was the only link Marree had to Jack's past.

The truth, like everything else, would be in Jack's private room at the George V as Calla had said. Why the big secret from her? She would have accepted, but he allowed her to remain in the dark.

These thoughts continued to overwhelm Marree as she checked in at the hotel lobby. After using the check-in details Calla had given her, the receptionist gave her a special card for the particular floor, which would open the door to Jack's private suite, giving Marree access to all his personal things.

Marree's French was limited, and although the receptionist seemed friendly, he could've been flirting with her.

She pressed the button for the top floor—the presidential suite. The elevator headed up, and her heart raced.

Marree knocked on the door. Perhaps, by some miracle, Jack would come to the door.

No answer.

She used the key card. When she entered, she saw the place was immaculate. The spacious main foyer had an extension that stretched along the front window with views over the Champs-Élysées. To the left was the master bedroom with a king-size bed. Past that was a marble bathroom, and to the right of the foyer was the study with large double doors. A small corridor led undoubtedly to the kitchen, dining area, and two small bedrooms.

Marree carefully slipped off her shoes and walked into the master bedroom. Where would she find Jack's safe? She couldn't get into the safe with her hands, so she went with the only other option that came to mind.

Jack was a high-tech thinking man, and the room was riddled with expensive computer screens.

Arranged in a rough pyramid shape, a series of screens, each a bit smaller than a phone book, stood on a desk from which short, thick tubes of different colored wires snaked away from the pyramid to small, rectangular boxes, each one a different shade of green, yellow, and red.

He must've been paying good money for this place, and Marree knew he was paying for privacy rather than luxury.

The bedroom was a massive space with a four-poster bed that covered one wall. With exquisite views over Paris, Marree gently opened the closet, but there was nothing there. Jack was not a clothes man—she had never seen him in anything but casual wear. She looked for writing, but there was none. His portable computer was also missing.

She moved on to the private bathroom, but no clues were to be found.

Jack had always taught her to look for the little things. She'd noticed nothing.

A black pouch was hidden behind the tap ware at the sink.

She went back into the foyer, and there it was, a small safe behind a curtain.

Jack had told her many times never to use force. One had to outsmart the security system, a small combination safe with small sliders. For a smart guy, this was an amateur move. But then again, no one knew he spent time here but Calla. She smiled, thinking of him.

After three attempts, the door opened, and inside were documents.

By eight in the morning, Marree was on her third cup of coffee. She hardly slept for the excitement of finally decoding Jack's past life. It made sense. Halona's creation of the perfect code—whoever possessed it was invincible. But what could this mean?

Marree went through Jack's files like a shark. She scanned for anything that would tell her what he had been up to.

In his closet, she had found his old backpack. It was faded olive green with the name of a college printed on it. She opened it up and took out his clothes and his toilet bag. She didn't look through it. It was essential to hasten.

She then checked the pockets of his clothes and came across a folded piece of paper and a key. She opened up the form and saw a list of names with numbers next to them, and then under each name, there were symbols and letters.

The key was to something in the hotel room.

She looked around and saw a small table that was pushed up against the wall. The top was made of glass, nothing special, just a piece of glass that might display something underneath it. Jack must've kept his laptop on that table when he wasn't using it.

Marree then waited for a long time.

She had been sitting there for so long that she felt her anxiety grow. The more she waited, the more it sunk in. Jack was not coming back.

She thought about the International Security Taskforce and the time they'd spent together, most of which she spent trying to understand the organization and Jack's work with the operatives.

Marree also thought about the time he had saved her life. He had once been the only one she could trust.

Marree opened the safe and found a tablet, then switched it on. She used a hacking chip from her handbag that opened up the tablet's system. Jack had a lot of money. She found his banking information, just the US accounts, but no transaction details.

Marree opened a folder labeled "International Security Taskforce." She found a photo of the ISTF building and was about to close the file when she saw something odd, a note with a list of names, including hers.

Fleming, Jack, A.
Johnson, Marree, F.
Gentry, Craig, A.
Dane, Peter, A.
Hansen, Jonathon, A.

Marree found another folder. This file had a logo from a company called Cyrus Tech Enterprises.

Marree went back to her overnight bag, grabbed her CIA laptop, and placed it on the desk. Loading her secure program, she latched onto Jack's tablet and penetrated his email program. As an analyst, this was easy, but Jack was cautious so she would find only what he would allow her to see.

It was difficult, but she opened his outbox and found an unsent email to Calla dated eighteen months ago.

She opened the email, a coded message, one quite suited for Calla.

Her eyes widened.

Jack had used a cipher known around intelligence circles as the Beale Hoax to encrypt a new cipher that locked a bioweapon prototype. No further details were in the email except a reference to a telescope.

Why a telescope?

She looked out toward the window to see a spy camera pointing at her when her cell phone rang.

Her heart skipped a beat.

"Who is it?" she asked.

FORTY-FOUR

PACIFIC OCEAN, ALASKA, 5:12 A.M.

OSKARA COULD BARELY BREATHE AS she took her morning jog. She drew in a deep breath and advanced further past coated icicles that clung to the cave walls. It had taken her two flights and Lent's private armored boat to leave Mahé and touch down at Granite Mountain Air Station, Alaska. From there on, a private helicopter had brought her to this facility.

There wasn't enough air in the place, and Lent had made sure of it.

She had to be ready.

A high-tech facility, made of glass and steel, deep in Alaska's Ice Caves, was beyond her. All underground, all openings led to the edge of a frozen lake.

There was nothing behind the empty glass except for an endless expanse of dark ice. Mounted with a mountainside, the construction facility resembled a fortress. A steel bridge ebbed out of the second cliff.

Lent Cyrus had built this facility. Somehow, he'd wired enough cables to power an ice palace that could rival any hotel in Siberia.

Within the center of the facility, a tall tower stood at its center that had to be over ten stories tall. Its snow-covered roof was coated in elaborate snow sculptures, powered by AI to keep it frozen underground. Pure vanity. Vanity.

A sweet, clean scent of ice wafted past her. She was in the outermost part of the facility. A slight breeze and a bit of condensation dripping off icicles the outer spaces of the facility misted the air.

She could see her breath as she ran. Walls and floors of the cave thickly coated with icicles, from ceiling to floor. This was where the best air was.

The main building, invisible to the public, was behind thirty feet of thick ice, and although the ventilation system worked well there, it was enough.

There was nothing like breathing cold ice air.

Many believed the caves had formed in the ice age. Perhaps they were right, and it certainly had earned its name as a 10,000-year cave. In this part, stalactites hung from every ceiling, and if it weren't for her firm-grip ice shoes, the floor glazed with thick ice made it impossible to do a run.

The natural bowling pin shape of the walls had trapped cold air inside. And it was here that Lent had built an establishment like no other jetting out to a frozen lake. Camouflaged within the ice, it was barely visible from the outside.

Once she made her way here with her men on ice motorbikes, twice she missed it. Like a spaceship, she was inside a building that seemed to float above the Earth on an ice mountain cliff.

A subterranean structure set into the side of the mountain, no one would find Jack Kleve here.

Not until they had what Lent wanted.

When she had done her five-mile run, it was time to go back.

She made her way through a barely visible steel door in the ice, a wonder of ice meeting technology that opened up into a high-tech monument spread on three floors. The room she entered was the size of a football pitch embedded in the ice where Lent housed a high-tech AI laboratory.

Two hundred hires worked for him here, most former SAS, Navy SEALS, and rogue intelligence agents from around the globe who wanted to make a buck. Others recruited from God knew where made up her little army to protect Lent and his projects.

Inside, a grand, white staircase with massive carved marble steps led down to the secret facility. Paintings and sculptures were everywhere, and marble-like rooms boasted a collection of art she knew nothing of but was sure it was reasonably expensive and rare.

She took an elevator to the top floor and entered the first room on the left. The room was bright, surprising considering it had no natural light coming in, but technology had done what it was instructed to. She'd only seen his mansions in Miami and Morocco, but here, in the ice?

An ice palace, all white, hidden in a cliff. It was a splendor; it was commanding. The walls and floors were clean, polished. Smart technology was everywhere, with cameras in every corner, like in a TV show.

While it was freezing and mostly snow and ice outside, the place was warm and comfortable inside.

She sank into a chair, and though everything in here was white and silver, somehow it never felt cold. Paper spread out on the table with Oskara's notes from the morning meeting posed unresolved problems.

After she'd changed, she fingered her black leather jacket, a cross between a bomber and a motorcycle jacket that was more than a year old. Her white T-shirt and pair of black jeans were tight, and she growled in frustration.

Oskara wondered what else Lent knew to create. He was a

genius, and there was no telling how many facilities worth billions he had made.

She dipped down on the white floor and wondered if someone like Cyrus would really ever care what she thought.

There was a knock at the door. Then it opened, and Kingsley, the tech chief, stuck his head through the opening.

"What is it?" she asked impatiently.

"When do these server problems get resolved? I can't work with a constant state of flux," he said. "I thought Jack would have talked by now. How can I progress on hacking his gene-editing research? What sort of place is this, anyway?"

Kingsley was right about one thing. Before Oskara met Lent, she'd never imagined he had a place like this. She drew out her tablet and checked the server's activity, then raised an eyebrow. "None of your men have figured out what happened to the servers?"

Kingsley sighed. "No, nothing yet. There was a power surge in some systems. It seems to interfere with the connection. It may take a while to sort."

"Damn it," Oskara said. "I need those servers up and running."

"I'm doing what I can, Oskara. It won't be until tonight. All I have are the most basic diagnostic tools. The farm is on the other side of the compound. It's going to be a major hassle to get there."

She frowned. "If you need me to send reinforcements, just ask."

"I don't need help. I just need patience," he said.

"I need results," she said.

He turned and left the room.

Oskara watched the door closely, then turned and looked at a cracked computer terminal she had smashed into a wall earlier. They had reconnected the external monitor to the system, displaying a downloading screen. It said it needed to update the software. It asked Oskara for a password. Then the frozen screen made her curse, and her hand grazed the shattered glass and plastic. She'd have to get it replaced and pushed a compartment under the table.

Just as she was about to resume her investigation, the screen froze, and the download started. A new window popped up on the screen. It read:

Platform Zeta is getting dangerous. The damage caused by the previous power failure has caused the engines to cross a threshold considered a failure point. It is now unrepairable. The Eye is monitoring the effects caused by increasing levels of inactivity. You have lost access to the satellites and are responsible for the failure. Falsify your position so that we do not link your actions to FR-IA. You must also assume command of the FR-IA and, by doing so, you do not have direct access to the reactor without going through a classified chain of command.

Oskara cursed under her breath. "Damn AI! Why hire a machine to get what a human can do? What now?"

It looked like she would need to access and restart the engines and service from the Eye, but she couldn't show her weakness. Lent would be disappointed and probably fire her on the spot, if not worse.

Though she couldn't be sure of anything, she thought he'd be a bit more amenable to her request for resources, if not exactly willing, but she had another idea.

"I won't take you making a mess of my base," she said when she stormed into Jack's holding room several moments later.

"What have I done now?" he asked.

Sexy as hell, he was sitting at his desk, idly stirring the

remains of his cup of tea and a game of solitaire spread out on the table.

She had to hold herself back, the same way she had when she shot him with a blank.

"I have a server problem. Help me with it." Oskara said.

"And why would I do that?" Jack said.

She drew her firearm.

He raised an eyebrow. "You really need to stop waving that gun. You know you will not use it, not until Cyrus gets what he wants. And by the sounds of your minor problem, you're not helping him get what he wants. So then tell me, why should I help you?"

She turned to a video monitoring app on her phone and placed it in front of him.

The view was to a Paris hotel.

Jack froze and registered the scene.

"Any further questions?" She asked.

Jack glanced up from his game. "Take me to your servers. I need to make sure the engine is going to last."

She held her gun at the ready. "I can't afford any further setbacks. Make those servers talk, or else…"

Jack leaned back in his chair. It creaked. "It's been a while since I got my hands dirty," he said. "Lead the way, and I'll do it. I'll get your system back online and set everything right."

Jack stood up and walked over to the door. He leaned against the wall for a second, watching her.

She frowned. "Just get the servers back online and don't get in my way," Oskara snapped.

"After you," he said with a smirk.

THE TENDONS in Marree's neck tautened. "Calla?"

"Marree? You okay?" Calla said.

Calla's voice was full of concern. Marree breathed a sigh of relief as he'd been waiting for this call. "I'm fine."

"Did you find anything?" Calla asked.

Marree's tension evaporated like smoke in the wind. "Jack was working on something."

"Something?"

"It doesn't say what," Marree said. "It's in an email meant for you, but he never sent it."

Passion thickened Calla's voice. "Looks like it was something that could change the world."

"Like? Says here in his notes the world is a pretty messed up place, and he wants to change it."

"Yes, that sounds like Jack," Calla added. "What other people was he working with?"

Marree rechecked the information. "Doesn't say."

Calla's voice was only a whisper in her ear. "Did he say anything more about why he was staying there in Paris? I can't seem to get the connection between that Paris trip and one we took to New Mexico."

Marree felt her confidence return. "I can help there. Jack used the decryption of the Beale Ciphers to encrypt a new cipher to lock a scientific project."

"So, he decrypted it? Does he mention a telescope?" Calla asked.

"Yes, but no detail. Just a line about it belonging to Halona."

Calla's tone sent apprehension coursing through her body. "So Halona must've helped him use it. It's the only thing that can decrypt the missing Beale cipher. Jack knew how to use the telescope. I know how to read the information. But sounds like he used it too."

Marree leaned against a wall. "Yes, to code and lock a bioweapon, but he doesn't give much information in the email."

"Halona wanted me to decrypt the cipher and, together with Jack, protect the secret. Along the way, Jack must've figured it was the safest way to protect the codes to the bioweapon."

Fear churned Marree's stomach. "Why would Jack create a weapon?"

Calla's voice was firm. "He wouldn't, but others could turn his science into one. The Beale cipher had not been decrypted, but Halona knew the secret was no longer safe if I could do it. So she wanted us to protect the ciphers."

"All for a treasure?" Marree asked.

"I don't know," Calla said. "Halona must've helped Jack with the cipher, and that's why Jack wanted me to be far from the telescope. He knew if I deciphered the Beale Ciphers, I wouldn't be safe. He protected us by hiding the telescope using it to protect his invention. No one has ever decrypted the Beale cipher or is likely to—

"Except you. If you have the telescope," Marree added.

"And if that happens, I have access to a potent weapon," Calla said. "Jack was keen on genetic science, and he swore to make sure he could connect gene science to technology and science crime lords. It looks like he was working on a highly scientific project that could be a bioweapon in the wrong hands. He mentioned he had left files in that hotel room he used at the George V eighteen months ago. I think something else happened in Paris."

"I'm sure there were many people who didn't like him. Perhaps jealous." Marree said.

"That figures. Jack was unbeatable in science and tech knowledge. Such a polymath. I wonder though if something else happened in Paris. With an enemy—

"What? No. Why would you think that?" Marree said, afraid of the horror in her voice.

"Not sure."

"I found a reference to a trip to New Mexico," Marree added.

"Okay?"

Marree's heart lurched to her throat. "And I'm worried about you. I'm—

"Don't worry. There's no reason," Calla replied. "We took that trip to help Halona. Sadly, we failed and lost her. I don't want to lose you Marree, you have done so much already. I have much to tell you, but I can't."

"Why not?" Marree said.

"Because this isn't the right time. I'm so sorry, Marree, but I will."

"What aren't you telling me?" Marree sensed Calla didn't want to do this, but there was no way out.

"Allegra will contact you soon," Calla said. "Stay put in that hotel room. I don't want to say it over the phone. We have to talk about this in person."

"Okay, but when?"

"When I find out what that bioweapon is and where it is."

OSKARA GUIDED Jack through the labyrinth innards of the facility toward her private server room. From the outside, the place might have looked like a military installation, but on the inside, it was anything but. Jack glanced back over his shoulder.

Servers lined Oskara's tech room to the ceiling, networking equipment, and other odds and ends. She led him down a long corridor, past several closed doors, then brought him to a particular entry, and she let him pass into the server room.

"I'll have it up and running in no time," he said.

Oskara watched him work. "Can you fix my link? And no funny business. I'm watching you."

Jack studied the several rows of machine servers, indeed high tech, and some of the latest installations he'd seen. The machine had failed. Possibly because of several uploads crashing transfer networks. If he worked discretely, he just might get the communication link he needed. They had been overpowering the servers. Why?

He ran a hand through his dreads. "My work requires an

understanding of all parts of a system," Jack said. "I've been bored for hours."

Jack's voice caught in his throat. And he saw an exposed wire in the machine's claw. It hissed and popped, catching fire, and then fizzled out of existence.

"What the heck was that?" she asked.

Oskara stood silently, then circled behind Jack and stuck a gun in his back. She was way too close, but would she know what he was up to. Most people could not read computer language, especially the ones he had written. The virus would be up in no time, and so would the tracking device.

He fingered the wires as Oskara watched him. Jack would have to hurry. He found an opportunity, promptly swiped the paperclip, and connected the chip to his watch, creating a link to his satellite.

An errant bead of sweat rolled down his cheek. "Your system caught some bad wiring in its operation. It's over-loaded and blew up," he said, studying the sophisticated length of the wall-to-wall servers. "I'll have this fixed in no time."

Oskara frowned, then walked over and stood by the door, gun at the ready.

FORTY-SEVEN

FOUR SEASONS HOTEL GEORGE V,
PARIS

MARREE PACED THE ROOM, her eyes darting like she was chasing something. A chapped and dry layer of skin covered her lips. She stopped in front of the window and peeked out. The city street below was alive with cars, trucks, people going about their business. As if she were in a cage, she felt trapped. Why was it taking so long?

Marree looked around the room. There was a chair by the window. She sat on it but couldn't get comfortable then stood up and walked away.

From what she had heard from Calla, they had shot him. Marree realized how little she knew of Jack and his life.

Marree wanted to hear from Allegra, but it would be a long time, and there was no way to get in touch.

She started looking at the file she had taken from Jack's safe. She had tried to put all the puzzles together in her mind, but it was getting her nowhere.

Marree could not think straight, and there was more to the Beale treasure than anyone could have ever guessed. Taking out a flash drive from her purse, Marree went over what she had found in Jack's cabin.

She looked down at the table. Marree had examined the cabin bit by bit and still nothing. Her past was a secret she hadn't disclosed to Jack or Calla. She could access her files to find the name of Halona, the woman who supposedly held the clues to the ciphers. Halona had been in touch with Jack and Calla, which is why they were now targets.

Marree opened a new tab on her laptop and found Halona's name on the CIA's secure website. Halona hadn't been in contact with the CIA for over two years. This made Marree's job easier. She could find an address for Halona and a phone number.

Her eyes felt heavy. It was getting late and Allegra had not been in touch. She kept reading, and heavy lids took over as she failed to remember anything she had read in the last few minutes.

Later, Marree awoke with the sudden feeling that she was being watched.

Marree's eyes moved to the chair by the window. It was empty, still in the same place as before. She sat up in an abrupt movement and looked around the room, but didn't see her. "Allegra?"

She waited for a response, but there was nothing, then glanced at her phone.

8:25 p.m.

Marree stood up. The room had darkened, and she turned on the light. No one.

She walked over to the chair and looked down at it. It was empty. Her back throbbed, her head ached, and her muscles felt heavy and damp. She could barely hear anything over the sound of her pounding heart and racing mind. Marree searched the room, but there was no sign of anything out of the ordinary, just the camera. It had to be the hotel's CCTV connection.

She went over to the window and looked down at the street. Around the corner, a taxi flashed its orange lights.

Leaving the window, Marree advanced over to the chair. There was a note on it. She picked it up and read it.

You should have told us the truth.

A sudden feeling of heaviness expanded in her core. Marree walked over to the door and opened it. She looked outside, but the hallway was utterly silent. There was nobody in the corridor and no one in the stairway. Marree reentered the room and closed the door behind her. The world reeled around her, the room's colors bled into one another, the edges of the walls came alive for a split second before vanishing. She forced herself to keep her eyes open.

Marree had been waiting for Allegra for hours. She must've fallen asleep.

There was a sudden noise by the bedroom door.

Allegra stood in the doorway, staring at her.

"Are you awake now?" Allegra asked, coming into the room.

Marree stood up. "I was just resting my eyes."

Allegra came closer. "How long have you been here?"

"A while."

"You look flushed." Allegra put both her hands on Marree's cheeks. "Your skin is burning."

Marree stepped back. "I'm fine. Calla gave me access and told me to come here and wait for you."

Allegra followed her. "Don't worry about that now." She put an arm around Marree's shoulder. "Why don't you lie down, and I'll get you a cold pack."

Marree turned to face her. "I'm fine." She pulled away

from Allegra. "I'm not used to waiting, anyway." She was about to say something else when she heard a noise in the bathroom. Her hand flew to her waist, where she had hidden the gun.

Allegra held up her hand. "It's okay. It's just Tiege scanning the room. Sit down. You won't be safe here much longer. I've asked Delgado to pick you up in a few hours and take you to safety. We need to talk."

"You dropped that note here?" Marree asked.

Allegra tipped her head back to stare at Marree. "Yes, and instinct tells me you know how to handle yourself. Why didn't you tell Jack and Calla you were CIA. Secrets around Calla, Jack, and Nash don't fare well. Did you know that?"

Marree's chin dipped. "I'm sorry. I should have."

Allegra would not let go of the matter. "You never told Jack, Calla, or Nash about what you did for the CIA, did you?"

Marree shook her head slowly. "No."

"Why not?"

Marree watched Allegra, guilt gnawing in her gut. She shrugged. "I don't know. I just didn't."

Allegra took a seat and then leaned forward in her chair. "You can't explain why?"

Marree ran her hands through her hair. "I just never did. Just never happened. I don't know why."

"It's because you didn't want to."

Despair weakened Marree's resolve. "What?" Marree was feeling more awake now, but the lights were still glaring. She squinted at Allegra but still didn't understand her logic. "I don't know what you're trying to say."

"I'm saying that you can't be part of a team like them until you learn to trust and be trusted," Allegra added. "Trust is big around those three, and they drew you in. My advice is you tell them everything, or I will."

"But that's not the point."

"Yes, it is." Allegra leaned forward again. "It's the whole point."

"Okay. I'll tell them, and I feel guilty enough I never told Jack," Marree said, her heart sinking.

Hands to her hips, Allegra rose. "In a few hours, Delgado will be here. Get some shut eye. You'll need it."

Allegra turned to leave the room. "One last thing. I have a house just outside of Paris. This will be my last contact with you for a while. You understand now?" She turned to look at Marree once more. "Once you decide if you want to be part of the team, be ready for what you'll find. Because some secrets are too dangerous to know."

CHAPTER
FORTY-EIGHT
LONDON, THE LONDON COVE

SOMA'S EYES darted from one display to another as they strolled into the London Cove.

Calla watched her thinking Soma must've felt out of place in the world she possibly didn't know existed. But she'd forgotten her emotions the first time she entered a cove. Calla was used to the operatives' coves now.

"How much more high-tech could the operatives possibly get?" Soma asked Calla, who took a seat at a sleek white desk behind a laptop in the large boardroom.

They'd spent hours inside the London Cove since Scorpion Tide had docked in the channel and remained off the grid.

"So this is a cove?" Soma asked. "What are these things? What happens here?"

Calla observed her new friend. It must've been a lot to take in. "It is my ancestry and a long story. But what you need to know is the operatives are my people, and I'm one of them."

"Jack didn't tell me much about them when he messaged me. It must've been part of the secret work he was doing," Soma said. "So you're telling me that there's been a group of people who know a lot more about this world, and they just live among us."

Calla wasn't sure what Soma meant by a group of people, but it must've been hard to take in. "These people have saved the world from global havoc so many times. They've worked with intelligence circles and governments for years. Most agencies and even ISTF don't know what they're doing to help them."

"Then why not just come out in the open and operate freely?"

Calla rose and went to the far end of the room, where a sizable metallic iron structure stood. She bent her knees, leaned over, and then lifted the desk until it was vertical. She then turned toward where Soma sat and focused on her cell phone on the table. A secure intelligence line.

Calla read out every single intelligence communication Soma had received in the last twenty-four hours. "And that's just the beginning. I come from a race genetically advanced in thinking, science, and execution. My genes differ from most human beings. In fact, they are human genes just several light years ahead of human anatomy. Don't ask me what else I can do."

Worry lines creased Soma's forehead. "Really?"

"But as you can see, my genes give me the ability to do much of what science dreams of. When I was a child, I could read codes and understand ciphers, symbols, and all kinds of ancient and technological language. It has helped me in my career, but now those wiser than me tell me it will help save our world from becoming more technologically dependent. Jack has helped me understand it for several months, and if this got out, I don't think the operatives would be safe. Soma, people are afraid of what they don't know."

Soma's jaw was still open when Calla set down the desk,

returned to the seat, and sank into it. "Can all the operatives do this?"

"No. There are varying degrees of ability. And there is still much we must learn. But one thing I know all operatives possess a form of edited genes that science can't understand, and if I have not confounded you yet, it was a science born centuries ago. Operatives' minds and brains can process information simultaneously and at a hundred times more than the average human. Ironically, most do not know they are operatives. I was that way."

Soma seemed to be thinking about something when she swung round. "That's why… There was this one guy…"

"Don't overthink it. Just see it as a certain race of humans who learn to develop faster than any other race. They just did it thousands of years ago. I descend from them. Now we need to get to work to find Lent."

"So you didn't need my help at all back there at Jack's house."

Calla shook her head and felt she could be honest with Soma. "Soma, it scares me what I'm able to do. Most of the time, I shy away from things like firing a gun. I never miss. My genes won't let me, and it has scared me for years. If it wasn't for Jack and my husband Nash… I'm afraid to hurt people, and not just physically. I don't fully understand yet what I can do, and it scares me. I've even lost a child. People who fear me targeted my unborn child, something I'm not even sure I'm truly over."

Calla wondered if she'd shared more than she had intended, but there was something about the comfort of Soma sitting in front of her. She had never warmed up to someone so quickly, but it reminded her of how she and Jack had first met. Soma had a Jack likeness, and for a moment she felt she had him back.

"I'm so sorry, Calla. Losing a child must've been very difficult," Soma said.

Emotion caused Calla's heart to quaver. "Let's put it this way, our child was a target for our enemy," Calla said, a lump crawling down her throat. "As a lead operative, the operative thought the safest place for me was in ISTF, the very organization that can harm operatives, ironically, is one I lead. Or led..."

Soma's hand on Calla's shoulder was comforting and Calla knew she wanted to ease her pain by changing the subject.

"ISTF has wanted to know more about Lent Cyrus for years," Soma said. "A world-renowned terrorist in intelligence circles. I marveled at how little the Western World knew about him. At the African Intelligence Agency, we've been onto him for five years. That woman we met back there, Oskara, is an assassin for hire. She rarely stays around long with any one employer. However, we've noticed that she's been working for Lent Cyrus for quite some time. The North African branch of the AIA has helped identify a Moroccan operation. Our blind spot is we don't know where in Morocco."

Calla's stomach coiled in a knot. "You say the African Intelligence Agency has had little luck in locating Cyrus?"

"Lent won't want to be found, so it will not be that easy." Soma replied. "If we've lost his tail in Marrakesh, he could be anywhere right now. The man is well connected."

"I gather he doesn't work alone," Calla said.

"Correct. He partners with the best out there, and that's the information we don't have. We would've expected ISTF to have it, though," Soma responded.

Calla didn't know how to find where Lent Cyrus was operating without more to go on in ISTF files. It had been days since she'd heard from Nash.

Maybe now she would have better luck using satellite tracking, as Nash and Jack had used recently to locate other criminals. She bit her lip. "Nash was working with Jack using satellite technology to locate the whereabouts of several terrorist facilities. Maybe he'd found something out."

"We should find out," Soma said.

Calla thought for a minute. "Wait. I think there's more to it. Jack is an old friend of Tad's. Tad surely must've known the whereabouts of Lent Cyrus. After all, how did he know I was in trouble and met me that day?"

Calla got a look again from Soma, but didn't comment.

A head popped into the room. Operatives Tayla, Eudora and Mal, and another man appeared.

"You've got the location, right?" Calla asked.

"I'm not sure," Mal said.

Calla had a feeling there was more to it.

Mal continued. "I can't be sure what we have, but we've picked up communication on one of our remote satellites. The strange thing is, Jack was the only one who knew how to manipulate that satellite."

CHAPTER
FORTY-NINE
ABU DHABI, 3:27 P.M.

NASH'S COMMUNICATION DEVICE BUZZED. He checked the number, didn't recognize it, and ignored it.

Abu Dhabi in August wouldn't be fun. With the heat index, the temperature in the shade could swing between 130 and 140 degrees. When it wasn't raining, which was more the exception than the rule in this part of the world, the city ironically charmed its three-and-a-half million people who mostly lived on its outskirts.

Nash's tactical gear added another five degrees. In this, the wealthiest city in the world, everywhere he looked from his position in the convoy, there were high-rises and jagged deserts. The world's highest sand dunes were in the vicinity.

Abu Dhabi was the most modern place he'd ever been to. At first, it was visually overwhelming to him. Against a clear blue sky, sunshine glared mercilessly down. Sound and colors assaulted his senses on every corner.

Small groups of three arrived at the palace, and they entered from vantage points.

Nash's men in tactical gear on each end of the compound waited for his command. The mission could be swift, but Nash didn't know what they would find. He hadn't seen this scale of tactical gear since the Cape Verde ocean incident.

Two fingers to his chin, he glanced back at the convoy of a dozen black vans and two Land Rovers behind him. This mission was one of the most dangerous he could have encountered.

If the sun was up and in the sky, he could glimpse the attackers operating any machine guns.

He looked to the east. If the mission grew too dangerous, he could order a retreat, only if necessary. However, his mission was to bring back Massoud alive, Salib's son.

The hotel seemed like a safe house and had several entrances, guarded by security forces, regularly patrolling the halls.

Splitting up was out of the question once they were inside the palace. They had to stick with the group.

Nash looked back at the palace. There were two other hidden entrances. One was too far from for his liking, more like a desert outpost. At least for now, it was the only means to their exit. He spied through the scope of his sniper gun and turned up the microphone. "I want eyes on that south entry and wait till I give the all clear."

Salib nodded. "Roger that."

"Is everyone set?" came Nash's next command.

Everyone nodded.

Nash observed the mission as a whole. He could march into the palace and bring Massoud out, but his instinct to follow the plan was too great. "Hold anyone that enters the palace or exits from it."

Nash took in a deep breath.

A knock on the door got the attention of the four men behind him.

An agent opened the, his walkie-talkie squawking something in French.

"Why?" the man said. He retracted his walkie-talkie. "They need someone out front. What's your command, sir?"

"I'll go," Nash replied.

The man led him to the back entrance, where a dozen agents holding sniper guns stood by.

Nash pointed to two of the soldiers. "You two go," he said. "The rest of you remain here."

The agents nodded and went outside and passed two more.

"The entranceways," Nash told the two agents. "Those two… go," he said, then stopped in his tracks when he saw her through the eye of the gun.

No!

He listened.

"Can I ask your opinion?" Margot folded her arms and stared at Mason Laskfell.

Alive! Mason Laskfell! Nash took a step back, and his skin tingled with discomfort.

Margot's face couldn't be easily read, but then there was that other face. Mason, a man killed over six months ago.

Nash listened.

"Can I ask your opinion, Qasim Nasir?" Margot failed again to mask her emotions. "I want to know."

A man garbed in Arab tunics stared at her, but he maintained his cool. "I don't think I know you, miss," he said. "Why should I trust you? Your connection to Laskfell is what has brought you here."

Margot breathed hard as Laskfell stood up. "Margot, you still haven't told me your solution," he said.

Nash stayed behind the gun. "What's he doing here?" Nash breathed to himself.

Margot rolled her eyes at the men. She was out of her depth.

Looking to the palace from the south, Nash turned back to the compound to make sure everyone had made it inside. He looked in the rifle, scoping to check on Mason and continued listening.

"Does Cyrus know you're here?" Margot said to the men, stalking forward. "Does he know you're in the Middle East?" She slid her eyes up. "Clearly, I've underestimated the whole situation."

Margot motioned for Mason to come forward. They walked between the security guards as Mason smiled at Margot. "Have you told them?"

Lips twitching, Margot stood behind Mason and eyed the soldiers.

Mason laughed, a dangerous laugh that Nash remembered so well. "Don't you think I taught Cyrus everything he knows? Be on the lookout," he said through his laughter. "They need to see what's coming. That's the way I've always planned it."

Nash got his men ready and gave the signal.

LONDON, 11:19 A.M.

THE OPERATIVES' lab boasted ample open space with tables displaying high-tech screening gadgets throughout.

Monitors covered the walls. Surrounded by muted, unnamed electronic hums, a faint hum, white noise, and the clack of a keyboard, few people in lab coats walked around.

"This is a highly technological area," Calla said. "I thought it might be helpful."

Soma progressed to a table, put her bag down, then walked over to a screen with two vertical lines of random letters and pressed a button on the side.

A box popped up.

"What's that?" Soma asked.

Calla looked at her. "Morse code. And that next to it is an ancient coding system."

"The basis for future code-breaking?" Soma asked. "Will it help?"

"Perhaps. Let's find out." Calla clicked on a button that said, "translate."

A series of letters appeared below the screen.

"What does it say?" Soma asked. "Can it help us with the telescope?"

"No," Calla replied. "Let's try something else. Don't be alarmed," Calla said as they walked into another high-tech area. "We're going into the quantum lab."

Soma didn't respond.

"It's not what you expect," Calla said. "Here, we're dealing with tiny code details. We're going to see if anything here can help us read the Beale Ciphers, somewhat like the Enigma machine. It's in case we can't use the telescope."

Soma looked around. "What a place?"

Calla took joy in watching Soma's amazement. It reminded her of her own amazement when she'd first walked into a cove. "This is the most advanced area of the lab. We can test things here that can't be tested anywhere else. Here it is. The quantum lab."

The door slid open, and Calla ushered Soma inside.

The room was like a small theater. In the center, a platform. Around it, an audience of twenty at least. They were watching a hologram—a display of the particle that scientists called the Higgs boson.

"That's the Higgs boson. Particles took on mass through the Higgs boson, a particle at the center of the universe," Calla said.

"It's enormous." Soma looked at it with fascination. "What's it doing?" she asked.

"Moving," Calla responded. "Because there are so many particles that it's interacting with."

Soma looked at her blankly. "Interacting with what?"

Calla sighed. "Each other, essentially. The Higgs boson makes all particles interact with each other. But that's not why we are here. Let's go to the back room. The quantum code machine room."

The room was empty of the usual clutter except for four

massive machines. The size of an office, the walls were lined with banks of steel cabinets, humming with rows of code machines and computers.

Made to not draw attention, the floor was all black marble, and in the far corner, every code machine known to man was on the counter.

Soma's awe was clear in her eyes. Her face said it all. Coves were mesmerizing to the naked eye, as they held every machine known to man, new, futuristic, and ancient. Surely if they could not operate the telescope, maybe something in here could help.

Finally, Soma spoke. "Everything leads to Lent Cyrus. It always does. But it makes little sense why such a terrorist whose focus has always been on gene editing and science suddenly wants decryption, leading to a treasure. It's not his style."

"That's something we need to work out. We've limited intelligence on Lent, but his reach into Mason Laskfell's world was deep from the sounds of it. Laskfell's aim has always been to exploit operative treasures or use them as a bargaining chip to reach his goals. I don't think this would be any different," Calla added.

Soma raised an eyebrow. "Who is Mason Laskfell?"

"Someone you wouldn't want to know. He used to be my boss at ISTF, a brilliant cryptanalyst, but then one day, he snapped, and something happened that drove him to turn on the operatives. He was perhaps the most powerful operative we knew and have on record. But he is dead. Right now, let's get back to the ciphers."

Calla sat down in front of three screens mounted on the wall. She pulled up the three Beale Ciphers, which she hadn't seen together, and stared at them for a long time, trying to find the connection between the three. There had to be something linking them and the telescope, but she just didn't see it.

"I think we may need better help on how to work the telescope."

"I see," Soma said. "Nothing here helping?"

Hand to her chin, Calla studied the information. "On the contrary, every telescope owes its existence to one secret archive. Don't know why I didn't think of it."

"Which one?" Soma asked.

"The Royal Observatory has a telescope collection. You can see planets and stars and galaxies and comets. There are some ancient telescopes from the eighteenth and nineteenth centuries as well. I think over there, they may know more about this telescope. Right," Calla said as she turned back to the computer, staring at the three ciphers.

"I just don't get it. There has to be something linking them. Something," Soma said.

Calla tilted her head toward her. "There is. Also, they have all the surviving historical paper records of observatory activity and technologies from 1675. This means that we can see from their records the role the British and the European states played to encourage discovery. We'll find documentation on telescopes and the technical ingenuity on the age of exploration of many continents, including the Americas. Telescopes went to the Americas from Europe. The mother of all telescope technology is in Europe, and the Royal Observatory will tell us much."

"What about the wall drawings and the photos Jack took?" Soma asked, wandering over and peering at the computer screen. "Interesting," she said. "I've seen nothing like it."

"Yeah, I was just thinking the same thing," Calla said.

Soma tipped her head back to stare at Calla. "Looks like gibberish to me."

"Ciphers often do, but there's something more sophisticated here. The cave wall drawings inspired Beale's Ciphers. To understand how to decipher them, we must know how he used the telescope. Lent was somehow connected to Halona's family and wanted to keep secrets hidden."

Soma's eyebrows knit."But isn't there little evidence he even lived?"

"Yet his ciphers have places like the NSA and GCHQ taking them seriously," Calla responded.

"I guess. There's one other strange thing about it," Soma said.

"Wait a minute," Calla replied, sitting up straight. "That's it!" She jumped up from her chair. "We've got to go to the Observatory."

Soma looked at her with alarm. "Now?"

Calla shrugged. "We must see what Galileo knew about such telescopes and what he wrote about them. Says here he too wrote ciphers. Backward!"

"Galileo?"

Calla could feel excitement in her veins. "Yes. Could be we have to read these ciphers backward."

DAY 9

THE OBSERVATORY DOME stood on a hill that took them ten minutes to climb from the Royal Naval College. Stars seemed to stare back at them through a dark, cloudless sky.

When they arrived at the entrance of the Royal Observatory, they had to wait ten minutes in line to get in. It was a solar eclipse evening, and the crowds wanted in with or without tickets. The Observatory was a large glass green dome, its base set close to the ground in Greenwich Park, South London.

Once inside, they moved to the reception. Large windows let in light that streamed down the entire front of the building, filling it with bright images of the cosmos. It was imposing, both in its size and with images of the stars that filled its glass.

Calla took a chance asked a woman to see the ancient telescopes used in Greenwich.

"Sure, we are occasionally open them to the public, but we haven't touched some of them in a long time. I can show you one of the first from the 1600s that was brought here for a study some years back," the woman said. "It's in the same place. Come with me."

A few minutes later, she and Soma climbed up a ladder onto the stage in the middle of an old observing room, where a giant telescope stood in the center.

"We don't handle it much. We installed a sort of insulating glass box around it," said the woman.

"A glass box?"

"Yes, it keeps it in good condition. Without it, the air in here would deteriorate the telescope," she said.

The telescope, with its many pieces of glass, was hard to see. Soon Calla was underneath it.

"No, it's not here," Calla said. "The message Galileo wrote on the telescope is gone."

"You serious?"

"Yes."

Soma was staring at the top of the telescope, which had thick metal poles on all sides.

"There's something here," she said.

Calla gazed at it and then saw what Soma meant.

Fine gray dust covered the telescope, and in between its base and the glass box were strange lines. Calla carefully grazed her finger along the lines. "Writing," she said.

"Yeah, I think you're right," Soma replied.

Calla thought hard. "Writing Galileo wrote on the tele-scope. It's not backward but turned upside down."

Soma's eyes widened in astonishment. "Upside down?"

"Wait, I've got something in my bag we can use," Calla said and pulled out a folded sheet of paper and held it upside down in front of the telescope. "Now, let's see if it fits. If the writing on the telescope is like a letter, then we—

"It is!" Soma finished. "The writing on the telescope looks like the letter A! That's why it seemed like gibberish. This is it! Yes, but where's the next clue?"

Calla gave a dry laugh. "If there is a next clue."

"What do you mean?" Soma said.

"Well, in the wall ciphers, the decryption said something about two paths," Calla said.

"So?"

Shoulders straight, Calla faced Soma squarely. "The two paths are messages. Jack also took photos of them."

"Which one do we use?"

"Either," Calla said.

Soma's eyes held a hint of disappointment. "What if the clues lead in different directions?"

"Hmm... Then, we just have to follow both, don't we?" Calla said.

"Let's go back to the telescope and see if we can figure it out," Soma said.

They held up the paper again and stared hard at the telescope.

"What Galileo wrote on this telescope is upside down—but the next are numbers and would be backward like this," Calla said, carefully tracing the pattern. "One... two... three... more."

"What does that mean?" Soma said.

"We already know there are only numbers in each block of the Beale Ciphers," she said, looking at the numbers outlined on the telescope. "One block won't make sense."

Hands to her hips, Soma observed closely. "It could be an acrostic."

"Maybe. Or maybe it could be a type of code called a Vigenere cipher, used with numbers instead of the alphabet," Calla replied. Then she added. "Vigenere cipher... Vigenere... Wait! We need to go somewhere that has an extensive dictionary."

"What about the British Library?" Soma said.

Calla stopped in her tracks.

The interruption came from behind.

Instant.

Vicious.

The noise was piercing, and then all they saw next was dust.

THE DOOR EXPLODED, and heavy bodies burst in.

Calla dashed for the back of the room and crashed into another guy.

He grabbed her and threw her against the wall.

She saw a woman coming with a knife and kicked her in the stomach.

The woman dropped the blade, and Calla picked it up before she saw another guy.

The door to the basement was in sight, but she could not see Soma. The stairway was dark, its walls chipped and peeling white paint. Impossibly long, the second-floor hallway stretched almost endlessly. She sprinted to it and pushed it open.

Then she heard them.

It was cold. The concrete walls had that dull gray look of a basement that's been sealed shut for years, with air so stagnant it smelled of mold and musty mildew. A rough and cold wall, like the skin of a winter's day, scratched at her arms as she flashed down the steps.

Once in the basement, she heard them again, ran, found a long table, and prepped her gun. Calla crawled under it.

Where was Soma?

She waited.

A loud gunshot pierced the air.

Gunpowder stung Calla's nose as the sound carried out the window and into the room at the end of the basement.

Soma!

A figure moved out of the far-right corner, past the pillars. She aimed, fired, and he fell. His body twitched. It was a flesh wound.

She wouldn't kill them until she knew who they were.

Calla surfaced from under the table and headed toward the stairs. The sound of people running greeted her when she got outside.

Calla heard a gun go off, a woman scream, and a man's yelp of pain. She felt a tightness in her chest and the urge to reach Soma, then saw Soma running away.

Some agents waited near an empty truck, and when they saw Soma, they chased. Calla fled after them.

Three of them got into a truck whose driver was a dark-skinned woman who slammed the truck door and a heave of air gushed Calla's way as it sped off. Her pulse raced as she waited. Would they come back?

She saw it coming just in time. Before Calla had time to react, dust exploded and rose in a cloud, and she retreated.

The gas stung her face, pungent enough to make her eyes water.

She took cover.

"Calla?" she heard Soma say.

"Soma?"

"Yeah, I used the cans when the attackers came for me. Come on, let's get out of here."

"You alright?"

Soma nodded.

They moved fast through the crowds until they reached a quieter street.

"Who were they?" Soma asked.

"I've so many people after me I've learned not to ask. Someone wants to stop me from reading the Beale Ciphers before they do."

A sheen of sweat formed above Soma's upper lip. "What now?"

Calla gave her a smirk. "I don't know about you, but I've had enough of this. How about we ask Galileo himself?"

Soma raised an eyebrow. "Huh?"

"Yes. It's time Galileo himself gave us answers."

DELGADO ARRIVED on Champs-Élysées to find the streets crowded. Allegra had told him to be careful. Something did not seem right. Delgado watched as a group of men dressed in black and wearing ski masks walked up to Marree and slammed her against their van.

Marree's eyes were wide open, but her pupils were dull, unfocused. Her lips, blue and cracked, they must've scared her. She screamed and tried to fight back. Marree's voice was thin, pained, angry, but quickly quieted. They overpowered her and threw her into the back of the van. The door slammed shut, and the van sped off.

Delgado took off after them. He ran across the street and chased after them until they pulled into an underground parking garage. The van vanished as he followed them down the ramp. He scanned the area until he found a security camera. He went up to it and looked at the security guard, who was leaning against the wall. Delgado walked up to him and showed him his badge.

"Did you see that van?" Delgado said, pointing at the screen. "Can you call someone?"

"What?" the guard said in French.

Delgado took out his phone and called Allegra. He explained the situation and told her what section of the garage they had gone into. Allegra asked him to wait until backup arrived.

"No, I'm going in," Delgado said.

Delgado hung up and flashed toward the entrance of the parking garage. He stopped at the security booth and told the guard to call the British Embassy immediately.

"What happened?" The guard asked as he dialed the number.

Delgado advanced to the entrance and saw another van pull in. He hid behind a concrete pillar and watched as the men dressed in black got out of both vans and gathered at the entrance to the parking garage. They had Marree. He didn't have enough backup. If he didn't act, she, too, like Jack, would be gone. They intended to harm her. Gagged, she begged with her eyes to let her go. Delgado's instinct was to run to her aid, but then he realized this might distract the attackers and allow them to escape with Marree.

He looked around and saw a window above him.

Once again, he called Allegra.

He told her about the van coming in and hung up.

Delgado pulled out his baton, broke the glass, then climbed into the window overlooking the road.

He fell and landed in a dumpster. As he climbed out onto his knees, he quickly got up and scanned the area the corner of the garage.

Delgado stood in the shadows and waited for the oncoming van. As it came up the ramp, he stepped into the light and aimed his gun at them. The gunmen pulled over and turned off the ignition, with Marree still inside.

"Put your hands up. I'm taking her back," Delgado said.

One crook stepped out of the van, pointing a rifle at Delgado.

Delgado fired a shot.

It went through the attacker's leg, who tried to limp back to the van.

"Stop," Delgado said.

He stood above the wounded crook with his gun pointed at the van.

Two of the ruffians stepped out with their hands up, and Delgado approached them with his gun drawn.

He pushed them against the cement wall and restrained them. A third kneeled over the wounded man. Delgado approached him and told him to get up when Allegra arrived with backup.

"Marree? Where's Marree?" she asked frantically.

"She's inside this van," Delgado said.

Allegra came back with the door opened, and a look of shock masked her face. "She's not here."

CHAPTER
FIFTY-FOUR

THEY WERE ninety minutes outside Abu Dhabi and deep in the desert. Yet, somehow a Royal Pavilion of villas, unparalleled and in seclusion, showed its majesty. The desert sanctuary was where Salib had taken his son, Massoud, and done the debrief. Nash hadn't settled. He couldn't reach Jack and Calla.

Being on the outskirts of Abu Dhabi would mean he would need a good hour to get to the airport and find out what the heck was going on.

Qasr Al Sarab, by Anantara, rose from the flame-colored dunes like a Mirage as the jeeps made their way toward the most luxurious desert hideout Nash had yet seen. It was an ideal man-made Oasis, but Nash was in no mood for pleasantries like unwinding in a *hammam* or traversing the Rub'al Khali by camelback.

The car parked outside a lush garden terrace facing the dunes with a desert panorama behind them. In all of several minutes, Salib dragged his son into the royal suite, with Nash following. The young man had been silent most of the way here, and Nash wondered if he would say a word to his over-bearing father.

"What were you thinking?" Salib shouted in Arabic, his eyes staring deep into Massoud's. "Don't you know how dangerous Mason Laskfell is?"

Nash stood back and watched as Salib interrogated Massoud.

How could Laskfell be alive? Nash had to get out after he saw Mason in there.

He wished he could walk away.

He didn't trust Massoud, even though he had saved his life.

"What were you thinking?" Salib asked Massoud. "Mason Laskfell is a dangerous man."

"Just wanted to make money," Massoud replied. "I know I haven't been the best son, but I wanted to change that. I wanted you to be proud of me. I studied science so I could be part of the big projects in the world. None of those have come my way. So I went after them."

"By getting involved with a criminal? He has had his eye on you since you were a child."

Salib stared at Massoud for a moment. "You've made your point, Massoud. I'm proud of you. That's why we rescued you. But…"

"But what?" Massoud interrupted.

"Do you have any idea how dangerous this guy is? You could've died if it weren't for Nash!" Salib said.

"I'm sorry," Massoud responded.

Massoud now looked down and shook his head, perhaps hoping Salib would not believe what he had just told him.

"What!" Salib shouted. "You're seriously telling me you did all of this because you forgot there is only one life! That's more dangerous than going to work for Mason."

"Ok, okay. I wasn't thinking," Massoud replied. "I knew

Mason had the technology to fund my work. I tried years ago to get into ISTF, where this kind of technology exists and develops at a rate faster than man can cope with."

"Then why did you continue working for him?" Salib asked. "Did you not realize how dangerous he was?"

"He gave me a straightforward job. For each mission I completed, he gave me money. Nothing dangerous or hard. I thought nothing would happen to me. Believe me when I say some projects Mason has access to are beyond this world."

Salib gave Nash a knowing look.

"Understand, Mason is not a scientist," Salib said. "But he wants the credit and the prestige that comes with being one. Because he has access to power, he can just buy this technology."

"I understand," Massoud said. "It's not worth my life, nor the life of my family."

"But Massoud, you're not completely honest," Nash said. "You haven't told us how you did it."

"What do you mean?" Massoud asked.

"There was no basement in that place. Where exactly were you working, and how was it all setup?" Nash asked.

"There was a well built and hidden lab, complete with wires to detonate if there were any breaches. I had to inspect the explosives myself," Massoud said. "It's difficult getting to them."

"Even if you got them in, how would you know where to detonate them? That entire house could've just exploded," Nash said.

"Oh," Salib said. "I'm sorry, Massoud. I couldn't let this guy kill you."

Massoud's head hung low. "If I can get just one more mission for him, the blackmail will work, and I won't have to work for him anymore."

"No," Salib said. "You'll not work for him anymore. He's a terrible man and has sent many people to their deaths."

"My brother is dead!" Massoud said, interrupting Salib. "He died because Mason gave too much credit to traitors at our intelligence agencies. That scientist sent his men out on a mission to kill the target. He got killed instead."

"I'm sorry for your loss, Massoud," Nash said. "But Salib is right. Mason is a terrible man and more dangerous than you think."

"Then what are we going to do?" Massoud asked. "We can't go to the police? Not the circles you to belong to."

"I'll explain what we're going to do," Nash responded. "We'll get ISTF back in there to get what you worked on. Mason doesn't know what he's up against. That whole place, and all the people in it, is going to be eliminated. However, you are going to help me, Massoud. I'm going to do what I do best. I won't be surprised this time. The rest of the people in that facility are going to be rescued. It's a spy program, and Mason is recruiting spies that can counterpart ISTF, CIA, MI6, you name it, any intelligence agency out there. That's when you disappeared. He took you from your family. The attacks seemed random, never realizing that Mason was part of them. He's a madman."

"What do you have in mind?" Salib asked.

"We need to cut off Mason's communication to the child spies, most probably grown up and deep in the world," Nash said. "To do that, we need… no, only I can cut it. When I do that, I'll go into the facility and rescue as many as I can. To do that, we need a place to work. I have my battle with Mason. Don't suppose you both know he was killed more than a year ago. Not sure how he survived, but I suspect Margot Arlington has something to do with it. After all, she supposedly shot him."

"Margot," Salib said. "She killed Mason?"

"Yes," Nash said. "She's a tough woman to understand."

"And once was a confidant," Salib said.

"That's probably how they got to Massoud," Nash said.

Nash walked to the edge of the window. He pressed the button on his watch. The response was not immediate. Nash waved Salib over. "I'll call Jack. We need him on this job."

"Jack?" Salib asked.

"Yes, you remember, Jack. He's a friend of mine," Nash said. "A good friend."

"I've a friend coming by. She's going to take us to a safe house," Salib said.

"I can't come with you," Nash said. "Massoud is safe, and you have him back. I can't reach Jack and Calla. So this might just have to wait a little longer. I need to go."

"I remember Jack. Yes, I remember him very well. He's extremely gifted with technology. Is there anything I can do?" Salib said.

"Only if you can get this watch to work. Jack gave it to me," Nash said.

"That will be tough with the comms down across the border and infiltrated by government comms. I suspect you need a secure link to Jack's satellites."

"Yes, I'll try to get a hold of Calla. She might know where Jack is." Nash said.

"Let me see that," Massoud said, moving to where Nash was.

Nash powered up the watch. "It won't link up. Jack specified a secure link. But something has gone wrong," Nash said.

"It's a spy watch?" Massoud asked.

Nash smiled. "Yes, you can say that. If Mason or Arlington do anything to hurt Calla or Jack, they'll regret it. I can't afford to lose them."

"I understand," Massoud said. "I'll help you. After all, you saved my life. Let me see that," Massoud said.

Nash handed him the watch.

Massoud fiddled with it, turning it over in his hands. "Yeah," he said. "I think I know what's wrong."

"What?" Nash asked.

"The communication with the satellite is broken. It sometimes happens if you're in a place that has a lot of interference."

"The tunnel to the palace," Nash said.

"Right. The communication must've been broken when you were in the tunnel on the way to rescue me. That explains why you heard nothing from your contacts."

"And this flashing?" Nash said.

"Whenever the watch tries to contact the satellite, it bounces its signal all around the room. It will keep flashing like that until the satellite can see you again and resend the signal that you're alive to its Nautical Sensory Signal."

A blue light blinked on the front of the watch.

"Ha! There it goes," Massoud said. "There's the satellite."

The blue light flashed three times, then went out. A red light above it flashed. Then the light turned into a dot and disappeared.

"The satellite has accepted the signal," Massoud said. "Now it has to transmit it to an NSS. That could take a while."

"How long?" Nash asked.

"Not sure," Massoud said.

"Can you fix it?"

"I can try. It's complicated. I've only seen prototypes, and if there's anyone who can fix it, it's your friend Jack, who must've made it specifically. I'd have to replace the satellite, reroute the circuit, and secure the motherboard. But it's not that easy."

Nash squished his eyebrows. "No? Why not? What do you mean?"

"I can't fix the watch until I get to the satellite. Then examine the board."

Nash ran a hand through his hair. Calling was no good. They had made a point never to use phones when he was on these missions. Therefore, he needed Jack. Maybe he could try Delgado. Even then, perhaps someone could intercept the signal and compromise this very secret mission. And why could he not reach Calla? She must be worried. If the watch failed to work one more time, he'd break his rules and call Calla.

The watch flashed red, then blue again.

Massoud studied it carefully as it pulsed with life. This was a good sign. Perhaps it would work eventually. Nash looked back at Massoud, who was staring at the watch.

"What's wrong?" Nash asked.

"The signal has been interrupted," Massoud said.

THE MAN HELD up his hand to silence Marree, and she obliged.

He was an imposing figure–Marree could tell that much, even from the silhouette. His shoulders were as broad as a curtain, if not more so. His face was an angry mask of craggy flesh, and his breath came in ragged pants.

The way they had shoved her in the van said one thing. They were in a hurry, but where to?

The assailant turned on a computer and illuminated it. In the center of the laptop's screen, a strange-looking eye popped up. It was like a common camera eye, however; it seemed more human with white streaks crossing over the pupil, like a cross, and a white sclera; the whites of a soft eye.

The eye thing moved and looked as if it was trying to look at Marree. The man hesitated and turned to her. He stared blankly, looking her up and down, circling her body from some vantage point where he was higher than her.

The eye moved and stared back at her.

"Marree Jackson, CIA?" a soft, robotic voice greeted as the Eye grew more prominent on the screen.

Marree didn't respond at first. She just stared back at the Eye with an unblinking gaze.

"I am," Marree's lips moved, but the words themselves didn't come through.

"You deceive even those close to you, like Jack," the voice said.

It was soft and calming.

"Lent? Lent Cyrus? You've invested in these smart technologies. That was my job, analyzing enemy advantages in technology and equipment," Marree said. "Jack refused to make a weapon for you when he was alive. It was you who had him killed, wasn't it?"

"What makes you think he's dead?"

Marree wasn't sure what was happening with her emotions. Had Lent lost his marbles? One couldn't be too sure about the company that he kept. "You can't threaten me in broad daylight," she told him.

He laughed. "Only if you want to see Jack alive."

It was a masculine, deep sound, and it made her ears ache. A woman who Marree was sure was an assistant at ISTF, Scarlett laughed too. She sat across in the back of the van with her. 'They,' as Marree knew them, Lent's people in the van, watched her with pity and disdain. They seemed to think she was an idiot.

Marree frowned. "What happens to me now? We know Jack didn't carry out the order. How can he when you killed him!"

She directed her anger to the Eye on the screen.

When she thought of it, most files at the CIA had referenced the strange laptop with the Eye that almost impersonated Lent.

"So stubborn, so loyal. Of course, he will or risk losing you."

"I don't know what you mean." She tried to keep her

words from trembling and her voice low, but it was hard.

The people in the van looked amused for a moment. Just how had Lent built this empire? Women hated him, and men feared him.

MUSEO GALILEO, FLORENCE ITALY,
21:59 P.M.

STARS WERE BLACKENING over the museum. Several frescoes from the Middle Ages decorated it, making it illuminate and colorful. Several paintings by the Italian Renaissance artist Giacomo della Porta adorned many walls.

By the time Calla and Soma passed through the upper floor, careful not to wake the alarms, the dimly lit museum maintained an air of antique mystery. Its walls were made of heavy wood and stone. A grand staircase led to a dome-topped center displaying astronomical instruments. The staircase welled with light from a shimmering dome overhead. An idyllic place, if it weren't for the antiquated machinery that creaked and groaned, the steel-plated walls and roof. Chunky, state-of-the-art metal detectors littered the floor.

Soma looked as if she was about to trip over something.

At the bottom of the basement, several floors below, the air was heavy with the smell of old wood and dust, old books, old instruments, old parchment, and old ink. It was a smell of age and loss, of a world that never changed. The smell of a forgotten library and archive.

An enormous expanse of glass was on the ground, covering

several thousand pieces arranged like floor mosaics in a square grid. The faint crunch of glass as they walked across the floor in this part of the archives made them stop. In the distance, they heard a low hum, a steady background noise that brought a sense of order to everything.

This was an archive room, no longer used or visited, and the entry had been easy. Through the fire exist and down the stairs. A thick layer of dust mainly covered everything in this part of the museum. As they walked, the dust clung to the bottom of their shoes. Paint on the walls flaked, and the wood of the corridor was rotting, failing to disguise the floor covered with dust and grit.

Calla and Soma could faintly hear them. Scientists filled the museum below.

She turned to Soma. "They are here for a purpose, and we must get to the telescope before they see us."

They had seen the scientists through the spy cam. They stood in front of artifacts from the great naturalist's life and works, studying them, researching them. Most of them carried Native American instruments.

A giant dome with a telescope stood in the room's center and aimed at the ceiling. A long corridor with a stairway led to the first floor, lit by tiny lamps on the wall.

"This way," Calla said, pointing to a door at the end of the stairs.

They went toward the door and made their way into a dark room.

They tiptoed toward the far end of the room, where a table stood with an old computer on it. Two doors boarded the far wall.

One was open.

They peeked in and found a second room with a desk with a tray and an ancient-looking tool on it.

"Is that it?" Soma asked.

"I think so. Looks just like the one in my research," Calla said.

"We have to get it."

Calla reached for the lamp, turned it on, and then studied the tool. It was ancient and looked like a wrench. It had been so long since she'd touched one of these.

"Stop!"

They turned to see a museum guard.

"Stop or I...."

"We need to knock him out," Calla whispered to Soma.

"Agreed," Soma said.

"Right." Calla said. "Did you bring the tranquilizer gun?"

"Not good enough," Soma said.

"We could throw one of these ancient books at him?"

"No, that will just hurt him," Soma said, giggling. "We need to knock him out."

"Fine," Calla said. "I'll hit him with my elbow, and you'll take care of the rest."

Calla observed the guard as he ambled toward them, ready to call the Italian police with a phone in hand.

She took a deep breath and started running toward him.

He saw her coming and took out his phone, and she raised her elbow and swung it toward the guard's face.

The guard dropped the phone to the ground with a thud.

Soma grabbed his neck with her hand and held him until he stopped struggling. "He was talking too much."

"You don't waste any time," Calla said.

"Neither do you."

Calla grinned. "Trust me, I am a museum curator. Now let's get what we need and get out of here."

TENSION ROSE in Nash's stomach as he left Salib and Massoud. He felt like he would be sick. He needed to get back inside. As he paced the halls to his room, he recalled what his telescope gun had picked up in the eyepiece. Sure enough, Mason Laskfell, the terrorist from hell who had once tried to throw Calla to her death, was alive.

How?

What was Mason up to? How could the bastard not be dead! He felt as if his insides would eat him alive with angst.

Nash looked at his watch and saw that it was almost five a.m. He was tired and hungry. It had nearly been seven hours. Maybe he was too late. "I won't risk Calla's life again," Nash said to himself.

He scanned information from a contact at the NSA in Maryland he'd requested on the way here. Mason was planning to leave a bioweapon at the center of every major city in Europe. The deadliest one ever, the 'Pale Noir'. Nash had been watching it for months.

Bile rose in his mouth, and he dialed Calla immediately.

There was no answer.

Strange. He was already late checking in.

Why wasn't she picking up? He would try again later and pounded his fist on the table when he entered his room.

He dialed Langley.

"Yeah," the tired voice on the other end said.

"Stealth, this is Nash. Mason Laskfell is alive. I know where he is and what he's up to. I need your help. I want to know what he's after. Is there anything about a spy training facility for prodigies that you can pick up? I was investigating it about three years ago." Nash asked. "Check anything in Africa and Eastern Europe. Maybe Asia."

"Nash, there are a bunch of facilities like that all over the world. You sent me out there to investigate months ago. There are facilities where agents train to be professional spies. They start young and work for the wrong people. Some were calling it the school of editing. They train there for eight years, and then they are sent into the workplace. There's no place better for training. Have you checked out anything on your own yet?" Stealth asked.

"No, not exactly. I got into the file mentioning a place in Italy. It was a project meant to create a better spy through DNA manipulation. They were looking to create new agents called MNAs. Mason Laskfell started the project seventeen months before he died. I figured it out when he had the symbol tattooed on his arm. There was a scientist there who was working on and off on the project. I tracked him down, and he was murdered several months ago." Nash said.

"Why didn't you tell me this before?" Stealth asked.

"The man I was tracking had a daughter. Soma Kleve was the name, I believe. She went missing several weeks before he was murdered. I kept her name out of it. Stealth, Mason was after her, and he would do anything to get her. I think it was all a cover to get me out of the way so he could find her and also what I feared, her brother, Jack Kleve, my best friend. I didn't want it to be true, but now I am more certain than ever. He must have used her for something, but I don't know what. This means Jack's life is in danger."

"Says here she escaped at age twenty-three," Stealth said.

"Now, he'll stop at nothing to get her. I need to do whatever it takes to stop him before he reaches Jack." Nash said.

"Nash, I… there's something you need to know. ISTF has been compromised," Stealth said.

His heart leaped from his chest. "What!"

"I'm sorry, Nash. I told you why no one could find Mason, because he was once the head of the agency. He knows all your tricks at ISTF. Everyone who worked with him traded their lives and the lives of their family, and some kept his secret after he resurfaced. I'm so sorry," Stealth said. "Calla Cress was called in to see the committee, and no one has seen her since, and the entire agency has been shut down temporarily. It's come out that Mason and his people were using the agency to sell international government secrets," Stealth said.

"That's why I haven't been able to reach her. I need to tell Calla that the agency is shut down, that her father should make sure that no matter what happens, she should stay safe." Nash sat and stared at the ground.

"Nash, she's safe," Stealth said. "She's on a wanted grid, but they are so secretive about her details. Almost apologetic, which tells me something is wrong."

Nash drew in a sharp breath. "Then I need to talk to… she may be on the run. Why didn't she…?"

"Maybe she was protecting those she cares about. Maybe even you… We need you to help us stop, Mason. He's been in touch with a certain Lent Cyrus. Someone he brought into ISTF briefly about fifteen years ago."

"Did you say, Lent Cyrus?"

"Yes. Why?"

"Lent was connected to an AI project started by Ashton

Vaxon, who also worked at ISTF when it began. Ashton, too, died. It was cancer, I believe. Or maybe something else. I wonder what this means," Nash replied. "When I joined ISTF after the KJ 20 Ops, they assigned me to look into it. I found incomplete information. Damn, just what are they up to?"

"You can save her from the hell she's about to be in, Nash. I've already sent you the files. Take down Mason Laskfell, for all the lives he has ruined," Stealth said.

Nash knew what he had to do and felt his stomach churn. "I'll be in touch. Stay safe."

Nash ended the call and looked at his firearm on the table. He turned and packed. There was one lead he needed to follow, with no time to waste.

DAY 10

CAFFÈ ROSANÒ, a three-minute walk from Accademia Gallery in Florence, was set in a stone building surrounded by glass. The way the sun bounced off the windows and refracted off the huge flat mirror in the front contradicted Calla's emotions. She wasn't hungry. Sounds in the café were subdued, as conversations and laughter and a jukebox playing Italian songs drowned out their thoughts. Soma ordered a black coffee.

They were sitting at the table when the curator walked in, a distinguished-looking man with white hair and a mustache. He said something in Italian to the waiter and then sat down across from them. The waiter soon brought him a coffee and a brioche.

"I'm sorry I couldn't come to the museum," Calla said, trying to avoid a discourse on why they were meeting the head curator of the Museo Galileo at the café.

"No problem. I'm just here for a change of scenery. Where are you from?" he said.

She bit her lip. "I'm a curator at the British Museum in London. My name is Calla Cress."

"Calla. That's unusual. It's Latin. It means 'lily'. Ah, it suits you," he smiled, and she felt herself wanting to smile back. "It's good to meet you and your friend," he said, shaking her hand and sending a brief nod Soma's way. "What brings you to Florence, can't just be Galileo?" he asked. "What can I do for a well-known historian like yourself? You explained little on the phone."

"I have an old telescope, but I don't know how to use it or what it might be worth. It also may be damaged. Can you tell me more about it and this tool?" she asked.

"May I see the items?"

"Of course." She opened her bag and took out the telescope and the telescope tool.

"It looks like a good one," he said, examining it. "A Galileo."

"A what?"

"A Galileo, made by the master craftsman himself named Galileo Galilei. It was made sometime between 1585 and 1610."

"I see," she replied, although she didn't see at all. "Just how did an Italian telescope end up with Native American writing and symbols. Also, why would it have a connection to a Native American tribe?"

"Several craftsmen in Italy were dreamers during that period. The symbols don't have any significance, as far as I know. Many explorers took such telescopes to search the New World."

She looked at the telescope again, taking in the details, especially the writing on its frame. "What can you tell me more about it?"

He smiled. "Well, I can tell you it's considered the finest antique telescope in existence today. Of its kind, that is. It would probably be worth over a million dollars if you sold it. But I can also tell you it's exquisite. And very rare. You might not have realized it, but this telescope has a lens made of crystal."

"Crystal? You mean glass?" Soma asked.

"No, crystal. It's less common than glass. It's much more opaque and much stronger. It's also heavier, which can be a disadvantage for portability. I'm not sure how old the crystal is, but this one appears to be in good condition. It looks to be simply a type of magnifying glass."

"What else can you tell me about it?"

"It's ancient. Like you said, it has symbols, writings, or ciphers of some sort on it. I'm not sure what they say, though."

"How can you be so sure?"

"Because it's a simple cipher. There are many ciphers, and they're all different. There are two general types, though— simple and complex. They used the simple form for basic communication across languages."

Calla stared at the telescope's symbols. "What if it's… an old forgotten story? Maybe even a lost history—something that's barely known? Like a lost language?"

"Oh, you mean something like hieroglyphs? I can tell you that's impossible. If it were, we would have never lost that 'language' because, unlike hieroglyphs, the symbols on this telescope are straightforward to interpret. Mostly, anyway."

"Uh-huh."

"The complex cipher, however, is usually used to hide single words within a sentence."

"Right," she said. "But what about the symbols? What if it's a language that's been lost for hundreds of years?"

"I'm afraid that's impossible. May I ask why you're so interested in this telescope?"

Calla tried not to give away much. "Well, I just found it."

"Where is it from?" he asked.

"We're not sure. It could be from the New World."

"What do you mean? You said this is an Italian telescope," he said.

Calla didn't have time to explain. "It is, but it could also be from the New World."

He raised an eyebrow. "Why do you say that?"

"Well, we know of a Native American tribe suspicious of new technology, no matter the century." She made a face. "When the Europeans arrived in the New World, they also brought a new language—and even the English language. The original language evolved into dialects of some Native American languages. I'm sure the tribe that adapted this telescope had a name for the language."

"They did, but it's no longer in use. Also, some..." he said, pulling out a file. "When you called, I did some digging when you mentioned a connection to Native Americans. In our archives, it says three telescopes were bought, one by an American family on the way to the New World."

Soma's eyes lit. "On the way to the New World? You mean..."

"Yes, the expeditions to America. There were Spanish, Portuguese, French, and English. Some documents said the Spanish and the English used these telescopes in the New World."

Calla wanted to know more. "You said that only three were made back then. Where are the other two?"

He shrugged. "The owner of the second telescope may be deceased, but that's all I know. They found a diary in Mexico with the information. Since it wasn't a current diary, no one ever tried to translate it. It was only about three pages. The owner of the telescope might have been looking for something specific, like the Lost City of Gold or a particular tribe."

"What of the third?" Calla interrupted.

He shrugged. "I don't know."

"When were they made, and when was this one purchased?" Soma asked.

"Made in 1585, it was purchased about two years later. There's more," he said, taking out his laptop and connecting to the network. "Eventually, a family bought that telescope for a piece of land in the New World two centuries later. The land was in the New Mexico region, sold to a certain Jefferson Beale. The land belonged to Native Americans, and he seemed to have made home and connected with his buyers. They seemed close in terms of trust."

"How do you know this?" Soma said.

"It's documented here. They passed it down through the family. In fact, they used it twice in the Civil War. The owners died during the war, but the telescope passed through the hands of their daughter. Then to her son, to her grandson, and so on and so forth till today. They then handed it down to the women in the family."

"When?" Calla asked.

"In the 1920s."

Conflicting thoughts flew rapidly through Calla's mind. "What happened to it in the 1920s? That's when Halona mentioned her family inherited it."

"It was sold, again. Perhaps stolen or bartered."

"Stolen?" Soma asked.

"That's all the information we have as of now. It ended up being privately owned by one person. A certain Mason Laskfell."

Calla's brain failed to come up with any logical explanation. Her breathing sounded labored, her panting breaths quick, short and stuttered. "Did you say Laskfell?" Calla felt her heart sink.

"Yes, but records show it was many decades ago, but somehow the family got it back. Then eighteen months ago, someone came back for it."

"How do you have this on record?" Soma asked.

"With such rare telescopes, we know a certain secret group has been watching when it exchanges hands. A certain Lent Cyrus is part of that group, the Black Horse Group. They call themselves keepers of history. Mr. Cyrus came to the museum not too long ago. He's a huge benefactor of the museum."

MARREE'S BODY ACHED, and her head spun. She felt like a truck had just run her over. Or maybe a bus, or a few.

Her hands bound, her vision was blurry. She was most definitely not in her hotel room, but in a small, dim room. Blinking a few times, she tried to clear her vision. It was no use. The room was so dark that she couldn't see anything except dark stone walls. Marree hobbled to the window, and from her height of four floors, she had to be in Marrakech. That's where Lent was last seen.

It had to be the old quarter, but this was not how it'd been the last time she was here. There was a massive marketplace outside her window, full of stalls and men selling spices and old books. A man was singing, but she couldn't pay attention to his voice. It sounded muffled.

All she could hear were the call from the mosque and birds singing, but she needed to pay attention. She heard a door bang shut, making a loud noise.

Startled, she jumped.

A laugh boomed across the room, making her shiver.

"Hello, Marree, sweetheart. You look ravishing."

His voice was like honey, smooth and soothing. It was the voice of a man who had done things outside the law, who had killed many times.

Lent walked over and stroked her bruised face.

Marree could only see Lent in outline, and in the dim light, he was a shadowy figure in a black suit and white shirt. Then he emerged fully.

She flinched and pulled away. The psychopath was in full analysis mode, his eyes deep and black. The warmth of his pupils sent shivers down her spine, like the eye of a hurricane. They were black and deep, like the ocean, not like the eyes of a person.

Marree recalled all she knew from her CIA files. He was what they called a gentle terrorist. A psychiatrist gone wrong. Takes you in slowly before he strikes.

Marree felt the air get sucked out of her lungs. How? Why? Marree stumbled backward. She found herself wedged between the dinette set and a kitchen counter.

Lent stalked toward her. His eyes grew wider with each step, a hint of cologne and expensive cigars.

"Did I hurt you?" he sighed. "I'm so sorry."

"What do you want?" she answered in a low, hoarse tone.

"Nothing, Marree. Absolutely nothing. This is your gift. It's what you deserve. Payback for what your friends did to me. Our first encounter was at the CIA, as you can recall. You decided not to give me a break. Imagine my luck that you made friends with the man I've been looking for, for years and years." He narrowed his eyes. "Thank you for leading Jack Kleve to me."

"But—

"You're a menace, and you need to be taught a lesson. You can't do anything about this. It will never end," Lent said and left the room.

She had never met the man, but Lent Cyrus was notorious

around the CIA. They tried to catch him, and he had evaded them many times. It must have been because nobody knew what he looked like. She had to be careful because he was a man who went by many names and equally many personas. The door shut, and she tried to move, but she couldn't.

She tried again.

It was still hopeless.

She tried once more, finding strength in her limbs. They responded, and she flew to the door, trying to bang it open.

"You've woken up," a woman's voice said.

The voice was distorted. She couldn't tell where it was coming from.

A light came on, shining in her eyes.

A thousand thoughts swirled in her head as she glanced around the kitchen prison. Small things seemed bigger as she stared at them. A shadow from the corner of her eye was large and menacing. She could barely breathe.

Her skin was slick with sweat and her heart was hammering in her chest. Low, hopeless whimpers emerged from the back of her throat. Marree started piecing it all together. It must have been at least twenty-four hours, and that's when she remembered it. Blackness.

This was Scarlett, who stood in front of her wearing a head-scarf, laughing. The clothes may have been local, but they were also sleek and fashionable, their colors bright and bold. Their subtle patterning only made them stand out.

This was the woman Allegra had mentioned. She had been an assistant to Allegra when she headed ISTF briefly. And she also worked for Calla and was the one who had betrayed her. Possibly also the one who had arranged the ambush of the ISTF building.

The tight cords around Marree's wrists were already cutting into her skin. Nothing compared to the pain in her left hand. "Why are you doing this?" she asked Scarlett.

"ISTF owes me," she answered.

"Owes you what?"

Scarlett did not respond.

Marree felt terror creep up her spine. They had kidnapped her in another part of the world. Nobody knew she was here.

Scarlett approached, gun at the ready.

BEDFORD COUNTY, VIRGINIA
9:27 A.M.

DAY 11

THE CURATOR of the Museum of Galileo had been helpful. Still, if they were to find what Beale truly wanted hidden, Calla had to find answers herself. Here in Bedford, New England met Appalachia, nestled in the foothills of the Blue Ridge Mountains, where forests and farmlands grew on gentle slopes. The village of Bedford, with its cobblestone streets and quaint shops, though picturesque, hid Beale's secrets.

Beale had bought land in New Mexico, but he had also brought the treasure here. Virginia, at least according to the papers published. With three cipher texts, the first unsolved one that was now itching at her nerves gave the treasure's location.

GCHQ had confirmed the second was solved and detailed the contents of the treasure. It was the third that had made her want to come here. Also unsolved, it listed names of the treasure's owners and their relatives. This had to be where Lent came into the picture.

After all, hadn't Beale stashed his treasure here, but everyone had overlooked one thing. The county archives.

Still, the town hall was a maze as Soma and Calla filed from room to room and information desk to computer records.

The town hall didn't organize records as they kept their archives back in London. There were many families in the documents, including Osa-Menglian, Halona's family. It would take them all night to locate the right family that had owned the land Beale bought.

Something else that stood out in more recent records became more apparent to Calla Cress. Just who was Peregrine Esperson? It noted the family was the first owner of the land. In fact, the Osa-Menglians worked for this family, the Esperson's. It was all on record. Besides that, there was no other detailed information about the woman Peregrine.

Someone in this city was very good at erasing information, but when had that ever stopped Calla from finding out something she wanted to know?

"I found something!" Calla said and rushed over to the small, cramped room where Soma was carrying around a heavy trunk of documents.

"What?" Soma said, dropping the trunk. "You'd think they would've digitized all this by now."

"Funding, a disease that doesn't catch museums," Calla said with a grin. "Peregrine is recorded a few times, and each time her last name changes. She is recorded here as Peregrine Vaxon and Peregrine Esperson, then Peregrine Esperson Cyrus as well."

"She was married to Lent?"

"Don't know yet. We need to see if they have any information on Peregrine Esperson. Esperson is the ancestral name linked to Jefferson Beale. That was her maiden name. What exactly happened to her, and who was her family? She was the first Esperson that owned the land. I found the family that worked for her family, the Osa-Menglians, Halona's family, and I'm sure they had her papers," Calla explained. "Says here Peregrine's family stole the land."

"I'll be right over. Just curious about all of this, Soma said, grunting.

"We can't handle the trunk. It weighs a ton and has over one hundred years of paperwork. We could never open it all up at the same time. We can either leave it for the town hall to deal with—

"Or we could do it together," Calla said. "I'm not going back to London without this information."

"Okay," Soma replied.

Calla smiled, wondering if her Samsonite strength would shock Soma a second time. "Let's do it together."

"You sure? It is heavy," Soma asked, a little nervous.

"Do you want to help me or not?" Calla asked with a smile.

"Yes, now which way?"

Calla made a quick guess. "Left."

Soma grunted as she put muscle in her lift. "I can't lift this!"

Calla approached. "Here, let me," she replied, then turned to hear a noise.

"I have heard of the Vaxons," the clerk said when she returned.

"Excuse me?" Calla asked, setting the trunk down.

"I've heard of them. Peregrine lived here in Virginia for a while with her husband, Lent Cyrus. They were very well off and ran the town here before the war. This area respected them. If you want to understand what they did for this town, understand their history. The Vaxons owned a shipping company that took one of the first steamships out to South America. This ship almost went down in a storm, and the only people to survive were the Vaxons. The ship went down, but many people believe they made it home. I cannot speak for the town as it was a long time ago. But I can tell you that the Vaxons were among the first settlers to come to the Americas. They made a quest to find gold, and that was how they came to own so much land. They are remembered as kind and generous people."

"Then why steal land from the Osa-Menglians?" Soma asked.

"Because of what was on that land. Yes, the Beale Cipher treasures," Calla said.

"How do we get into these trunks without breaking our backs?" Soma asked.

"Not until after our lunch break. Besides," the clerk said, "our archives are safe unless the government takes them over. So you could wait till we have more help after lunch."

"I see," Calla said.

Calla used the chip in her brain and accessed ISTF records on Cyrus. Though sketchy on his operations, there was so much more to Peregrine. She was taken from her family at twenty-five and was never seen again. Her husband, Lent Cyrus, sent communication looking for his missing wife. However, he received no response. They reported her missing. A few months after that, Vaxon, a former ISTF consultant, also went missing, and no one had seen since.

"Did ISTF ever see Vaxon after that entry was made?" Soma asked Calla when she shared the information.

"Not that's recorded. But as you can see, the Osa-Menglians, Halona's family, were just a typical family, with no recorded legal trouble. And if they had ties to the Vaxons, or Espersons, and indeed Lent Cyrus, they might have erased it," Calla said, now drawing out the telescope. "But why this telescope?"

Soma paced the room. "It's a screwed-up connection between several families, a treasure, ciphers and gene editing."

"It could also be a love triangle," Calla said. "Peregrine knew both Lent Cyrus and Vaxon. But she was married to one. The question is, who?"

"However, if she was taken from her family, and that's most likely what happened, given the current information, she would have been taken from Lent," the clerk said.

Calla called Tiege at the Operatives Intelligence Center. "Tiege, do we have any records on file relating to a Peregrine Esperson? Also, does she have any MI6 or CIA files?"

Tiege came online. "Yes, we have a file on Peregrine Esperson. It's not an MI6 file, though. It's CIA, and it's top-secret. I could get a copy of the original and unearth information on the Vaxons."

The line went dead. "Tiege?"

Nothing.

She sat down in the chair. "Tiege?" Calla called again and looked up at Soma and the clerk.

The move was sudden. The clerk whipped Soma into a stronghold grip, then thrust the pistol into her back.

"Give it to me," she said, her eyes unwavering at Calla. "The telescope. Now!"

Calla shot Soma a glance, who shook her head without an ounce of fear.

The clerk's gun pressed harder into Soma's back.

Calla dropped the telescope, and it fell down to the floor, landing with a thud.

The clerk snatched it, gun still in Soma's back.

Calla could make one move to repossess it, but not without harming Soma. And the gun could go off. "Not an archive worker after all?"

"Never said I was. You assumed."

In one movement, she radioed into an earpiece, thrust a needle into Soma's neck. Soma collapsed to the ground.

The floor shook as a ground trapdoor opened. The clerk rolled her body into it, and it closed shut before Calla could reach it. All she could do was look at Soma spread out on the floor, motionless.

THE WHITE HOUSE, WASHINGTON,
9:12 P.M.

THE PRESIDENT'S chief of staff was watching and listening from behind a closed door. He didn't like the argument; he didn't like the American Ambassador to London.

Margot Arlington, he'd heard about her, but she was talking the president's language.

Margot, US ambassador to London, leaned forward in her chair toward the president of the United States. "I make it my business not to gamble."

"You're an ambassador," the president said.

"I'm a diplomat. I negotiate with people," she said. "In this case, Mr. President," Margot said, "let's find out what the people want. They want to know you control this, and I can make the deal in London. And if they want to buy the bioweapon? Maybe they'll feel safe if you are ahead of this. Then they buy it," Margot said. "I mean, it's their money, not ours."

The president shifted in his chair. He didn't like Margot's cavalier attitude.

"They can't buy it," he said. "They can't even touch it. We do not even know it exists for sure."

Margot leaned back in her chair. She was a stunning woman, still in her early forties, and her thick black hair was cut short, with bangs and tendrils that framed her face and fell to her shoulders. Her eyes were dark, and she had a beautiful smile, which she flashed at the president. She knew he was a handsome man, but he was old, and Margot was in no hurry to get involved with an old man, not after what she had been through. She had been married to an old man for twenty years, and she had lost everything when she left him.

"I know they can't touch it," Margot said. "But they can have a say in how it's used."

"They can't have a say in anything."

"Let's be partners, Mr. President," Margot said, and she glanced at him.

He shook his head. "I don't know… it's too risky."

Margot's eyes bulged. "We stole it from a private seller. Who are they going to threaten? It's theirs. Or it's ours. Either way, we have a right to say what happens with it."

"I don't think so," the president of the United States said.

"No, even if we can't stop them, we have to have control. What are you afraid of?" Margot snapped. "That they'll use it? Or that we'll have to use it?"

The chief of staff observed the interchange. She was outspoken with the president, and he respected her for it.

"Either way, it's theirs unless we act," she said.

The president of the United States shook his head. No one was going to tell him what to do, especially not an ambassador. "The American people don't want any part of this."

"Are they going to find out?" she asked. "The weapon is buried underground, in a tunnel under safety glass. Alaska, to be exact. It's already on US soil."

"They'll find out," the President said.

Margot smiled. "And everyone will know that the United

States has the power to wipe out any country they do business with. Isn't that what you want?"

The president pursed his lips. He didn't reply.

The chief of staff knew it reminded him too much of his wife.

Margot sat back in her chair, and she examined the president with a slight frown. She had known him for years, and she knew his strengths and weaknesses during that time. He was a knowledgeable, sometimes brilliant man. But he had no finesse and didn't understand the needs and emotions of other men.

"It might come to that," Margot said.

"What might?"

"Americans cutting up the market, taking all the money. Making themselves the only buyers in town. If the other countries won't buy from us, then we scrap the tunnel and bury it, or sink it, whatever. We'll guarantee it. If we do, they'll have to buy from us. Then, when it's all over, we'll sell them the weapon for a tidy fee, same as always. Jack Kleve's weapon stays out of the wrong hands. America makes sure that the world is a safer place for democracy."

"And what if our allies find out?"

"So what?"

"They won't forget."

"Why do we care?"

"I care," the president said.

"I care more," she replied.

"You care more about yourself than you do about your country. If you had not been a great campaign supporter, I might be inclined to...."

Margot's mouth hung open, and her eyes shrank to the size of pinheads. The president had never talked to her like that. His speech was near perfect, and the room did not give away his thoughts.

Taking a long breath, she leaned forward toward him. Margot didn't read his face or estimate his mood. "You don't have to worry," she said. "I'll not run for the presidency again."

The president didn't reply.

From what the chief of staff knew, Margot had never actually seen the weapon before, but Mason Laskfell had assured her he knew what it was.

CHAPTER
SIXTY-TWO

THE EXPLOSION RIPPED, taking down half the wall to her right. Calla had to get Soma out before they tore this place into pieces. Not on her watch, she thrust toward Soma and hauled her to her back. It took two attempts to lift Soma's limp body. Whatever they had put in her had drugged her unconscious. Calla prayed it wasn't lethal.

Smoke swirled around them as she staggered forward. Laying Soma flat to rest against a wall for a moment, so she could find an exit route. She couldn't think of an alternative.

Calla poked her head out past a hall and couldn't see anyone. Rubble was dropping from the upper level. Every other direction was clear. Soma didn't move but was breathing as Calla jerked a radio from her belt. "Tiege, come in. Do you read me? This is Calla."

No response.

With one heave, she reached for Soma and moved. Debris fell. Calla's mind raced as she scoured for a clear exit. She needed a straightforward approach to rescue Soma. As she reached for her phone again, it clattered to the floor.

She made a break for it. Before she could reach the exit, a

slab of concrete slammed into it, missing them. Calla drew back and heard a muffled sound coming from her watch. She had never taken Jack's watch off.

Jack?

His voice was in her mind. It had to be. She checked the watch on her hand.

"Run, Calla, she has left an explosive!"

The sound was in her head. Was it real? No? Was it? Jack? How could it be?

"Jack? Is that you?" Calla said.

"Yes! Get out of there, now!"

Confusion clouded her senses. She had to be hallucinating. Real or not, she obeyed his prompt to find a way out. She charged for the only open door they had, the grand entrance.

A table blocked it. *"Someone's in there, Cal. Stay calm. I can read your position from my satellite. Put your gun in your hand. Take one clean shot thirty degrees to the left, and you are clear to the outside."*

Jack?

That voice, she knew it.

"Stay calm, Calla," she told herself. "Tell me where you are. Jack?"

The table still blocked the exit. It was the only way out, and she moved to the edge of the table.

Another explosion rocked the area.

Crawling to the side of the table, she aimed across the hallway. "I will try to clear the debris and take a shot. Give me a measurement on the computer, then read my exact location. Remember, I only have thirty-degree of movement."

"Don't worry, I'll get you and Soma out of there."

The table was in her way. The exit was too far away. If she could make a clean shot.

The shot came. "Jack?" she said. "Where are you, Jack?"

She saw no one.

The shot had been clean. The man with the gun at the door was gone.

And now the exit was in sight. Calla put a powerful arm around Soma. "Jack?"

She moved faster. Whatever was happening, she needed strength.

Rubble loosened around her, and beneath her feet, it slid away. She lunged forward, and her feet landed on solid ground. When she looked behind, the downhill was an inferno.

Soma coughed.

They were out now. That's all that mattered. That call had come just in time.

Jack? Alive? In her head?

The watch sprang to life again.

CHAPTER
SIXTY-THREE

CALLA HOBBLED to a café in Bedford looking for a place for Soma to rest. She had done what she always did in such situations. Kept moving.

The café was tucked away at the end of a street corner. Small and cluttered, it sat at the end of a quiet curve in a quiet street. Housed in a single-story building made of gray brick, the windows are lit with yellow lights. Even at this late hour, it was busy with people talking and laughing. The clink and clatter of cutlery, dishes, metal cups, and glasses made her head hurt. Calla took a sip of her cappuccino and glanced around, scanning the room.

She spotted a man with his back to her, sitting alone in a far corner. He wore a dark coat and had a black scarf wrapped around his neck. He was looking at her through the reflection of the mirror on the wall, staring right at her.

Calla felt a frigid chill sweep through her and signaled to Soma who was coming to.

The man looked like the same man who'd blocked her exits at the town hall. She had only watched him and didn't think he'd noticed her.

Maybe she was wrong, but she couldn't shake the feeling that the man was waiting, waiting for what? They had the telescope. Well now, she was no use to them, maybe just a nuisance. Maybe it was FBI. She had no time for that. She was still a fugitive. It could be any of the intelligence forces instructed to turn on her.

All hers and Soma's travel across borders had been carefully orchestrated between Delgado and the operatives.

Calla looked away, then glanced around the café, quickly taking in the dark wood paneling and the antique mirror ahead of her. Still, she wasn't just looking—she was checking over her shoulder to see what the man would do.

She felt his stare, intense pressure on the back of her neck, making her skin crawl.

Soma paused. "We've got more company."

"Who?"

"Not sure. Could be anyone. We have few friends right now."

When it came, it was swift. Loud and targeted. The bullet came from the open door, not the man. There were more. Calla ducked, took two lunges, and brought the gunman to the floor with her while Soma fired back.

A group of attackers in dark tactical gear came charging in. Black clothing, with a military style design to it, they had come prepared with tactical vests, belts, and helmets. Boots thudding, gloves and balaclavas covered heads and faces. Only their eyes showed through the glass helmets. A pungent chemical smell tainted the air.

Café goers sprang in all directions, looking for the exits, screaming as they took off.

Calla rose from her position and gripped a chair in her hands. Shaking with fury at the ambush, she threw the chair at three men, taking each down with her toss. Two rose to their feet. One troublemaker laughed. "Come quietly. This is the CIA."

Damn it. Them now!

Just how wanted was she that the CIA would bring four against two? Before Calla could answer, a man lunged for her and took hold of her. His partner fired before Soma could move.

The man was so close that Calla could see his tongue flick out to lick his lips. She kneed him and then he fell to the ground. He rose slowly, the gun still in his hand. Calla stood frozen in place while he looked right at her, his mouth opening and closing like a fish's.

She remained still until she heard the chair swing. He'd read her mind. She was a fraction late. The one who had grabbed the chair turned and ran with it. It hit her in the jaw, and she reeled back.

Calla shot up and saw a table in front of her.

Soma grabbed it, wrenching it from the floor and throwing it at him. It hit his leg, and he stumbled, falling to the ground.

"Are you all right?" Calla asked Soma.

Soma nodded.

Calla watched the men writhe on the floor. She was not having a good day. "This way. We need to leave now."

The blow was swift. It knocked her out cold.

CHAPTER
SIXTY-FOUR

CALLA'S HEAD hurt as she struggled to regain consciousness. The pain in her head was excruciating. When she opened her eyes, she could only see a few inches in front of her. She was being carried, looked up, and saw the face of Soma. The drugs had to have worn off. Calla remembered it well.

"Please don't die, Calla. I can't do this without you."

Calla tried to speak, but her mouth would not move. She tried to reach up to touch her head and felt something wet and sticky. Blood. She was covered in blood.

She slipped out of consciousness again.

Soma stopped walking and put Calla down on the ground.

They must have come out of the café and were now in a hotel room. Soma must somehow have reconnected with Tiege.

Soma's shoulders slumped in despair. "Calla, are you okay? Will be safe here until we can get a flight to London safely."

Soma shook her gently.

Calla opened her eyes. She had been dreaming, but the

image of Jack stayed in her mind.

Soma's voice rang with anxiety. "Calla, I need you to wake up."

Calla looked up at Soma. "Jack is alive."

"What?" Soma stared at Calla in disbelief. "How do you know that?"

"I don't know." Calla touched her head and winced at the pain. "I just do."

"You were talking to someone in the town hall."

How hard had that blow been? Surely she'd hallucinated Jack's angelic rescue. "I was just imagining."

Soma motioned forward. "No, Calla, I've just spoken to him on your watch."

Calla nodded.

Soma reached into her backpack and took out a first aid kit. "You need to lie back and let me clean your wounds. You're bleeding pretty badly."

Calla tried to sit up to better look at Soma, but she felt dizzy and fell back down on the bed. Where was the voice in her head coming from? She heard it again. His voice. Her head must've been hit harder than she had imagined.

"*Cal,*" the voice said. "*It's Jack. I'm okay...*" then it trailed again.

"Jack is alive," Calla whispered.

Soma was concentrating on cleaning the wound with a wet cloth.

"Jack is alive. I heard his voice..." Calla trailed off.

She flinched and tried to sit up as Soma put gauze on Calla's head wound after cleaning it with a bottle of antiseptic.

"I heard him," Calla said. "I'm going to find him. I hear him in my head, my heart."

"Calla, you need to rest. You have been on the run... they kidnapped Jack. He doesn't know where he is, and that watch is his only connection to the outside world. He fixed the satellite communication, and you can speak to him telepathically through AI software connected to your pulse and central nervous system through the watch." Soma held Calla down as she tried to stand. "Calla, you've been through a lot. You must be concussed and were walking around after a serious blow to the head but, you're bleeding pretty badly. You're going to need stitches, but I'll do what I can now. Stay still."

"Can't believe Jack is alive," Calla said, examining the watch and trying to patch it to the operatives' networks. He's alive. That's all that matters. And now I'm worried about him," Calla said.

"How will we find him?" Soma asked. "We'll search every inch of the planet for him. Are you able to use the watch to reach him again?"

"No. I can't get it to work." She drew out her cell. "Tiege, hi… yes, I'm okay. Can you patch me into a satellite?" Calla said. "We need to find Jack. He's alive. I'll explain later."

"We also need to get the telescope back," Soma said. "We have to figure this out. Now. Before we lose him forever."

Calla patched the watch's internal chip to a network Tiege made available. The satellite signal crackled to life. It was a low bandwidth satellite signal, but clear enough.

"We're receiving you, Jack," Calla said. "Can you hear us?"

Tiege's voice joined the network. "Can you hear us, Jack?"

"Hi," Jack said through the wires patched to their senses. His voice was tired but strong.

"Is this real? Is this really you?" Calla said, tears biting at her eyes. "How? How is this possible?"

"Yes, it's me. All I know is they have me here to build a weapon for Lent Cyrus. He stole my technology and has it somewhere here. There also seems to be a very pertinent desire to understand the Beale Ciphers. You can't let them, Cal. You know what that will do. I've scanned the area. It's just outside of my range of sight. I do not know where I am, but it is a high-tech facility, and there's lots of snow…"

"Jack?" Calla said. "Soma…"

There was silence for all of five seconds. *"Soma? Are you there?"*

"Yes," Soma said. "I went to meet you as you promised in Mahé, but we were attacked, and I found your friend, Calla."

Calla could tell he was tired and weak.

"How long have I've been here, Cal? Do you know?"

"Ten days, and I'm being blamed for your murder. ISTF is after me."

"Cal, I wish I was there. They must've drugged me. Some things are fuzzy. I know they had me out the entire time they transported me here, wherever here is," he replied. *"I've had no contact with anyone outside this place. Not till now. Tiege, can you hear me?"*

"Yes," Tiege responded aloud.

"Let me tell you a little about this facility. Maybe you can find it on your radars. It's protected by security systems. I think I can disable them from here, but they're going to know someone is messing with them soon. They'll send someone over here to check. I was in the server room and know they are using government-grade links. That's how I patched my satellite and could connect on the watches. Don't know how long till they find out."

"Be careful, Jack. We will find you," Calla said.

"I have infiltrated their systems," Jack said. *"I found out about this place from a couple of guards I knocked out."*

"All right," Calla said. "Can you get out of there before they figure out you're messing with their security systems?"

"How?" Jack asked. *"I have no way to leave here. I don't even know what country I'm in,"* Jack said.

"We'll get to you. If it's the last thing I do. I promise, Jack," Calla said.

"Is Nash with you? I could not reach him on the watch," Jack asked.

"No. I've been too scared to contact him. I was afraid they would kill him like they tried to kill you."

CHAPTER
SIXTY-FIVE

JACK MOVED to the small window that looked out to a bridge and a frozen lake. They had moved him after his breach of the systems.

In the distance, Jack saw a tall, cylindrical head of a shuttle pod rise from beneath the snow and ice. It rose slowly, piercing the ground and revealing itself. A Throm mini-shuttle, the largest he'd seen, because he had designed it that way. Its cylindrical head had wings extended to the sides, giving it a narrow profile. This could not be happening. They had found it and brought it here.

Tad was the only person he had told. He had helped with a few pieces. Jack had wanted to create a global vaccine engine. Should the Earth ever have an uncontrollable disease, you could immunize or vaccinate the world from the skies, from shuttles and flood the atmosphere with the vaccine. That was the purpose of the machine. His dabbling with gene editing was just to further research in the area.

"What was that?" Calla said.

"It comes up every day for an hour for testing. It's the

shuttle they took off my designs. Tad must've told them. I used an engine set up in the Pacific where they found it. Lent wants me to arm it. That's why I'm here and they are trying to get the telescope. You can't let them."

"It may be too late," Calla said. *"Why the interest and why target Halona?"*

"Halona's family are the heirs to the telescope that has been passed down from generation to generation ever since Beale wrote those ciphers. Though they knew of the legend and heard the reports that it led to a treasure of gold and more, the family always knew there was something more Beale had done, but they never knew how to unravel the mystery. They just knew it connected to their ancestors and could be done by a telescope. An extraordinary Galileo, one in three, the telescope unravels ciphers like the Enigma machine. They want to decipher the cipher because Halona used the telescope to write a sophisticated cipher that arms the weapon. Once they know how to read the ciphers, they will know the codes to the weapon."

"Oh, no, Jack," Soma said.

"That's why Cal and I could tell no one about the ciphers and the telescope. Supposedly, Squanto brought the telescope to the New Land when he'd returned from Europe and is a great ancestor of the Osa-Mengalins. He gave it to the family. Beale then had a love affair with one of Halona's ancestors and grew attached to them. On the Osa-Mengalin's land, the treasure was discovered. I understood from Halona that Jefferson Beale wanted the treasure to go to their family, even though his family had bought the land. He created the ciphers inspired by the caves, that were special and mysterious to her ancestors, using the Galileo telescope. Halona had been trying to read the ciphers in full, but knew she needed someone. You, Cal. The cipher that arms my tech I only have half the picture."

"What's the connection to Lent Cyrus, though?" Soma asked.

"Lent Cyrus and a certain Ashton Vaxon were once partners. They came into contact with Mason. This was several years ago when they were both working on something with him at ISTF. Nash and I looked into it before you joined ISTF, but we could not find much. Later, we found out Peregrine, Ashton's wife, claimed the land on which Halona's family lived through some misunderstanding we still don't understand. Beale's treasure was on that land, and it belonged to Halona's family. Nash and I found out that Ashton, Laskfell, and Cyrus teamed up to create a drug to save Peregrine's wife, who had a curable medical condition, possibly cancer. Laskfell only agreed to do it as he believed Ashton had something valuable… access to the Beale treasure and cipher through his wife. Ashton and Lent agreed. Both men loved Peregrine and were rivals in life but partners in crime. Both men wanted her to live, even though she later married Ashton.

"Laskfell wanted my research on gene editing and my program shuttle to use as a bioweapon when the time came. Well, you and I know Margot Arlington shot him before any of that could happen. So ISTF closed the case when Laskfell died and before you took over. This whole thing comes down to love and hate. Laskfell's hate of anyone having more knowledge than him and Lent and Ashton's love for a woman who was connected to a cipher mystery. I also must tell you that Halona decoded the cipher with the telescope and used the decryption to close my shuttle program. That's why they need the cipher. We kept no copies of the decryption because we had the telescope."

"We've lost the telescope," Calla said. *"So we've lost anyway to decipher the cipher. You were the only one who knew how to use it, and I'm sorry."*

"Don't be, whatever you do," Jack said. "don't let them

unravel the cipher. I'll do my best not to let them arm the bioweapon. There is a link you may want to check out in a Zurich Vault. Look for Amos Lancaster. I never got a chance, but you may be able to."

"I'm worried about what Lent Cyrus might be up to. His people have taken over ISTF. I learned he has been privately funding gene editing for years and has connections in government intelligence agencies," Calla said.

"Are you okay? How about Marree? Nash?" Jack said.

"Yes, I'm fine. Marree's fine. I spoke to her yesterday." Calla said.

Jack heard a noise, then peered through the tiny window to see someone open the shuttle door. The interior was brightly lit. Someone stepped out of the pod. Wearing a suit, with a white, blue, and red cape on the front, a white M with a red circle behind it. On his chest was a biohazard symbol framed in white with a red circle behind it.

Jack turned back to the call. "I just saw someone."

"You know him?" Calla said.

"No," Jack said.

"Who was he?" Soma asked.

"A man possibly of Chinese origin. He's being held here like I am. He was walking to the front of the hi-tech facility. It's protected by many security systems, and he was in some sort of security uniform."

"Has that happened before?" Calla asked.

"Maybe twice? Maybe three times?" Jack said. "Calla?"

The sound of the watch was faint, but she could make out the words clearly.

"Jack?"

"Right here, Calla. Soma, Tiege, I'm back."

The sound was definitely more unmistakable this time. "Yes, I can confirm the man in the shuttle was Chinese. I've met him in the common rooms before. He knows more than I do. He, too, is a prisoner here.

"*Jack, you need to find him,*" Soma said.

The watch's signal buzzed, and it went dead.

SIXTY-SIX
3:17 P.M.

DAY 12

LENT THREW her on the floor.

Marree shivered. All she could feel was the cold seeping into her bones.

Lent's looming big afro and athletic build came into frame.

"Why?" Marree said.

"You're about to meet someone that I think you've missed. You can equally convince him to do something I've wanted him to do for the last few days," Lent said.

Her gaze focused on him as he sneered, his dark eyes looking Marree over from head to toe. "I thought you were supposed to be a powerful woman, but you sure don't act like one."

"Why don't you show me the way out?" Marree said, rising from the floor slowly, her lip dripping with blood.

"I need to explain something to you first," Lent said, still leaning in close.

Marree tensed, but stood still.

"I have a situation. I have to break through the security of a secure installation with a bioweapon that will wipe out the entire Earth if you do not cooperate."

Marree knew Lent was a powerful psychiatrist who knew how to lure his patients into a conversation they didn't intend to have. He had used the skill for years.

He pulled a device from his pocket. "I've got help on the inside. All I need to do is get my hands on some information that I can use to get into that installation. I believe your Jack is the only one who can give that to me. Now Marree, your job is to convince Jack. I'm sure you have every skill to do so. Including the one you used to lie to him about your CIA past. I've already told you that time is of the essence."

Her eyes narrowed. "I don't believe you."

"You don't have to. You just have to use Jack to get me in. And I'll do the rest. Look."

Lent gestured to a screen. It showed what looked like a live feed of Jack. The man was a real psychopath to go this far. Jack was dead, and now he teased her senses with his image. "I'm going to need Jack's help to get me past the security. And I don't want you to try anything when you see him in person."

"I'll try to keep that in mind," she played along.

"Good. Now I'll have my bodyguards come to get you in fifteen minutes."

"Where will they take me?" Marree asked as Lent walked away.

Lent had a sizable group of bodyguards. Marree shivered as she thought of why exactly he had so much security. Was he planning or going on a huge mission with a huge target?

Lent stopped to call someone on his phone. He turned away from Marree and faced the monitor. The man on the monitor looked to be a clone of Jack. Marree could see a resemblance, but she quickly dismissed that notion. How could a random person with Jack's face be a clone of him? It had to be their way to get her to cooperate and do whatever it was they needed.

Marree then heard a voice saying that her time was up. Marree's thoughts were racing. She tried to reason with Lent.

"Lent, I don't know what you want from me, and while I normally don't just go into something blind, I can't trust you.."

Lent's bodyguards pulled up Marree and dragged her through a massive establishment of technology.

Was this place really in the mountains? But just where were they taking her? Undoubtedly, the whole thing about Jack was just about to get her talking about something. She didn't know what. Was this some sort of elaborate ruse for Lent to bring her and Jack in and kill them both? The thought galled her. But Jack was gone. Why the mind games?

"I've been planning this for a few days. It so happens you got in my way," Lent said.

Marree walked into a room behind Lent. Her heart leaped when she saw Jack, and her entire body quivered from head to toe, not from fear of Lent, but from the ghost, Jack's ghost. Her hands covered her mouth, her eyes widened in disbelief. She stood frozen in the moment's intensity.

Jack looked unharmed, but she could see Jack was with guards. She was going to shout out, but noticed Jack was struggling to get free. She couldn't tell if this was because of the guards or some other reason. Marree didn't know what was happening. How could Jack be alive? She longed to run to him and hold him. She had grieved for days, but Jack looked strong. It was his eyes. His eyes said it all. He was resisting as much as she was.

"It better be done within seventy-two hours. I'm on a time schedule. When I return in seventy-two hours, he'd better have answers," Lent said.

Lent left them alone. Marree knew it would only be for

minutes. She dropped to him and placed both hands on his cheeks. Tears stung her eyes. "Jack, I thought…"

"Say nothing," Jack said. "This bioweapon works. I did a test in a lab here. He uses mountain animals."

Jack was clearly very uncomfortable with this. For a moment, Marree was uneasy. "Jack, if the weapon works, it could harm many people."

"It was never designed as a weapon. It was designed as a vaccination aid. Gene editing does incredible things, but only in the right hands."

"I know, Jack. I know you only ever wanted to help. I am so sorry, Jack,"

"For what?"

"For lying to you. More for not telling you the truth. I was at the CIA when we met."

Jack froze for a minute.

CHAPTER
SIXTY-SEVEN

LENT TOSSED a stone into the bright water as he faced the lake. He allowed the charm of Lago Maggiore to distract him for several moments. Only two people ever came here with him, and they moved ahead of him through the entrance to the church and the portico made of Renaissance-style arches, a fusion of three chapels.

Lent knew he had made the right decision to bring her here, where the nuns of Santa Caterina del Sasso needed more money than pertinence from God, and we're happy to welcome any of his ventures.

Certain their silence had been bought handsomely, the nuns enjoyed the tranquility and anonymity in a sanctuary where art and history merged in the most wonderful of architectural structures.

The men in front of him stopped on the balcony that leaned out toward the Borromeo Gulf, Stresa, and the islands, and Lake Maggiore's eastern shore which could be reached by taking a super-modern elevator that runs inside the rocky ridge.

Sister Theresa waited with the Reverend Mother, Katharina. The nuns felt out of place here in a thirteen-century tired location that used to be home to a Community of Augustine monks in the 14th century. And somehow, these nuns were given a small and less prominent place alongside the community of oblate Benedictines who now ran the monastery. The nuns provided the administration, a strange way to combine a community of men and women. But why did he care as long as they took care of his prodigy, who would border twenty-two years old today?

Sister Theresa and Katharina had a connection to Lucy. They had also been very discreet about the way he had planted Lucy after her training for five years.

Lent glanced at the blossomed girl who was as strong as any other operative he'd ever met, and yet she did not know who she was.

"Have you been giving her medication?" Lent asked.

It was sister Theresa who answered as Lucy stood beside her and stared blankly.

The amnesia drugs were working and he would lessen the dosage once she was ready.

The Lombardy air seemed to suit her Lucy as she went about her day. Perhaps a little better than the Swiss air where she spent most of the last twelve years.

Her complexion now had a bit more life and her eyes were brighter than he had ever seen.

A child, a Chinese prodigy, only a girl. His collection was becoming complete, especially after he had lost Soma and never pinned down Calla Cress. She would've been the ultimate test candidate.

His Lucy. Lucy had been in training for a good number of years now. His little child prodigy was the next best thing he could get, and even if he took everything away from her, she might just understand what he was up to. She was the one thing that could stand in the way.

He moved into the room where Lucy was. Lucy had had every luxury that she needed and had forgotten all her immediate family members thanks to those drugs that he had given her. Indeed, it was as if she had been reborn the minute that he had brought her.

God knew these children had more than he could have ever trained them into, and they were in substantial form.

The drugs he had used on her and the training had given her gifts that he could never have been able to have himself. He could never have known that she would have been like this. He could not have Jack in the same way. Nor Soma.

He had a big attachment to the girl.

He felt so sorry for Lucy; she had escaped his system and now she would have the punishment for it. These damn operatives kept getting in his way. Agreed, the operatives had existed before the Great Flood, so they say. They had been on Earth way before the current humanity. They had something special, especially that Calla Cress.

If only these children could appreciate what Lent had done for them. He had sent them all here. Soma, though not an operative, has been exceptional, but she's found her way out. He wouldn't let Lucy be the same. And there she was, trained at his school.

But Soma was someone else now. A lesser life than hers.

He was their greatest teacher and a man who they could never beat.

Soma Kleve had been a small girl with danger and greatness in her. She had proven her ability. He loved her like a daughter, and she was an outstanding student. Soma would have had a great life there, too.

Perhaps she would have been as good as Calla Cress.

The last that he'd heard, she lived in Venezuela and then moved back to Africa. He had done much for her, and all she ever did was disobey him. That would change now for all of them. The trick he had pulled at the lake would be Calla's worst nightmare.

"So that will be everything, won't it?" Reverend Mother Katharina said.

"Almost. The last payment will be sent to you shortly. You will be told where to deliver her. I'm very impressed with how well you have looked after her."

Sister Theresa's eyes narrowed into Lent's own. They spoke of a vengeance, perhaps a vengeance for all women subject to a man's power. Yet Cyrus knew the sisters needed his money and silence more than they needed anything else.

HE COULD SEE the evening air traffic as Nash hurried through the military airport. Glad to be back online, his one thought was to find Calla. Calla possibly didn't know Mason Laskfell was still alive. Delgado was in France, still with the Scorpion Tide. He would start there.

He stopped at the Porsche rental place once he landed at Nice airport.

A woman approached the counter. "Hello Mr. Shields, I see we have your usual car. The type of Porsche is a splendid choice, fast, well balanced, built to last. We also have the new 911GT2 in stock. We would be eager to send you a quote."

"I just want the car."

"Yes, Mr. Shields, I have your usual car ready for you. Here is your rental agreement. Please sign this for us."

"I'm buying this time," he said.

"Of course. The 1984 Porsche 911 Series Carrera," she said smiling.

"Do you have a Titan 2.0L in a base model cabriolet. Porsche makes the original model,' he asked.

"I do have one."

Nash found the car where the Porsche lady had said it would be. Parked alongside a series of other models. The car was the quickest route to the yacht and because he had to take it through the French countryside; he knew they would not want it back after he was done with the desert trek to the airport. He drove out into traffic at breakneck speed.

Fifteen minutes into the ride, he looked in the rearview mirror. Someone was following him.

The car behind him sped up.

Nash pushed the car to pass a bus.

The car behind was closing distance. As Nash came to a straight patch, the car behind swerved to hit him.

Nash spun the wheel to the left and the right. It bumped the back of his car.

The pursuer was still alive. Nash gunned the engine and careened around the cars ahead. The car edged up beside him on his right. Nash hit the turn signal and veered left swiftly.

He had to shake the following car now. Nash turned again sharply to the left and the right as the car broke speed limits. Nash dropped back to let them by and turned onto the last stretch.

"Got ya." Nash drove faster through Provence's countryside.

The follower's car slipped back behind him. They were now equal in speed.

Nash turned sharply into the path lined with lavender fields. As he raced over the small hills, he floored the accelerator. He could hear a much louder engine behind him. It was unclear to him what the psychopath gained from following him. His pursuer was out for blood. Calla had taken his place as head of ISTF, something that pissed off many people. Maybe this guy was one of them.

He couldn't lead them to the yacht and had to take a detour.

He got on the road toward a farm and entered the quiet road. Legal police speed limits did not matter anymore. Nash pulled out his gun that he grabbed, slung onto his back. The car tried to push him off the open space on the cliff.

He swerved again to the left and the right.

The pursuer still followed.

Nash drove faster and pulled onto a dirt road.

The pursuer in a haste swerved left and his car went straight into the wooden side of the monstrosity of a tractor parked by the farm. A huge chunk of wood came off the side of the enormous machine and hit his car.

Nash hit the accelerator, and the motion spun the front of the car around to the side.

He went to the car to check on his pursuer.

He circumvented to the front of the car to check the extent of the damage to the fender. Despite the damage to all the lights, the engine was still in good condition, but signage, lights, and the engine head had been damaged.

As he continued his investigation, he feared the worst. There was no one in the car.

Nash stood for several seconds watching the car. It was then he saw the watch Jack had given him light up. Navigating to its GPS function, he breathed a sigh of relief. Calla's signal had returned.

THUNDERSTRUCK. Once. Twice.

Calla's head still hurt from the wound in Bedford as she laid her head in her hands.

Damn it, Calla. Get your mind back on track.

You're supposed to be the one with the answers.

The sky darkened suddenly. A storm had rolled into the harbor as Calla paced the deck of the yacht. She had reached the top rung of a ladder and glanced at the dark rolling clouds overhead. To prepare for the storm, Delgado commanded the control program to shut all the yacht's windows, and Calla proceeded below deck of the extensive boat.

The wind gusted, causing the coast waves to slap the side of the Scorpion's hull. The yacht could handle anything, including going into camouflage mode, or even avoid detection by sending a mirror reflection of itself hundreds of meters away. The control program of the Scorpion Tide had taken over the boat's functions, leaving no trace of their presence, only the wind rippling the water around the yacht, which was rough, as large waves chopped around them, yet the sturdy ship held its stance.

• • •

Delgado caught up with her. "I'm sorry, Calla. Marree was taken before… I tried," Delgado said, looking straight at her.

Calla sighed. "I know you did, Delgado. You're a good man, and I'm proud to sail with you. You've saved my life so many times."

His voice was sincere, dampened with heavy emotion. "I wish things were different. I mean for you. You don't deserve any of this after what you do to keep us all safe."

Delgado didn't like to lose. But then again, neither did she. Everything was gone, the telescope, Marree, Nash, and Jack. How did she get here?

Allegra joined her on the protected deck and handed her a glass. "Take this."

"I don't need a drink now," Calla said, shaking her head

"It's a sedative. You're going to need it. You've got a flight to catch."

"And where exactly am I going?"

"Zurich," Allegra said.

Calla took a sip from the glass. The whiskey went down smoothly, warming her from the bottom up. The storm was rolling in from the south.

It was time to change direction, and she looked up at the sky, catching the flickers of lightning across the horizon. Clouds covered the night sky.

"We've located an account. Actually, it was Nash who did so and alerted me before he went on his mission. Money has been flowing to and from this account for years, as well as other goods. There is a vault as well."

"What's in the vault?"

Allegra raised an eyebrow. "That's what you need to find out."

"Interestingly, the account is registered to Vaxon's widow. Peregrine Esperson."

"Her again. She binds three men, Vaxon, Cyrus, and Laskfell," Calla said, reaching for the drink again.

"All have a strong interest in genetic engineering," Allegra added. "Especially Cyrus."

"And he has Marree and Jack."

"Yes, he does."

"But you're the one who has all the answers. That vault in Zurich will show you what we are up against because the clock is ticking now. An interception we picked up on an unidentified satellite mentions five cities."

"You think that's where they will start with the bioweapon?" Calla asked.

"Yes. I do."

Allegra's voice had never sounded so urgent and so strange.

Lent was targeting DNA medical institutions in five countries.

Calla was not exactly sure why. She paced the deck and then turned. "Are you sure?"

Allegra nodded. "I've sent out operatives to gather information, and they are yet to come back. But I know only you can do this job. Beat Cyrus as his game. Let's put the world back in order. Let's find Jack, but you need to know what's in that vault. Our sources show that's how the three men interacted. They each had access to that vault. Why?"

She paused for a while. It appeared she was processing something somewhere in her mind.

"What is it?" asked Calla.

Allegra's disturbed expression made it clear to Calla something had just agitated her.

"Which countries has Lent started with?" Calla asked.

"The latest shows the US, UK, China, and Germany. The weapon is already in position from an unknown location."

"All Jack wanted to do was help spearhead a global vaccination program, should one be necessary, but clearly, Lent has another idea. He has made his demands to MI6, and also we are taking control. He'll release the weapon if you do not decipher the Beale Ciphers, for him. The message arrived this morning, but if you get to that vault, you'll be one step ahead. He also demands any information that Halona gave you."

"Okay. Soma and I will check it out. Send me everything you can find regarding the DNA database they are targeting. I want every bit of information that you can find. Also, find any cross-sections to Jack's work on DNA research," Calla said.

They both knew Jack had been working on human genomes using DNA.

"I will send you everything that I can," Allegra assured Calla. "I'm currently helping MI6 in investigating these targets. But we cannot be sure that I'll actually gather any information regarding the preparations that Lent is making to carry out his attacks."

CHAPTER
SEVENTY

JACK PUT his eye against the peephole and scanned the hallways. Lit by dim light, he couldn't see to the end. They would soon let him out in the main areas for dinner, as they did every night. The hallway had a sickly sweet smell. One that Jack did not particularly enjoy.

He returned to the bed in his cell and checked his watch. He had to save the power source.

He remembered him. Zeng was an expert in bio weaponry. He usually worked with the military, but Lent had pulled him from the field to work from the lab this time. His being here was not voluntary. That was what he did, build monsters. He changed existing weapons to suit the military's needs. He was here to work on Jack's technology.

The treasure's worth was just a grain of sand on the beach compared to the tech in this ice palace. Jack couldn't really understand what Lent needed the treasure for. After all, he had a lot more money than the cipher would fetch today. But perhaps there was something more that was driving Lent into this madness.

Once, Lent had been a brilliant man of technology on

paper. Perhaps a visionary like himself who had wanted to change the world. But something along the way had happened, and Jack was not sure what. He couldn't worry too much about that now because he had to get out of here and take Marree and anybody he could.

At dinner, Jack saw a Zeng reading a newspaper, sitting across from a bodyguard with a full head of hair, wearing tactical gear. The guard was just staring out the window.

For a moment, Zeng glanced up and looked at Jack, then down at his food.

Jack watched Zeng closely. Later that night, Jack heard the guard's footsteps. Time for another interrogation. The guard led Jack again into a bright room with more tubes than he recalled the first time.

Jack shuddered as they strapped him into a steel chair, unsure what they would do next.

A sudden burst of flashes of light blinded the room. The guard's head turned toward the door. He shut his eyes to shield them from the blinding light. A strange scent hit Jack. Not pleasant, but not unpleasant either. More like an aura that spread around Jack, even to the tubes strapped to his arms.

When he opened his eyes, Zeng stood in front of him. The guard was on the floor, gasping for air.

A fine karate chop to the neck if he knew one.

It totally took the man aback, and left him unsure whether to react.

Zeng threw a punch in a second guard's stomach, who'd charged in after him.

The big man fell back.

As Zeng leaped on top of the man, he threw another punch at him. And another. The man looked as though he couldn't get up.

Zeng pulled a device out of the guard's chest, then turned to the computers. He clicked away. "I've found a way out of here, and I need your help," he said to Jack before unbuckling him and pulling his restraints off. "This place is a big maze, but I can figure it out and get out of here and take anybody we need to."

"Who are you?" Jack asked.

"Zeng Weisheng. I won't hurt you, Jack," he said with an accent. "We're going to help each other."

"You know who I am?"

"Anyone who knows technology and science knows the chief tech officer of ISTF. They must want you bad to bring you here."

Jack suddenly realized what was going on. Zeng was helping him. He seemed to have a plan and had possibly been here much longer than Jack cared to imagine.

"Be quiet now, Jack," Zeng said as he led him to the door. "We don't know what all Lent has up his sleeve."

A door at the end of a dark hall opened, where two guards were waiting. The pair hurried. In an instant, Zeng had his arm around the man's neck. His other hand pushed a device to the side of his head. Immediately, he lost consciousness.

Jack took on the other guard, and they continued down the hallway.

"Lent Cyrus has been building an ice palace that is penetrable to signals communication. I worked for the Chinese government, but then I left with my family to go to America many years ago because I didn't want to work on this bioweapon. Somehow Cyrus must've found out that I knew and could complete what they had started after he bought the technology from underground groups. The next thing I knew, they took away me from my family. I've been here ever since. Ironically, for being in a prison of some sort, I've had every luxury you can imagine."

"What have they made you do?" Jack asked. "What do they need you to complete?"

"They need me to complete your work. They've known about your work for a long time, and you'd be tough to crack. Literally."

Jack's arm muscle flinched involuntarily. Must've been the exhaustion. "I put a glitch in the system so that only I will be able to release the system."

"I see," Zeng said. "Smart, was it an Engler code you used? Is that why I couldn't get to it?"

"Even simpler. A historical code."

Zeng seemed torn between his inability to crack Jack's code and the desire to move. "My number one thing is to get out of here and get to my family."

"How long have you been here?" Jack asked.

"Eighteen months this time," he said. "I broke out once and got as far as the beach. Contacted a submarine I developed not too far from here, so I could get out. If we can just get to the beach, this thing here," he said, looking at the device he'd taken from the guard. "This can contact the submarine, and we are out. That Russian submarine owes me a favor."

"A beach? Where are we?"

"Alaska. In the middle of Bering Sea, by my take. In the North Pacific Ocean between Russian and Alaska. We're on an inhabited US island, at least. That's what the US thinks, on hundreds of millions of acres of nothing but raw frozen land, St. Matthew's Island, to be exact. Lent started this facility thirty years ago, building a weapon launchpad and aiming to gather as many bio-weapons as he could. It's a sick hobby."

"This rings a bell. The Aleut tribe initially inhabited the place, and the last activity here was the US Coastguard attempting a radio station in the 1940s. It makes sense why he chose this place, and his decades of investing in tech have allowed him to build an empire here."

They heard a noise behind them and hurried into the next hallway that led out deeper into the facility, where Jack figured the halls lined the inhabited rooms of the facility from the outside. Zeng entered the snow-covered tunnel first, with Jack behind him. "This place is immense," Jack said.

"All the rooms are connected to another room. By the way, when you get to the end, you will see what I mean," Zeng said.

Jack followed him down the hall coated with snow. In front of them was a door. Zeng stopped and then opened it. He walked in, and Jack followed.

Jack saw a dark red tunnel stretching into the background. At the end was a vast, sinister-looking white tunnel. This was it. That's where they could get out.

Zend turned back. "On my earlier attempt, I took a photo of the blueprints and mapped out the coordinates. This passage leads to our escape. We'll make our way to the end, and the guards won't be able to see us."

The pair walked for another ten minutes and came to the end of the tunnel.

Jack breathed in an enormous sigh. "Can you show me the coordinates, the blueprints? I can send these to the Scorpion Tide with my watch."

"Suit yourself," Zeng said, airdropping them to Jack's watch, "but why would you want anyone to come here. I just want out."

They approached and walked to the door of the south wing. Zeng placed the device on the door and pushed it back. He then activated it. They made it through the door. It was very slow.

All Jack could think about was finding Marree. Just where was she in this big establishment? Somehow, he felt Zeng knew.

"Now, let's see if we can go up to the top to a platform above this ice prison. Lent will never expect that. We must find the others. But we have to be quick," Zeng said.

But behind them was what looked like water. They couldn't go that way. "We can swim," Jack said.

"We can't take the risk. That is not water. It is frozen nitrogen. Trust me," Zeng said. "Come on, we can make it."

They walked down another hallway. Then Jack saw a door, far down at the end. They had made it to a tower.

"This has to be the platform above the rooms where they were holding us. This is where we will find others."

They heard a guard approach them. Zeng slammed him into unconsciousness.

Jack again followed him up, and they both walked through the crack in the door. Jack saw the platform above them. They both walked over and made it to the top.

"We can't leave yet. I have to find Marree," Jack said.

JACK STUDIED THE FACADE. "Think I know where they are holding Marree. But you and her need to leave fast. I'll hold them back as you escape. I saw a bridge controlled by smart technology spanning the nitrogen lake. I'll hack it and steal a device from Oskara's tech room that will help us."

Jack and Zeng heard the noise of the water wheels grow louder. They moved back through the tunnel and found a passage, a narrow tube carved out of the rock, a tunnel no wider than a man, but long. Rough stone walls, cracked and dimly lit by a green light cast from the ceiling, they hurried through it.

Jack rushed through and hurried down the stairs to a dark area. Separated from the rest of the facility by floor-to-ceiling glass, where Marree was being held.

"Here, use this," Zeng said, handing Jack a chemical that looked like ice but colder. "It will melt the lock."

Marree stirred when the door slid open.

She rubbed her eyes. "Jack?"

He drew her into his arms.

"I'm sorry, I was just trying to help."

"Sh… They are tracking us, and we're running out of time. We have to hurry. Zeng will get you out of here. Go with him and use this watch to contact Calla."

He turned around, and they saw Oskara standing in the doorway. She stared at him as if she'd been expecting them, her features frozen in place like an ice sculpture.

Marree's eyes drew wide. "She has a gun!"

Jack used one move, tired of the woman. This time, his hand struck her firing arm. The gun dropped, and he picked it up.

Jack fired a warning shot, and his nose burned with the scent of gunpowder.

Oskara drew back.

Jack then turned to Zeng. "Lock this door from the outside when you get to the bridge. I'll do the rest." He handed Zeng the gun. "Go!"

They hurried back out of the tunnel and outside toward the nitrogen lake. A small control room separated them, and the outside.

Jack moved forward, crunching ice under his boot until he reached the bridge's edge, with Zeng and Marree hurrying behind him.

"I'll go back now," Jack said, drawing Marree into his arms. "Zeng can get you out and has the coordinates to this place. If we all leave, we may not make it, but guys can. I'll hold them off."

Gunfire exploded behind them, echoing in the frozen wasteland. The blasts were so close and loud that the echo hurt their ears.

A staccato of semi-automatic rifle fire split the air, the shots missing their feet on the frozen bridge's edge, and sounded like meat slapped on a butcher's block.

"Jack. I can't leave you," Marree said. "They'll hurt you."

"I'll be fine. Just hurry. Allegra will know how to contact Nash and Calla."

She agreed reluctantly.

"Good luck, Jack," Zeng said. "You sure?"

"Yes. Oskara needs a distraction. I'll be it. Now go!"

Jack hurried and arrived back at the small entrance through which they'd left. They wanted him, not Marree, not Zeng. If Zeng had not cracked the code to his machine, then he was what they needed. He understood now. Halona was a target for what she knew about the ciphers and the telescope. Jack turned around and made his way back to the building.

Inside the control room of the bridge, he found Oskara awake and standing. Beside her stood a familiar face.

Scarlett.

CHAPTER
SEVENTY-TWO

DAY 13

OSKARA SHOVED Jack in a leather chair of the executive wing overlooking the entire facility, a long, open room with a balcony at the back. The glass of the balcony extended to the edge of the exquisite lounge, rising above a thirty-foot vertical drop. Embedded inside the frozen cliff at the edge of the waters, a rotating eye moved in the far corner of the room. Come to think of it, he had seen a few of those around here. Lent had made a fortress worth Jack's admiration.

Oskara had been less kind when she'd marched Jack back into the establishment with her men. Jack knew it had been the only way to make sure she would not focus on the others. He was confident she didn't know they were missing. They had to believe he had escaped alone.

"Next time you decide to take a walk, just make sure I'm right behind you," Oskara said.

"I wasn't aware you were that attached to me," Jack said with a smirk.

At that moment, Scarlett walked into their room, her brows

twisted in anger. "Hey, this isn't the price that we agreed," Scarlett said.

"I have paid you well. Now get your things and get out of here."

"That was not Lent Cyrus's deal with me," Scarlett said.

"Sweetheart, as far as deals go. I'm the one making them," Oskara replied, throwing an access card on the table. "You've been given all the information you need to know. You'll find everything you need there. And everything is in order. The helicopter is waiting to take you."

"I want to stay. Cyrus promised, and Mason Laskfell as well. You don't work for a man like Mason without learning a few tricks."

At the mention of Mason, Jack's eyes narrowed. Scarlett had been working for Mason all this time.

"You've been paid enough and have enough money, so find another way of making your living," Oskara said.

A shadow dropped on Scarlett's face. "This isn't about money. I've been trained in all areas of this."

Scarlett had worked for Lent and was not above using people, but this Jack had not seen coming.

"Scarlett, what did you do?" Jack said. "It was you. That's why Mason hired you. What did you do to Calla?"

"Cyrus knew about her," Oskara said. "She'd been one of his first targets. Those that we could indoctrinate, we could use. Scarlett was one of the many who were used to build what we've started, but she's of no use to us anymore. Now get out!"

Oskara's men were swift with Scarlett, unforgiving, and all Jack heard were shrieks, and boots dragging on marble, once they'd led her out of the room. Then silence before the door opened again.

This time, Jack's emotions were uneasy. The words he'd planned to say to Oskara remained in his throat.

As a figure stepped into the room, the warm air filled with the smell of cigars, the sweet smell of vintage whiskey. Jack looked into the eyes of the man who had betrayed him from birth. He watched him through gritted teeth and balled fists.

"I guess it's time you learn your father helped to get you here," Oskara said.

Anger welled in Jack's gut as his father walked to the table and leaned against it. "I don't suppose you are going to throw me out too?" he asked Oskara.

"The deal is done with you too. You both have what was agreed. Now move!" Oskara said.

Jack's father looked at Jack as Oskara lifted an eyebrow in contempt. "Jack is to return to his quarters," Oskara commanded the three agents still in the room. "Make sure this one leaves with Scarlett."

The men walked Jack's father to the door, and it slid closed once they'd gone through it.

He hated him. Damn, he hated that man!

Oskara watched him. "Let's get you back to your room and forget about them. There are other things for you to worry about."

SEVENTY-THREE

ZURICH, PRIVATE SWISS BANK,
10:26 A.M.

DAY 14

CALLA STOOD outside the private bank, looking up at the facade, studying it. The concrete on the outside had a very high sheen to it, and from certain angles, she could see her reflection. Dressed all in white, which wasn't practical, she had a good excuse. She was trying to be invisible.

It was easy getting into the bank. She'd worked out the details with Tiege and Allegra.

Getting out, well, she'd have to improvise.

Security here was well trained. Entrusted with more than US gold bullion, the bank held personal treasures no one knew about. Bombproof, an intricate security system that used voice recognition, inside a team of robots moved pallets. No humans were allowed past a certain point—the vaults, and that's exactly where she needed to go. She had to be one of those robots.

Calla waited a few moments and turned to Soma. "Now."

Soma dropped her through a dark manhole a street away

from the main entrance. The air in the tunnel was heavy and felt like it was pushing in all around her.

Dressed in a high-tech operative tactical suit, a white and silver combination, it was made of a rare fabric and shiny, smooth metal. Mimicking an aluminum shield, the fabric glimmered silver and almost looked like chrome. The suit would look like a metallic figure to human eyes as it refracted light from even the tiniest speck of dust. The suit protected Calla from any laser alarms and would only register her as a robot on alarm systems.

It was like a second skin.

Dark around her, the only light came from the city above, but she could see everything. She landed on concrete, mud, and grime. Moving slowly in silence, Calla found the vault's bunker door, where the contents were dropped several hundred feet should the bank ever be in trouble, like now.

Calla radioed Soma. "Okay, set the alarm off. That'll have security drop the vaults to my level within thirty seconds. They are strung onto steel elevators that move two hundred miles an hour."

Tiege was online. "You'll have just ten minutes, Calla. That's how much time security needs to check for breaches in their systems. I've wired a command via the London Cove. You're now Calla the robot."

Calla acknowledged the message. "Thanks. Okay, Tiege, release in 1, 2, 3, 4…"

It took three corners to reach the concrete slab of a door. The siren pierced her ears several feet above as Calla slid inside the door. "Tiege, I've found the robot area. From here on, you would need to camouflage me."

"Roger, your suit is now active. Metallic and laser-ridden like those robots," he replied.

Calla moved.

Heading to Row 27, her eyes zeroed in on a serial number Allegra had sourced. It belonged to Ashton Vaxon.

Alarm bells rang in her head as she paced into the dark room. Rows of white cases had dropped onto lanes of orderly counters, each with millions' worth of personal wealth and treasures, yet something focused her attention elsewhere.

A robot, with a bolt of blue light on its head, flashed by behind her.

She froze.

Lifelike, it moved in silence and slowed before returning to her spot. It studied her. With each step, mechanical legs had sprung into motion, and its head swiveled back and forth, identifying threats.

The robot's footsteps sounded like marching boots, each footfall filling the vault with echoes that bounced off the concrete walls.

Calla heard Tiege in her ear. "I'll deactivate it. Walk right past it."

Calla continued to Row 27. "I never thought Mason would go this far. For years I believed he really cared about defending the world, not destroying it," she said.

"He hadn't done that kind of science for years," Tiege said in her ear. "Seventeen seconds."

Calla studied the digital screen of the third box in Row 27. "Bingo. I need the combination," she said.

Tiege read it in her ear.

The large box slid open, and she went in.

Her eyes widened. "Good God!"

SEVENTY-FOUR

CASSIS, PROVENCE, SOUTH OF
FRANCE, 11:12 A.M.

NASH TOOK a moment when he reached the Provence village and stopped the ignition. With his car destroyed, he would need to get new transport.

Damn, he really liked the Porsche.

As he slid the car into the outskirts of Cassis. He had to get to the Scorpion Tide. Finally, his phone had a decent reception. Yet, still, Calla's phone rang with no pickup.

Nash wouldn't call himself a worrier, but he was damn uncomfortable with this. He parked the car a few streets from the harbor and entered a busy café.

Being on these missions always made him nervous because it wasn't wise to connect to Calla for their safety. That was the life of an expensive hired agent. But he only took life-saving missions worth something to the greater good. Since he'd met Calla for the first time in his life, he cared if he lived.

On his phone, he connected to the NSA's secure files. From inside the café, he could see out the front window as the newscast of morning news blared from the TV set.

Once his espresso arrived, he took a sip, and the drink hit his tongue like a hot coal. The espresso was bold, robust, and bitter. The coffee burned, leaving behind a tingling, metallic taste that lingered for minutes.

The servers took all of two minutes to connect.

His heart racing, Nash checked the evidence. What he saw reeled him back. Calla was a fugitive wanted by the ISTF and Interpol.

Calla's photograph was attached to it. Just how...? Nash knew Calla was innocent. Anyone who could smile while being accused of killing anyone must be innocent.

His phone soon needed recharging. Before he could charge it near the bar, what he saw made him stop as he connected to his system at the Scorpion Tide. There, he had access to most international intelligence systems. The MI6 one stood out.

Mason Laskfell had set the whole thing up. The evidence had been fabricated and planted. MI6 had just got wind of it only a few hours ago when a bioweapon threat reached them. Another name stood out.

He should never have let someone who worked for Mason work for them.

Scarlett.

She had been their blind spot and Mason's way in.

Nash's steps were swift when he left the café.

THE ENTRY HAD BEEN swift into the vault. Small, the space was well-defended with cameras, but Tiege had disabled them.

The interior was a massive room filled to the brim with sleek, state-of-the-art electronics. It housed a single golden statue of a man. His face was shadowy and expressionless, his skin deeply weathered and gray.

Ashton Vaxon buried his treasures here and Mason Laskfell must have known it, too.

The air inside felt like it had an electrical buzz. Every electronic component within the vault hummed with a silent expectation.

Calla wiped her brow as a second robot paced the grounds. Its steps echoed off the vault's interior. With Tiege's hack of the security systems, no one took note.

The solid walls echoed with the high-pitched whine of machinery, a red glow pulsing from the furthest corners.

Soma's voice popped into her earpiece. "Anything?"

"I need to find Mason's trail," Calla said as she went through the items in the vault. "This wasn't the plan. Mason was supposed to be heading the prevention of bio weaponry, not funding it. He sold out to Lent Cyrus."

Calla went further. Her eyes grew wide at the loot inside.

Filled with various items of wealth, art, and gold, they glimmered under the bright lights of the security cameras.

Several gold-plated ornate statues of kings and queens, each looking oblivious to the treasure they were guarding, were placed throughout the vault.

There were piles of gold bars that could fill an entire bathroom. Some of it glittered like snakeskin. Hundreds of items needed to be sorted through, but she was after something else.

"Mason was planning to take control of the world with a bioweapon," she said as she laid out her hands on the table with enough loot to fill the Louvre. "He was planning more disasters, and we're going to deal with each one," Calla said, her eyes falling on a broad black box on the table in the center.

Calla made her way toward it and opened the box. It had a tablet. She retrieved a chip from her suit and placed it into the table's memory slot. "Tiege, can you hack it?" she asked in her earpiece.

It took Tiege three seconds, and they were in.

One file, in particular, drew her attention. "Tiege, can you copy this file?"

He was on it before she'd finished her sentence. "Twenty seconds, Calla. I can only hold the systems so long before they scramble and reposition."

She studied Mason's signature on various documents and government deals. ISTF stamps were all over them.

"He had plans to start up a spy ring to bring in various government personnel from different countries," Calla said. "Each country had its own team. Then Mason would turn them and those who knew about the plans into agents, including children."

"Children?" Soma asked.

"Children and teenagers. It was a full recruiting program."

Tiege's voice was clear and loud now. "Ten seconds, Calla."

She stopped. "Of course! ISTF was the biggest target. He planned to frame ISTF from day one, not lead it."

As she turned to leave, once the file had been copied at one hundred percent, a document caught her eye. At the bottom was a copy of the Beale Ciphers and several documents relating to Halona's family and Jack's. There was also a copy of the telescope.

This time Tiege's voice had an urgency. "Move, Calla. The vault will seal you in," he stressed.

Calla's eyes turned back to the vault entrance, and the door began to move.

CHAPTER
SEVENTY-SIX

CENTRAL ZURICH, 12:22 P.M.

THE PATH LEADING up to the station's main entrance greeted Calla and Soma as they hurried into the station, to wait for a straightforward way to the airport. Blending in a crowd was all they needed. A stone fountain with a sculpture of a winged woman at its center stood in the middle of the paved pathway.

A spy's life had its benefits. Calla had changed into a simple black dress with knee-high black boots on leaving the bank.

Her emerald eyes grabbed attention when they weren't hidden behind a pair of sunglasses.

A breeze lightly grazed her shoulders as they hastened through the wide corridor leading to their train's platform number and they found an empty bench.

Calla unrolled papers she'd snatched from the vault, the ones she had tucked into her boot.

Everything in there was short of a larger conspiracy. Cryogenically frozen, Peregrine's body was stored in a freezer somewhere in Eastern Europe. Here, such science was under development. The picture and forms she read proved it. A signature on the medical records was not Lent's, but a name becoming more familiar by the day—Ashton Vaxon. Who was this?

The medical papers contained a formal request for information on Peregrine's health status. She was terminal. Peregrine had made too many enemies to include a picture of herself on that document. She had kept her dossier small, and she had not left a single record of her existence anywhere. These papers were the only record that she had been there. Upon her death, Ashton was instructed to destroy her materials.

How had Mason come across these papers? What was the connection to Lent Cyrus? Why was he interested in Peregrine, and why was she frozen, and where was she?

Peregrine had orchestrated the entire thing. From the drugs to the mercy killing, cancer, cryogenic freezing, and even the false death certificates. Underneath, more evidence showed the prototypes of an AI surveillance camera embodied in a round device called *the Eye*. It was all part of the plan.

CHAPTER
SEVENTY-SEVEN

DAY 15

ALLEGRA'S PLANE waited for them at a private airport strip outside Zurich. Soon, they were airborne.

"Ms. Cress," the pilot announced over the intercom. "We will touch down in Venice soon. Miss Driscoll will meet you at St. Marco Square."

Soma's reaction to children and teenagers in Mason's program bothered her. There was an address close to Zurich in the mountains. It was an address they felt led to a place they both didn't want to voice.

Lucy's eyes stared back at Calla from an old photograph she'd always carried in her wallet. Time was running out, and she needed to find Jack, whose watch had been inactive now for twenty-four hours. Something in what she had found in Lucy's room eighteen months ago was puzzling her. Lucy's cipher in the diary, the hidden tech room in her bedroom, the disappearance, the connection to Beale's own wizardry at putting ciphers together.

The diary's pink pages were covered with scribblings.

Lucy's handwriting had mimicked Beale's ciphers. Numbers in random order, moving along the page scribbled by a ten-year-old.

Lucy's diary was old. The pages were falling apart. Ink splotched all over the pages, meaningless numbers, words, fragments. Without the telescope, how could she read this?

Calla stopped at a random spot on the page and traced a line through a cluster of numbers. She then moved to another location and traced another line and did this several times, then stopped and looked up. What did the telescope do that she wasn't getting. Without the telescope, it was hopeless. The numbers in the diary were so tight and tiny that Calla had to squint to read them. The first page seemed to be a note. Calla continued reading.

She played with the notepad against a pocket mirror. The ciphers looked like a regular string of code in the mirror, but it looked like an unbroken string of numbers from any other angle.

Calla consulted charts on the phone Tiege had given her as Soma returned to the seat beside her. She tried to find a correlation between the ciphers and the map. Her eyes tried to find any kind of pattern in the mirror. After all, wasn't that how a telescope worked? Then it hit her as it made sense. Beale's ciphers could be read this way.

A mirror laid flat in front of her was too tempting when she pulled up Beale's cipher. The second one.

Without a word, she reached out and placed her hands on each side of the glass. She could make out her own reflection and that of the window.

Calla watched the two reflections, that of herself and the cipher.

It wasn't until she studied the entire text that she saw the faintest hint of a pattern in the ciphers.

She had a single hope. Calla took a deep breath and

focused on what was about to happen. There was a pattern emerging. Names, places, and facts were becoming apparent. Locations as well became clear from the design in the ciphers.

Her hands clenched over the mirror, and she focused her mind and tried to make the cipher look more easily decipherable.

The theme was clear, and they were all routes and directions to places they had discussed with Jack. She found a simple message in the cipher, and as she looked closer, she studied the mirror and saw an entire line of words as the cipher appeared. She saw a phrase and she shuddered.

SEVENTY-EIGHT

VENICE, ST. MARCO SQUARE,
10:27 A.M.

CALLA AND SOMA sat at a café several hours later, thinking and sipping warm coffee at St. Marco Square.

The location on an address they'd seen in Switzerland was an old spy school in a monastery, and no government agency knew about it. Lent Cyrus had kept it under the radar, and he seemed to use religious establishments to his aims.

Calla sat across the table from Soma. Her tongue felt too thick to form the words. "That had to be a painful experience?"

Soma's chin dipped. "Yes. It was."

Passion thickened Calla's voice. "Soma, I'm so sorry."

Soma gave her a careless shrug. "Don't be. The spy school strengthened me."

"But Soma, it's not right. Who else did they put in there?"

"We'll bring it down," Soma said. "I don't care how big an army it is."

Calla touched Soma on the hand. "And I'll help you."

A welcoming smile curved Soma's lips upward. "So we're partners now, eh?"

"I guess so."

Soma stared at the people in the square as tourists crowded it. Calla didn't know what more to say. If Soma had gone tried to go back to the facility, it would have changed so much.

"Listen, Soma. We just need to strategize. We are severely outnumbered, and going into that place would have created too much havoc. I promise you and every other victim of that place that I'll get to the bottom of it. Allegra's late. It's not like her. Let's go. Delgado has docked."

They started walking toward the dock and took the little boat toward the Scorpion Tide. "Hold on," Calla told Soma.

It was then that she felt it. "Something's wrong."

"What do you mean?" Soma asked.

"I don't know," Calla said, trying to stay calm. "I don't know."

But that was a lie. She knew exactly what it was. And so, without another word, she and Soma turned around.

The explosion came just as they got to the shore. A blast that ripped out at sea. With all the power of the sea, it came like a wave, like water shooting out of a reservoir.

Where her yacht had been was a cloud of smoke.

A harsh, acidic odor drifted in the air as the smoke cleared.

Her heartbeat fast. Sweat stung Calla's forehead, and she wiped it away.

The ringing in her ears was deafening, as if someone had slammed a gong as she walked by.

Calla stood motionless. The smoke from the explosion was billowing, creating a thin veil that cut visibility by half. A haze hung over the area, nearly as thick as the fog on the Thames.

Soma shook Calla by the shoulders. She yelled, "We have to get out of here!"

Soma's eyes were wide, her hair disheveled, and the skin on her neck red and raw as screams erupted in the square. Her hands pressed hard against Calla's shoulders.

Calla was breathing hard, as if she'd been running. She just couldn't move. Not her yacht, not her people. No. Her heart was beating. Someone had blown her boat up, and she had no one left and nothing left.

Nothing remained. When Calla's senses returned, she turned around.

Soma was gone.

She felt a cool hand cover her mouth, and then it pulled her back.

SEVENTY-NINE

NAIROBI AIRPORT, KENYA

THE MD-83 GROUND-SERVICES vehicle drove down the ramp and positioned itself in front of the plane's tail before slowly making its way under. Its steerable trailer-mounted lift-gate was only a few feet below, which itself was almost level with the ground.

Kaarlo Kleve had not seen Nairobi for years and wanted to hurry as the plane door opened. Black rain clouds, casting their noonday shadow onto the city, seemed to match Nairobi's reputation.

Kaarlo made his way out and into arrivals, which were exceptionally long today. A tall, burly looking man greeting him at arrivals looked, well, not exactly friendly.

The man was dressed in a smart but not formal business suit and a tie. He was always late. No wonder it had taken him a few minutes to find the correct immigration queue.

"Welcome to Nairobi. My name is Mr. Ibrahim, from the AIA," the man said.

Kaarlo nodded a greeting.

"I see you're in a good mood," Ibrahim said.

Smoke billowed from a Bamburi cigarette that a porter

stuck in their gums. It bothered Ibrahim as he lost his patience with the gatekeeper in front of them as they made their way out into the car park.

"Listen, I need help to get my son back. I have served you for many years. Enough is enough. My spying on Lent Cyrus was supposed to help my children, not endanger them. I lied to them and my wife for years," Kaarlo said.

A half smile creased Ibrahim's mouth into a mocking grin. "What do you want from us?"

"This all started with you guys. You couldn't stay away from my children and were so drawn to their talent. They have my son, and we need to get him out. Lent is holding him. God knows what happened to Soma. I'll not risk my children's lives anymore." Kaarlo said.

They arrived at the African Intelligence Agency office in Nairobi forty-five minutes later. Kaarlo and Ibrahim were ushered into a windowless office at the end of the corridor on the first floor.

"When you took this job," a man across the desk said. "The deal was you were in it for life, regardless of what it might do to your family."

Kaarlo swallowed hard to hide his stab of disappointment. "Correct, but you didn't keep your part of the bargain to protect them. I lied to my wife and children for years."

"Do you want me to tell my bosses that you have violated the contract by being in contact with your children?," the man asked. "You're spying on a British spy, ISTF to be exact, and you do not call us? What do you want us to do? This is the first time you have come running to us."

"That was before I knew Jack was with ISTF. The deal is done. I just want my son back. He is all I have now! Damn it!"

"Calm down, man," Ibrahim said. "This is what we're

going to do. It's way too dangerous to get to Lent Cyrus. If you want to go, we'll give you the arms you need but won't give you any men. You went into this with your eyes open. You knew what you were doing."

Stark reality struck Kaarlo by force. "I don't want to fight."

"Not my problem, okay. These coordinates will help. Get to this man, Makumbe, before 6 a.m. He's being held in the old, abandoned jail just off this road. That's all I can help you with now."

Jack's father left the safe house and wandered into the streets of Nairobi. His wife had left him, and he would never forgive himself for lying to his children. He thought of his daughter Soma and his son Jack, growing up alone without their father. One day, he decided that he had been away and up to no good for too long. He just wanted to get his son out of there. At least he knew he was alive.

Kaarlo pulled out his cell and dialed a number. "Tad, we need to act now. I know where Lent Cyrus is. You following the coordinates I sent you? The AIA is in. Let's see what we've got. Makumbe is in a small jail in Nairobi and knows how to get to Lent's African operations. We've called my contacts at the American Embassy for more information. Hurry! The Embassy says we need to find Calla Cress. She's a British spy. Do you know her?"

He heard a voice on the other end of the line say, "am afraid I do."

DAY 17

LIGHT STUNG CALLA'S EYES. The vehicle kept moving. When it stopped, she rose and pulled herself together. There were other people in the car with her.

Then she heard the sound from the mosque and morning prayers.

Calla stared at her boots, covered in shards of glass from the car's smashed window. She must've stood and slammed back against the glass. Had she been trying to get out? Calla hadn't realized it before, but her lip was bleeding.

Several moments later, the truck stopped in a village, and all the people were getting down from it. She grabbed the bag from the seat next to her and exited the vehicle. A man with a long beard sat by the roadside in meditation. He opened his eyes and said something to her in Arabic.

Just where was she?

"My instructions were to leave you here," came a voice from behind her. The truck driver waved her out of the way and continued his journey.

Calla dropped to her knees with a wave of emotion.

A man made his way to her and pulled her up. "You must cover your hair with this," he said. He handed her a black veil, which she pulled over her head. "I need answers. I need to know where my friends are and what happened to them. You must help me," she said to the man.

"This is not a good place for you," the man said.

What was he talking about, and just who were these people?

"She has to follow us. Bring her to safety," someone behind her said in Arabic. Calla had learned the basics from Nash.

The voice came from a very tall, handsome middle-aged man with a striking goatee. She could've sworn he was the spitting image of someone she knew very well. Calla couldn't hide the surprise of seeing the face in front of her. This was indeed Jack's father.

The last she remembered was in Venice. The explosion.

The third face she'd only seen a few days ago. Weariness sapped her body's strength. "Tad?" she said.

And now, these two were her only hope of getting out of this place.

"Calla, are you okay?" Tad said.

His demeanor made her curious. "Where are we?" she asked.

"You're in Africa, Algeria, to be exact, close to the Moroccan border. We're with the African Intelligence Agency. Lent paid us to get rid of you, just like they did me."

She turned back to the man with the goatee. "You're Kaarlo Kleve, Jack's father. I've known about you for some time."

"After Lent had what he needed from your friends and me, he moved the problem to the AIA," Kaarlo said.

Warily, she leaned forward. "You guys have been under-cover for decades. More covert than any intelligence agency and very efficient."

Fatigue stole the sparkle from Kaarlo's eyes. "Yes, we like to work alone, and under the pretense that African agencies are second to others, that's how we strike."

"You're good. But now I need to go," she said.

Tad shook his head. "Lent has a habit of bringing people here that he does not need. He likes to subject them to the desert," he said.

"So, what will you do now? What he paid you to?" she said, wiping blood from her lip and shoes as she glared at Kaarlo, the man who had betrayed Jack all his life.

Kaarlo arched a quizzical brow. "I'm so sorry things had to be like this," he said. "They used me to get to my son. The first thing we have to do is get you to safety."

"I'm so sorry about everything, but you have to trust me for now, okay?" Tad said. "I need you to come with us. We need to get out of here."

Had she heard wrong? She had had enough of this. A lot of bad days. But enough was enough now. "Where's Soma? Where's Jack? You let them blow up my boat," she said, the thought stinging her core as she recalled the events.

How had everything led to this? To nothing? Had she lost everything? She could not let the emotion defeat her.

"We need to move," Kaarlo said. "Enemies surround you. They can track you down in this village. We just need to make some time. You're probably going to need a doctor. You were bleeding badly."

Calla wiped the blood from her lip as Jack's father stared at her for a few seconds and then spoke. "We need to get you out of here before Lent finds out that you survived that tranquilizer."

"You spiked me? It was you in Venice? How did you know the tranquilizer did not hurt me?"

"Because I made it. Now come on, we need to go," Kaarlo said.

Her eyes peered into his soul. "I'll only go with you as far as a decent connection. But from there on, I go alone."

CHAPTER
EIGHTY-ONE

CALLA SET the bag down on the table when they entered a small house several moments later. A doctor gave her a painkiller, dressed her arm wound and gave her something for her bleeding lip.

How had it come to this? She had to break free. No one knew the truth behind the Beale Ciphers except for her.

She licked her cracked bottom lip and winced at the pain. Tears ran down her face, this time from frustration and rage. "Bastard. How could you, Mason?" she whispered to herself. "How could you?"

Calla clenched her teeth and took a deep breath. A deep secret she kept with her best friend had cost her everything, her husband, and everybody around her.

Now she was in a village somewhere in north-eastern Africa, unable to find answers. The only thing that she desperately wished for was to get out of here and find Nash. As soon as she had a decent connection, she would call him. The time had come.

She curled herself into a ball and hugged her knees. Dried blood still clung to the nook under her nails. The dryness in her throat was killing her and she stretched for the decanter on the small table.

"Calla."

She turned around.

Tad stood in the doorway. "I've found the signal you asked for."

Calla nodded and gestured for him to come in. "Well, speak."

Tad walked in and cleared his throat. "It's coming from Alaska."

"Alaska?" Calla stood up.

Tad took out a satellite image on the laptop. He pointed to a specific area. "This is it. St, Matthew's Island between Russia and Alaska."

Calla went over and looked at the laptop. Her gaze turned back to Tad. "What's the exact location?"

"It is approximately 767 miles from Anchorage. In the middle of the North Pacific."

"That's where Jack is," Kaarlo said, entering the room. "I can use my connections in Russia to help. I know how to get there."

Calla pursed her lips. She had tried the watch only twenty minutes ago. At first, she'd felt like Nash had connected, but maybe it was just in her head. Jack had said the satellite had not been stable.

She looked at the laptop. "I'm going."

"We'll come with you."

"No, you won't."

ALLISONVILLE, INDIANA, 4:21 P.M.

LIGHT SPILLED in through the windows, illuminating the white marble. Margot came down the sweeping staircase of the four-story mansion. She passed the grand front doors, hinting at the wealth inside.

She'd done well for herself, and Mason had to agree. He'd taught her much.

Mason poured himself a whiskey as she entered the grand lounge.

"Why didn't you let Vaxon sell it to you instead of Lent?" Margot asked. "That wasn't the plan."

Mason shrugged. "The Eye's camera technology was something I worked on. It was a deal between the two of us."

"You're saying that he can see everything and everyone?" Margot said.

Mason sipped his liquor. "He did well."

"You're not very clear," she said.

Mason's lips pursed. "I hardly think so, at least not without some rather significant help."

Her patience was walking on a tightrope. "I, um, I have concerns about what we might find out," she said.

Mason said his drink down on the table. "I see. Another thing. I don't think he's all that he appears. Watch him. Go slow."

"What do you mean?" Margot asked

"Never mind. I don't know what to do. Maybe we should just sell it all."

"Sell what?" she asked. "What we know. Tell me more about the Eye spy camera technology," she said.

Mason hesitated for a few moments. "It's a technology for embedding additional wavelengths within light. A pretty old idea."

She stared at him for a long time. "That's a pretty strange concept. How does it work?"

Mason's eyes met hers. "You see everything, even in death. When I started working on it, I was thinking about it as a concept for communications: embedding a signal in another signal and switching it when necessary. Think of it as a way to send imperceptible signals. After a while, I realized how useful it would be for surveillance, maybe even into one's thoughts. It makes little sense on a purely theoretical level. But it's possible."

This time we have a felt she needed a drink moved to pour herself one. The sick knot of tension in her gut dissolved. "And so you went to market."

"Not exactly. Massoud, Sheik Salib's son, was a promising young developer who needed a project. He developed it, and then I didn't want it going to anyone."

Margot raised an eyebrow. "That's why we held the boy?"

"He was the next best thing to Jack Kleve. I never got to finish the work. It's just… components. Chips and lenses and threads and tiny motors. Ashton Vaxon had other ideas. Something more sinister. Spying where people didn't think was possible."

Margot wanted answers and she approached him slowly.

"You give me the impression you intend to sell it. Does that mean that it's illegal?"

"It would seem so. The enforcement would depend on the use you put it to. Plus, how do you keep the NSA out?"

She raised an eyebrow. "Is it in operation now?"

"Yes."

"Where?"

"Let's see... everywhere," he said. "You can't stop its surveillance unless you go to the source."

Margot's curiosity got to her. "Where's the source?"

"Now, I can't share all my secrets, can I?" Mason said. "But you might say it's being controlled from Ashton's grave."

"Just tell me what you're going to do now," she said. "Shields has always been onto you and me. What do you think?"

"We wait," he responded.

She raised an eyebrow at him. "Wait.?

"Yes. Lent knows what to do."

CHAPTER
EIGHTY-THREE

THEIR EYES WERE adamant as Calla gathered her things. "We can go with you," Kaarlo said. "We'll help you get past the desert. Tad and I have camels in the village. It's not that easy to cross the desert. You'll need an armored vehicle. Lent's people are hostile, and there are few watering holes. Other people have gone without finding their way out. Did you not see the battered trucks?" Jack's father asked. "They attacked us. That's how you got hurt. Plus, you're in no condition. You can't go alone. There are enormous dangers in these parts."

"I think I can manage," Calla said.

Kaarlo picked up their things. "What are you doing?" Calla asked.

"We're going with you," Kaarlo said.

"But..."

"I'll not lose my son again," he said. "I lost him many years ago and I'm not losing him again," Jack's father said.

"I'll leave you at the edge of Rabat," Calla said. "I've arranged for you to be paid for the transport. My father will see to it. After all, you respond to money well."

"Listen, I betrayed Jack, but I didn't mean to," Kaarlo said.

Calla hadn't expected this level of honesty from Jack's father.

"When he was a teenager, I planned to leave him behind."

Calla raised an eyebrow. "Why?"

Kaarlo leaned in. "I had no choice. I had to keep Jack safe."

"From what?"

"The children's spy recruitment of gifted children. It is a covert organization that seeks super intelligent kids. They invite them to a summer camp that's run by nuns. They're very strict and have a very high skill set for one's age. Jack was about fourteen."

Calla sniffled and wiped her face with the back of her hand. "We have to get Jack out of there. That place is a death trap and there are many secrets inside. I don't care how dangerous it is. We have to rescue Jack."

Hands to his waist, Kaarlo drew in a sharp breath. "Both our objectives are the same, but you will stay."

Calla couldn't help but feel she understood Jack better than his father. "I know, Jack. Though he resented what you did to him and the family, he hates your choices but always gives even his worst enemies the benefit of the doubt. Your reconciliation will be for another day. So tell me, why the loyalty to the African Intelligence Agency?" she asked.

"They spared Jack from Lent's recruitment. They helped me protect Jack from afar. Until he joined university. At that point, they assigned me to watch him. Jack was doing incredible work in science and research, and the AIA thought he could one day be an ally."

"What happened next?" she asked.

He shrugged, "Nothing. I started drinking, got involved with the wrong kind of agents. After university, Jack became successful and MI6 recruited him, and I imagine you met him when ISTF recruited you both."

Kaarlo wasn't a weak man or a codependent man, but he

was a man who had been broken by a life of secrets that he didn't want anymore. Calla drew in a deep breath."I promise you, we'll find Jack. Let's go to Rabat. You must stay there. Otherwise, Lent will suspect something."

Several hours later, they drove in silence. Tad briefed them about the Sahara Desert and how they had to cross some of it to avoid intelligence radars. In Rabat, they'd find help. Her desire to find Jack and Nash was stronger than Tad's need to ease his conscience.

She rechecked the watch. It had more life than before, but as much as she willed her mind to connect with Nash, he didn't read her signal.

The desert was an empty void, endless sand, harsh sun. As the heat grew, the desert showed its true colors. The dunes were like mountains, hard and unrelenting, impassable, without the right vehicle.

They were still several miles from Rabat as the four-wheel-drive crushed desert sand. She knew they would not let this go and only hoped that Tad would change his mind. The last thing she needed was a sour reunion with Jack, Tad, and Kaarlo in Alaska.

Through the open window, dust clouds tossed through the air and caught at their throats.

"We need to find a rest point," Jack's father said. His voice was harsh, and his eyes were clouded. "We'll stop here and rest."

It was a matter of pride. Calla checked the watch. It was a weak signal, but she would contact Nash as soon as she got to Rabat.

The continued desert ride was going to be harsh, but she had no choice.

An hour later, they reached Merzouga, near the Algerian

border, the gateway to the Sahara. It was a small city, mostly a series of alleyways and the main road leading to a central square. A few cafes and shops lined the streets, but most business was done in the desert.

Calla rolled down the window as the men stepped out of the car. They headed toward a café, leaving the key in the ignition for the air conditioner.

The air smelled of sweat and salt, a mix of desert plants with the scent of the hundreds of camels that called this place home.

It was now or never. Calla hurried from the back and climbed into the driver's seat.

She turned on the ignition.

The car started. Calla drove down the road, weaving around camels as she passed the café. She saw the men turn to look at her as she passed, then shifted gears and pressed the gas a little harder. She turned onto a main road and drove toward the inner Sahara, going faster and faster.

The engine revved loudly. She was going to find her men and felt a bubble of laughter in her throat. "I'm sorry, but I have to do this alone. Thank you for your help!" she called.

Rabat was approaching as she drove into a desert village, its Arabian architecture scattered across the hills as she had never seen them before. She hadn't seen this part of the world for many years. She parked her car on the desert road and looked around for a familiar mark. With the supplies she needed for the desert in hand, she tried to reach Nash again, but the watch's signal would not allow her. She'd not had a cell phone since Venice and continued into the desert toward Rabat.

Forty-five minutes later, she saw it. The wind sounded like a thousand dry palms rubbing together. Loud, it whistled and howled around the four-wheel drive.

A pillar of wind and dust swarmed around her car. As it approached her, it was four stories above her. Trying to outrun the storm, she drove as fast as she could.

Calla could feel the slashing sand bite at her skin through the open window. It bit at her as she tried to outrun the enormous cloud that was heading her way.

She rolled up the window and was now speeding toward death.

It was no use.

Her front tires drove into what could only have been a well of sinking sand. The front wheels dug into the sand, and the car dipped.

The seat belt held her as she watched the world get bleaker and bleaker. There was no road, no building, no person, nothing. Just a pillar of sand, sucking her car toward it at an alarming rate of speed.

CALLA TRIED to open the side of the door, but it was all happening too fast.

Stuck, her vehicle sank faster than she wanted and would submerge in minutes.

She squinted against the bright sunlight and remembered her first history class. *"If you're in trouble, never try to win by brute force. It's more efficient to win with ingenuity."*

She needed to escape, and there was only one way.

Calla reached out to the door handle and touched it. The car lurched forward as the sand below her gave way. Calla knew what she had to do, but didn't want to admit it to herself. After a moment, she steeled herself and reached for the handle again.

She was about to do the one thing she knew she shouldn't, but couldn't breathe. Hands trembling, she rubbed her eyes and blinked a few times to get them to adjust to the darkening light.

Her shoulders were raw and red, her hair a tangled mess, but her eyes were clear and alert.

This wasn't the place she wanted to be. Something itched

her skin, but she couldn't pinpoint what it was. Her arms felt like they were covered in lead. The pounding of her heart overrode her pulse. She could hear it pounding in her ears.

Calla wanted to get back to the surface before the car disappeared from sight.

Then darkness. A lot of darkness.

NASH FLEW OUT OF NICE. His flight took longer than expected, and he hoped he wasn't too late. Through the watch's signal, he had sensed an emotion that frightened him, but he couldn't get the device to work.

For twenty-four hours, he'd been following its signal. Salib had insisted on joining him when he reached Cairo, and together they flew to Rabat. There, Salib's contacts organized a desert vehicle.

Salib sped up the four-wheel-drive closer to the spot. Then, Nash saw the taillight of a car flashing in the desert cloud.

He knew Calla could barely breathe, and it seemed as if her mind was stumbling in and out of reality.

Curled up in a ball, her knees pressed against her chest, her eyes squeezed shut.

He had to do something and went back to the armored truck and found a rope. He found it, tied the end around Salib's rope dispenser, shuffled to Calla's vehicle's tailgate, then laced the cord around its back.

Calla's car sank deeper, and he could barely catch her through the window.

Using the rope for leverage, he moved fast and started pressing the button to pull on Salib's winch.

The car moved, but not enough.

Calla was unconscious, trapped. She couldn't open the door.

Nash tried pulling again, ignoring the sand clogging the spaces between his fingers. He could feel the heat from her engine that was still running.

His hands made sense of the rope, and he tugged on it again, using all his energy. The car moved, and he motioned to Salib to use his vehicle to pull harder.

Calla finally moved, moaning and pressing on the window.

Nash pulled, but the car was not getting closer to the surface. He started yanking at the rope again.

Calla was becoming near unconscious, and he didn't know what to do if she didn't make it.

Nash hauled again. The car raised somewhat as Nash turned around and pulled in desperation.

The engine of Salib's vehicle churned. Nash yanked again, using all his energy.

The car moved, and he motioned to Salib to use his vehicle to tow harder.

Finally, the car was out of the sand. Determination filling him, Nash wedged the door open.

Calla was still lying in the seat. He looked back toward Salib's vehicle and saw that he was pulling it to the surface again. There was no time to waste.

Salib kept pulling with his winch. As the car neared the surface, Salib turned the wheel and brought the car closer.

Nash tried to pull Calla out, but something trapped her in the seat. She didn't respond to his efforts to reach her.

He struggled to pull her out through the window, her seatbelt still buckled.

Nash wrapped the rope around his fists and pulled. Then he moved to the other side of the car and took the cable, pulling until the knots were unlaid.

Salib joined him.

Nash stopped for a moment and looked at Calla. Her face was blue. She was not breathing.

Salib yanked out a hammer.

Nash held his hands on the door as Salib struck. It wedged open, and they pulled her out, and Nash brushed the sand from her face.

She was cold to the touch, but it was impossible not to try to resuscitate her. Nash slowly cut off the seatbelt, but her body was half-conscious.

He took her hand. There was no time to waste. Nash grabbed at her nose and began giving her mouth-to-mouth as well. She stirred. Then coughed.

"Calla? Thought I had lost you."

Her head moved from side to side as she came to.

"Calla, I thought you were dead," Nash said, stroking her hair.

Eyes open, her breathing was steady. She looked at him with clear eyes. Skin still pale, at least she was conscious.

"Nash?" Nash? How did you....how did you get here?" she asked.

All she could do was fall into his arms.

"I'm here, beautiful.," he said, kissing her eyelids. "Why didn't you tell me? Why didn't you—

Tears stung her eyes. "Nash, I couldn't after I saw what they did to Jack. I couldn't lose you too."

Calla smiled slowly. "You going to tell me off for swerving, or are you just going to enjoy the moment?"

The corner of his mouth rose ever so slightly. "You nearly died out here, so I think I'm entitled to a rant or two."

"Only nearly?" she said, raising an eyebrow.

"For someone who almost died, you're chirpy," Nash said, smiling.

"I guess you'll just have to make sure that doesn't happen again."She took his hand in hers, then shifted her attention to Salib. "Can we stop talking so we can go find Jack?"

Nash laughed and helped her up. "Not until I know you're okay."

CALLA WOKE in a stranger's bed, draped in white silk. The linens were crisp and smelled like lavender, like fresh linen. The walls were the color of the sea, and she blinked, trying to orient herself, then checked her reflection in the mirror on the dresser. A scent of flowers and vanilla drifted from the vase by the window.

"Calla?"

An Arab man stood in the doorway as Calla's eyes opened. "Do you know where you are?"

The man was young, with kind eyes.

"Who are you?" Calla said.

He smiled. "Massoud. I'm a friend."

Calla sat up on the bed and felt as if her head was about to explode as the man left. And then she saw him.

"Allegra filled me in on what's happened. I got to Nice, and when the Scorpion Tide wasn't there, I spoke to Allegra," Nash told her, taking a seat on the bed next to her. "I think I got to Venice a little too late. Allegra told me they would look for you in Nice, so Venice was the safest place. I guess not.

They followed you. Cal, I'm so sorry. I'll never, ever leave you like that. Baby, I didn't know—

Calla's stomach churned, glad to see Nash. She plastered her lips to his and drew in his scent. As if to convince herself he was real, not a dream. She pulled back. "Nash, the Scorpion Tide is gone. He blew it up. And Jack ....",

"I know, beautiful. Jack, where's he? I've been trying to reach him since I heard about the Scorpion Tide," Nash said.

Calla was back on her feet. "Something happened to Jack. We have to find him."

Nash had a mask of concern on his face. "Calla, why did they come for you and Jack? What is it you and Jack have that they so desperately need, and will kill for it?"

Her heart welling with relief to see Nash, Calla drew in a deep breath. "The Beale Ciphers. A bunch of secrets and artifacts related to them. A telescope, pictures, and numbers that Jack and I discovered in a cave. A family living out in New Mexico of Native American ancestry gave us the tip."

He raised an eyebrow. "I don't understand. That's a treasure story that's been around for years. Isn't it a hoax? It can't be... who would... are you sure?"

Calla shook her head. "This goes back to a woman by the name of Halona. Jack dated her several years ago, and her family was connected to the Beale Ciphers. Jack and I can decipher the ciphers, but we need to be together, and there was this telescope from Galileo. It's gone now…"

"Of course. I trust you. I'll not let anything happen to you and certainly will never leave you like that ever again. I've got my entire team here with me. We also have a small team at the Cove in London, and Allegra has picked up some pieces, but they still outnumber us."

"The Scorpion Tide is gone. Everyone is looking for me. I'm a fugitive now, Nash."

"Not on my watch. We're going to fix this," Nash said,

stroking her face. "Continue going despite the odds. We will do it together."

She was tired and had not slept well in days. "Nash, don't you understand that Jack and I are not bulletproof, and we can't always stay one step ahead of these guys."

"Not today, beautiful. You've been through one heck of a week. I have a pretty good idea where Lent Cyrus is. We have to be careful because they can't know that we're on to them. They need time to get to their next target, and we have to be there. Allegra will use this information, and she'll use it to get more eyes on them." He kissed her tenderly.

Calla wanted him and hadn't realized how much she'd missed him. She could feel the heat from his body.

Nash put his hands on her face, stroking her cheeks. He pulled her close to him, kissing her. He was so close she could hear his heart beating. Nash kissed her neck as he undid the buttons on her shirt.

Calla was in a world of her own. This morning, God knew she didn't care about the world around them. She wanted to be close to Nash.

Calla pulled away from his lips, and they were both out of breath.

Nash was taking off her shirt and kissed her lips again. Calla felt the weight of the last few days release in her as tears streamed down her eyes. She had missed him, almost like the time she thought she'd lost him.

He wiped tears from her eyes, and was about to pull away, then whispered, "I missed you so much."

Calla didn't know what to do when he took his shirt off, as the evening rays of sunlight hit them both, she looked into his eyes. All she could do was smile. They needed this moment. There was no one else in this world but them.

CHAPTER
EIGHTY-SEVEN

DAY 18

CALLA DIDN'T KNOW how long she'd slept when she opened her eyes.

Nash was dressing, and he slid put on his gun holster. "Cal, Allegra's here now with help. She has one of our bases on standby. We'll go there and plan how we extract Jack. It's time for White Wolf Extraction. When was the last time you heard from him?"

"Okay," she said.

"We must move fast." He walked over to a wall and hit a button. Lights came on, and the window raised.

He stepped out to a balcony, looked at the hovercraft on the sea, and went back into the room. "She's here. We must go. We've come up with a way to find Jack. He's being held on a remote island in Alaska. Marree and a scientist by the name of Zeng checked in about an hour ago."

"I'll be ready in a few minutes," Calla said.

She took a shower as fast as she could. When she was finished, she combed her hair and pulled on a pair of pants and a shirt that a woman, whom she now understood had worked in Nash's family for years, had laid out. Just her size. She had barely finished when Nash and Allegra walked into the room.

"I've also enlisted help, Salib's son, Massoud," Nash said. "Interestingly, Massoud, a hacker only second to Jack, was also at that spy facility you discovered in Switzerland. Massoud, somehow like Soma, escaped, and along the way, he ran into our good friend Mason Laskfell. Mason is alive, Calla. I saw him with my own eyes. Allegra will help us rescue Jack."

Calla took a moment. Had she heard right? For a moment, she sank onto the bed. "Where's Soma? Did you find her? She's Jack's actual sister. She's become like a sister to me too."

"We'll find her," Nash said.

"And Mason, he's alive? Nash, we saw him get shot. Margot—

"Well, they conspired," he said. "Yes, something must've happened between him and Margot Arlington. They're working together. I've always suspected it, but little did I know she would help him cheat death," he said.

Calla headed for the hovercraft with Nash. Allegra hugged her at the foot of the stairs on the dock. "I'm glad you're okay. Let's go get Jack. Follow me."

"Any news about the Scorpion Tide? Delgado? The crew?"

Allegra drew in a quick breath. "I don't know yet, Cal. It was a terrible explosion."

Calla put her head in her hands and rubbed her face slowly. Soon, they got into the hovercraft, and it moved out to open water. Calla had to know. "How is it that Mason Laskfell is alive? How in heaven's name? What happened to him?"

Allegra turned to look at Calla as the hovercraft chopped the waves. "I don't know the details, but the plot thickens. There are more surprises in store for you. It's not as straightforward as you had expected. Mason planned his death.

Another party somehow got him out. We don't know the details about that either."

"Who? What party?"

"Margot Arlington. The former US ambassador to London," Nash said. "It's the only answer I have. She must've got him out. There's no one else."

Calla bit her lip."Where's she?"

Allegra shrugged. "We don't know the details of that either. Calla, we must understand the Beale Ciphers. That is what Lent has wanted all along. He wants you and Jack and Mason must be helping him. If you don't give him the decryption or what's at the end of the Beale Ciphers puzzle, he will unleash something dangerous. That's why he wanted ISTF completely incapacitated, starting with you, Jack, and Nash. Plus, Lent used technology to spy on individuals through cameras."

Calla understood."That's right, the Eye. I saw the proto-types in the vault in Switzerland."

"He hacks any camera close to individuals, and he can spy on your life. That's how he got onto the Scorpion Tide on your wedding night. He used your guest's mobile phones and kept jumping from one to the next to find precisely where Jack was."

Calla turned to Allegra. "It wouldn't surprise me if Lent and Laskfell go back a long time."

Calla thought back to what she had learned in the vault and in the warehouse. Something Allegra had said confirmed what she had feared about Aston Vaxon. He wasn't what he seemed.

EIGHTY-EIGHT

NORTH PACIFIC OCEAN, BERING
SEA, ALASKA

DAY 19

WHISKERS OF FROST caught in the tree branches, hanging from tips of icicles. The blades of the submarines were coated in a frosty pink gel as they boarded the speed boat to St. Matthew's Island. An island many had said humans can't conquer, but Lent Cyrus had. According to Zeng's intel, it was a fortress deep in the frozen rock within a natural cave that had been built over forty years.

Calla radioed Allegra, who'd stayed on the navy ship. "You sure about this?"

"The government owes you and Jack a favor, so I pulled one and steered command of HMS Siren. She's the most trusted ship in these waters and can send a chopper once we find the location."

Calla knew it was a tough call, but Nash had led many a mission like this. He could find anything that wanted to remain hidden.

The forest ahead was covered in a blanket of snow that fell from the trees like rain. Some trees were over fifty feet tall, and others were sparse and flat. Branches were covered in a white coating of ice, their trunks frozen to the ground. Ice on the ground was slick and hard to walk on. It had been that way since they'd left the ship.

Calla, Nash and Tiege led the team of twelve operatives in winter tactical gear. As they moved in a single file, their breath made an icy cloud around them.

Wisps like white fog snapped like lightning in the daylight. It wasn't their clothes that kept them warm; it was their willingness to endure the cold.

Snow fell in their hair and clung to their winter suits, made of lightweight fabrics that looked like silk but were made of a woven mesh that allowed for breathability.

"We're going to the north side," Nash said, checking the coordinates from a watch he pulled from his tactical vest.

"We're northeast. Seventy more feet to the ice cave entrance. Zeng's blueprints are accurate. It's below us. Then at the edge of the cave is a connecting bridge over a liquid nitrogen body of water," Tiege said.

Nash nodded. "This is probably the place. I want you to secure the ropes. If any of us fall, we won't go all the way through. Calla, you're with me. Tiege, stay with the rest of the team until my signal."

"We'll stay here and send a patrol of two to gather information," Tiege replied.

"There'll be a couple of special units to infiltrate in the area. A helicopter will be used and drop us right within a few miles of the caves once the target is recovered," Nash added. "It will not be a simple job. Lent's forces will be weak if we do it right," Nash said.

Half an hour later, the helicopter landed in an open space in the hills a hundred feet away from the entrance to the caves.

The rest of the team couldn't follow them on the narrow

path. Only Nash and Calla. They would cross the frozen bridge, and that would be their way in.

They moved forward.

"Tiege, we'll stay on the radio, get Jack and then come back this way," Calla said.

Nash's eyes met Calla's. "Okay. You ready for this?"

She nodded and moved swiftly behind him as they made their way further, deeper into the ice cave. According to Allegra's intelligence, it would be a good half hour before they broke through the main external facade of the ice structure where most tourists came. Still, their mission was to go deeper. Several operatives went ahead with a drilling machine that would get them to the outer facade of the ice structure.

Once the operatives got to the spot on the map Allegra had given them, Nash held off the group. "Calla and I will break-in. We'll find Jack and bring him back. At the moment, all we know is this is the way out, so it might be a good idea to wait here. We'll be in contact via earpiece communication."

The operatives began using a high-sonic machine to drill through the ice. Large enough to fit a man, Nash proceeded followed by Calla. They emerged to the other end into a wide space that was as dark as night. Nash turned on the flashlight and looked around. "There it is. That's the door."

On the other side was a wide, solid door with a security system at the entrance. When they got to the little box by the door, Nash deactivated the security system using a hack, and the door slowly slid to one side.

They found themselves in a tunnel lit by fluorescent lights that led up to a steel elevator. Nash pressed the button, and the elevator opened.

Calla stepped in and pressed the button for the bottom floors. The doors slid closed, and the elevator began its descent, moving down fast. She noticed the temperature drop as they descended. By the time they reached the lower floor, she was in awe of the place. The doors opened, and they faced a room covered in ice, from the walls to the furniture. Everything.

As they advanced, there were several rooms with walls made of glass. Some rooms had a single piece of furniture, all white. Some had several, and some had none. All the rooms were empty of people.

Calla placed a hand on Nash's shoulder. "What is this place?"

"We're about to find out," Nash responded.

The halls had various staircases that led to nowhere. A chill ran through each room. Calla noticed several footprints in the ice leading up to where they continued until they got to another steel door. This had to be the central space where they had built the facility. Possibly shrunk its size to keep the main rooms warmer.

Nash used his silencer to blast the lock open and drew the door to one side.

Inside, a warmth overwhelmed them as they entered a narrow tunnel. After they scanned the area, they continued to another door.

"Jack?" Calla said quietly, aiming to reach him on the watch.

The watch blinked. It was working better than it had for days.

Jack came online, the watch responding. He gave instructions through the waves and through the watch's satellite signal. *"I've hacked the signals here. I'll open the door."*

Calla and Nash then stepped into an expansive room. A few steps further, the room led to a reception area and a bar. Several people in white outfits and silver suits went about their business. Lent had gathered engineers and some of the world's brightest minds in the world. A trick Mason Laskfell must've taught him.

They hardly noticed Calla and Nash enter.

Nash and Calla made their way to the ice bar, dimly lit by tiny lights. Bartenders dressed in red suits with black ties, all of them cordial. No one looked up or acknowledged them. Calla and Nash took seats at the busy bar.

They waited, planning their next move. It wasn't long before a bartender approached. They had made it this far and had to maintain their cover if they were to find Jack.

The bartender smiled and nodded. "Can I get you folks something?"

Calla and Nash studied him before she spoke. "Water."

He smiled and went about fetching the water. Leaving the bar area, they headed to an elevator.

"Jack? Which way?" Calla said.

The answer came to her via the watch. They stepped into another elevator, which made its way up to the ice palace. It stopped for a moment and then moved again.

This had to be where Jack was being held. No one was in the lobby when they stepped out of the elevator. The lobby led to an open balcony. They left the dimly lit hall and progressed down the stairs and out into the snow. The wind blew in the background, as the snow whipped against their faces and hands.

They hurried through the snow toward the North Wing. Jack had mentioned they needed to find the third door.

When they reached it, Nash fired his silencer.

The doors blew open.

Warm, humid air from inside poured out. Calla could hear a crackling fire in an elaborate room. A man was sitting on the floor in front of it, and he didn't move. He could've been a statue, and they advanced and shut the door behind them.

"Jack?" Calla called out.

He didn't move.

She took a step closer and could hear a muffled voice.

Determined, Calla took another step and gasped as Jack slowly came to and turned his head.

He studied her and then touched his head.

He was bleeding.

She circled behind him. "Jack! You're okay," she said.

Nash began opening his restraints, and Calla saw they had attached him to a pole in the center of the room, at least twelve feet away from the fire.

Jack was standing now. Nash grabbed the metal straps attached to his ankle and loosened them. Jack swung around to face her as Nash continued to work the restraints, and after a few more seconds, the last straps were undone.

She locked eyes with him. "It's okay, Jack," she said.

Nash slung Jack's arm around his neck. "Let's go. We only have a few minutes."

THEY HURRIED BACK the way they'd come. Jack's feet dragged behind them as Nash moved him in step. Soon his feet responded.

What drugs had they given him?

Once outside, Calla radioed Allegra. "Has the chopper left?"

Allegra's response was swift. "She's on her way to you now. You have Jack?"

"Yes, he's responding. For a moment there, I thought we'd lost him," Calla said.

"You guys need to have a little faith," Jack said slowly and smiled.

Nash checked the perimeter. "I couldn't talk to you using the pulse watch. I didn't know they hurt you, Jack."

"I'm okay," he said, shivering in the cold.

Calla did not know how long the chopper would be, but eventually, someone would follow. They moved ahead to the bridge to the main gates.

Then a bullet zipped past their location.

They ducked.

There were three behind them, on foot.

Nash returned fire and handed Jack a pistol as they charged to the bridge's control room. When they arrived, the door was locked.

"We're going to have to break it down," Calla said, placing her hand on the cold ice wall and felt something change. She kicked a boot into its middle, and the wood broke.

"Let's go," Nash said.

They found a place to climb and jumped to the other side of the control room. They hit the ground with a loud noise and hurried toward the bridge where the chopper would meet them.

"Everything okay?" Tiege spoke in their earpieces.

"We found Jack. We're coming back your way," Nash said.

"Hurry," Tiege said.

Jack stopped suddenly, his senses coming to him.

Calla nudged him. "Jack, we have to go."

Jack wouldn't move. "We can't. I… we need to disarm the weapon, and I still don't know where he's keeping it," he said.

"It's in the lake on the other side of the bridge," Calla said.

Jack gave her a brief, lopsided grin. "How do you know that?"

"I saw it. On the blueprints Mason held in Zurich. They planned this with Lent for years," Calla answered.

"Mason?" Jack said,

"Yes, Jack," Nash said. "He's alive."

Jack's shoulders lifted in an awkward stretch. "I'll ask about that one later."

Urgency made Nash's chin tight. "Let's head there, but we need to get past three security points according to this device," he said, pulling out his GPS. "Wait, maybe there's another way here," Nash said as he pointed to a room.

"It's like a tech hub in here," Calla said. "Let's try to get in."

They scampered to an outpost shed.

Jack's eyes grew wide. "This is where I saw Zeng a few days ago. He was coming out with a biohazard suit."

They could see the frozen lake.

"I think the lake is moving," Calla said.

"Like some sort of machine that is keeping it frozen," Nash added.

On the other side, they saw an elevator.

Jack's face settled into hard lines of determination. "Let's try to get into that."

A breath of exasperation whistled between her teeth. "I think it just goes down."

"We should still try," Jack responded.

She nodded, and they rushed to the elevator. Soon, they split up, and Calla paced carefully to a row of three white outposts filled to the brim with servers. A myriad of computers blinked life to the facility, but which one controlled the Eye? The thing she'd seen in the vault. What seemed like a small door on the outside led deep into the ground, where hundreds of machines churned. Jack and Nash joined her.

"We're in some kind of server room," Nash said. "This is where he has been controlling the bioweapon."

Jack stood firm in his assessment of the facts. "And comes up like a shuttle. That's what Zeng was doing that day."

Calla surveyed the room.

Nash's long legs strode across the floor. "Which one is it? Which one turns it off?"

"That's just it," Jack said. "Unless you have the decryption of the cipher, you can't. Am afraid I never thought I'd need to use it. That's why I let Halona do the encryption. She knew she was in danger, and that's why we were in New Mexico, Cal, to decipher the Beale Ciphers once and for all. Halona wanted you to know it all. She was the only one who knew the code." He turned to Calla. "Unless—

Jack's words shattered her confidence.. "Jack, the telescope…."

A bullet clipped the edge of the control panel counter, and they turned.

NASH AND JACK exchanged fire with Lent and his men. The tension in the air was thick and foul. Oskara's face was becoming all too familiar to Calla now.

Oskara's aim was sure as she tossed a weapon, a mechanical device with four sturdy legs sprouting from a single metal base that curled into a bulbous ball and clung on to Calla. Ropes spread from the robotic device and coiled around her.

Nash fired, and Oskara dropped the device as Calla stumbled and fell back free from the constraints.

Calla watched as Nash took on three and Jack, two in hand-to-hand combat.

The struggle led the men and the assailants back out into the cold toward the lake.

They stumbled, slipping on the ice and cracking it with their footsteps.

Calla only watched for seconds before Oskara reappeared, then sprung up and booted Oskara in the gut, the fall bringing her to her knees. The fight was a blur of fists and boots.

Oskara reached for her device and tossed it again.

It caught Calla in the legs this time and wrapped itself around her.

Oskara moved forward. She was tall, her body well-muscled and lean, but not skinny.

Calla struggled against the restraints holding her, but it was of no use. The robotic ropes tightly bound her arms and legs; she could not break free. Feet bound, the restraints felt like they were made from steel.

"Too bad you can't see the complete picture, Miss Cress," Lent said. "We've never met, but believe me, I've known you a long time."

Calla winced, unsure how long he'd been there. She raised an eyebrow, "Move before I do damage."

Lent sneered. "Feisty, aren't we?"

The psychiatrist he was, it felt like he was reading her mind.

"It's a shame, really. If only you had seen my true purpose in this world," he said.

"Purpose? You've got a purpose?" Calla asked, anger welling in her. "You're just some rich guy who wants people to think he's some kind of savant so you can make even more money for research and weapons. You were using Jack for that. Why?"

Lent looked up distracted, as if lost in his own thoughts as he paced slowly.

Calla worked her bonds over and over, waiting for him to get back to her.

He didn't take long and was still smiling, like a madman. No, a man of business, clearly enjoying his work.

Calla felt her blood boil.

"Nobody serves me," he said, almost in passing. "And none must. It's only because of how I've been chosen to bear this burden that I can act with impunity. Peregrine was fond of three Beale Ciphers and was related to the man in St. Louis, the man who wrote the pamphlets."

He laughed again.

Calla narrowed her eyes. "You killed her, didn't you? You killed your wife."

He swung round. "I wouldn't exactly say that."

"You think you're so different, but you're just a leech, sucking blood from people's lives!" Calla said.

Lent shook his head and scoffed at her, his face turning red. "You think that this world is real? Do you think the people in it are real? We're the same. Operatives with a mission!"

"I don't plan on bringing back the super race, the operatives. You're just a coward, hiding behind your money and your power!" Calla said. "Why did you kill your wife, Peregrine?"

"You don't understand." He shook his head, smiling. "You understand nothing."

She felt confident she could withstand his anger. "Enlighten me."

"There was a Peregrine when she was very ill. She was scared, but they took her hand and told her that everything would be all right. I told her I loved her. She looked at me, and I could see the light in her eyes. She knew we would be together forever. He and I loved the same woman, and neither one of us wanted to see her go. He got careless?"

"He? Who? Ashton Vaxon?" Calla asked, tugging at her restraints.

"You catch on quick. He married the woman who should have been mine and look what it did to him."

"So you killed him and married her?" Calla replied, her skin heating.

"He's still with us. Sometimes too much so. He inhabits this whole place. This…" He grunted and looked back down at Calla. "She died. The doctors told me it was too late for them to save Peregrine. I sat with her, holding her hand, until the last moment before she died."

"You're just insane. You're..." She didn't have time to finish her sentence.

"What's the matter?" he asked mockingly. "You don't like this in-depth look at my psyche? Do you think you chose to come here? The truth is. I brought you here. They say you read thoughts, especially when in danger. I'm intrigued. You can read the thoughts of that thing! What's it saying to you. Where's Ashton hiding? I know he's here. I built this place so I could watch his every move. I hear him but can't find him."

Lent was bordering on madness as Calla watched him near her. "What?"

She tried to get away from him, but the restraints held her fast. Calla scrambled for what felt like hours. Her movements were like those of an automaton until she felt her back against the wall.

"You can stop now," he said. "It's over."

Calla looked up to see that she was next to a dark, narrow shaft. Daylight shone from the bottom. Come to think of it, it wasn't daylight. It was an inferno. A furnace.

She looked back at the deranged man and stood, hands bound. "I've seen what you can do," she said. "You're pathetic."

"Let me explain it to you then." He turned away from her, pulling a small, shiny gun out of his pocket. He looked to the west and then to the east, then aimed the gun up at the ceiling and fired. A long, unending tone pierced the surrounding air.

A clicking sound followed. Was he turning the pistol on her? Oskara stood observing, grinning.

"No!" She knew what was happening. The click was the sound of a mechanism activating. "No!"

It was the bioweapon. He would release the pathogens. She watched the machines fire up, anger welling in her.

Lent smiled at her. "You won't survive this," he said.

Calla scrambled away from him. But there was nowhere to go, not while bound like this. A sudden strength entered her will, her body. Genes honed from genetic science she didn't always understand made her spring. She didn't look when she jumped.

She was halfway down a dark, narrow shaft seconds later when a large, orange spark flashed to life at the bottom.

The machine was almost active.

THE POWER in that spark was like a lightning bolt burning through the walls. Calla felt the air being sucked out of the shaft, and her back hit the wall.

It was hot, and she barely had time to wonder what had happened before another flash of light burned past her. She had to act now, before it was too late. She took a deep breath and snapped off the restraints holding her wrists. The power surging through the system was building, and her heart was hammering in her chest.

Wasting no more time, she wrapped her arms around the curved ladder, struggled to the top of the shaft, and burst into the server room.

It was then she saw Lent, who stood over the machine that controlled the servers. He had a lever nearly pulled back.

She advanced, searching for any weapon to use against him. As she looked around, she saw the hack job he had done. Oskara stood beside him.

Wires connected to the power, and she saw the arc of electricity the servers gave off, crackling and fizzling.

Lent swung round with a look in his eyes of complete satisfaction. She wouldn't let him get any closer to that machine and progressed slowly.

The building shook. It was going to blow.

The windows blew in.

The lights went out, and debris fell from the ceiling.

Calla ducked as a pipe that swung down toward her head. Oskara had seconds and turned to the door, slid through it before a second explosion that rocked Calla backward and threw her into the wall.

Lent watched, anger swelling his face as a second machine burst into flames.

"No!" He ran to it. "This weapon will do what I set it."

Calla's eyes widened. "Don't Lent! Get out now! Would you trade your life—

An explosion.

He was relentless. "The weapon. Peregrine! I promised you more than Ashton."

He was losing it. A psychiatrist who deserved to be in his own chair. Calla made a move for an air hole by the door, her only way out.

There was another explosion. All Calla saw was smoke. The building was nearly on fire. She charged for the shaft and threw herself down as a loud explosion sounded behind her.

CALLA DOVE DEEPER into the shaft that spit her out into the lake as the server building behind her exploded. Her feet hit frozen water several feet below the shaft's end. A hand pulled her out of the water and toward the bank when she came up for air. It took all of two seconds to realize it was Jack.

"You okay?" he said.

She nodded, trying to avoid the clattering of her teeth.

"Let's go," Nash said, putting his jacket around her.

They charged to the bridge, now a half-burning structure about to collapse. It was so weak that an ordinary wind would have torn it to pieces.

Beneath the flimsy construction, a large puddle of oil had been spilled, and a cloud of black smoke trailed from the oil as it burned. From a distance, they saw Oskara at the end of the bridge.

She released a detonator that bombed the rest of the bridge's surface.

They couldn't get past, and the destroyed path made it impossible to move.

"There's another way on the other side," Nash said.

Calla wrung her hands together. "Okay, let's get over there. We have to get across."

They spotted a helicopter pad shaped like a horseshoe. Its edges and the surrounding area were secure, well-fortified, and planted with razor-sharp spikes and crosshairs. It must've been Lent's own chopper. Ready to soar, its blades hummed and whooshed, awaiting departure.

The guard didn't see them as he chatted with his colleagues. The surrounding area was littered with rocks and small boulders, but the security were armed with laser weapons.

"I think I can take care of the guards," Calla said.

She crept from the bushes, hurrying as Nash joined her. Calla entered the clearing, keeping their gait as quiet as possible. The lasers still pointed at her, but their attention had veered away. It was hard to tell if it was from smoke, sweat, or fear, but she moved and landed one blow in each guard's middle. Their faces blanked, their eyes like cold marbles.

Jack jumped into the helicopter and the blades hummed as Nash and Calla hurried behind him and then got into the aircraft. The beast rose above the frozen lake as Oskara's men fired at them.

The engine chortled as Jack aimed the chopper's guns and fired. Oskara and her assailants dropped back as the surrounding ice broke.

"That should deal with it. I don't think they'll be coming after us," Jack said.

"Something's wrong here," Calla said. "Turn back,"

"What?" Nash said.

"Trust me, Jack, turn back to the lake," she insisted.

They flew, heading straight for the center of the frozen lake. "I can see the pole. Vaxon is in there. Lent's eye," Calla said.

They quickly flew over the frozen lake and spotted a long electric pole. A hundred feet high and three feet wide, it ran vertically from out of the lake. The perimeter of the frozen lake throbbed with electricity.

"What's that thing?" Jack said.

"The Eye. AKA, robotic remains of Ashton Vaxon," Calla replied.

The Eye was a giant disk filled with metal wires. Lithe and thin, it was triangular and spun slowly, like a lazy snake.

"What are you talking about, Calla? Who's Vaxon?" Nash asked.

Calla tried to ignore the cold in her bones. "He's lived electronically in that. Lent killed him but kept his intelligence in that thing. The human brain is the most powerful machine ever known to exist. Doesn't surprise me we've taken inspiration for AI and robotics technology from the human brain. Lent has been one step ahead of anybody else."

Nash raised an eyebrow. "Nothing shocks me anymore."

Calla continued. "I guess being a psychiatrist also helped. Lent had been studying Vaxon for years. My guess is they were tech investors together and with the technology Vaxon recreated himself with artificial intelligence and the Eye. They built much together so it doesn't surprise me that Jackson was onto let's plan, he was just one step ahead of him. Vaxon's been here a long time as an AI that has learned in isolation here for decades, learning about the world, waiting for a day to avenge Vaxon and Peregrine."

"Who's Peregrine?" Nash asked, studying her.

"Lent and Vaxon loved the same woman, Peregrine," Calla continued. "She owned information on the Beale Ciphers so dear to her, and both men swore they would unearth the ciphers and even find of the treasure. They were rivals, and one, Vaxon, married her, which made Lent mad. But she was also very ill, and it's still not clear what happened to her except she's frozen in a vault in Switzerland. Lent was furious and killed Vaxon. But not fully. God only knows what he meant to do with Peregrine. Mason has helped Vaxon stay alive through AI. I found files that Laskfell kept on all of this in Zurich. Both men came to Mason for help, and he played them against each other. They are operatives. Vaxon has been living like an AI that controls this place, and Lent has been hunting him for years. That's why he built his palace here and hired experts to not only find the ciphers, but for them to keep his existence here so the AI could operate the weapon. The three men needed each other. Mason, Vaxon, and Cyrus, and one woman came between them all. To stop this madness, we have to destroy that AI," she said. " I think the helicopter will only let one person down. I should go," Calla said.

Calla jumped off the chopper, straight for the lake before either man could stop her.

JACK HAD to land the chopper. There was no sign of Calla when he stepped on the ice of the frozen lake. He moved as ice crunched beneath his boots.

"Jack!" Nash roared.

Lent dropped to the ice, cracked it with his marred body, and sank under the surface, hauling Jack with him.

Where had the man come from? His face was scarred from fire and ice. Jack only had seconds to turn before he was swept under.

Lent's grasp was firm, taking Jack as a powerful anchor under the frigid water.

Jack couldn't move quickly because of the weight of his clothes. Then he remembered the pistol still in his pocket. He retrieved it, raised his head, gurgling as he moved, and shot. The water had made his body numb and he could see the sky, and Nash restrain Oskara.

"Jack!" Calla screamed, appearing.

He gasped for air as he rose above the surface of the water.

Calla charged for him.

Bullets from Lent's handgun whizzed by Jack's head, and he fired back.

Jack didn't care if he was going to die. Lent was going to die first.

Jack struggled, his leg caught in Lent's lifeless, solid grip. He put the pistol in front of him and took a deep breath. Looking down, Jack didn't have to fire. The waters had taken Lent's life.

Cold water stung at Jack's throat as Lent's lifeless hand dragged him to the sea's depth.

CALLA FLUNG herself in the water, and her body temperature dipped.

Could this be happening again?

Jack was fading from her gaze, and she couldn't hear him. Everything was slowing down. The lake was growing, shimmering like an oil slick and stretching further away from her. This is it, she thought. She'd failed. She'd let Jack down. Again.

Fear welled in her chest. It was worse than the fear of the lake. It was the fear of losing Jack. Again.

She thrust after him.

Images of Lucy drowning came back to haunt her. The thought paralyzed her senses, and she felt as if her entire body couldn't move.

Why was she so afraid of the frozen water?

Naturally, she was an excellent swimmer, but something happened inside her when water and ice and freezing temperatures met. This combination paralyzed her.

Calla's body temperature dipped further, and icy water consumed her. Only the image of Jack struggling propelled her forward. She looked up for a second to see Nash. He would surely jump in. Nash always put others ahead of his own life. She had to reach Jack before he could. She was closer.

She smacked her lips, trying to get the water out of her mouth.

Her lungs seized, and she remained submerged.

She saw Jack again, silhouetted against the bottom of the lake.

Nash held fast onto a rope he tied to the helicopter for security. He tossed the other end near her, and she dove further after Jack. She was the only one who could get to Jack as he was slowly going further under.

She couldn't breathe. Somewhere from deep inside her, the desire to reach Jack was greater than the fear of her own death. The energy warmed her veins, and she felt a sensation in her body again.

Her eyes opened. The sky was still there. It wasn't fading away. Life was still in her, and she felt the surrounding water, but it wasn't cold anymore. It was warming up. She reached for Jack's jacket and tugged him to her. It was hard to move, but she couldn't let go of Jack. Nash was right. She had to survive.

Calla pushed Jack upward. He was unconscious. She couldn't leave Jack, not like she had left Lucy. She was cold, but didn't care. Her father had a name for that feeling. He said it separated men from the boys and women from girls. Those men and women, he'd say, were made of the power to hold their breath in the frozen water. She'd never really understood what that meant until now.

An athlete and a swimmer, Calla had been training and good at sports since she was eight. She used to hold her breath in the pool for so long that the referees had to blow the whistle on her.

Calla loved the feeling of pushing herself to the limit. It

gave her a sense of control that she could do almost anything until that day with Lucy.

This was the first. Since then, she'd never really needed this skill. She felt cold, but felt in control. Calla was losing stamina and knew she could swim into the ice. She knew she could go deeper and needed to.

Calla pushed, and her body moved forward. It was like she was being propelled from behind. She was being dragged into the depths of the water.

Calla was struggling. It was hard to see. The water was icy cold, and the blood had rushed to her head. It was only for an instant.

Just as quickly as she felt out of control and struggled, the feeling was gone.

Calla had strength in her arms. She could feel herself racing to the surface with Jack. Kicking hard, she moved fast, not getting tired. Calla did something she hadn't done in training and pushed further with all her power. She broke the surface and was out of the water.

"Nash!" she screamed in one gulp.

Nash and the team came and pulled Jack out of the water and covered him with a warm blanket. Nash administered CPR. He then glanced at Calla for a second as Jack failed to respond.

Nash tried again.

Jack's cough was the response he needed and Calla breathed a sigh of relief as Nash helped him into the chopper. Swinging round, Nash reached for Calla's hand.

She shook her head. "Take care of Jack. I've got a plan, but you have to trust me," she said, determined. "I won't let them do this to us anymore. That camera, that Eye has to go."

"Don't do this," he pleaded. "I trust you, but—

"I have to," she said and dove under, invincible.

CHAPTER
NINETY-FIVE

CALLA HURRIED toward the base of the pole and climbed up without time to think. It was like she was in a trance, breathing hard.

Her arms felt like jelly when she finally reached the top of the pole.

She climbed the last two feet, ignoring the sharp ice that bit into her fingers that bled when she ripped open a metal box.

The air was frigid, but she didn't feel it. She picked up the tiny, black metal object, holding it in her palm, and pulled its wires apart. She dropped to the ground, lying there on her back.

Calla felt as if water was moving in her veins. She could feel the cold, the darkness. She'd learned to swim underwater with instinct and had learned to hold her breath.

This was Lent's secret. Vaxon's brain in an AI capsule. A man in an AI box. He had died years ago and frozen his brain into an AI machine that fed on ice and cold temperatures and used mind control to manipulate those who worked for him. There was only one way to destroy him.

Calla reached for her firearm and shot the box into pieces. It was over.

Then, like a flash, her whole perspective shifted. Where once she'd been an observer, she understood the AI. She read its code; she was inside the machine. Calla, too, could be seduced by it. And she had a choice. It wasn't the survival of the fittest. The camera had stolen much of her life and that of others. It wasn't about winning or failing at all. It was a choice between man and machine. Man, woman and science.

Calla closed her eyes, her body in agony. When she opened them, Nash stood above her. "I'm never letting you out of my sight again," he said.

Her lips clattered from the cold. "Don't, baby, but I have a cipher to read, a treasure to find and hide for good."

DAY 20

THE HILLS STOOD quiet as the sun rose. A magnificent house atop the hill radiated in its whiteness, protecting the privacy of those who lived within.

The drive was long, at least ten miles from the exit of Interstate 50. They could hear only the roars of the car.

Nash, with the help of a few ISTF agents behind, drove as fast as he could.

His vision was focused on the road with the aid of his night binoculars. The lights from the dashboard were the only thing that could be seen in the vehicle. Jack eyed him. "How are we going to get in?"

The question shook Nash. He stared ahead on the road. "We'll get in," he said. "You can imagine my surprise when I learned Laskfell's death was a lie. He had planned it from the beginning with Margot. She promised to keep him alive, and in return, she got the best end of his deal. Mason Laskfell has access to technology that belongs to the operatives, and he will continue to exploit it. They planned it all along. She shot him with blanks. And because we were not in charge of ISTF, we never got to see what happened with that body. He's been in hiding all this time." Nash said.

Jack sighed. "Sounds like these two have been in a love nest for a while. It's his only weakness, isn't it?"

Nash drummed the steering wheel with his fingers. "She's his weakness, but now she's also become our most valuable asset at catching him."

They arrived within minutes. The car screeched to a halt as they passed the security gates. ISTF agents hopped out of the car, their guns pointed at the house.

Nash and Jack exited the car. They joined the rest of the agents as they approached the main door. Nash held his hand up to his throat mic and signaled for them to get ready. Except for the agents at each entrance, who kept the gate open as the convoy drove in, none were yet in the house.

They'd come with enough men. Nash and Jack wanted it to be swift. With the president on board, they would take both Mason and Margot into custody.

They approached the house, and Nash signaled to his team.

Searchlights turned on, bathing the yard in light.

He signaled forward.

Agents crept up to the house, and Jack was the first to make up the steps.

He stopped mid-stride as Mason emerged with a pistol aimed at him. Nash's blow came from nowhere when it hit Mason from behind.

Mason dropped the weapon as more agents ran up the steps past Jack.

Nash kept the weapon aimed at Laskfell as they secured him.

"Wait," Nash said to Mason. "You like to cheat death, don't you?"

Mason pinned him with a glare of fury. "I'd watch my back

if I were you. You, Kleve and Cress. This is only the beginning."

The agents shoved him forward. It was then they heard a scream at the back of the house.

Laskfell took his chance, shoved his hand in his pocket and retrieved and object he tossed to the ground. The lights went off for several seconds. When they came back on, Laskfell had vanished.

"Let's go get him," Jack said.

"No," Nash replied. "Not now. I have a better idea."

Nash and Jack were first to arrive to see Margot cornered in a back room of the house, eyes wide with fury. A shaky hand held a pistol forward. "Shields, you're supposed to work for me. For the government."

"I do," Nash replied, his gun securely aiming, "but you're not it. Not anymore."

Her finger pressed.

Nash was faster, discharging a bullet that hit her pistol, spinning it out of her hand.

The shock of the explosion of Nash's gun sent her dropping to the floor. She lay silent with her arms propped behind her as agents surrounded her

"He left you behind. So much for loyalty, Arlington," Nash said.

Men restrained her as he walked toward Margot, studying her snarling face.

Several moments later, Jack walked up behind Nash. "So, should we go after Laskfell?" Jack asked.

"Not today. I put a tracker on him," Nash said. "And plan to follow him soon." He lowered his weapon as they took Margot away. "Jack, call a team in, and check the house for anything helpful." Nash turned toward his men. "All right, everyone, let's get to work."

Jack gathered the men together. "Clear every room on this

level and check for any smart technology. If Laskfell has been here, it won't be far."

Two agents led away Margot in handcuffs, and Nash shook his head as she left. Why she had held onto Laskfell, he would never know, but now, they could follow him. Besides, with Margot in custody, they had Laskfell where they wanted for now.

ONE WEEK LATER

THE SMELL of fresh mountain air wafted in their direction as Calla and Nash rang the doorbell, unsure who they would find in the chalet. The town was as quiet as a church at night, perhaps why Calla always found it soothing.

"You sure you can do this?" Nash said, squeezing her hand.

"Yes," she replied. I think I'm ready. I could only have done it with your help."

Nash's eyes were sincere. "What you did in Alaska to save Jack's life was short of a miracle. Cal, you broke through your fear and Lucy will be thrilled to see you."

A young lady opened the door. Though she was now twenty-two and six years Calla's junior, Lucy still looked the same as she stepped aside and let them through.

Moments later, Zeng and his wife, Sue-Lynn, joined them in the vast living room with large French windows overlooking the lake. Calla felt a sense of release overwhelm her.

Sue-Lynn began. "I told you, you never had to blame your-self, Calla,"

Calla nodded slowly. Her eyes were on Lucy for a long time before she spoke. "I'd thought you drowned in that lake there," she said, eyeing the lake out the window.

Lucy's eyes were alive with determination. "I did," she said. "And then I lived."

"How's that possible?" Calla asked. "I mean, you were dead. And twelve years have passed. How did you survive?"

"I was in the water for minutes then learned to breathe with the water covering my nostrils."

"And you didn't drown?"

"That's right," Lucy said. "When I was a newborn, I couldn't breathe. That's what my parents told me. I learned how to live after I was declared dead. It has served me well, but he waited for me by the lake. Lent Cyrus had been watching my family for years."

"I'm sorry for what happened to you, Lucy, and I've missed you," Calla added.

"Me too, Calla. You didn't give up and found my clues," she said, smiling. "When I was born, I wasn't breathing right," Lucy said, "and I was blue. It terrified my parents. They were afraid I wouldn't live and gave me a drug that would help me breathe. But some of the side effects meant it could stop my heart for a few seconds. That's what happened in the lake. My heart stopped, and when I was vulnerable, Lent took me away. And then you never heard from me again. So in the room and in the diary, what you found was really linked to that. My condition helped me with codes and ciphers just like you. So you and I are very similar."

Calla felt her heart sink and drew in a profound breath. "You've been brave, Lucy. I can only imagine what those nuns did to you. Lying to you for years, drugging you for months and yet you've turned into this marvelous woman. I admire you and I'm so sorry for what happened to you."

Lucy drew Calla into a hug. "Yes, I'm glad you're my friend. Jack also saved my father's life. He was taken so they would keep me alive. They wanted to use your friend Jack the way they used my father, for what they know and for their brilliance. It's a strange thing that people can't deal with brilliance, isn't it? It scares them. And that's what I always saw in you, Calla. You have a brilliance people fear. It scares them, and they want to eliminate it. I knew that all those years ago."

CHAPTER
NINETY-EIGHT

TSARINA'S GOLDEN CHAMBER, MOSCOW

THREE DAYS LATER

MOSCOW'S TSARINA'S Golden Chamber rose nearly 140 feet. Unmistakable by its gold, the dome's architecture was intricate. They entered the building through an arched door and found themselves in an imposing hall, lined on either side with rich red carpets. A series of stained-glass windows overlooked the city. Ornate tapestries hung on the walls, intricately woven with gold and silver thread.

In the center was a stately staircase with an enormous crystal chandelier hanging from the ceiling and a gigantic dome towered above them. Marbled gold material shimmered in the candlelight as they arrived.

As they made their way down into the building, the lavish surroundings impressed them. The official reception room of the *tsarinas* of Russia glimmered with the wealth of the past.

A few moments later, Calla, Nash, Jack, Marree, and Allegra entered a sizable golden chamber with a single desk and three chairs in the middle. They were told to wait there by a man at the reception counter.

Marree went to the corner of the room and examined a tapestry hanging on the wall full of rich colors, exquisite patterns, and details.

Jack paced around the room as Nash sat down on a chair and waited.

After a few minutes, the man came out from behind the desk and sat in one chair. He now faced Calla. He got out a cigarette and lit it.

Nash spoke first. "We're here to sign the papers."

"By all means, Red Fox, I take it ISTF wants to keep this quiet," the man declared. "I am agent Kuznetsov with Russian Intelligence. Sign here."

"I can't sign," Jack said. "It is not my name. It should be hers, the head of ISTF for many more years to come."

"For now, let's keep ISTF out of it. I'm still debating whether to go back," Calla replied.

"Of course," the man answered, prepping the papers in front of them and handing her a pen.

Calla signed without her eyes leaving his face.

"So this is what they used Beale's gold for, decorating your ceilings?" Jack said.

"Yes," Calla said. "It was a debt to Russia in the Cold War so they wouldn't attack the US. One of those Cold War secret agreements," Calla said.

"How did you know?" Jack asked. "What led you to this?"

"I'm a British Museum curator in charge of the Byzantine and Roman collections. Something there in my work alerted me to the history of this place. I learned that what you see now above you is Beale's gold. The Russians hid everything in plain sight."

Marree advanced. "Incredible."

Calla grinned. "Jack, it started when we were in New Mexico almost two years ago. While we were there, something didn't ring true to me. First, it occurred to me that Beale had found out more than he was saying. Beale landed on two very important things. First, he learned how to do Native American encryption based on a language that had never been written. So he knew nobody would ever find that treasure unless he allowed it. When we were in that cave, it was the first time that language I had known and studied ever had any sort of written form. In our case, it was symbols. Later on, when you said Halona explained Native Americans met with the Europeans who brought these telescopes, that's when it hit me."

"What?" Marree said, watching her as the man sneered.

"Someone in the sixteenth century created a crypto machine that was a fascination to the Native American tribe. They married a language that could never be written with a brilliant machine at hiding ideas. This was Beale's inspiration. The ciphers began with an argument over land all those years ago. Then developed into the battle for the ownership of the telescope."

Head back, shoulders straight Nash moved forward in confidence. "Trust you to figure out any code, doesn't matter what it is. It's as if the world has secrets answers only for you to find them."

She giggled. "From what I can see, Halona's family lost the land. Still, they kept the telescope which for Peregrine's family turned out to be more valuable than the land they got out of the deal from the courts. This was all in the documents at the town hall in Bedford. So, in a nutshell, these families knew what happened, that there was a treasure to be found, but each had a piece of the puzzle that the other couldn't do without. And the feud continued. Beale came into this picture because his family married into Peregrine's family, who eventually married into Vaxon's family. Lent, in love with Peregrine, swore to get the ciphers to settle a promise he made to her, whom he froze cryogenically to save her from suffering from fatal cancer, or so he thought."

"Wow, that's something, Calla?" Marree said. "So why are we here?"

Calla's lips twitched slightly at the corners. "To make sure ISTF British interest stay at bay. There's more. Beale came across the encryption system started by the Native Americans and was Peregrine's great-great-great-great-grandfather. The encryption using a numbering system relied on a telescope and a series of hidden messages in a mountain cave. They brought the telescope to the Native Americans from Europeans who moved to the US during colonization."

"But where did the gold come from?" Marree asked.

"West, perhaps California. Mined by Native Americans who hid it in the caves. When the Europeans arrived, they found the gold and added some of their treasure taken from various expeditions to it. Beale moved it to a different cave. After I decrypted the cipher using a mirror, it all made sense. Most telescopes use curved mirrors to gather and focus light. That is what I did, and set it against the ciphers, but read it in reverse. It's not a puzzle. Actually, it's a map. If you look carefully, the numbers draw a map. A sixteenth-century map, to be exact. You'd have to set it against a map from the time they found the gold. That's why everyone went wrong. They were using modern maps. The map outlines the desert. There, a treasure was hidden only meters from Halona's family home. Laskfell found the gold, swindled Lent and Vaxon, then made a deal with Russia on behalf of the US government using his ISTF credentials, all top secret. It's precisely the same method used in the cave drawings."

"Beale wanted to return the gold to the Native Americans, Halona's family. His family." Allegra added.

"Yes, his family, Halona's and Peregrine's, are all linked. Her only misfortune is she fell in love with two men," Calla said, eyeing Nash and Jack. "Vaxon and Cyrus. She only had months to live."

"How did you know?" Jack asked.

"Lucy's diary. Lucy had a hidden tech room as a child where she'd spend hours looking at ciphers and set them against modern software."

Marree's eyes were eager for answers. "How does Vaxon, the Eye, fit into all of this?"

"Vaxon's wife's family, that is Peregrine's family, stole the telescope and the link to the decryption in the caves from Halona's family. Halona's family somehow retrieved it, understanding also that there was a treasure in the New Mexico mining caves with tons of gold that nobody knew of. It was on their soil. Beale forced his wife's family to reveal the same information and find the gold in the mines. He then moved some of the treasure and left the bigger treasure. He encrypted the ciphers so that he could come back and retrieve them, but he never returned, and no one could read his ciphers. Halona's family had an argument with Beale's family over the ownership of the land, and it ended up in the courts, and it's recorded at the town hall in Bedford County. Halona's family lost the case, but they could keep the telescope and knew the cave drawings' exact location. They didn't know where exactly the gold was, both that which was taken by Beale and that which remained in the cave. The thing that Halona's family owned was a crypto machine, a telescope that could encrypt and decrypt ciphers."

"So the US government never learned about this?" Jack asked.

"No, Laskfell, an operative, using operative intel, did. The sad part is that when Laskfell found the gold, he couldn't transport it without the US knowing," Nash added. "We confiscated the gold and the US government later paid the Russians to stop an attack on US soil, another potential biological assault. The fee was paid in gold, and that gold was stored at Fort Knox for a while. I took a trip there, and they didn't bank on me finding it in their files."

"So, ladies and gentlemen, I urge you to look up at the ceiling."

The small group turned their faces upward.

Calla drew in a deep sigh. "What you see up there is about thirty percent of the gold that Mr. Beale found. The Russians believe they could hide it in plain sight as a sign to the Americans that something of theirs now belonged to Russia."

"You know so much, Calla. I admire you," Marree said.

"Oh, don't. Despite what I do, this place will always be special. It's a reminder of a truce between the East and the West. And we are here to sign and keep that truce. No one needs to know that because the gold is real. Many will continue to decipher Beale's pamphlets, and so that history will remain buried."

"I would like to see the inside of the place if it's okay?" Jack asked the man.

"Of course," he replied and handed them a copy of the signed documents, which Allegra placed in a safe briefcase. "This Tsar didn't think he was going to meet his end at forty-four. After the revolution started six days after the Tsar abdicated, the royals tried to reclaim control, but the people felt they could do it better and overthrew the Tsar. So they actually did to the Royal Family what no one thought possible, killed two members."

When the others followed the man for the grand tour of the chambers, Allegra stayed back, her hand on Calla's shoulder. "Well, Calla, never again will the British government challenge your decisions as head of ISTF. Congratulations."

"I don't know Allegra. Betrayal is hard to swallow. How often does the hunter become the hunted? ISTF remains a place that may still one day be compromised. Perhaps it's time to do things differently."

"Like what?" Allegra said.

Calla sighed. "For one, there's still a problem. Scarlett was spotted in Prague with Mason Laskfell."

EPILOGUE
MAHÉ, THE SEYCHELLES 11:27 A.M.

FIVE DAYS LATER

MAHÉ WAS splendid at this time of year, a perfect example
of what a paradise should strive to create, just as Jack remembered. The Coco de Mer trees swayed in the wind, the soft
green of the grass. A carpet of tropical flowers, their scent
overwhelmed his senses. Even the softness of the breeze
couldn't stop the emotional waves that had been swamping
Jack since Scorpion Tide approached his home island. It even
felt stranger with Soma and his best friends by his side.

Now, it didn't seem as scary as he thought it would. He
had left many memories here, secrets too, but he also had to
stop fearing his past. Had he not been a boat boy and the
determination to do something better with his life, he
wouldn't be where he was today.

"We can come with you," Calla said as they stood on the
deck of the yacht, ready to dismount.

"I have to do this alone," Jack said. "To think my father was
working undercover all these years. It's not even logical."

Nash raised an eyebrow. "Jack, you've got one of the most

logical brains I know, but sometimes emotions get the better of us. Calla and I are here. If you're not ready to do this, you can come back another time."

Calla flashed him a smug smile. "You know, Kaarlo pretended to be one of the bad guys. It was to protect you and Soma from ever being recruited by that spy school."

Soma had not left Jack's side since they been reunited on the Scorpion Tide. "The minute I found out, I had to find you, tell you, but that's when I realized they had kidnapped you. Our father has not made great choices, but without him, we would have never found you in that place."

Delgado moved onto the deck.

"Now tell me how you protected the ship and the crew?" Calla asked.

"Same way Nash taught me," Delgado replied. "The Scorpion Tide had remained incognito in Venice that day. Nothing it felt right since they had taken Marree in Paris or Jack for that matter. From that moment, Scorpion Tide was always in camouflage or reflection mode. We had had enough penetration, and I had to be careful. I guess you don't know all your yacht's secrets. The Scorpion Tide projected a mirror image of itself from afar. That's electronic reflection mode and what the radars saw. That's what Lent blew up and anything in his weapon's wake."

Surprise rendered her speechless. "I see."

Jack turned his attention to his long-lost sister as Soma made her way forward through the small crowd. "Nash told me how he found you in Venice when you'd been taken."

Soma gave Jack a stiff nod. "Nash made sure I was okay before heading out to find you, Cal," she said with a peer at Calla. "I envy you. To have men like Jack and Nash in your life."

Jack couldn't help the chuckle rising to his throat. "You have them too. And now I have you," he said.

Soma's smile was infectious and warm. "You got that right!"

Marree took Jack to one side. Her eyes were warm and soft with compassion. He knew she had much explaining to do, like the whole CIA thing, but like everyone here, she was family. Especially after what they had all been through. He had to trust he and Marree would work out their secrets, just as Calla had worked out hers. It wouldn't be easy.

Marree took his hand as if she had read his thoughts. "'I'm sorry, Jack, Really sorry. It'll be okay."

Delgado, Soma, Nash, and Calla stayed on the Scorpion Tide as Jack jumped into a small speed boat to Mahé with Marree. He wanted to do this alone, but needed Marree to be in on this. When they arrived at the African Intelligence Agency Headquarters, Jack was told to have a seat and wait.

The main offices were scattered in small buildings across the hillside. White marble colonial columns, blue framed windows, and the sweeping views of the Indian Ocean greeted them.

The building they entered was square with two floors and the windows boasted bright blue frames, not your typical intelligence agency. He was led through the front doors into a cavernous salon that hugged two magnificent pillars and then a large office.

Blinded by the sunlight penetrating the tall picture windows that lined the office, he felt warmth return to his skin. Even more large windows further along looked out on the Indian Ocean, giving no hint at the taller buildings on the other side of the glass.

"Mr. Kleve," a woman said. "You can go in now."

"I'll be out here if you need me," Marree said.

Jack followed the woman to his father's office. He finally understood when he walked in.

Sitting at a desk, the tall man, his father, sat behind a desk with a gentle-looking leather chair.

Kaarlo stood. His trousers were slightly more casual than most, but tailored. A khaki belt circled his waist, and his cotton shirt was buttoned up and pressed, but it did little against the heat of the African sun to stay that way. The minute taste of the leather and the polished desk and chair sent a faint flavor of spices and tobacco.

Jack and Soma had been wronged, but he could not hold hate forever. It would eat him up, and he wanted to move on with his life. He now knew why he could not commit to Marree. She represented stability. Something he had not had all his life. Not until he became wealthy through hard work.

His father was just as technologically savvy as he was and was the first hacker of his kind in Africa.

"Dad," Jack began.

"I know you have a lot of questions," his father interrupted. "But I have to say I'm proud of you, son."

"Not sure how to take that," Jack replied. "I never even knew you existed," Jack said. "I saw you die."

Kaarlo squirmed under Jack's steady stare. "I was undercover, and I couldn't get close to you or Soma. I joined the AIA at age twelve, and my first assignment, after the agency trained me years later, was my family. They recruited me because of you and Soma and then brought Fiora in to ease your mother. She couldn't stand the lies, so she left."

"You never had contact with mother after that?" Jack asked.

"This is still a very sensitive subject," his father said. "Though most of the things you asked about are true. You have a special group of friends," he said, eyeing Marree next to him.

Kaarlo then moved to the desk and pressed a button that pulled out a series of smart chip cards. He selected one and held it out to Jack. "The AIA found many operative technologies in Africa and confiscated some. I'm going to pass them on to you. We also found something else. All of Mason Laskfell's operations across the globe. I think you should have this intel."

Jack felt it should've eased his worries, but this changed everything.

JOIN THE ADVENTURE

SHORT REVIEW

Thank you for joining Calla, Nash and Jack on this adventure!

As an author I highly appreciate the feedback I get from my readers. It helps others to make an informed decision before buying.

It only takes a few minutes. If you enjoyed **The Decrypter and the Beale Ciphers** please consider leaving a short review where you bought the book or by going here.

www.rosesandy.com

BE THE FIRST TO KNOW

Be the first to learn about new releases and other news from Rose Sandy, by joining **Real Time with Rose Sandy**, a podcast and fun e-update. See you there by going here:

https://rosesandy.com/signup/

JOIN THE CONVERSATION

While you are at it, swing by the official Rose Sandy Facebook page (www.facebook.com/rosesandyauthor) to join a community of adventurers, history and technology enthusiasts.

Finally, if you enjoy pictures of travels, book inspirations, historical mysteries, science and technology thrills, check out my feed @rosesandyauthor on the Instagram app.

IN THE DECRYPTER SERIES

Book 1: The Decrypter: Secret of The Lost Manuscript
Book 2: The Decrypter and The Mind Hacker
Book 3: The Decrypter - Digital Eyes Only
Book 4: The Decrypter - The Storm's Eye
Book 5: The Decrypter - The Pythagoras Clause
Book 6: The Decrypter and the Beale Ciphers

She's a museum curator, a doubter, and a skeptic. It all changed when the British government asked her to decrypt a code written in an unbreakable script on an ancient manuscript whose origin was as debatable as the origin of life. Then there was the issue of her long-lost parents.

Using her knack for history and technology, she bands with two faithful friends and is thrown into a dangerous journey of cyber espionage investigating the criminal, the unexplained, the scientific and the downright unthinkable.

More here: https://rosesandy.com/the-decrypter-series/

WHAT READERS ARE SAYING ABOUT THE DECRYPTER SERIES

"Takes you on a ride and refuses to let you off until you reach the very end."

"A brilliant read! I recommend this to anyone who enjoys mystery, suspense, thrillers, or action novels. The detail is astounding! The historic references, location descriptions, references to technology, cryptography…. this author really knows her stuff."

"An action-packed adventure, technothriller across several continents like a Jason Bourne or James Bond movie, but with an actual storyline!"

"Brilliantly written. I loved the very descriptive side, which was a good way of visualizing and getting to terms with each new place, as the action takes place in several different countries."

"The description is so rich, so immensely detailed that it just draws you in completely to its world."

"There is great tension and chemistry between the two main characters, Calla and Nash, that has you begging for more."

"The historic references, location descriptions, references to technology, cryptography…. this author really knows her stuff."

There is great tension and chemistry between the two main characters, Calla and Nash, that has you begging for more."

IN THE SHADOW FILES THRILLERS

A CROSSFIRE BETWEEN TECHNOLOGY, SCIENCE, AND INTERNATIONAL ESPIONAGE

Book 1 - The Code Beneath Her Skin
Book 2 - Blood Diamond in My Mother's House

A series about intelligent women caught in the crossfire between technology, science, politics, international espionage, and the men who drag them there.

Guaranteed action adventure in each book, you'll fill the need for thrills, savor satisfying cliffhangers as you follow a secret organization, **The Shadow Files,** and two of its former agents around the globe.

Sworn enemies, one is on a mission to safeguard the globe from economic corruption, and one swears he'll protect the victims.

Each book can be read as a stand-alone story. More here: https://rosesandy.com/the-shadow-files-series-2/

ABOUT THE AUTHOR

Rose Sandy never set out to be a writer. She set out to be a communicator with whatever landed in her hands, but soon the keyboard became her best friend. Rose writes suspense and intelligence thrillers where technology and espionage meet history in pulse-racing action adventure. She dips into the mysteries of our world, the fascination of technology breakthroughs, the secrets of history and global intelligence to deliver thrillers that weave suspense, conspiracy and a dash of romantic thrill.

A globe trotter, her thrillers span cities and continents. Rose's writing approach is to hit hard with a good dose of tension and humor. Her characters zip in and out of intelligence and government agencies, dodge enemies in world heritage sites, navigate technology markets and always land in deep trouble.

When not tapping away on a smartphone writing app, Rose is usually found in the British Library scrutinizing the Magna Carta, trolling Churchill's War Rooms or sampling a new gadget. Most times she's in deep conversations with ex-military and secret service intelligence officers, Foreign Service staff or engrossed in a TED talk with a box of popcorn. Hm... she might just learn something that'll be useful.

For more books and updates.

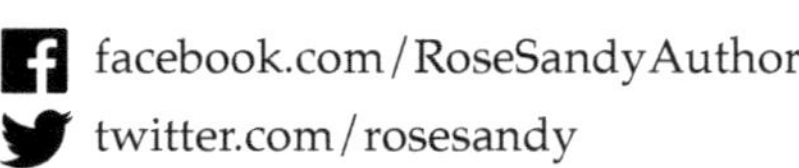